MISCHIEVOUS MAX

And the Beast of Silvernails

Beau Durand

Durand Publishing

Colorado Springs

Durand Publishing

3405 Sinton Road 236
Colorado Springs, CO 80907
Visit our Web site at www.durandpublishing.com

First Paperback Edition: August 2019

Durand, Beau, 1971–
Mischievous Max – And the Beast of Silvernails: a novel / by Beau Durand. —
1st ed.
p. cm

Summary: Max Hunter has a habit of getting himself, and his siblings, into trouble. One day he discovers a murder in his favorite hangout—an old dilapidated barn—, and sets out on a journey to identify the murderer. With the help of his seventh-grade friends, he not only uncovers WHO the killer is, but learns the small town of Pine Plains, NY, and its citizens, have many secrets—some of them normal, some of them down-right scary.

ISBN 978-1-7333983-3-6 (Paperback)
[1. Witches — Fiction. 2. Murderers — Fiction. 3. Middle schools — Fiction. 4. Schools — Fiction. 5. New York (State) — Fiction.]

[Fic] — dc22
HC:
PB:

RRD-C
Printed in the United States of America

DEDICATION

This novel is dedicated to my big sister, Lisa, who died decades too soon. It's also dedicated to my brothers Brian, Craig, and Curt. I'll always remember the times we shared growing up in New York.

CONTENTS

THE SAD TRUTH IS THAT MOST EVIL IS DONE BY
PEOPLE WHO NEVER MAKE UP THEIR MIND TO BE
GOOD OR EVIL.

–HANNAH ARENDT

TO ASK IF I AM MISCHIEVOUS IS THE
UNDERSTATEMENT OF ALL TIME.

–MALCOLM GETS

SOMETHING'S ROTTEN IN THE BARN

Before slamming the front door, Max's mother thrust a steel bucket at him. She pointed to the hen house and said, "Max, you won't collect eggs and shovel horse manure forever. You're in seventh grade now." She knelt and pointed at him. "I want you to think hard about what you want to be when you grow up. I expect some ideas tonight at dinner."

Max replied, "Yes, ma'am," and gulped. His mother's finger twitched inches from his nose.

"I mean it," said Beth Hunter.

Max stood there, not knowing what else to say. His mother had something on her mind. Her eyes swam and looked misty when she spoke. So, he let her do the talking.

"You need to focus. Stop messing around and getting into trouble."

Max flinched. "I'm fine mom. Everything's under control, really."

Beth shook her head. "Your father and I worry, Max. You're getting older." She paused and sighed. "Girls are going to ... well ... start coming around. Now that you're starting football, those other boys, like that bully Tony, are going to test you —"

Max huffed. "Seriously, Mom, don't worry. I promise, I'll do my best." Max flexed his arm. "Besides, I've got like thirty pounds on that jerk, Tony. No one is going to mess with me."

"It's going to take more than muscles to get ahead in life, Max," said Beth. "You have to go beyond what people expect of you." She pointed at his eyes. "And you need to wear your new glasses, for a start. Your father expects great things from you, Max. You're crafty. You're smart. Don't let that go to waste."

"I won't, Mom."

"I'm serious." Beth Hunter clasped Max's shoulders. "Take some chances. Face some new obstacles. Remember, failure is part of winning."

Max rolled his eyes. "I guess so, mom…"

He stood as ridged as a board while his mother hugged him. Then she patted him on the shoulder, and without a word, opened the screen door, letting it slam behind her.

Max rushed down the steps and across the farmyard toward the chicken house, not looking back. He swiftly collected the day's eggs, piled them in the bucket, and placed the lot on the house's front porch for his mother. He rushed to catch up with his siblings, who were already racing away on their bikes, laughing.

Every golden color of fall whizzed by while Max Hunter peddled furiously. The nip of fall stung his nose. Cool air burned his lungs.

He beat his older brother and sister through the trees easily enough, down the steep Silvernails Hill, and into the sudden darkness of the valley. His Diamondback mountain bike was under his control—no problem. He jammed the hand breaks tight after crossing the Silvernails bridge skidding through the dust and under a grove of birch trees along the creek.

He dumped the bike and trotted off into the high weeds yelling, "Come on! We don't have all morning!"

The small hamlet of Silvernails, nestled deep in the maple and oak-covered hills north of New York City, wasn't a town at all. It was an easily dismissed intersection; a small strip where two old railroads met many decades before, though the tracks were long gone. The Rojan Kill creek—a winding scar cut through the forest canopy—formed the boundary where Silvernails ended, and the sleepy town of Pine Plains began.

Like Max, townspeople raced their cars up and down Silvernails Hill and over the creek's bridge daily, oblivious of its history. It was just another bridge. Another stream. Another blur.

A dilapidated, rust-red barn stood near the intersection in a dark patch of silver birch trees and a large weeping willow. Like a wary soldier the barn leaned, creaking under the slightest breeze. Massive spider webs overran its innards. Decaying moldy leaves littered its floor. It smelled of damp rot from years of disuse. Tractors and farming equipment had been removed long ago, leaving a dusty, cavernous shell, locked tight.

The decay of the barn never deterred Max, his sister Riley, and big brother Joe. They would squirm through two detached boards at the base of its termite-ridden rear wall to tell stories or play cards. The hole remained well-hidden on its back edge, where the lonely creek ran by mere feet away. Stands of cattails and stinging nettles obscured the dirt trail the kids created between the hole and the road.

The barn stood adjacent to the Rojan Horse Farm, where Max had secured a weekend job. He made his money working with thoroughbreds, shoveling horse poop, and painting miles of paddock fence with thick, black, acidic tar.

On this chilly Saturday morning, Max made a terrifying discovery.

✂ ✂ ✂

"Guys, get a load of this!" said Max, who had slithered through the damp, moldy leaves on his belly.

Riley followed him in, stretching and grunting as the air squeezed from her lungs.

"You're getting fat, sis," said Max, laughing.

"Shut up and help me —"

Max bent down, grasped his sister with both hands. He lurched backward, freeing her from the clutches of the building's ever-shrinking hole—but not without scraping her back on a splintered board.

"Ouch!" Riley gritted her teeth and groaned. "I've grown three inches this summer, you know." Riley wiped the dirt and slimy leaves from her plaid shirt in disgust. She reached behind herself, checking her back. "Mom's going to kill me. She just bought this." She squinted at her fingernails and made a growling noise. "I just painted these yesterday, too. Now, look."

Riley noticed that Max was distracted. Her younger brother stared at something dog-like, furry, and quite dead.

"What'cha got there?" said Riley, who kept her other eye on the hole in the wall—Joe had not yet emerged. Joe was the oldest at fifteen and in high school. He had become less prone to things like dirtying his clothes and trespassing with his younger brother and sister.

"You coming, Joe? Max's got a special treat in here..." Riley pinched her nose closed, staring at the dead animal.

"I think it's a dead pig," said Max. "Hard to tell, it's all bloated." Max proceeded to pick up a stick and poke at the carcass.

Riley rolled her eyes.

"Dude, you'll pop it. You'll be sorry."

"I think I'll stay out here this time and keep watch," said Joe, his voice muffled by the chattering creek echoing against the barn's walls. "Don't you have to be at work soon, Max? I see the manure spreader climbing the hill. Cindy's on the tractor. And we need to get to track, Riley."

If Cindy Norris hauled horse poop up the hill with the spreader, it meant she had finished in the large, steel training center and was prepared for Max's arrival. Max would muck stalls in the two larger barns farther up the hill. However, the dead pig proved much more entertaining.

It wasn't every Saturday that Max and his siblings were hustled out of bed extra early and forced to "run along" so their parents could clean the house together. Max had persuaded Riley and Joe to bike with him to the farm after chores. He'd go to work, and his brother and sister would continue into Pine Plains to run cross country. Max had just joined the football team, but Coach Charlie had canceled practice for this Saturday.

"Look," said Max, dismayed, "its snout is missing. So are its ears."

Riley inched over to look, hoping the thing wouldn't pop, spraying her with its putrid, liquefied insides. She'd seen woodchucks before, dead and bloated on the side of the road on a hot summer day. Like dirty little bombs, sometimes a car would hit them. They'd explode.

The pig looked very much like one of those chucks.

"Be careful," said Riley.

Max poked at the thing's face, searching for an eye.

Something caught his attention in the upper corner, shining through the spider webs.

"Do you see that Riley? It looks like a doll. Kinda small, though. Looks like some silver buttons for eyes, different sizes…"

"What's a doll doing up there?" said Riley, shuffling around the pig sideways.

"It's on a string or something," said Max. He grunted while clamoring up on a stack of rickety old boards precariously piled below the creepy toy. "I'm gonna snag it —"

Max reached the top of the heap. The boards were ancient, cracked, and littered with chunks of glass and debris. Sharp rusty nails jutted out in every direction.

Standing on his toes, making sure not to scuff or dirty his new Nikes, Max leaned against the wall. He reached high with his arm, barely scraping the foot of the dangling toy. He pinched it between two fingers, clamping down hard on its rough burlap material, before losing his balance and falling backward.

Max screamed and tumbled to the floor. Boards flew in all directions. A plume of dust wafted into the cold, stale air, sparkling as it hit a flat wedge of sunlight streaming through a broken window. The maneuver cost him his arm. A snap, followed by a grinding crunch, and what sounded like a loud pop, rang out. Max hit the floor with a thud.

Max cried. "My arm! It burns, and it's bleeding…"

Joe scurried through the hole. He had no issue appearing when it was "absolutely necessary." He ran over to the commotion and plopped down next to Max. Riley stood there, brushing dirt off her shirt. Joe grabbed Max's bloody arm.

Max shrieked.

"Are you seeing this?" Max half-cried, half-stuttered. He quickly dragged his bottom across the dirty floorboards, away from the exposed pile of old beams.

The doll had landed near the bottom of the stack. Next to it, a glossy white human leg jutted out from under the boards.

"Oh, my god," said Riley, who narrowly tripped over the corpse of the dead pig while backing up. She scratched her ankle on a rusty nail. "Ouch!"

"A person's leg!" Joe lost his breath. "Look at its rotten black foot, and the tattoos —"

Joe stopped. His face turned white as the blood left his skin. His pounding heart competed with the noisy creek outside. The walls of the barn closed in on him.

"I'll get help, yes ... the best thing to do," said Joe, stammering his words. "Uh ... you stay here, Riley. Wrap this around Max's arm." Joe handed his sister the gray hoodie he wore. Though covered in dirt, it would serve to protect the protruding bone until help arrived.

"I'm running up to the barns. There's a phone in the office."

"Don't wait for Cindy," said Max, who sat holding his arm against his chest, but appearing more lucid. "Just call 911."

Joe wasted no time. Max didn't have to tell him twice.

N N N

Max propped himself up against a gnarled, bark-covered support beam with more rusty nails sticking out. Chains and old keys dangled and clanked.

"Are you ok?" said Riley, panting. She looked ready to faint.

From the corner of her eye, she saw the gentle hue of the pale, grayish, hairless leg protruding from under several thick beams. Underneath would be the rest of the person, or whatever remained. The idea of the sickening pig behind her, the leg under the boards, and Max pushing back his pain caused a shiver to run up her spine, momentarily numbing her scalp, its hairs standing on end. Her eyes swam. She suddenly trembled as though the Devil himself had appeared.

"We're standing in a murder scene, you know that?" said Riley, trembling.

"Not only murder, but someone has a disgusting way of treating animals … what a freak!" said Max. His eyes flashed between the leg and the pig.

Riley was distracted by the doll, which sat propped up on the beam it landed against, relaxing, almost staring at her.

Max stared at the doll too. One of its button eyes was wider than the other, and both were silvery-black. Someone had made its body from tan burlap. The stitches were fat and woven from a dark thread. The fabric was rough-cut, and strings fell from the ragged seams. A single white thread had been tied around its neck. On its chest, a small red, fabric heart had been sewn clean and tight. What looked like droplets of blood-stained its legs. Two needles poked out of its neck.

"I wonder what this means," said Max. He had calmed down but remained visibly scared. "Who do you think did this, Riley?"

"A psychopath."

"Do you think they know we've been here before?" Max cringed at the thought someone else used the barn. What if they knew he regularly played there? His body shuddered. A full, aching fear drove the pain from his body.

Judging from the look on Riley's face, his sister felt the same way.

"I hope Joe's fast," said Max. "We're surrounded by death."

"Mom and dad are going to kill us."

"But we found a dead person. Maybe we'll be heroes," said Max.

"They specifically forbade us from playing in old houses or barns in the area, yet here we are, again, stupid."

"You're stupid!"

"Remember what happened to us in the old house up in the woods? The one abandoned decades ago?"

"I remember it was your idea," hissed Max.

"Your choice to go, kiddo."

"Yeah. I broke my ankle going through that floor, didn't I!"

A similar incident happened to Max before. A hunter's lodge far behind their property in the woods had been abandoned, boarded up and rotting for years. Max had found it after the family first moved upstate from Long Island; his dad had taken a new job and promised the country would be just as exciting as the city. Of course, like all kids, curiosity got the best of Max, and he enlisted Riley and Joe to help explore the abandoned lodge. Max, unfortunately, had stepped on a rotten board, fell through the floor, and became stuck; bad things happened when his parents showed up with a band of police to unstick his sorry butt. Not only had he broken his ankle, but his dad's black belt had marked his butt for weeks afterward. Plus, his dad had grounded him. Now he would have to relive the experience again, but this time, things looked much worse.

"I can't look any longer," said Riley, backing away from both the pig and the leg in the boards. "It stinks in here, too."

"Smells pretty bad, yeah," said Max, wrinkling his nose. "Could smell worse. Probably happened within the last day. Remember when our electricity went out?"

"Mom was so mad," said Riley, remembering the October snowstorm that took out all the trees, littering the road with branches and two feet of snow that shut the town down for two weeks. "We lost all our food. It smelled terrible."

Riley looked away, but Max stared at the leg.

I wonder who it could be, he thought.

"Do you think that doll is connected to this?"

"Like some Satanic ritual in the movies?" said Riley. "Yup. Can't think of anything worse. Murder is murder, bro."

"Not when some criminal probably planned it." Max squinted, looking confused. "Look at that poor pig." The pig lay mutilated in front of them. "I don't see no blood anywhere."

Riley surveyed the floorboards. She saw no sign of blood in the extremely dim light—no puddles or streaks. The pig's size suggested in no way had it been pulled through their hole in the wall. The dust around it remained undisturbed.

Riley cringed. "It happened somewhere else?"

"Yup."

"I don't like this one bit."

Max huffed. "It's like they just appeared here, too. But how…."

ท ท ท

Ten minutes passed in a heartbeat. Heightened voices and commotion reverberated through the barn's decaying walls.

"He's in there!" said one voice. Joe had returned, saving the day as before.

Something obscured the light coming through the siblings' makeshift entrance into the barn. Riley and Max watched as a pair of thick, callused, aged white hands scraped the dirt and damp leaves outside, revealing a gray-haired, bearded man. Charlie Wise, Max's PE teacher and football coach (who volunteered as a fireman on the weekends), peered into the barn.

"Are you kids, ok?" grunted Charlie. He noticed Max holding his arm and growled at the sight.

Riley quickly cut Max off. "Get in here. Max broke his arm. There's dead things around us."

Charlie grumbled something about the football season and backed out of the hole. His hair caught on the ragged edge of a support beam, and he cursed while pulling his head free. Additional voices erupted outside as more vehicles stopped along the road. Voices shouted from outside the hole and at the front door, sounding panicked.

"Gotta remove some of them, there nasty boards," said one man's voice in a southern drawl.

"I got a sledgehammer in back, Jerry. By that hole there."

"What about the front?"

"Imagine using the front door, man. Duh!"

"Man, it's chained shut. It's all rusty. No one's been here for a long time."

More voices rang out from the front of the barn.

"Yup, all chained up. This freakin' old lock's rusted. No one's getting in here without breakin' in," said another man.

Sirens, far away at first, grew louder.

A vehicle skidded to a stop in front of the barn doors, sending dust through a gap underneath. The sirens sputtered with a beeping sound and stopped. More sirens yelped from behind.

Joe appeared under the opening in the back wall. He looked up in the direction of his siblings.

"Police and an ambulance are here, guys. Sit there," commanded Joe. "Don't move an inch."

Inside, Max eyed the doll. He knew that once adults entered the barn, everything would be part of a crime scene. He needed something from his terrible day.

"I'm taking it," said Max, breathing a bit heavy.

He gathered his strength and slid toward the dead leg, not more than six feet away. Closing his eyes, he reached across the bare, rotten foot, and snatched up the creepy, bug-eyed figure.

"What are you doing with the toy?" said Riley, alarmed. She frowned. "I can't imagine having an ugly, old doll like that. It's nothing like my old Hairdorables doll or Barbie, but I did cut the hair off those, so…"

"It's mine. I found it. I got it off the ceiling."

"It's evidence, dumb —"

"Not if they don't find it."

"What are you going to do with it?"

"Keep it. Find out what it means."

Max looked around. He needed a place to stash his find. The paramedics would be looking him over, so he couldn't stuff it in his tattered clothes.

"Riley. Put this in my windbreaker. Tie it up. Tight," said Max, insisting his sister help him.

Pounding commenced on the front door. Clanking, and rattling from splintering metal bounced off the walls inside. A whacking sound jarred the building as chains snapped and broke.

"Quick!" Max tossed the doll to his sister, who effortlessly caught it. "Come on, hide it for me, please?"

The creepy thing crackled inside.

"Odd stuffing," said Riley, "sounds like crinkled paper. Don't they normally have cotton or something soft inside?" She looked closer. "Looks like some hair sticking out from the seams, too."

"Who cares." Max waved his finger at the windbreaker.

Riley obeyed.

"What harm could it do," said Riley. She picked up the windbreaker, stuffed the doll in one sleeve, and bound it into a ball. She tossed it to Max, who flinched, protecting his broken arm. He batted it back to her with his foot.

"Hold onto this thing for me."

"If you insist."

"Thanks," said Max.

"Don't mention it. I mean, ever," demanded Riley. "We're in enough trouble as it is."

N N N

The rickety, but heavy front doors broke open, sending splinters of wood into the barn. Coach Charlie, together with several police officers, a couple of paramedics, and Joe, rushed in as the morning sun illuminated the barn's secrets. The whole group stopped as one, yards short of Max and Riley, overtaken by the site in front of them.

"Holy mother of God," said Charlie, gasping. His triple chin gyrated as his plump glossy red face dropped. He made the sign of the Cross with his hand, from shoulder to shoulder.

The extent of the carnage and the barn's other secrets had not been as apparent in the dull light. Max and Riley had no clue what other items hung above them.

Overhead, suspended from the rafters, were four more fabric figures hanging among tarnished ice picks, rusted rabbit traps, and metal twitches used to keep horses in line. Two had long hair attached—girl dolls. The other two, in Max's opinion, must have been boys. All four dangled with a thick string tied around their necks, cinched like Hangman's knots. None of them had red hearts sewn on like the one hidden in his coat.

The mutilated pig rested on its side in the center of the barn. Not only had its snout and its ears been skillfully cut off, its tail and one leg had also been removed. A gaping, perfectly round hole punctured its side.

Where the stack of boards revealed the battered, tattooed leg, several more boards higher up had given way, exposing a severed neck—minus the head.

A paramedic and police officer bolted from the barn, heaving as they did, throwing up their lunches into the bushes flanking the doors. A younger police officer, new to the Pine Plains, rushed over to where Max remained frozen from the carnage around him. The officer fell to his knees and hovered over Max.

"Did you see anyone else around here, son?" said Officer Green.

"Just us, sir," said Max. "No one else ever comes here."

Two swarthy, overly muscled paramedics shuffled toward Max, creating a wide gap between him and the pig.

"We're going to need the coroner, sir," said another officer. "Get on the radio and get them over here." He patted Max on the back. "Moreover, get Sheriff Hunter. Tell him Max is at it again." He glanced at Max. "You're lucky you're so athletic, Mister. Your break could've been worse. So much for this football season."

Coach Charlie, standing farther away, growled.

Max and Riley grimaced at each other.

The paramedics went to work tending to Max's arm. Riley stood aside with Joe and waited for their parents to arrive: Sheriff Ace Hunter and their mother, Beth. The farm's horse trainer, Cindy, had returned with the manure spreader. Aware of the commotion down the road, she continued tending to the horses since the entire town of Pine Plains seemed to have arrived.

Max had gotten himself into trouble yet again.

Silvernails Road remained blockaded for the remainder of the day, except for one gap where a police officer let traffic pass by. One hundred feet off the road, the barn had been quarantined; yellow crime scene tape hugged it like a belt. Large and small vehicles with flickering red, blue, and white lights remained parked out front. Scores of investigators combed the site, which now ceased to be Max's secret hang out.

Broken in the Hospital

Max's crusty eyes flew open the morning after his grisly discovery. A bolt of pain shot through his arm and shoulder. The muscles in his back clenched into little knots. His head pounded.

He had slept well, considering his injury. The large, pencil-lead thick needle in his arm delivered a steady stream of mind-numbing medication.

The hospital insisted on holding him overnight because of his exposed wound. The bone had broken through the skin, exposed to rusty nails and decomposition from the pig and the dead body. Max had overheard the doctors discussing bacteria before fading out. Sepsis, toxic shock, and other things more horrible than the break itself issued from the mouths of adults in the room. Some nurses had even laughed, which annoyed Max.

His arm had been wrapped in gauze and braced so he couldn't bend it. The cast had not yet been applied and molded.

Max studied his purple fingers. They protruded from the end of the bandages like bloated sausages. Black, dry earth still filled his nail beds.

So much for clean hospital conditions, thought Max.

Diagnostic machines beeped, and blurted, feeding off his energy from the sticky, cold pads affixed to his skin. Wires spread out in all directions like tendrils.

And, Max noticed he only had on a white robe with a floral print!

"Where's my underwear?" he shrieked. He didn't recall permitting them. "Rude, inconsiderate...." He fished around with his free hand under the robe, inspecting under the sheets, to the left and the right of the bed, ensuring everything was in place. He noticed the white counter next to the aluminum sink contained jars of gauze, cotton, tongue depressors, and other goodies; they would make their way into his pockets. He always took souvenirs.

Max looked toward the door, sensing movement. He spied a dilapidated old female nurse passing by.

"Ma'am," said Max, his voice hoarse from a dry throat. The nurse had turned her back toward the opening, fiddling with medical instruments on a tray in the hallway. Max yelled again.

"Hell-O-O! Nurse! I need some help. Please!"

The nurse whipped around, dropping a clipboard and spilling sharp stainless steel instruments all over the floor. She berated herself quietly, muttering incomprehensible, sharp obscenities under her breath. Max never heard such language; he would chew a chunk of Dove or Ivory soap at home had he spoken them himself. He preferred Ivory, of course—no flowery scent or sticky aftertaste.

"Oh, I'll be right with you, young man. Hold your horses," said the nurse. She dropped to her knees, using her liver spot-covered, thin-skinned hands to scoop up the instruments. She placed them back on a tray dangling over her head.

She better not hit that thing with her head, thought Max. He imagined the sharp instruments falling once again, but this time impaling her in the back of the neck.

The nurse grunted, slowly wobbling from one leg to another until she stood up. She twisted her body left and right. Cracking noises resonated from her spine. She turned around and hovered in the doorway of Max's hospital room.

"What can I do you for?" she grunted, out of breath.

"Ma'am," said Max, "do you know when my parents will show up? When is breakfast?"

The nurse stepped inside his room. Her jittery hands snatched up the patient's file next to the bed.

"Looks like your cast will be applied in another hour ... you'll get breakfast ... your parents should be here by noon. Then you'll be discharged."

"Do I get any cool pins or screws in my arm?" said Max, excitement beaming from his face. Then he cringed as more pain shot down his arm.

"No, honey, the doctor wanted to make sure your wound would properly heal, but there's no need for additional equipment," the nurse informed him. Then she paused. "You can call me Nurse Carver, for now, sonny." Stretching and yawning, reaching her arms to the ceiling, she barely looked awake.

"Did you work all night?" said Max.

"Every night, yup ... here with all the sickies. You should rest some more sonny. The doctor will be in soon. Then the fun begins." She shot him a not-so-nice wink, like she knew something he didn't, looking a bit too excited.

"I just want to go home," said Max, cringing from the pain and coming torment.

"I hear you there, boy."

The two exchanged a casual, friendly smile.

Nurse Carver turned in the doorway. She held her bony hip with one hand and groaned from some unknown malady. Max turned his attention to his broken arm, wondering what it would be like to wear a cast.

N N N

An hour had passed, when a young male doctor arrived with a broad smile full of perfect, white teeth.

This one must've gotten some sleep, thought Max; *poor old nurse; happy young doctor!*

Max wondered if money had anything to do with it. Oh, the things he heard on television and in the news. Max knew doctors made good money, but as for Nurse Carver, he could only guess.

"How you doin' there, Mr. Max?" said the doctor in an energetic tone. Max wasn't sure how excited he could be considering his predicament.

"Oh, I'm just ok," said Max, who had been dozing. He squinted his eyes until they came into focus. His eyes fixed on the doctor's name embroidered on a stiff white coat: Jordan Devlish, MD.

"You ready for an awesome cast?"

"Ready as I'll ever be, sir."

"I'll get this thing over with, and you can have something to eat. You might throw up if you eat first." The doctor was frank. Max preferred the truth and cracked a sly smile.

Max bit down, grinding his teeth.

The doctor tore the white, sticky pads from Max's skin carefully ripping them off one at a time. Max was happy he didn't have any hair yet to go along with it. Next, Doctor Devlish extracted the needle from Max's arm, covering the wound with a firm cotton pad and more tape.

"The nurse is almost here. We'll get you back there and get it all taken care of," chuckled the doctor. He saw the look of frustration in Max's eyes.

"This happens all the time, little man. Easy as apple pie, or so they say."

The doctor flashed another white, toothy grin. His skin looked smooth and blemish-free. His hair sat stiff, perfectly coiffed in a high undercut like some fitness model.

This guy can't be more than twenty-six years old, thought Max. The fact the doctor looked young put Max at ease. He wasn't old and shaky or smelling like some weird chemical preserved his aged skin (like his experience with the other doctors).

"Hey, Doc," said Max, "what sport do you play?"

"Rugby," said the doctor. "And I don't suggest you start anytime soon, mister."

"I'm supposed to play football this fall… and I run."

"Way cool, little dude," said the doctor. The doctor quickly scribbled a few things in the patient file and rushed out the door waving.

Max passed the next twenty minutes in silence. Nurse Carver returned, still hitching around on a bum leg.

"Ok, son, time to move you to the other room," she said, storming into Max's hospital room. "Do you need to go pee? Or number two?"

"No, ma'am, none of those," said Max.

"Let's get it done then. It looks like your father is arriving sooner than expected, probably in the waiting room before we even finish." The nurse dragged a rusty, rattily wheelchair over, motioning Max to hop off the edge of the bed and sit in it.

In a flash, he scooted off the bed and plopped down in the chair. He clenched his teeth; another sharp pain shot through his arm. A muscle spasm raced through his shoulder.

"Yeah, I know it sucks," groaned the nurse noticing Max's facial expressions while fiddling with metal parts on the chair. "Wait till you get to be my age…"

Max looked up at the woman hovering inches over him. Paper-thin skin hung over her sun-deprived, bony cheeks. Her breath smelled like the horse barn, like dung and moldy hay. Max wrinkled his nose and did his best to hold his breath.

N N N

Another thirty minutes flashed by. It seemed like an eternity as the doctor applied Max's cast. The doctor was happy Max's wound didn't seep puss or bleed but informed him he'd need to come back to have it re-dressed in a week. A new cast would be applied.

"Can I have the same color next time?" said Max. "I love blue."

"Any color you want, young man," said the doctor. "Your dad's waiting outside, but do you want some breakfast first?"

"Can I just go home?"

"You sure?"

"Yeah. Thought my whole family would come. I feel a little barfi anyway, so I'm glad they didn't."

"NURSE!"

"Yes, doctor," said Nurse Carver, outside in the hallway. She entered the room and bent over to prepare the wheelchair for Max. Max noticed two bandages on the back of her emaciated neck. He couldn't keep from laughing.

"Did you spill those things again?" Max squealed with delight.

"The supply tray is very unsteady," said the nurse, acting defensive. She fidgeted with the wheelchair parts.

Nurse Carver stomped down on the brakes, ensuring the wheels locked. She forced them back up, releasing the brakes, and shoved the chair up against the examination table. "Go on, get in the chair." She tapped her foot and sighed as though everything bothered her, including Max.

"Hold on, give me a sec," said Max. He half-jumped, half-slid off the table, taking the paper liner with him.

"For crying out loud," growled the nurse. She reached over Max, under his legs, and snatched up the paper.

"Watch your hands," said Max, shrinking from her probing fingers. He still had a robe on...and nothing else.

Max backed into the rigid blue, cold vinyl seat and placed his slippered-feet in the footholds. He gave the nurse a sideways glance.

"Someone didn't sleep well yesterday, did she?"

"I sleep just fine, thank you," the nurse snapped. "You stay up all night..."

"I'm the one with the broken arm," grumbled Max.

The doctor had been working over the sink in the examination room. Listening to the two bark at each other, he chuckled under his breath.

"It's a nice day outside," said the doctor. "Maybe you should head on out of here, young man. Also, you nurse; I think you need a long break. Go out. Grab a coffee. Enjoy the day."

"Your father is waiting outside, Max." Doctor Devlish pointed to the long, glary hallway.

The nurse took the breaks off the wheelchair and lurched her charge toward the hallway door. Max rolled his eyes at the doctor and prepared for the bumpy ride to follow.

Grumpy old thing! Max felt even more miserable than the tired, sleep-deprived nurse.

His newly casted arm resided in a dark blue sling draped over his shoulder and around his neck. The cast rested heavy like cement. How he would ever function in school, he couldn't fathom. Gone would be his first season on the football team. He knew Coach Charlie was pissed. Gone, maybe, would be his job at the horse farm. He'd have to talk to his boss Cindy because the holidays were coming and he needed cash. Worst of all, his favorite hang-out spot became a crime scene.

The hospital's long halls were far from the dingy interior of his barn. Light blue-green walls gave away its clinical, sterile nature. Stark white ceiling tiles surrounded bright, blinding lights. Shiny, putty gray tiles covered the floor. Not a speck of dust or dirt remained.

The wheelchair careened forward, driven at a frightening pace by the less-than-delightful woman behind him. Left around a table. Right to miss the janitor coming from the broom closet. And a slight skid as Nurse Carver jerked the chair ninety degrees into the waiting room.

Max came to a sudden, skidding halt a foot from his father's tapping black police boots. The tapping stopped. His father jumped to his feet, startled by the sudden intrusion.

"I'm sorry, Sheriff Hunter," said Nurse Carver. "We can get going in these things sometimes —"

"As I recall, you have a couple of tickets in the system, Ms. Carver, for this very issue," said the sheriff. He stood up and tucked his thumbs into his thick black belt.

"Which I am preparing to pay, you bet."

"This week would be nice, but I'll give you a break because my son has a broken arm. You've been so kind and careful in taking care of him."

Sheriff Hunter looked down at Max's cast. "Blue? What kind of craziness is going on there? Whatever happened to basic, run of the mill white plaster? No wonder you're in trouble."

"For what?" screeched Max.

"Being somewhere you know we'd never allow. Always doing things differently."

Officer Hunter worked hard and preferred to command respect everywhere he went. Keeping up an image meant everything in a town where secrets hid around every corner, and the gossip ran like sap from the golden maple trees in fall. Ace may have been Max's father, but his family came second when he clocked in as the town's sheriff and worked in the presence of the public.

"If I weren't there," said Max, "you'd all never know about the body in the barn. You never said anything about not going in —"

"We'll talk when we get home, now get out of that thing. You only broke your arm for crying out loud." Sheriff Hunter pointed a stiff finger at the wheelchair. He shook his head. "You better toughen up, boy... If you ever plan to be a policeman like me —"

"Oh, you better get going then," said Nurse Carver, duly noting the sheriff's sour mood. She helped Max to his feet.

"For crying out loud," said Officer Hunter, "he's not a baby. He didn't break a leg!" He rolled his eyes at the nurse's unnecessary need to help his perfectly able son and strutted to the front desk to sign Max out.

The discharge nurse quickly loaded the clipboard with forms. Sheriff Hunter leaned against the counter, and she flashed a broad, cavernous smile while slipping it to him. The secretary to her right, a younger girl fresh from college, peeked around her and grinned.

"Hi, Sheriff. How's your day going?" The secretary swooned at the sight of the sheriff, laying on the charm and tossing her blond hair.

The discharge nurse moved, blocking the secretary who protested with a grump on her face.

"Don't mind her, sweetie, she's new. How's your equally handsome son doing?" She planted her elbows on the counter and rested her flawless, tan chin in her palms while leaning in toward the sheriff.

"His arm's just broken is all. His butt's going to be a bit red later too, so I'd say he's just fine, Miss Julie."

"Well, sounds a bit harsh —"

"Did you hear what they found in the barn he broke his arm in?" said the sheriff, looking down and signing his name on the form.

"No, do tell." Nurse Julie's cheeks glowed a deeper shade of pink, the more she talked to Max's dad.

"A dead body, and a gigantic, mutilated pig. Like one of those crop circle animals. All cut up."

Nurse Julie's face dropped in disgust. She looked at Max, who had joined his father at the counter.

"Mom's waiting, I'm sure, dad," said Max, ignoring the nurse on purpose. He tugged on his father's sleeve and grumbled. "Can we get going, please?"

Nurse Julie smiled and flashed her blue eyes. She shut her mouth with a pout when Ace didn't react. Sheriff Hunter was known as a "looker" and a "hottie" among the local women, turning heads wherever he went. The ladies of Pine Plains, and the surrounding towns like Sharron, didn't mind or care, how they acted around him. They were all very forward in expressing their interest.

Sheriff Hunter shrugged his broad shoulders and turned, slipping the clipboard into the nurse's polished hand before heading to the sliding glass doors dividing the waiting room from the parking lot.

Max had already rushed to the police cruiser, leaving his father to flirt. He knew he could use his father's interaction with the nurse as ammunition when the black belt came out. Max could avoid both a spanking and a grounding. His mom wouldn't suspect a thing if he got what he wanted.

WELCOME HOME MAX

Officer Bernard Reese waited at the Hunter family's farmhouse for the sheriff to arrive with Max. Being Sunday, his wife made him promise to be home in time for church, though she knew the current tragedy in Silvernails meant he'd be working days, nights, and even on weekends. Bernard dedicated his days to the department, but Sammie always recited church rhetoric: "You can't be more dedicated than y' are to God, Bernard. He's yer savior, remember. Get yer butt home in time to do his excellent work, you hear me?"

Bernard stalled in returning home. He preferred to hang with Mrs. Hunter and her family.

While just married, and with his first baby on the way, the excitement had already waned for Bernard. Sammie, though pretty, had already turned into a brute, demanding his undivided attention: no ogling other women; no beer with the guys; no, no, no. His place remained at home with her. He could never leave unless he was on duty. Oddly, the sheriff always demanded Bernard work overtime—thank the Lord! That's what Bernard told Sammie, anyway.

Ace always backed up Bernard.

Mrs. Hunter handed Bernard a big mug of scalding black coffee.

"You're the best Beth," said Bernard, cradling the hot cup and smiling.

"Well, you better hurry up. Ace's about to walk in. He said you two are headed to that old barn after he drops Max off."

"Yup, this one's a real mess. That crazy son of yours better be happy a broken arm's all he got," said Bernard. "At least he's a well-built boy for his age ... should heal easily." Bernard took another sup of coffee and set the mug down. "How's Riley?"

"Oh, she'll be fine. A scratch is all. Should heal up."

Bernard watched Beth tinker with dishes in the sink. The hot water from the faucet steamed the window glass while she scrubbed the morning's breakfast from the griddle. A couple sighs, and he knew thoughts raced through her mind.

"How are you holding up?"

"As good as anyone around here, I suppose," said Beth, letting out a more profound sigh and turning around. Suds dripped from her hands.

"I just don't understand something as insane as a violent murder and the mutilation of an animal. In OUR town."

She wore the worry every local mom had, hearing the news of such a grisly murder, and being so close to it. Beth felt it more than others, though. Everyone in her family had some role to play in the fiasco, and she couldn't get away from it.

"You all going to issue a curfew, or maybe...." Beth stopped herself and decided not to make any suggestions.

The front door to the house flew open, startling both Beth and Bernard. Thumping rattled the ceiling as Riley and Joe rushed down the stairs.

✎ ✎ ✎

Sheriff Hunter entered the house, dragging Max by the ear. Max cringed but didn't fight his father's quick temper while stumbling alongside.

"Beth, this boy needs a time out." He whipped around and released Max from his vice-like hands. "Max, get up there to your room, you're grounded."

"But dad," said Max, "I didn't do anything wrong. Can't I at least eat first?"

"Not till you take some time and think about WHY you have a cast on your arm. This is no joke, Max." Ace cleared his throat while unbuckling his belt, setting it and his gun on a side table. "And now you can't play football, either...."

Beth had dashed into the living room, leaving Bernard drinking his coffee at the counter. Bernard remained with his back to the kitchen door. He had no interest in family drama. His day would already be filled with death, and the wretched, stinky barn. He continued to sip his quickly-cooling coffee.

"And, you're going to school tomorrow, so you better rest up," continued Max's father.

Beth dropped to her knees. "Max, honey, how's your arm? You poor thing!" She fussed over Max as though he were a broken crystal pitcher.

Riley laughed, clutching the stair's oak railing. She relished the moment her brother would finally receive an honest punishment. Joe felt more sympathetic, easing over to his father's other side and peeking around while his mother probed Max for undiscovered issues.

Ace threw his hands up, took his hat off, and circled the sofa to the kitchen where his officer sat. "He's all yours."

"Mom...."

Max cried. He pressed his head into Beth's shoulder and sobbed, unable to help himself. Nothing this horrific had ever happened to him before, and the realization of what he had experienced finally took its toll.

"Oh, you've been incredibly brave, seeing all those things. And your poor arm."

"He's fine," said Riley. "Come on, Max, let's go upstairs."

"But I'm hungry," Max whined, unable to hold the infantile sound back. "The hospital didn't give me any food."

Ace yelled from the kitchen, having overheard the commotion. "He refused to eat, the nurse told me at the desk."

Beth whispered in Max's ear. "Which one?"

"The one with the teeth, Mom," he said, his eyes wet and nose stuffed.

"Not the secretary?"

"No, mom. The other one."

Beth knew the nurses well. The women of Pine Plains knew of their wandering eyes at Sharon Hospital and their history of straying with married men. She also knew the discharge desk where Ace checked Max out. She shot her husband an accusing look while hugging her son. She whispered in Max's ear: "I'll take care of it."

Max got a peck on the cheek before his silent trek upstairs with Riley. Joe crept up behind them.

"I'll bring some food up, honey. What do you want?"

Max turned while climbing the steep, wooden steps. "Grilled cheese?"

"You go rest, I'll be right up," said his mother. "Grilled cheese and tomato soup."

"Mom?" said Max.

"Yes?"

"I know you're waiting for that answer from me... I think I'd like to become an investigator someday. Just so you know."

Beth winked and waved for Max to go upstairs.

Max spent the remainder of his Sunday staying out of the way. His father had left with Bernard to investigate at the barn. Max played board games with his siblings in his room and theorized what, or who had created the horror they all witnessed Saturday morning.

Max's bedroom made use of the third-floor attic, the highest place in the farmhouse. A floor to ceiling, arched window overlooked the two red barns on the property's eighty acres. Behind the barns, Max grew his prized pumpkins which had swelled as the end of the summer drew near. The fall festival would be upon them, and he knew he'd be the winner in the largest pumpkin contest. He could see it all from his bed, with its frame pressed against the window.

Max also possessed the doll.

Riley had stashed the doll in the back of Max's bottom drawer, behind his socks and underwear. Max found it the most impressive and creepiest thing he had ever seen.

Max smelled money when he thought about making them for a profit at the festival. Who wouldn't want to buy something connected to the murder? With Halloween coming up, and the state of fear the town would be in, the dolls would be a winner. Max agreed with the politicians he saw on TV, "Never to let a good crisis go to waste." If he couldn't work with the horses for a while, sales would have to be the next best thing.

The day ended. Max fell asleep full of grilled cheese. His mind burst with ideas he intended to share with his friends the next day in school.

A FAMILIAR RIDE

A crisp September, Monday morning arrived. The events of Saturday were fresh on everyone's minds in the small New York town of Pine Plains. Especially at Max's house.

It was customary on the Hunter farm for alarms to sound at four o'clock on weekdays, each member did their share.

Max tended to the chickens and collected eggs.

Riley helped milk the six heifers.

Joe cleaned stalls for the cows, goats, and feathered creatures.

Beth prepared breakfast.

And Sheriff Ace Hunter oversaw operations and prepared for his long day at the station, always grumbling over how he needed a career change.

This Monday was no exception, regardless of a complaint, head cold, or broken limb. Sheriff Hunter accepted no excuses.

"Max!" said his father. "You're still on chicken duty. Get a move on, buddy."

Max stumbled around, half asleep. In a new pair of blue jeans, a black T-shirt (ripped to accommodate the enormous cast) and white sneakers, he descended the steep stairs to the living room. He slid into his father's vast hunter-green, light down vest (the only coat he could put his arm through), and headed out to the chicken coop, not too far from his prized pumpkins.

"Man, it's cold outside," said Max, who opened the rear door with one hand and stepped out onto the porch. His siblings ran out from behind him, blowing their breath into the air, and creating steamy white clouds.

"Not too cold, maybe forty degrees," said Riley. She veered toward the barn to milk the cows.

"At least you don't have to shovel poop," said Joe, dreading another morning of animal feces—just what he needed to smell like during the day at school. Being the oldest and having to handle a sharp pitchfork, Joe was the sole user of the pointed tool until Riley turned another year older. Riley already complained about milking cows being dull, and how she wanted to do some real work, like Joe.

Max smiled. "Maybe if you would get those grades up, bro, dad would split chores between all of us."

"You're an accident waiting to happen, Max," said Joe.

"I use a pitchfork at the horse farm all the time. Cindy trusts me."

Riley kept out of it. As the middle sister, she couldn't support either side and win, often keeping her mouth shut. If she ever did get in trouble, Max was usually at fault. Her youngest brother often succeeded at pointing the evidence in Riley's direction.

Max watched as his mother worked on Riley, who just turned fourteen and, as Beth liked to say, started "blooming." She often called Riley her third son, because the girl spent too much time aiding Max in his meddling; she got into trouble just as often. Riley also refused to wear dresses, opting for jeans, and plaid shirts. Her hair hung in a twisting mess, long and knotted in spots.

In the last month, Beth managed to convince Riley to try manicuring her hands and toes. Riley agreed and found she enjoyed painting her nails.

Riley called to her brothers while running across the yard. "Let's see how the cows like these!" She flashed her freshly painted, bright red fingernails, and proceeded to grimace while making squeezing motions with her hands.

From inside, their father yelled again. "Get your butts to work! The school bus comes in an hour."

Max tried running for the barn, intent on feeding the chickens and collecting their eggs. He didn't get far. The brick-like cast on his arm forced him to stop. Leftover anesthesia continued to wear him out. He was forced to walk to the barn, slowly, and his brother and sister passed him laughing. He knew he had an exhausting day ahead.

↗ ↗ ↗

Max snored the entire ride to school. The diesel fumes he regularly complained about engulfed the back seats of the school bus. He always got a headache, and his complaints about the unsafe conditions and possible asphyxiation made him very unpopular with the school's mechanics. They'd come back each time saying, "There's nothing wrong with our bus, no sir, nothing at all." Word would get back to Max's father, who'd berate him later at the dinner table over exaggerating so much.

The bus finally careened down Main Street, whizzing under the street lights in the center of town, around the pharmacy, and down the county road to the school.

Max awoke from the crashing of metal as the bus barreled over several speed bumps in the parking lot. Mr. Tom wasn't known for taking anything slow, and he always rushed to get the rowdy kids off his bus.

The orange behemoth lurched to a stop, and the doors flew open with a snap.

Max took his time. Not only had Ace filled Max's backpack with books, but Max's broken arm throbbed.

"You got those books, bro?" said Riley.

"Yeah. I need to get used to it, I suppose."

"Ten weeks?"

"At least." Max cringed. "It's throbbing today. I can't stand it."

Riley patted his back as they descended the stairs to the sidewalk.

Kids massed on the front lawn, waiting for Mrs. Elliot, the school's secretary, to open the doors. Max noticed the usual girls huddled together. They whispered and shot glances at boys who ran around, chasing one another through what remained of the dying green turf.

Farther down the sidewalk, closer to the gym, several police cars sat empty. Officers wrapped in black, thick-looking tactical gear, with bright green reflective vests, and casual ball caps, paced around. Bernard and Max's dad had not yet arrived.

Riley whispered in Max's ear. "I bet we're going to have an assembly today … because of the murder."

"YUP," yelled Joe, who had been standing nearby, listening in. "Dad's going to be coming too. We're going to get some tips on how to protect ourselves."

Several students spotted Max and rushed over. His blue cast gave him away. Anything out of place became a target for wild teenage gossip.

"Wow, what happened to you?" said Kevin, Max's lab partner in science.

"Super cool, Max. How'd you do that?" said the new French exchange student, André.

Bethany Waters had a different opinion, though no one asked. "Again? What's wrong with you? A blue cast?" She stood there with her arms crossed. Her shiny brown hair projected out in two pigtails. Her mother bought her designer labels, but Bethany always had something cruel to say.

Max hated her guts.

"Shut up, Bethany," said Max. "Does anything nice ever come out of your dirty little mouth?"

Bethany clammed up fast. A look of shock spread across her face. No one had ever responded to her that fast. Certainly, not Max Hunter. He was two grades below her and, despite being powerful for his age, was an easy target. Or so she thought.

"The bone splintered in half and tore straight through," said Max.

"But how?"

"I fell, simple as that."

"Yeah," said Riley. "Slipped on some hay, fell pretty hard." She lied.

"What are you going to do about the fair?" said Kevin.

"Yeah, your pumpkins are getting huge from those pics you showed me," said André.

"I'll manage —"

Laughter amongst the police officers stole their attention.

Sheriff Hunter arrived. He pulled his personal, lifted black suburban behind the other police cars, and shut the engine off. The laughter fizzled as the officers straightened their uniforms. Fake looks of seriousness took over their faces.

Max surveyed the boys running around on the lawn, acting like idiots.

He couldn't help but think the police could link any of his classmates to the grisly murder in his barn. Even the police officers themselves farther down the sidewalk. Any of the teachers in school, people he passed on the roads, and even his boss, Cindy, who lived and worked just up the street from the barn, could be suspects. Not one of them looked like the murdering type.

He still needed to call Cindy, too. Better yet, he could get his father to bring him to the farm after school because the crime scene was across the road.

"What do you think, Max?" said Bethany, breaking Max's concentration.

Max hadn't paid her any attention. "Think about what?"

"Didn't you hear anything I said?"

"Believe it or not, I have more pressing things on my mind, thank you."

Bethany huffed, and let out a dramatic sigh. She put her hands on her hips.

"The creepy girl over there. The new one...." Bethany pointed toward the entrance to the school, and a strange new girl Max had never seen before.

"Now, she's a looker," said Riley. "She's so freakin' pale."

"I think they call it Goth," said Joe. "The black hair ... and look at her fingernails...."

Even from far across the yard, the girl's black fingernails were hard to miss.

She dawned straight black hair with sharply cut bangs.

Her leggings were a patchwork of black, white, and gray squares, and she wore black flats, and a baby doll top—also black. Unlike the others in the yard, she didn't wear a jacket and braved the crisp fall air without shivering.

Max also noticed something peculiar: while the other kids ran around, letting out breaths of white, steamy air into the bitter morning, the girl acted like it was a warm, sunny day. Her breathing didn't fog up like the other kids.

"I think she's cool looking," said Max. "Must be from the city."

"I'd say so," said Bethany, "but she'll never fit in around here."

"Oh, I think you'll be best friends," said Max.

"What do you mean, loser?"

"I mean, she dresses well, like you." Max tried to be kind. "Everyone else around here dresses like farmworkers."

"You know what grade she's in?" said Joe. "She looks a bit older — "

"No one knows anything yet," said Bethany, acting defensive.

Max stared. The girl pretended like no one looked at her, and kept to herself by the unopened doors of the school. Not a single student approached her; they stood around in packs, engrossed in their childish, cliquish drama.

Joe glanced at the girl over his shoulder while strutting toward his father. Max took note of his brother's interest.

"Ask dad what's up!" said Max. "And take your time…."

Joe waved him off with his hand.

The school bell rang with a shrill, buzzing convulsion. It was broken. The school never got around to fixing it, no matter how many kids complained. Max shielded his ears with his free arm, lowered his head, and headed in the direction of the opening doors.

The pale girl had disappeared.

N N N

Once inside, Max veered right. He had lucked out, receiving a locker close to the central office near the entrance to the school. His father had demanded it for his own children's safety—it was one of the perks of being the son of the town's sheriff. Riley's and Joe's lockers flanked Max's. He never heard the end of it from his friends, or from some of his new team-mates, Jay, Xander, and Tony, who happened to be walking by at that very moment.

"Man, Coach Charlie's pissed!" said Tony. He spied Max opening his locker, and narrowly missed running over several kids while thundering across the hallway.

Tony Collins was an enormous boy for being Max's age: thirteen years old, five foot ten, and a brute on the football team. Coach Charlie found Tony was a solid bet because his father owned the local excavating company and (everyone knew) being rich paid Tony's way into anything the kid wanted. Tony was intimidating, though. Unfortunately for Max, the kid was also the school's worst bully. He leaned on Max for test answers and special favors.

Max dreaded the boy.

Tony whacked Max's cast with the back of a hand. "You were supposed to round out the team, man. Coach Charlie was counting on you, bruh." He hit Max's cast a second time, sending sharp shockwaves of pain up and down Max's arm.

Luckily for Max, Mr. London, the history teacher, passed by and stood between the two boys. Mr. London loomed a lot larger than Tony, towering over him and everyone else in the school.

"Your locker is on the second floor, Mr. Collins. Times almost up." Mr. London pointed to the stairs, saying nothing else. Tony attempted to hit Max's cast a third time, but a fast arm block from the teacher cut him off. The two exchanged a silent, tense stare.

Tony stormed off up the stairs, but couldn't resist talking back over his shoulder.

"You gotta face me some day, Hunter." Tony's voice echoed and faded as he disappeared around the stairwell's corner. He laughed. "I'm your worst nightmare…"

"Thanks, Mr. London, I owe you," said Max, embarrassed.

Mr. London smiled and patted Max on his back. "This is just the slightest moment in time, Max. You'll get your chance. You're almost Tony's size, anyway." Mr. London puffed out his chest. "History favors the bold, young man. Someday you might even be sheriff of this town. Who knows what you can do. You can do anything you want."

The teacher turned and walked back toward an open door.

Max had thought about a future in law enforcement. The genes were in his family. With many of his friends being groomed for careers after graduation—six full years away—Max had preoccupied himself with the idea of being like his father. Though, in just under a day, and under his mother's orders, Max decided her preferred investigating to issuing speeding tickets.

Max decided to take a chance—as his mother put it—and unmask the murderer.

И И И

The Stissing Mountain Middle School and High School were connected, forming a sterile, lifeless square box. White tile covered the floors. The walls were tan cinderblock. The classroom doorways had been painted a basic white with no distinguishing features except their nameplates.

Beyond Max's locker on the ground floor were the large, double doors to the library, followed by the large auditorium, and the gym. The building was curved like a giant U. Outside, behind the school, a large garden spread out with several trees, and memorial markers with plaques memorializing students who had tragically died throughout the school's history.

A commotion resounded near the auditorium as the sheriff, and his officers entered the building.

Joe came running down the hall directly at Max.

"It's definitely an assembly..." said Joe, out of breath. "In place of the first and second periods, the whole school is in the auditorium. Plus, our parents are coming."

"Man, they could've brought us to school, instead of that smelly old bus," said Max, irritated. Even though no one believed him, Max felt gassed to death on his rides to and from school. But, he had a plan to get back at driver Tom and the whiny mechanics, which, unfortunately, made the bus smell worse than it should. Under one of the front seats, Max had taped a plastic bag of broccoli with several small slits cut in it. The broccoli slowly rotted, making the front of the bus smell like nasty, broccoli farts. The mechanics could never figure it out. They never looked under the seats. Max waited to see how bad it would get. The other kids would just have to deal with it.

Max rummaged around in his locker, grabbing the books and supplies he would need.

"Wait till after homeroom, idiot," said Riley. "If we don't have first and second —"

"My third period is science. Aren't we getting a new teacher today?" said Max.

"Yeah, Mrs. Jacobson is out of here. Or so I heard," said Joe.

"Probably some old fart," said Max.

He slammed the locker shut with a BANG. The sound gained the attention of the officers at the other end of the hall, including his father, who pointed at him, duly noting Max's lousy behavior. Max knew he'd hear about it later, which ensured the day would be that much more miserable, but it was nothing new.

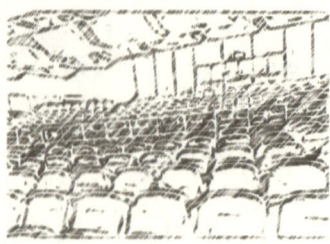

THE BIOLOGY TEACHER

The new goth girl sat at the first table in the entrance to the cafeteria, commonly known in the morning as Homeroom. Max didn't pay attention when he barreled through the doors, and, being chased by other students, tripped and nearly ended up in the new girl's lap.

Max's science books spilled on the floor when he fell to his knees. He landed on his side at her feet, avoiding his broken arm in the process. His body made a dull THUD. He grunted, losing his breath.

"Oh, my, are you ok?" said the girl, surprised.

Max looked up, rolled onto his back, and viewed her upside down. Her black hair hung over his face like a mop. Her glossy black eyes grew wide, and she held back a laugh.

"Go ahead, laugh, it's a little funny ... I suppose," said Max.

She smirked and bent over to retrieve his school supplies. Max teetered onto his side and squirmed up onto his knees, making sure to avoid the clumsy cast in the sling.

"How did you break it?" said the girl, nodding at the cast.

"Just a fall."

The girl huffed at his response like she didn't believe him. She placed his things on the cold white bench attached to the folding table and extended her hand.

"I'm Maxine, by the way."

"Oh...."

"And you?" She got close to his face. Too close. Max blinked several times and backed up.

"Well? What's your name?" said Maxine.

"Um ... well...." He didn't know what to say.

How strange, thought Max, *our names—the same, or darn close to it.*

"It's Max. Yeah, right. You can laugh."

The girl perked up. An unmistakable look of delight spreading across her face.

"Too cool!"

"Too weird," grumbled Max, who had begun collecting his things, avoiding any eye contact with the new Maxine. The fact they shared a name unnerved him. He felt the day couldn't get any stranger or annoying, but he was wrong.

Having overheard Max's discussion, André and Kevin fell into hysterics as they hustled toward the unlikely pair.

"I wonder. What can we do with this?" said Kevin, elbowing André.

"Max, Maxine... Maxi Pad? Beaucoup des options —" André stopped, unable to speak through the avalanche of giggling erupting from his mouth.

"Don't even start," said Max.

"Too late," said Kevin. "You're stuck with us for six more years."

"Well, not me," said André. "Just a year ... then back to Paris."

Maxine interrupted, noticing Max's frustration.

"So, I see you're in Biology." She pointed to his textbook.

"Yeah, seventh grade, but we have some new teacher coming —"

"One of my parents is the new science teacher," said Maxine.

"Your mother, or your father —" The bell cut Kevin off, followed by a woman on the loudspeaker. Her scratchy, piercing voice directed the students to line up in Homeroom, by grade, and follow their teacher's aides to the auditorium.

Ms. Stout stood at the head of the line. She slouched with her hands on her broad hips, and the usual look of disapproval on her plump overly blushed cheeks.

"Be quiet. Get in line. Means you too, Rickey." Ms. Stout arched an eyebrow at Rickey Masterson. Puberty consumed Rickey, who was now covered in freckles, angry pimples, and fidgeting from not taking his ADD meds.

None of the kids liked Ms. Stout. She never smiled, even when Max told the best jokes in the world. Why she chose to work in the school, none of them could ever fathom. She clearly disliked kids. Even the teachers kept their distance.

Ms. Stout always smelled like bacon. However, she was in charge, so the class lined up fast and kept their mouths shut, hastening an end to the torture.

Ms. Stout grunted and whipped around: "This way, kiddos." She led them through the cafeteria doors and down the hallway past Max's locker, past the library, and to the large wooden doors of the auditorium. Outside, two police officers stood like statues, smiling and welcoming each of Max's classmates with handshakes and the occasional pat on the shoulder.

On Max's way through the door, a muscular arm held him aside while the rest of the line passed. His father stood behind one of the doors and made his presence known.

"Hey."

Max turned and flinched at the intrusion.

"Hey, dad."

"How's that arm?"

"Fine, I guess. It really hurts, though, kinda throbbing."

"Oh, you're used to screwing up … remember when you broke your leg?"

Max remembered. His sister regularly reminded him how they all got into trouble following Max into that hold hunter's house deep in the woods.

"Sorry, dad. I'll try not to do it again —"

"It won't happen again." His father squatted to catch Max at eye level. "Now, I want to remind you NOT to talk about the incident—what you saw—in the barn, ok? I mean it."

His father's face grew stern, and his brow creased. He forcefully grasped Max's shoulders with his enormous hands.

"Promise," said Max, though he held his free hand behind him with his fingers crossed. How could he possibly keep something like this to himself? In such a dull, little country town (where talk of hunting season or the start of fall football took center stage), Max and his friends were always trying to come up with something new and exciting to do. So, he squeezed his fingers tighter, hoping the extra effort would seal the deal—he had some plans and wanted to know whom the leg belonged to, who committed the murder, and what the dolls had to do with it.

Max knew he'd need his friends to help investigate.

"Now, we're going to let your classmates, and the town, know about the murder, but nothing else," said Ace. "We're giving some tips on what to look out for, and how we'll protect the town, ok?"

"Yes, dad, I understand," said Max. "Can you help me with something, though?"

"What is it?"

"Can you take me to the horse farm later, or sometime this week? I want to talk to Cindy. I still want to do some work."

"Oh, I don't think you should work while your arm is healing," said Ace. "Plus, that nasty barn is right there, and if there's a murderer on the loose, I want you as far away from the scene as possible, except when you pass by on the school bus."

"Can I at least stop? See Cindy? Just for a bit?"

"I'll take you for a visit. You can pet the horses."

This satisfied Max. He'd get the chance to work his way into something, he always did. Maybe a side job, or at least plan on when he could come back. He was also angry. He needed Christmas money and didn't know what else he could do. The doll entered his mind, and his plans to create more of them to sell at the fair. He always thought of ways to make his own money.

"It's a plan, dad."

Max gave his father a half-hug, wrapping his useful arm around the sheriff's neck and choking him playfully while growling like a bear.

Sheriff Hunter stood up, took a big breath, and headed into the auditorium while anchoring his hat to his buzzed head. Ms. Stout commanded the entrance and wasted no time directing Max to the row his classmates sat in. One spot remained open on the aisle. Maxine sat in the second seat.

"You're in my grade?" whispered Max, surprised. The girl looked a lot older, more like a Sophomore. Max even noticed Joe giving her an extra glance when they were outside.

Joe had perked up when he saw Maxine in front of the school. Now Max had something new to hold over Joe's head.

Joe kept his distance from Max when other students were around, but at home, they'd share stories from their day and play video games.

Joe always won. Riley would always jump in and add her girly-stuff, but she was more of a tom-boy, as Beth put it, so it wasn't all bad. She never talked about boys, considering she was at "that age."

Ms. Stout, who had been standing nearby, put her finger to her lips and hissed: "Shush!" The auditorium fell silent. Sheriff Hunter and his deputies briefed the school, and the community, about the recent murder and their plans to protect the town.

ᴎ ᴎ ᴎ

Two hours passed. Many people asked questions the officers couldn't or refused to answer. The auditorium emptied amidst grumbles from dissatisfied townsfolk who demanded more answers. The students had begun to fidget, and the teachers worked hard and fast to get them out and to their third-period classes.

A general sense of annoyance had taken over the occupants of the school. Everyone understood the murder. The murderer had not yet been found or named and remained on the loose.

Police activity would increase.

Students and school staff were to take special care not to go anywhere alone. And the most horrible part of all, the one thing no one in the community liked, especially the kids (which created a heavy tone of anger and resentment throughout the rest of the school day), was the new curfew imposed in the town of Pine Plains by the Sheriff's Department. NO children were to walk unattended. Buses would not run until the sun came up each day.

Absolutely no children were to be outside of their homes after five o'clock each day unless attended by an adult.

The implications were far-reaching. Fall sports would suffer, afterschool jobs and activities would be cut short, and parents would have less time to themselves.

In Max's science class—third-period Biology—chirps of dissatisfaction sputtered from the lips of everyone in the room. At least until the new teacher arrived.

Ten minutes into the class, the door opened. A curious-looking person entered the room, escorted by the principal. Heads turned as they walked in, with several students uttering a dull, but drawn out, "Oh!" under their breaths. Max did the same, and while he understood Maxine had said one of her parents was the new teacher, he hadn't prepared himself.

"Hello, class," rumbled the principal, stepping aside as the new teacher took up residence behind the desk, in front of the blackboard. "Please welcome your new Biology teacher, Dallas Finn."

Among the shocked faces, Maxine gave a low wave. The room turned into a sea of open mouths and confused looks until Max broke the stalemate.

"It's nice to meet you," said Max. He didn't know how to address the new teacher. No one in the room could tell if they were a man or a woman. Maxine had stated it would be one of her parents.

"Hello class," said the teacher, "you can call me Dallas. I prefer Dallas to any other name, so please call me Dallas for the time you are in my class."

"Are you our regular teacher, or a sub?" said one boy.

"There will be no substitutes. I don't get sick. I am your regular teacher from now on—both Biology and Chemistry, grades eight through twelve."

"Please, class, give Dallas a big welcome," said the principal who began clapping.

"Welcome, um ... Dallas." The class hesitated. The kids typically addressed their teachers as Mr. or Mrs., and their last names.

Dallas quickly ushered the principal, Mr. Jake Fischer, out of the room. He stumbled through the door, just missing plowing his head into the top of the door because he stood almost seven feet tall. He slapped his head to keep his badly-placed hair-piece from catching and falling off.

The new teacher noted the white clock on the wall. Little time remained. Dallas wasted no time ripping open a brown leather briefcase on the desk and pulling out a pile of sealed envelopes.

"Ok, class. Now that introductions are over with, I want each of you, row by row, to come up to my desk, and take one blank name tag,"—the expressions on the students faces revealed their aversion to the changes as the new teacher whipped out a Sharpie and a stack of name tags—"AND ... ONE envelope."

Muttering ensued as each of the students stood up. Max approached the teacher first as the others fell in line behind him.

Arriving at the desk, Max looked at Dallas Finn in the face and forced a smile. He felt nervous more than scared. The new teacher was a sight—something the town, as far as Max knew, had never had before. He, or she, looked quite spectacular.

If a man, the teacher was very fine-featured, wearing a well-pressed Armani suit, with perfect close-cropped blond hair, and had the look of a scholar. If a woman, the signs were even more obscure. Dallas had flawless skin and was well perfumed, with perfectly manicured hands and high cheekbones, a long neck, and was exceptionally well poised. Dallas also had an English accent, or Australian, something Max knew meant class, at least from what he heard on television.

Dallas had no rings on, and no necklace—no jewelry of any kind. It didn't take Max long to size up the new teacher, using investigative tactics his father had taught him to get a read on people—something that came in handy, except, in this case, he still couldn't figure it out. He knew it would be too soon to press Maxine about it, he had only known her for a couple of hours, and it would be rude.

Max accepted the name tag with a smile, wrote his name in black Sharpie, and left the desk with one of the thick sealed envelopes. Max knew each student behind him would be tearing the teacher apart in their heads, trying to figure Dallas out. Oddly, as Max watched the line form, not one student frowned. They seemed quite excited, even happy.

Max sat in his seat and waited for the line to finish passing by.

Dallas explained what was expected of the eager students.

"Quiet please, we only have five more minutes, so let me explain," said Dallas, who stood still, waiting for the last of the students to settle into their chairs and face forward.

"What are the envelopes for?" said Carmen.

Max had decided Carmen was one of the prettier girls in the class. He had partnered up with her during several labs when Kevin had the flu. He liked her oddly vast knowledge of biology and anything anatomical, and she never hesitated to tell gory stories. She was a strange one, too.

"Good question," said Dallas, who hesitated, and created a game out of the moment. "Can anyone guess what's inside each envelope? Anyone? Not you though Maxine.... "

Heads turned toward the new girl, who had been inconspicuous in the back row, but whom Dallas outed. Dallas had not told the class Maxine was family, only Max knew.

"Lottery tickets?" yelled one boy.

"No."

"A teacher evaluation form?" said another.

"No, you can't evaluate someone you don't yet know," said Dallas.

"A prize?"

"No."

Hands kept popping up, but none of the students got the correct answer. Another girl—Emily Puckett, a poor farm girl from the outskirts of town—raised her hand.

"It's a science project or several science projects, and we are going to get into teams."

"You're quite correct, lovely," said Dallas. "You win a prize, Emily."

Emily looked down at her name tag. She had not yet written her name on it or pasted it above her heart like most of the others. She smiled, though, happy someone knew her without a tag.

"After class, Emily," said Dallas. "Let us finish up first. Everyone open your envelopes and behold the wonders inside."

Envelopes crackled. The sound of tearing paper pierced the silence of the room. Max's classmates extracted the folded documents inside and read the words printed on them in script with a fountain pen.

"You will see a number on the top right side of your paper, class," said Dallas, directing the students to areas of the room with swift motions of arms and hands. "Ones meet in the corner next to the fish tank; twos meet by the lab rats; threes meet by the skeleton; fours by the front door; and fives in the middle of the room. You have five minutes to debate, make a plan, and we'll pick this up tomorrow when you return."

Max had a three on his paper and ran to the corner by the skeleton, as did several other students. Maxine sat among them.

"How interesting," said Maxine. "How ironic."

Max chuckled. "So, we meet again."

Several other students joined the group to discuss the new science project. Max and Maxine decided to meet at the school's library later in the week to do research.

The new teacher, Dallas Finn, watched Max and Maxine with curiosity and flicked a finger at Emily to come to the desk for a chat.

CAMILLA THE LIBRARIAN

Biology class ended, but not without producing its share of new gossip.

While Dallas Finn took second place in the realms of teacher and student gossip, the weekend's murder, and the body now at Dr. Paris Esteban's morgue, took first place.

Max Hunter couldn't hold back from telling his friends what he knew, despite his father's warning.

In the hallway, and during the fifteen minutes between the third and fourth periods, Max spilled his guts to a small but eager crowd.

Max surveilled the hallway, making sure evil eyes weren't watching.

"I was there. You can't tell anyone I told you." Max whispered. "So were Riley and Joe."

"You saw the murder?" said Kevin.

"No, it happened before I got there. I fell on some boards and uncovered the body."

"So, you broke your arm at the murder scene?" said André.

"Yup, the bone tore right through my skin." Max had to inject drama into his story. He liked the faces the other kids made. "A dead pig was dumped in the middle of the floor —"

"No way. Awesome!" said Kevin, almost drooling. "What did the body look like?"

"Oh, we only saw the leg. It was nasty, covered in tattoos … and the foot was black, rotten."

"Gross."

"Yuck."

"I need to know who it was," said Max.

"A woman?"

"Couldn't tell," said Max.

André laughed. "Like the new teacher—how do we figure out the gender?"

"I have an idea," said a girl in the group.

Everyone turned their heads.

Carmen Esteban regularly kept to herself and sat next to the window every day. She wasn't altogether bad looking, Max and the other boys thought so. With straight blonde hair falling down her back and delicate features, she physically looked better than most other girls.

But she was strange. The energy she gave off unnerved Max. Her peculiar habits made everyone nervous. Her thin little fingers would tap on her desk. She startled those around her by chewing pencils until they splintered and snapped in half in her mouth.

Carmen spoke up, shocking Max.

"What are you thinking?" said Max.

The other kids looked at Carmen. No one said a word. They didn't want to upset her, fearing what she might do.

"You know my mother, don't you?" said Carmen. "Dr. Paris Esteban? She's the town mortician."

"What's a mortician?" said Kevin.

"You're in Spanish, aren't you?" said André. "Now, take the word 'mort'... spell out M O R T. what does it mean?"

"Dead."

"So, what does a mort—tician, do?"

Kevin rolled his eyes. "They deal with dead people, duh."

"Actually, guys, she fixes them. She gets them ready for viewing after they're dead, so families can see them before they are buried. So, they won't rot and stink."

"What does fixing dead people have to do with anything?" said Max.

"Well, my mom has access to the morgue."

A moment of silence overtook the kids. It didn't take Max long to figure out Carmen hinted at having access to the morgue.

"You mean we can get in there? See dead bodies?"

"Well, we'll have to figure it out. The morgue doesn't just allow people in," said Carmen, who took a moment to look around. Like Max, she made sure she only told her fellow students, and no one else would hear.

"She has a key."

Unbeknownst to Max and his friends, Bethany had skillfully crept up on the group. Her gruff voice pierced the moment as Max considered how to enter the morgue, when and whether the leg and the person it belonged to would be easily accessible. If he could have a look at the tattoos, and other things on the body, maybe he could give the person a name and discover what happened.

He had to know.

"What are you all scheming over here?" said Bethany, pushing her way into the circle.

Kevin jumped at her pronouncement. Bethany's face appeared directly over his shoulder. He could feel her wet, clammy breath against his face. He shrank away, twitching and batting at his ear lobe.

"I heard something about a morgue?"

Max cut her off. "We're just talking about the dead person they found."

"Gruesome, I agree," said Bethany. "Shouldn't you all be heading to your next class, though?"

Several heads bent down, looking at cell phones. One minute remained until the fourth period.

Bethany laughed, "You didn't hear the bell? Wow, you're all so busy over here scheming —"

Max whispered to Carmen and his friends. He turned his back to Bethany.

"Let's meet up at lunch … at the far table. Ok?"

Heads nodded "yes" as the group scattered. Some ran down the far hallway, while others climbed the stairs to the second floor.

They all left Max to defend himself from Bethany, who had not yet gone.

"So," said Bethany, "what's up with the Carmen girl? She's all bug-eyed over you."

"She's just trying to be nice, Bethany. Maybe you should try it sometime."

"I am nice. The prettiest. The —"

Max cut her off before she could make him puke from her long list of outstanding personal attributes.

"I gotta run."

"I'll see you at lunch then, save me a seat!" Bethany skipped away, happy she had invited herself, as always.

Max shook his head and rubbed the blue cast in its sling. His arm pulsated, and it itched. Nothing he did made his skin stop crawling. He growled to himself and sprinted up the steps to the English class.

И И И

Another forty-five minutes passed as Ms. Ballinger droned on about yet another fall writing project. The students were required to write a paper about someone they admired and compare them to someone they did not respect.

Max scowled when he considered the difficulty of the project. There were no people he felt strongly about, though he sat there thinking about Ms. Lurchner, the AP English teacher. She had rejected him from her class, saying Max "was not up to par."

I have all A's!

Max would often walk by her door, seeing many kids he knew playing games and laughing. He always felt she gave some undeserved preference to them. She was also a ridiculously tall, intimidating woman with buzzed blond hair; Max felt overpowered when next to her.

Ms. Lurchner was the person he didn't respect.

A finger tapped him on the rear shoulder as Ms. Ballinger continued to discuss the assignments.

One of the kids whispered, "Hey, Max, you should tell us more about what you saw in the barn."

Max whispered back, "In just a few minutes. I think she's finishing."

The teacher put her hands on the desk and stopped talking.

Sally McBride stood up. Coke bottle glasses grossly magnified her eyes. She pulled the stack of papers from the teacher's hand and handed them out to each student.

Several heads leaned in toward Max as the girl made the rounds.

"It was nasty," said Max behind his hand, working to ignore Sally's startling face. "We found a giant dead pig. No clue how it got in there. The opening of the floorboards is too small."

"What did it look like?"

"What do you think a dead pig looks like?" said another girl.

Max responded, "Oh, it was much worse. It had a hole in it. It was bloated and stinky. It had parts missing."

"Do you think they're keeping it in the morgue with the dead person?" said André.

"I dunno —"

"Yes," said Carmen interrupting. "Apparently, it's in a big freezer, next to the drawers they keep the people in."

Max leaned in and looked her in the eye. "I really want to get in there."

The door to the classroom opened. The school's librarian, Camilla Fox, exceptionally well dressed, waltzed in. She sailed past the rowdy students toward the teacher's desk.

Camilla towered over the kids. She had pencil-thin arms and legs, a long thin neck, and pointy chin. She always wore her brassy hair up in a bun, with a pair of tiny, black-framed bifocals on her nose. Her defining feature? Her bright red lips. She wore the same shade of lipstick every day, and it contrasted sharply with her collection of slate gray, silk pants suits.

Ms. Ballinger tapped her small wooden mallet on the desk, as though she were a judge.

"Students, students…" she called out. "Ms. Fox has printed some materials for you—a list of items you will need when researching in the school's library."

"Hello, Ms. Fox," the students droned in unison.

"Hello class," said Camilla, "please take one of these on your way out, and review them at home. You will conduct research next week in the library under my supervision, just as you will for your Biology projects. I trust you will prepare accordingly."

The librarian was very straightforward and formal. Though the students had only known her from the spring semester, it was fall, and she had already created an indelible image in their minds, especially Max's.

Max had been in her grasp once before after placing books back on the wrong shelves. Misplaced books alone bought him detention. Ms. Fox forced Max to clean the library every day for a week, take out the trash, and clean toilets all while she stood watching, with her arms crossed, and an insane smile on her long face.

Max caught her eye in the classroom, looking in his direction. The hairs on the back of his neck stood up.

"I don't know about her," said André. "She reminds me of stories from Europe, especially Russia, about a creepy witch who lives in the woods. She lives in a house built on chicken legs, and she eats kids."

"She kinda looks like Angelina Jolie," said Carmen.

"She reminds me of the evil one from the Wizard of Oz," said Kevin. "Look at that nose."

"Mon Dieu," said André in French, "she's looking at us. I think she's looking at … me."

The librarian said something privately to the English teacher, turned, and made her way to the door. While leaving, she whipped her head around toward Max and the group of whispering teens. A sly, thin smile drew her ruby red lips apart at the corners. Max caught a bright glint in her eye while she slipped silently through the door.

"That was weird," said Kevin. "How did you deal with THAT last year during detention?"

"She seemed less creepy last year, but now…" Max stopped talking. André filled in the blanks.

"Yeah, NOW she's extra creepy," groaned André. "Cast her in stone, put her up on one of our churches in France, and she'd fit right in. She'd probably scare the other gargoyles away."

Some light chuckles erupted from the group. Max continued his explanation of the body's condition. He also invited Carmen to offer her opinion. She was the daughter of the mortician, and she did have a way for them to get in. It also meant she was Max's new best friend.

"Besides the pig, there were a lot of crazy tattoos on the leg, and I think something shiny on the ankle, like a bracelet."

"Jewelry is kept in a special drawer," said Carmen. "But first, we need to get in."

"When is the morgue empty?" said Max.

"Oh, after seven o'clock."

"But there's a curfew now," said André. "No one gets to go anywhere —"

"Unless we have a supervised thing, like, say, a sleepover," said Max. "We can sneak out when everyone's asleep. Break-in." He turned to Carmen. "Is it easy to get the key?"

"Yeah, but that's not the issue. We do live several blocks from the morgue and mom's offices. So, it's close. But —"

"Are you open to hosting a sleepover? Would your mom go for it?"

"That's the issue. Let me see. Mom will be surprised. I'm not the most outgoing, so having other kids over would be a first," said Carmen.

"Don't our parents tell us change is good?" said Kevin, butting in.

A game plan formed. Max saw more pieces fitting together. He'd get to be an investigator for the first time, and have his most unique adventure yet.

The school bell roared, signaling time for lunch.

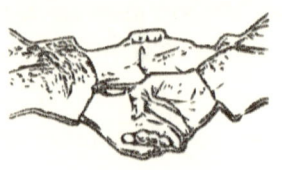

PLOTTING

Lunchtime at Stissing Mountain was always chaotic. Max made sure to arrive first so he could get his tray and reserve the corner table. It had a window view out onto the East Lawn. He preferred that spot to all others, it overlooked a stand of twelve pine trees he and his friends planted on Earth Day several springs before. Now about three feet tall, the blue spruces would grow big and tall and mark his place at the school forever.

He liked to mark his territory, it was something he learned from his four pugs, Rufus, Jack, Trapper, and Buddy.

Max's friends had not yet shown up. He waited with his tray of turkey and gravy, mashed potatoes, and mixed vegetables.

His mind drifted to his garden, and the gargantuan pumpkins he would need to harvest. On the farm the garden was his sanctuary. A place he could do what he wanted. He also had a small graveyard populated with over fifteen handmade headstones, each marking the location of chickens that had died—the chickens with names. There were no markers, yet, for pugs, something he dreaded. Max loved his dogs.

A tray slammed down next to him.

"This slop again?" said Kevin.

"I like it," said Max. "It's better than that greasy pizza."

"Remember when you had that turkey last year? When you spat it all over Bethany?"

Max laughed. "Yeah, that was horrible. When that other girl said something funny, and I had a mouth full of the stuff? I couldn't stop myself. Man, she was so pissed."

"Yeah, it was in her hair, all over her face, on her clothes... She looked like a wet cat."

"Do you think that's why she hates me so much now?" said Max.

"Oh man, she doesn't hate you. She has some strange thing for you, dude."

"Maybe," said Max, "she has been acting kind of strange."

"You're like a magnet."

Max took a large fork full of turkey and potatoes covered in peas and carrots.

Someone else tapped his shoulder.

Max whipped around, chomping on his meal.

"So, what are we going to do?" said Carmen. She smiled and sat down on the other side of Max, easing up close to him on the table's bench. Max smiled back. He had peas and carrots stuck between his teeth.

"So that's how you get them to like you," said Kevin.

Max shot Kevin a hateful look. His lips mouthed the words, "Stop it."

Carman grinned. "I like your freckles," she said. "It's like ... you have constellations across your nose."

"Look over here," said Max. He pointed to his right cheek. Eight freckles formed a perfect rendition of the big dipper.

"That's super cool."

Kevin stuck his arm out toward Carmen, pulled up his sleeve, and showed off his spot.

"Look," said Kevin, "I have one. It looks like the sun."

A large, round, crusty brown patch—a birthmark—spread out over Kevin's upper bicep. Carmen shrank back and grimaced.

"It's not that bad," said Kevin.

More students entered the vast, vibrating lunchroom. A new level of noise drowned out the conversation at Max's table. Max took advantage of the commotion. No one would be able to hear them talk.

Maxine plopped down on a bench. She positioned herself on the other side of the table, opposite Max. Her head of black hair blocked his view of the blue spruce trees out in the yard.

"I told you, man, you're a magnet," repeated Kevin.

Carmen extended her hand to Maxine. "Nice to meet you. What's your name again?"

"Maxine."

"Too spooky, but kinda cool," said Carmen. "The two of you, with the same name."

"My name is not Maxine," said Max.

"You know what I mean."

Carmen's eyes danced across Maxine's face—the standard evaluation between girls when they spotted new pray.

"I like your hair. No one I know here would dare do that."

"Well, I am who I am," said Maxine. She seemed more interested in what was going on with Max.

"So, what have you guys got planned?"

"Carmen is going to help me break into her mother's morgue," said Max.

"She doesn't own the morgue, she just takes care of the bodies in preparation for burial," said Carmen.

"Why would you want to do that?" said Maxine.

"I want to see the body," said Max. "I want to find out who it is and what happened."

"I guess I'm out of the loop. What happened? Who got hurt?" said Maxine.

"Max discovered the body, that's how he broke his arm," said Carmen.

"Yeah," said Max, "my dad's the Sheriff, and the body belongs to the murdered person, like what they talked about during the assembly, in the auditorium. Remember?"

Carmen scooted closer to Max, snuggling up against his side. Kevin rolled his eyes and let out a sigh.

"Pure magnetism."

Max inched away from Carmen. She moved too fast for him; he just had his thirteenth birthday after all. Sure, he thought she looked cute. But he found Maxine oddly interesting as well. The school year had also started a few weeks earlier, and now he found himself embroiled in a major murder investigation.

On-time, as always (he could set his watch to it), a sharp, hot pain shot through his arm and up through his shoulder, forcing the muscles in his back and neck to spasm.

"Yikes," screeched Max. His teeth clamped, reacting to the pain. He closed his eyes, trying to stuff it away.

"Are you OK?" said Maxine, noticing his grimace.

The girls looked to Kevin for answers.

"Yep, the bone ripped right through his arm. Right, Max?" said Kevin, being dramatic.

"You're so strong," said Carmen. "This only happened on Saturday?"

Max nodded his head. He kept his eyes shut, focusing on the pain going away.

Carmen continued talking.

"Well, I have an idea. I'll speak to my mom. Maybe this Friday night we can do the sleep-over?"

"That sounds like fun," said Maxine.

"I can get my mom's key to the morgue. We can sneak out when it's late. We live just two blocks away," said Carmen.

Max let out a deep breath. "Unfortunately, my parents grounded me for two weeks, but my mom might fold."

"How many people?" said Carmen.

Max opened his eyes, fluttering his eyelashes, and gained his composure.

"I know I want my sister Riley to help, and you too, Kevin…"

"Can I come too?" said Maxine.

An unpleasant look crossed Carmen's face. A tense silence overtook the table as Carmen hesitated with her answer.

Girls! Thought Max.

"I have some skills," said Maxine. "I make a great lookout… Plus, it would be cool to see the body."

"Did you know that it's headless?" said Carmen. She wanted to freak Maxine out, to dissuade her from coming along, but Maxine's eyes glowed with excitement over the prospect.

"Too cool," said Maxine

"I want to see it, too," said Kevin.

Girls outnumbered boys at the table, three to two when Bethany showed up. She parked herself next to Maxine and leaned on her elbows.

"Hey, Max," said Bethany. "I brought a sharpie. Can I sign your cast?"

She was the first to ask Max that vital question. He'd have to carry around anything written on that cast until the doctor applied the next one. Luckily, he knew it was in a week. So, he gave in, which made Bethany unrealistically happy. She knew how to fake excitement, how to blow up any situation and make it more than it was.

Max and Kevin looked at each other, each of them shrugging. Max cringed again as another slice of pain shot through his shoulder.

Bethany wasted no time. She whipped out a fat black Sharpie, much larger than Max expected, and made her way around the table, pushing her way between Max and Carmen. Maxine sat there staring. Max noticed she was very observant.

Bethany went to work on the cast. Carmen shot Max a quick look, placing her index finger up to her mouth, letting him know not to say anything to Bethany.

"Sounds like a plan, man. Right, Kevin?" said Max. He also looked Maxine in the eye when he said it. Maxine shook her head, "yes," indicating she understood.

Bethany kept writing, but she wasn't stupid. She listened in.

"What's this plan?" she said.

Max changed the subject. "Oh, it's almost harvest time at my house. I have to get my pumpkins ready for the fair."

"Oh?" said Bethany. "For jack-o'-lanterns?"

"Oh no, my parents gave me two acres to grow my stuff. I have three huge pumpkins for the Giant Pumpkin contest. One is almost nine-hundred pounds. The other two are closer to three-hundred. We have to use the backhoe to lift them."

"That's totally wicked," said Carmen.

"Oh, so you live on a farm?" said Maxine.

"We have a big old farm on the outskirts of town, some cows, goats, and chickens. It's not one of those gross dairy farms you smell everywhere else."

"Max also works on a horse farm," said Kevin. He eyed Bethany, who composed a paragraph on the broader part of Max's cast. "You know the barn where they found the body, where Max broke his arm? The horse farm is right across the road."

"Yeah, that was my favorite place to hang out —" Max looked down at his cast laying heavy on the table. Bethany finished her poem.

"What's that supposed to be?" said Max. "It doesn't make any sense."

"It's called a haiku. An advanced, simple, Japanese form of poetry," said Bethany.

"Where did you learn that?" said Maxine.

"My mom. She teaches us things the school won't."

"What else does she teach you?"

"Oh, how to sew, how to knit, crochet, woodworking, pottery. Things like that."

Max found something about Bethany he liked. She knew things he didn't, things he wouldn't dare ask his mother or father to teach him. He did need to learn how to sew better—the creepy doll still lay buried in the back of his underwear drawer. He needed to disassemble it and cut it into pieces.

"Hey Bethany," said Max, "are you open to showing me how to sew properly? I mean, I can do it. Can't hurt to make sure I do it right."

Bethany laughed, but the sound came out more like a sputtering giggle.

"Silly, why would you want to sew? You're a boy. Don't you run track and field, play football, things like that?"

"Yeah, but I have a project I want to work on. It requires sewing, and you probably know how to sew better than me."

Bethany's cheeks blushed.

Maxine and Carmen watched, both looking perplexed.

Kevin continued to observe, fascinated by the display from the girls.

"Well, I suppose," said Bethany. "I'd have to come to your house, or we can use the Home Economics room."

"What about your house?" said Max.

A communal gasp left Carmen's and Maxine's mouths.

"Oh no, my parents won't let boys over," said Bethany. "But I'm more than happy to teach you something new." Bethany put her Sharpie away and pinched Max on the cheek. She turned, and headed for the packed food line.

After Bethany left, the girls moved in closer. The cafeteria rumbled as kids massed around the tables, gorging themselves on turkey and gravy-drenched potatoes. Or the other choice, greasy pizza with plastic cheese.

Kevin sat down to eat his food.

Max took another bite of the mashed potatoes.

"So, is it a go?" said Carmen. "Do we have a tentative plan for Friday. Are you coming over to my house? Of course, my mother will chaperone."

"I'll work on my mom as soon as I get home," said Max.

Carmen let out another sigh. "And yes, you can come too, Maxine. I suppose it will be nice to get to know you better."

Max had not told Carmen that Maxine was the daughter of Dallas Finn, the new biology teacher. He decided to wait and allow Maxine to mention it.

"It's a plan," said Max. "We can use my digital camera for pics of the body. We get in and get out when everyone's asleep—like we were never there."

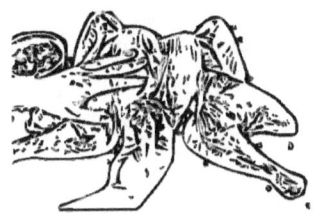

STUFFING THE BIRD

Max suffered in the rear of the big yellow bus going home. He claimed the last green seat next to the exit door, trapped in the suffocating bus with his thoughts

His father obsessed over the criminal investigation, unable to pick him up and take him to the horse farm. The Sheriff promised they'd go the following week.

Max propped himself up on his knees in the corner of the seat. He attempted to open the double latched, back window to vent the stale air inside, but failed and gave up, remaining pinned in the corner like some animal.

The bus passed dried out fields littered with corn stumps, and groves of de-fruited apple trees. The maples had turned red, yellow, and orange. The oaks were now a deep crimson. The last of the dry hay and straw had been harvested and bound into huge round bales. The land looked barren, dry, and dusty, with sticks jutting up, ready to be plowed under to rot until the following spring.

The colors of the fall streaked by on that chilly Monday afternoon. So, did the thoughts in Max's crazy brain. He replayed his walk through the school with Maxine.

"You know, Max," he remembered Maxine saying. "I know people are going to try and figure out Dallas. Dallas is a good person, and has been like a mother since adopting me."

Max knew people as male or female, and still found he couldn't understand anything other than that. He sat thinking about his limited knowledge as a seventh-grader, wishing he could grow up faster. To understand more.

He'd need it to become a good investigator.

Maxine had offered up another tidbit of information that disturbed him.

"I bet you didn't know that I am related to your librarian too, Camilla, did you?" she had said.

Max had asked her for more information and found out that Camilla and Dallas were cousins. Both were from Europe. Maxine asked him to remain quiet about it, concerned it would create some sort of commotion within the school, outing her and getting her into trouble with the other students.

Maxine knew she also looked different. She preferred to lay low. She didn't like the attention.

Max, of course, understood. He liked his privacy, too, though he found it difficult with his dad's position in the community. Being the Sheriff's son included more responsibilities than other kids had dumped on them. But being Max Hunter, the Sheriff's son, also had its benefits.

While Max's mind tossed around the many strange coincidences of the day. Curious new people and revelations about his own family made his skin crawl.

Bus driver Tom's loud, droning, unamused voice blared over the loudspeaker. "Mr. Hunter, are you special? Do you need to be on the

Sped bus with Little Joe and Sammie, and the wheelchairs? I can arrange that."

Max got the point. He sank down on the thick, spinach-green bench seat and fastened the belt with his clumsy free hand. His sister Riley remained in her secret world, engrossed in a book on the other side of the aisle. She peaked up momentarily to smirk at Max.

He stretching to the right so he could peer toward to front of the bus. His fellow school mates were uncharacteristically quiet. He knew the looming curfew had taken its toll, initially creating excitement at school. Upon sinking into their young skulls, it filled them with the dread of being captives in their own homes.

Max twisted his head to look out the rear emergency door and spied several cars following the bus. Officer Bernard Reese's police cruiser followed several yards back. He appeared to be drinking a cup of coffee.

Behind the cruiser, a red Jeep Wrangler followed. Dark black, tinted windows hid whoever drove. Max had seen that Jeep before in the teacher's parking lot, but never knew to whom it belonged. Unable to see inside, he still didn't know. A splash of pigeon poop had also smeared down the bus's window, along with splatter from some mud, making it even harder for Max spy.

The bus arrived at a fork in the road where the old Patchin's Mill still stood. The slow-moving stream crossed under the street, through the base of the mill, and into the water wheel itself, which continued to turn as it had for decades. To the right, the road led out to the sprawling countryside and the stink of the dairy farms. To the left, it wound past the Rojan Horse Farm and the site of the murder—Max's barn. Past that, at the top of the steep Silvernails hill, the road forked again, and the bus would head to the Hunter Farm, where Max lived four miles deeper into the forested countryside.

Officer Reese, with the red Jeep behind him, continued to follow the bus but stopped. He veered off the road while the bus wound its way up the hill. Max looked hard to get a glimpse of who got out of the Jeep before he lost sight of it. Though several huge yellowed oak trees and some bushes stood in the way, as did the smeared white pigeon poop, he saw the Jeep's door fly open. A tall, thin woman with a bun in her hair, stepped out.

"What'cha you doin', Max?" said Riley, who had been staring at her brother.

Max ignored the bus driver's commands to sit up straight and buckle his seat belt. He slouched below the window, out of sight.

"It's her. I know it is," said Max in a low whisper.

"Who?"

"Ms. Fox ... Camilla."

"What about her? She's just a librarian."

"Maybe," said Max, "but she's the one with the red Jeep. She just followed Bernard down there to the barn. Just got out of that Jeep."

The revelation blew Max away. How could the librarian—the one who made him do all those horrible things for placing books on the wrong shelves—have anything to do with the crime scene? If the hair on his neck stood up before, now it shot through his skin like little needles. He didn't like where things were going—not one bit.

The bus careened away, thundering over bumps and into potholes as driver Tom laughed. The kids complained, screaming, "Ouch!" and, "Awesome!" over the rattling and crashing. Bus driver Tom hooted even harder, looking back in the mirror directly at Max.

He does it on purpose, thought Max. *He most certainly does.*

Max curled up on the cold vinyl seat and waited for it to stop. His body quivered.

ᴎ ᴎ ᴎ

The bus reached the farm in record time. Max sprinted from away toward the farmhouse like a crazy person fresh out of jail. The solid blue cast strapped to his chest didn't slow him down. He opened and slammed the front door behind him and headed straight to his mother, who hummed to herself in the kitchen, preparing a chicken for dinner.

Max stopped by her side, looking down.

"Which one this time?" said Max. He stared wide-eyed at the gutted bird now stuffed with citrus wedges and precooked, salty bacon. He wrinkled his nose from the potpourri mixed with raw meat, and his mother's love for Chanel, which she wore every day.

His mother smiled. "None of ours, not this time," she said. "I went to Peck's Market today instead. No worries. You don't need to pour any cement and make another chicken grave, I promise."

Max felt relieved the chicken her hand punctured didn't have a name or a nesting box in the back. He looked up at his mom, figuring he'd get to her before his father got home; he had plans and wanted answers before it got any later. The sun would set soon.

Beth looked at the satellite clock stationed over the sink, where she prepared the bird.

"You better get your chores done and cover those pumpkins. We're supposed to have a hard freeze tonight. Also," —Max's mom pointed to the clock— "you have exactly one hour before that darn curfew starts. Get out there, get in here, before your father gets home."

"Can I ask a huge favor, Mom?" said Max. He wanted to get it over with during her good mood.

"Sure. What is it, honey?"

"We got two new projects assigned in class today. They are, I'm sorry to say, group projects." Max put his finger in his mouth and pretended to barf. His mother chuckled. "Anyway, several of my teammates are going to do a sleepover Friday night, Mom, to work on them, and wanted me to come. Can I? Please? I'll do anything…" He pleaded before he needed to, adding pressure.

"You know what your father said. You're grounded —"

"But this is school-specific, Mom. It's half our grade. I promise, we're not going to have any fun, it's basically girls and Kevin. Riley can come to keep me in line."

Max scratched at his cast and clenched his teeth again, pretending to be in pain. It always worked for him, and the cast made it more real.

"Carmen's mom will be there the whole time. We won't go anywhere after five pm, just the projects, I promise."

Max didn't think of it as a lie. His friends would work on projects, and one of them would be to break into the town's morgue. So, it wasn't a total lie.

Beth finished stuffing the naked, gutted chicken. She looked at the clock and back to Max while scraping chicken fat from between her fingers.

"Well, let me see. You better get your butt out there right now and get those chores done, or the answer is a definite NO. Got it?" Her words were quick and firm.

That's all Max needed to hear. A maybe, in his case, always turned into a yes. He hugged his mom. She eyed his cast and spun away from Max, telling him to wait.

"I have this antibiotic ointment your sister needs to use and these pills. Can you have her come in right away? I don't want her cut exposed while she's messing with those cows." Then her voice boomed louder, "Do we know this Carmen's mother?"

"Hold on, Mom, I'll get her right now," yelled Max. He ignored his mother's further questioning.

Max dropped his backpack on a dining room chair, zipped up his coat, and flew through the door, letting it slam behind him. The clock's big hand had moved through ten minutes, leaving him with fifty minutes outside. He had pumpkins to cover, chickens to feed, eggs to put in the pot, and he intended on stopping by the shed to check on doll-making supplies. He didn't want to tell his mother Carmen's mom was the local mortician, it might conjure up images his mother didn't need to see. So, he pretended he didn't hear her.

※ ※ ※

Max's father arrived home a couple hours later. Officer Reese accompanied him in his own patrol car. Exhausted, the two men entered to house to find dinner ready. The pack of pugs skirted around their feet. Their faces were always a welcome sight, they made sure everyone entering the Hunter home received a warm yet soggy welcome as they sniffed and blew their snoots in excitement. Sheriff Hunter reached down to pet the squirmy, black-faced crowd, looked around the living room, and into the kitchen. The pungent smell of a bird and a fresh, hot apple pie filled the house.

Max had picked a few small, decorative pumpkins and some multi-colored gourds for the table. Riley helped with place settings. Joe finished vacuuming the floor. Everything had to be neat and tidy, and to Ace's liking when he got home each day. He expected nothing less from his kids.

"Dinner's ready!"

Beth's voice rang through the house. The pugs stampeded the kitchen, leaving Ace behind to brush the hair off his black pants. He and Officer Reese removed their coats and made their way into the dining room.

Max sat in his place at the table before anyone else. He had taken a pretty blue pill his mother had given him, and not only did the pain subside, but the room seemed to move. He saw two of everything. Remaining still, he waited for his eyes to focus. His father sat down next to him.

"How was your first day back?"

"Long, Dad, you were there," said Max. "Lots of changes at school, some new kids too, and a new teacher. I have several projects assigned. I got the chickens done —"

Max's eyes were heavy. He slurred his speech.

"Beth," said Sheriff Hunter, "what did you give this boy?"

Beth yelled from the kitchen, "The pills the doctor gave me. Vicodin, anti-inflammatories…"

"Max can hardly keep his eyes open."

Joe and Riley stomped through the living room and into the dining room, where they hustled into their seats.

"How was your day?" said Ace to his kids.

"A little stranger than usual, Dad," said Joe.

"Yeah, besides the assembly…" said Riley.

"Seems to be the case all over town," said Ace.

Officer Reese cleared his throat and jumped in on the conversation.

"Seems our victim had their fingerprints removed. Sliced clean off —"

Ace shot him a "not at the table" look.

Max looked up with his blue eyes crossed, looking pukish. "You mean you can't identify them?"

"So far, no. Ms. Fox, who owns the land, was no help either. She didn't seem too disturbed about the condition of that rotten barn of hers, or what happened."

"How much does she know?" said Max muttering, and dazed, but doing his best to get any information he could.

"Just the body, nothing about you, don't worry." Bernard knew about Max's spring detention with the librarian and what he had endured.

"Of course," said Bernard, giving Ace a wink, "if it happens again...."

"It won't," said Max, staring at his plate and looking a bit pale.

"Liar," said Joe. "You can't help yourself. You're a sociopath."

"Just curious is all," said Max.

"Just grounded, too," said Riley, a big smile on her face. She giggled and shot looks at her father.

Beth brought the chicken in on a platter garnished with spring potatoes, carrots, and orange wedges, setting it down in the center of the table between two burning red candles. She took her place at the head of the table closest to the kitchen, folded her hands, and waited.

"Max?" said Ace.

With a sigh, and his head still down, Max recited the standard "thank you God's" and "bless this meal's" routine at their table. Each of the family members took turns, and today was Max's, despite his drug-induced, comatose state. His father accepted no excuses. Max knew he'd never get a break until he rested six feet under in Evergreen Cemetery.

"Thank you, Max. Everyone, dig in," said Beth.

Beth smiled and waited to load her own plate. Max stared at his but looked up when his mother nudged him with her hand.

"I'll take care of Friday, ok?" she whispered, spooning some potatoes onto his plate.

That's all he wanted to hear.

"This is going to be one hell of a week," said Bernard, who speared a carrot with this fork. He nibbled on it like a rabbit enjoying its last meal.

"Honey glaze?" said Bernard.

"Why yes, and cinnamon," said Beth.

Bernard savored the carrot, treating it like a juicy steak. Riley giggled even louder. Max just wanted the room to stop spinning.

DR. ESTEBAN

Sheriff Hunter had driven Max to school on Friday morning, knowing he wouldn't see him until Saturday. His wife Beth had gone against their standard grounding protocol; Max had been given two weeks in his room for his misadventures. However, Ace decided not to complain. Riley would be at the sleepover with Max. Joe would spend the night at another friend's house. And Beth promised Ace a "date night" to remember. After a week of investigating the Fox Barn Murder, as the newspaper now called it—bringing unwanted attention to the school's librarian, the owner of the land the barn sat on—a night off would be just what he needed.

Max knew his mom would come through. She always did.

His plans to enter the morgue illegally would get him in serious trouble if anyone found out. If they did, he'd never see the light of day. Both of his parents would ground him, and stick to it. While he understood the repercussions, he felt somewhat responsible and viewed his plan as heroic.

The group planned to sneak out of Carmen's home late in the evening. Carmen convinced her mother to go to a neighboring town, Red Hook, for some late-night dancing with her girlfriends, which also included plenty of booze, keeping her away.

The new curfew came in handy after all. It would keep people off the streets and out of Max's way.

"Could this have come together any easier?" said Max, who had survived school and paced on the sidewalk with Carmen, his sister Riley, and Kevin. They waited for Carmen's mom to drive up in her Volvo.

Maxine had not yet appeared. Max had not seen her since the third-period Biology class. Ms. Fox had come in again to address the students on the following Monday's library research schedule and had pulled Maxine out of for some mysterious reason. Dallas Finn didn't seem thrilled at her departure, either.

"I sure hope Maxine doesn't have an issue," said Max.

Carmen huffed, her arms crossed. "We'll be fine without her."

"But we need everyone, things can't start going wrong now," said Max.

Riley patted him on the back. "Calm down, bro, she'll be here."

"But it's almost four. The curfew begins in an hour."

"I'm sure my mom will be here in a minute," said Carmen, who reached down and grabbed Max's free hand. She clenched her fingers between his like they were a pair.

Kevin let out a, "Wow."

Riley backed up, putting her hands up and acting like she didn't want to get in the way.

Max stood stiff. Carmen's hand felt warm. The wind blew, and the temperature dropped fast, but he didn't want to show his surprise. He shot Riley a look to somehow save him.

Riley didn't budge.

Dr. Esteban barreled down the school's driveway. Dust and leaves flew up behind her.

The Volvo skidded to a stop in front of the four teens.

Carmen's mother flailed inside, motioning with her hands for them to get in while she fixed her eyeliner and lipstick.

Carmen yelled at the boys to sit in the back. She opened her passenger-side door, commanding the front seat.

Dr. Esteban stared in the rear-view mirror as the kids climbed in. She traced the shape of her lips with a dark red pencil and watched the unruly bunch argue over sitting too close to each other.

"Isn't another girl coming?" she said.

"Yes, Mom, Maxine... I don't see her yet," said Carmen

"Our time is running out, dearie," said Carmen's mother. "The sun is about to go down. We need to stop at the mortuary on the way home."

"You still have your party tonight, don't you?"

"Of course. I trust you with the house." Carmen's mother eyed the kids behind her. "And for you kids sitting back there, we have a surveillance system at our house—audio and video—so no messing around, you hear?"

Max put several fingers up, Riley and Kevin followed.

"Scouts honor, ma'am," said Max.

Kevin blurted out the first thing that came to his mind.

"So, miss, I mean doctor, Esteban, how do you become a mortician?"

"Well, I wasn't always a mortician, I used to be a doctor. I prefer to fix dead people—make them appear alive."

"Do they look as beautiful as you?" said Kevin, who had been staring at her in the mirror.

Carmen's mother smiled. She found Max's friend cute and blew him a kiss.

"Oh, Mom," said Carmen, who rolled her eyes and whipped around in her seat to frown at Kevin. They engaged in an eye lock, both trying to keep from blinking, but Carmen had Kevin beat. He lasted a few seconds before bursting into laughter.

"So, what's this project you kids are working on?" said Dr. Esteban.

"It's for science class, Dr. Esteban," said Max. "It's for biology. It's due in a week. The girl, Maxine, who should be here in a moment—one of her parents is the new biology teacher."

"Oh, that girl," said Carmen's mother. "I heard she was a bit strange."

"She seems that way at first. She wears a lot of black, but she's cool once you get to know her," said Max.

Carmen's eyes darted from Riley to Max.

"It's not like you see her a lot," said Carmen.

"Well, actually, she's in my biology class and my English class. We talk a lot in the hallway," said Max.

"Where is she now?" said Carmen, looking out the window while hovering over the rear-seat.

"Can you sit down sweetie," said Dr. Esteban, who looked past her daughter through the passenger side window.

The front doors to the school had opened. The secretary leaned against them with her shoulder, herself up.

Maxine clutched a stack of books to her chest and looked down at the pavement. She veered toward the Volvo with a frown on her face.

"Oh," said Max, "looks like something happened. I know Ms. Fox needed her."

"The librarian scares me," said Kevin.

"Yeah, and just think, we need to spend the day with her on Monday," said Carmen.

"Isn't Ms. Fox your librarian?" said Dr. Esteban.

"Yes, Mom."

"If it makes you feel any better, she gives us adults the creeps too."

Max opened the car door for Maxine, and she squeezed herself in. They were like pancakes in the backseat. Max didn't mind, neither did Riley, but Kevin grunted. He was shoved against the other door, crunching himself up into a ball, and acting wounded.

"Are you ok?" said Carmen.

Maxine wasn't in the mood for talking, but responded. "I'll be ok. I'll tell you all about it later. I'm kind of hungry, I left my backpack at home."

Carmen's mother assured them she had pizza on the way, but "None of that greasy trash," she often called it.

"We have a refrigerator full of stuff," said Carmen. "We've got extra bedrooms, plenty of room, and…" —Carmen made sure her mother had nothing to worry about— "will get that project underway, so we all get A's next week. No television."

"And no one … I mean no one, leaves the house during the curfew, got it?" said Dr. Esteban.

Not one of the teens failed to cross their fingers when they promised to adhere to the rules. Carmen knew her mother would be good and drunk, and would end up at one of her girlfriend's houses until late the next morning. Carmen had wanted to see the morgue. She always wanted to see a dead body.

Doctor Esteban sped away from the school and headed straight to the mortuary where she embalmed people in the basement and aided in burial services above. She held a private office to see individual clients, located on the upper floor.

Always above the speed limit, with her heavy foot, she made the short trip in record time.

The facility consumed a large old Victorian, faded from decades of harsh winters. Like all the other Victorians in town, it stood in line with other pastel-colored homes lining Main Street several blocks from the center of Pine Plains.

Dr. Esteban plowed the car into a pile of multi-colored leaves, situated under an enormous, century-old oak tree. The leaves exploded, creating a kaleidoscope of color.

"Stay here. I'll be right back."

Carmen's mom left the car and stampeded up the cracked and buckled walkway, disappearing into the faded purple of the front door.

Carmen whipped around in her seat.

"This is where my mom works, and the morgue is a few blocks down that way." She pointed down the road, whispering, "My house is a few blocks farther than that ... and an easy walk. There's just one issue..."

Max studied where she pointed, so did Riley. They looked at each other in surprise.

"All this time, and I never knew the morgue was so close to the police station and firehouse," said Riley.

Carmen corrected her. "Actually, they're connected."

"How are we supposed to get by that without being noticed?" said Max, his voice cracking.

"Yeah, they kind of know who we are," said Riley.

"It doesn't matter," said Carmen, "they're not supposed to see us. They're never supposed to know we were there."

"Well, it's supposed to be dark, and there are lots of yards for us to creep through," said Kevin.

"And the last place anyone would be expecting to see kids during the curfew would be at the police station," said Maxine. "It's kinda perfect, actually."

Dr. Esteban came rushing back toward the car, just like she said she would. She climbed in with her cell phone pressed against her ear.

"Yes, yes, three large, with all the toppings I told you… How much?" She barked at someone in the pizza shop while sliding into the driver's seat.

Max sat rigidly. He felt confined and unable to move, and at the mercy of Carmen's mother.

She put the car in drive, blasting back through the pile of leaves and out onto the wind-swept road.

As they turned and headed toward the morgue—and the police station—Max spotted the red Jeep at the Stewarts' Convenience Store and gas station. Maxine sank low in her seat and covered her face. Ms. Fox was out of sight. Dallas Finn fished around in the ice chest on the side of the store. Several bags of ice sat on the ground nearby.

"There's Dallas!" said Kevin.

Maxine sank even lower until only the crown of her head remained visible.

"We're almost there, guys, just a few more blocks. Wow, the sun is going down fast," said Dr. Esteban, looking at her watch.

The summer sun-faded and the early sunset of fall gave way to a cold, quick blackness. Though not yet five o'clock, few cars passed. No kids played in the yards or scurried down the streets. The town remained on lockdown. The few creatures that moved were an occasional dog skirting across some lanes, or a confused squirrel. The wind whipped up fallen, waxy leaves from the many oak trees that lined Main Street.

A light haze had also developed. In Max's mind, like a daydream, he considered how they would go about their task. He pictured a more relaxed time for his classmates under cover of night and the weatherman's forecast for fog. For once, the freshman weatherman at Accu-Weather had it right.

With the rusty gas station and the red Jeep behind them, Maxine propped herself back up.

"What was that about?" said Max, surprised by Maxine.

Maxine tilted her head to whisper in his ear. "I'll tell you later. My aunt and I are not exactly on the best terms. She and Dallas got into a scuffle earlier."

"Oh?"

"And, of course, I got dragged into it, like always. Camilla expects more out of me than Dallas. There's always something I need to do for her." Maxine pressed the stack of books tighter to her abdomen, guarding them like a dog defending its bone.

Max looked down at the stack, reading the spines on each: Advanced Molecular Biology, Third Edition; Calculus One; The Quintessential Urban Dictionary; and the one that caught his eye, Be Your Familiar— A Witches Guide to Animals and Spells.

Maxine caught him looking, and shifted the books.

Dr. Esteban slammed on the brakes, sliding yet again into another pile of leaves in front of their home.

"We're here," said Carmen.

Her mother turned in her seat.

"Ok, Carmen is escorting you guys inside. I'm not coming in, I'm going straight to the restaurant. Again, you guys behave yourselves. Have a good time. Also, watch for the pizza man."

"Yes, ma'am," said Max, who felt obligated to say something. While stepping out of the car, he glanced at Maxine's books. Not one subject was offered in seventh-grade. The last book wasn't even something covered in school!

N N N

Once inside, Carmen gave the grand tour of the house—another Victorian—and introduced them to the spare bedrooms. The group ended up in the kitchen just in time for the pizza man to knock on the door. When Carmen opened the door, instead of a man, the delivery driver was one of the seniors from high school, Bethany Waters' older sister Melinda. She wore the black and red pizza shop ball cap, with her brown ponytail protruding neatly from the back.

"I have three, four-cheese, chicken and veggie pizzas," she droned, reading off a greasy receipt taped to the top of the box. "That's thirty-three fifty."

"Ok," said Carmen, "here are two twenties. You have change, right?"

"No duh, I do, one sec—" Melinda dug through the pocket of her black pants and produced a wad of bills.

"Oh, just keep the rest. I forgot it's for your tip. It should be enough," said Carmen. "Aren't you Bethany's sister?"

"Yup." Melinda checked her watch, disinterested in the seventh-graders in front of her while blowing a bubble gum bubble. "I have to get my butt back to the store … I have fifteen minutes to get home before the curfew begins. Totally sucks."

"Yeah, be careful. Thanks for the pizzas."

"No problem."

Melinda tipped her hat like a boy playing baseball and ran off to an old Mitsubishi Mirage sputtering blue exhaust in the driveway. Max peeked around Carmen. Together they watched Melinda back out.

Melinda clutched a half-lit cigarette in her hand and thinking no one saw, took a few puffs with the car window open. She tossed the smoking butt out onto the sidewalk. The car shot down the street, back toward the center of town, it's taillights fading into the thickening fog.

"I sure hope she makes it," said Carmen.

"What do you mean by that?" said Max. "She's the school's star shotput thrower. She cleans up in field hockey too, and she has all A's. I think she can make it back to Tower Pizza and home in time."

Carmen handed the stack of pizzas to Riley, closed the door, and locked the deadbolt.

"Pizza!"

Everyone clapped.

"I thought you got four pizzas," said Riley. "There are five boxes here."

"Cool!"

SNEAKING UP ON THE DEAD

At eight o'clock that evening, the large red front door to the Esteban house closed behind Max and the four fidgety teens. The fog had thickened, which would have required the use of flashlights on any other night. Due to the curfew, Max remained serious about prohibiting flashlights considering the morgue and police station shared the same building.

They stumbled over cracked, uplifted cement at every seam in the walkway. Tree roots had bulged the ground underneath. Slick, damp leaves lead to even more unsure footing.

Max whispered when they reached the green mailbox sitting precariously on its stand. Blue paint had been scraped off on the stand's white surface. It had taken a beating in the past from the Volvo and Dr. Esteban's other nights out with the girls, nights she came home late smelling of vodka and nachos … and cigarettes.

"Are you sure your mom is staying out late?" said Max.

"She won't be home tonight, not with five kids in the house. She has her limits, believe me."

"Come on, guys," said Kevin, "let's get this done. The building is just a few blocks to our right."

"We'll have to go slow. I can't see my hands in front of my face," said Carmen.

Maxine took the lead and strutted forward without hesitation.

"Wait up, we can't see," said Max.

"I have great vision," said Maxine. "I can see farther than the rest of you. I should lead the way if we want to get there sometime tonight."

"We shouldn't stay on the sidewalk. Anyone can see us," said Riley.

"Exactly," said Maxine. "I'm going to take us through the yards. The bushes should give us some cover."

Obstacles tripped them up while following Maxine to the morgue. Cars had parked along the streets. De-leafed, prickly shrubs lined potholed driveways. Porch lights glowed like mini lighthouses warning anyone approaching something big loomed nearby.

Maxine led them over decorative rocks and small plastic picket fences, occasionally stopping behind an obstacle when a car (cutting through the fog) inched near them.

The streets were barren. Random sounds hummed within the thin-walled homes they passed. An unseen kid or two played video games or watched superhero movies on a TV with its volume cranked up. The last house on the block, owned by Mrs. Hellen Biggs, had a yard overgrown with weeds, torn window screens, and odd sheets in place of curtains. But none of it shielded the passing teens from Hellen's raging voice. She engaged in a fight with an unknown man over "custody." The group moved a little faster while passing.

"Are you sure we should still do this?" said Riley, whose eyes darted every direction at the slightest hint of activity.

"As I said, it's the best time if you were ever going to do it. Consider the fog a gift," said Maxine. She peeked over another shrub and waved to the others behind her to follow.

One block from the morgue, Maxine led the group back across the sidewalk and behind a parked van. "We need to cross the street," she said. "Come on."

At the intersection of Main Street and Railroad Avenue, across from the Post Office, Maxine dashed out into the road and out of sight.

"Wait!" said Max. He ran after her, as did the others. No cars could be heard coming through the fog, but within seconds Max smacked into the side of a Mitsubishi Mirage. His broken arm, still in its sling, slammed into the car's partly-open driver side window, and a loud CRACK and POP—and a shrill, yet muffled, scream—rang out into the still night. Max held onto his casted arm, tears rolling down his cheeks. A flurry of "be quiet's" and "they'll know we're here's" came from the others.

Riley leaned down, helping Max. He had become as pale as the fog. Maxine strode around the backside of the car to help, but Carmen took over. She ushered Max and Riley around it to the sidewalk.

"Did you break it again?" said Kevin.

"Don't know…" Max groaned.

"That was loud. Was it the car or his arm?" said Maxine.

"It's only been a week, it can't possibly be any more broken," said Kevin. He received a dirty look from Max, whose eyes had clenched under the pain.

"Can you continue?" said Carmen. "Do we need to call it off?"

"No," said Max, whose head began perspiring, "I'll be fine. We need to do this. It's the reason my arm's broken in the first place."

"We're just a few buildings away," said Maxine in a rushed manner. "At least we're on the other side. We need to get going, the longer we're out he—"

A siren blared close to where the group stood in the fog. They ran around the car and through a neighboring parking lot leading to the rear of the police station and the morgue.

A stand of dense, silvery-white birch trees formed a wall between them and the lot which sat vacant except for one police cruiser. Closer to the building, a black Cadillac hearse sat empty.

"That's the rear, over there. See the door?" said Carmen, whispering and crouching low to the ground in her white Capris.

Carmen raced past Max, rushing to the door with a very bright light hanging over it. The glare cut through the fog flooding the back lot and the hearse. Carmen put her hand up, indicating for the others to stop and remain in the dark. She looked around, crept up on the door, and peered around the other side of the building before returning to open it.

She mouthed the words, "Get over here." The others sprinted as the door opened inward, and Carmen stepped through it.

И И И

Once inside, Carmen closed the door, drew a few black curtains over its window, and whipped out her flashlight.

"See the stairs, right there?" she said, preparing to descend into the darkness. "At the bottom is the morgue. The freezers have the bodies. There are tables where they do things and grates in the floor for body-fluids that spill. Watch your step!"

Max followed Carmen closely down into the bowels of the building. The stairs were steep, covered in slick gray tile and slippery like the leaves outside.

"How do they wheel dead people down here?" said Max, who, like the others, kept a firm hand on the railing.

"There's a service elevator on the other side at one of the entrances the police use," said Carmen, whispering.

Max never thought about the elevator, which he saw many times when visiting his father at the station. He never knew the local morgue and police station were connected. They always entered the station through the front.

They reached the bottom. Carmen pushed her way through a couple swinging doors. She reached around the edge and flicked the light switch, lighting up the cavernous room.

Max wrinkled his nose at the smell. An image of the barn barreled back into his mind. The morgue smelled a lot like the rotten, damp, and musty barn in Silvernails. Max picked up the stale and sharp, yet sweet scent of death, now all too familiar to his sensitive nose.

"Reminds me of the butcher house by the school," said Kevin, who pinched his nose. "The men preparing cows and pigs, you know."

"More like Friday's at Peck's Market," said Riley, "when the old meat smells up the rear of the store… I hate that smell, except you don't smell fish here, at least."

"It's clean. They use Clorox," said Carmen.

"Maybe they need to use more," said Riley. Disgust puckered her nose and lips.

Large silver sinks flanked the room on one wall. Two silver examination tables stood in the center. Another set of doors lead to another hall. On the far wall, two large stainless steel freezer doors and several small silver cabinet doors sparkled.

"They keep bodies in the freezer on wheeled carts, but also in those drawers on the wall," said Carmen, pointing to the smaller of them.

"What about that pig?" said Max.

"That would have to be in the big freezer. The police had quite a time getting that thing in here."

Max took small steps toward the wall of freezers. He noticed white tags affixed to the doors of the smaller units. Large cards had been attached to the larger fridges with magnets, listing their contents in bold black letters.

On the front of the small drawer closest to the freezers, the tag's name read "Jane Doe," with the date of the body's discovery, and the statement "Police Property."

"This is the one," said Max, letting most of the air escape from his lungs.

He caressed the cold metal with his hand, feeling along its top edge and slipping along its polished chrome hinges. He placed his hand on the stiff handle and tugged, releasing the catch instantly. The spring-loaded drawer popped out several inches.

Max jumped back while exclamations of disgust and horror rang out from behind him.

"Oh, I'll do it," said Maxine, who plodded forward and grabbed the front of the drawer, yanking it out. She waited for no instructions and took her impatience out on the drawer.

Max stepped aside while Maxine muscled her way backward. The drawer and the black plastic bag containing the body glinted in the light.

"See, not so bad," said Maxine.

Maxine's reaction fell flat. Within seconds her face changed. Both Max and Maxine covered their noses with their hands.

"What's that smell?" said Kevin. He retreated backward farther toward the door with Riley and Carmen, each of them cupping their faces.

"So much for refrigeration," said Carmen wrinkling her nose.

"Is this what they all smell like?" said Max.

"I don't think so, then again, I never come in here."

Maxine giggled under her hands. "This is disgusting. We still need to open the bag." She sighed. "Fresh bodies smell so much better —" Maxine licked her lips. She stood as still as a statue.

Max looked at her with wide, terrified eyes.

Maxine's ghoulish expression startled him. She wasn't upset or scared in the least.

"Go ahead, Max," said Carmen, urging him, "this is your idea… At least get it done fast."

Max focused, he knew he had to be reliable. He never had issues with other things, being naturally curious. This time, however, the rotten smell acted as both a deterrent and a punishment.

Maybe my nose will get used to it, thought Max.

He did the reasonable thing and removed his hands from his face. He inhaled a drag of the musty, putrid air hoping to adjust to the smell.

His stomach clenched.

His acidic throat and esophagus contracted, signaling the approach of significant barf. Max resisted. He took another breath, this time with his mouth—keeping his nose shut—and choked down the mess.

Max couldn't make a scene in front of the girls. He would never hear the end of it. The girls would think him weak and not much of a boy. Kevin couldn't keep his mouth shut, he'd tell others in his class. Max would be a laughing stock and the recipient of never-ending jokes for the rest of the school year.

Max stuffed his fear aside, took another mouth full of air, and approached the black bag, which was laid out in front of him. The clasp on the zipper ended at the front of the drawer. From his recollection of crime shows, that's where the head would be. The bag looked short, and he cringed at what might be inside. What remained.

To his right, Maxine and Carmen appeared.

Riley and Kevin remained by the door with their noses covered. Kevin stood by the door's window, watching for movement. He listened for noises from the police station above and the exit in the back by the hearse.

"Go ahead, kid, let's open this thing up!" said Maxine.

"Yeah," escaped Carmen's lips in a hiss. She held back her breathing, but curiosity got the better of her. She always wanted to know what her mother saw. The people she worked on.

The pain of smashing his arm into a car on the way to the morgue took a backseat to Max's fear of seeing what lay in the black bag. Everything he had planned for was laid out in front of him. He had to know.

Max's hand shook. He reached for the tab. It all played out in slow motion. His trembling fingers grasped it and, numb from anxiety, unzipped the bag from head to toe.

On the other side of the body, Maxine reached for the edge of the bag's opening. Max did the same. They pulled the zipper part, revealing the body parts inside.

Carmen half-screamed, half-groaned, "Oh, my God, it's horrible!" and turned away.

The stink intensified with the opening of the bag. Max looked mortified, eying the dismembered parts laid out inside. Maxine stood frozen, her eyes glued to the contents.

"What do you see?" said Riley. "Does it look the same?"

"It's more than a leg, sis," said Max.

Inside the bag, Max and Maxine viewed what remained of the person from Ms. Fox's barn. Laid out in the same position they'd be in if the entire body remained intact were two legs, a torso, and arms and hands, but the police never found the head. The whole body lay in pieces, each one cut skillfully.

Max's heartbeat thumped loud enough for others to hear. His breathing quickened. He witnessed the extent of what had happened to the "Jane Doe" hidden under those boards.

"Well?" said Riley. "What is it?"

"Quick, Riley, I need the camera," said Max. "I don't know how long I can look at this thing."

Riley fished around in her jacket pocket for the thin digital camera. Grabbing it, she sidestepped her way to Max, reaching out with her hand. She made every effort to stay as far as possible from the open black bag.

Riley whispered, "You're gonna have some nightmares from this, aren't you?"

Max snatched the camera as Riley swung it. He mouthed the words "Thank you" with an annoyed look in his eyes. Riley learned how to set Max up. Now he'd most definitely have nightmares thanks to her suggestion.

With a big gulp, Max took the camera and aimed it at the bag and the body parts inside.

"Ok, Maxine, just hold that open for me."

Maxine complied, but could not keep her eyes off the carnage before her. Max snapped pictures, verbalizing what he saw and mimicking the forensics lady from TV.

Snap!

"There's only a stump where the head used to be," said Max. He gulped.

Both Riley and Carmen inched closer. Max continued.

Flash!

"There's a long slit running up its body. It looks like a Y with stitches," said Max.

"That would be from an autopsy when they opened it up," said Carmen, still not close enough to look and see herself. "Mom weighs the organs. Cuts them out and stuffs them back in."

"Ok, well, there's that white stuff. Gauze, I think. Wrapped around the chest and lower down. I still can't tell if it's a he or a she."

Carmen huffed. "The white card says Jane Doe, so it should be a girl."

"What else do you see?" said Riley growing more interested.

"Tattoos," said Max.

Snap!

Intricate tattoos covered the body parts. Max snapped a series of photos before throwing up into a grocery bag he had stuffed in his pocket. He'd hurl the longer he stood over the corpse. Maxine looked no better, though, she looked sickly pale all the time.

"That's a birthmark, there," said Maxine, pointing to the shoulder. "I have one too, so I know it's one. It looks like a bird —"

"It's a pigeon, I think," said Max. "And look at that design going down the ankle. It looks like a dragon … and a name."

"Harvey Duke, I think," said Maxine. "What do you think, Carmen?"

Carmen inched to the edge of the bag and peered inside with one eye. "I think you're right. Maybe their name? Maybe, someone they knew?"

Max spied the ankle bracelet and took a picture of it along with the blackened food that had begun to melt like wax. The stench reminded him of their thawed freezer when all the meat had putrefied.

"Are there gloves here?" said Max looking around the cold, sterile room.

Three boxes of different sized gloves sat on the counter next to the sink. Having spied them, Riley rushed over, limping on the leg she scratched in the old barn. She took the smallest pair. She heaved them through the air to Max, who, to her surprise, caught them with little effort.

"Good catch, bro," said Riley, who arrived at Carmen's side and peered into the bag. "I see why Coach Charlie is so pissed. You ruined his plans. So much for the football season."

Max eased the gloves over his free hands. He reached into the bag and took hold of the anklet, coaxing the jewelry down the pale leg and over the rotten foot and mangled toes.

"What are you doing? You can't do that!" said Carmen. "Someone will know. We can't risk it. I can't believe mother left it on the leg, it's supposed to be locked in that special drawer."

"But we need this. It has a lot of fancy beads on it. It's a clue."

"But it's there for a reason. Someone will know."

"People misplace things all the time. Besides, we need it more than this poor sap." Max who turned his glove inside out, encasing the bracelet inside. He shoved it in his pocket. "As far as they know, it's supposed to be in the drawer."

"Do you have enough photos?" said Maxine, who had become even paler. She looked like a vampire standing over her victim. The look of sick disgust revealed how she felt inside. Like Max, she couldn't last long before the night's pizza came up.

"I do," said Max. "We should get going —"

"Not yet!" yelled Kevin. "You still need to get pics of the pig, remember?" Then something caught his ear.

Footsteps.

On the floor above the morgue, the boards creaked. Someone walked from the opening of the police station to the far end of the building. They stopped. A loud THUD followed.

Low, but still understandable, the voice of a man scolded himself for dropping something. His voice emanated through the floor and reverberated through the air ducts connecting the building's rooms.

Officer Bernard Reese moved about. Max knew his voice well.

"Oh no, what do we do?" said Kevin acting panicked.

"We keep going," said Max. "Let's get into the big freezer, get some pics and get out of here. No one knows we're here."

Max turned. Without hesitating, he opened the freezer closest to the drawer with the body on it. As the cold air met the room, fog spilled out and down onto the floor, revealing the dark innards of the freezer. Max flicked on the light switch next to the opening. It illuminated everything inside, which, to his delight, included the large hairy brown pig.

"My god, that's huge," said Maxine, who appeared over his shoulder.

"You should see what's left of it," said Max, who proceeded to poke the camera in to snap more pictures.

Maxine stationed herself in the opening. The pig remained unwrapped. The full extent of its tortured body was visible to everyone in the room. Various parts were missing, just as Max remembered from the rotten barn.

"Someone did a real job on this guy, it's horrible," said Maxine.

"Yeah, it's a lot worse than the police let anyone know. We're not supposed to talk —"

"And, yet, here we are, Max," said Riley, groaning. She had returned to her position near Kevin. "If ANYONE finds out —"

"Your choice to come," said Max under his breath, snapping pictures in rapid succession.

"I came to keep an eye on you for mom." Riley acted offended. She crossed her arms with attitude.

Max's hand trembled. He dropped the camera on the hard cement floor. It hit hard, bounced, and skated across the surface and under the table with the body on it. Max let out some words that he knew would get him a mouth full of Dove Soap if his parents had heard.

The sound of Bernard's boots crossing the wood floor stopped just over the center of the morgue.

"Dude, he heard you," said Riley. "We need to get going. NOW!"

FLEEING THE MORGUE

Max had no idea if Bernard had heard the commotion below. After Bernard stopped, the sound of the door upstairs slamming made it clear more than one person had returned to the police station.

Distracted by the noise upstairs, Max made a horrible error in judgment.

Within seconds of hearing the sounds, Kevin opened the swinging doors to the stairs. Riley followed and stood by him waving to the other girls to hurry. Max slapped the light switch on the wall "off" as Carmen swung the door closed behind him.

Max launched himself toward the table where the camera had fallen, slipping on some liquid. He stumbled and did a face-plant on top of the open black bag with the body parts inside. Liquefied insides burst through the torso's unhealed stitches drenching his coat and splashing droplets of goo on his chin and cheeks.

Max screamed, pushing himself up and off the body. Maxine grabbed the latch on the zipper and closed the black bag. Carmen slammed the table into the wall and it shut with a loud click.

"Quick. Go, go, go!" screamed Riley. "I hear someone upstairs."

Max ran past the others and burst through the doorway and up the steps. The stink saturating his coat repulsed him. He easily forgot about his arm and the camera.

Carmen and Maxine followed with Riley and Kevin at the end. They raced up the steps, slammed through the back door, and out into the fog.

As the five dashed through the thick grove of birch trees they heard angry, confused yelling emanating from the building. Bernard and other officers raced around looking for whoever had broken into the morgue.

Max ran out of breath. He stopped several cars down the road behind a large Cadillac Escalade.

Carmen raced up to him. "You forgot something." She held the camera and handed it to Max who had bent over, his chest heaving from lack of oxygen.

"We have to keep going. They'll find us," said Riley looking over her shoulder and listening to the commotion at the station.

"What we need to do is get back to the house and pretend nothing happened," said Kevin.

"I agree," said Maxine. "Follow me."

"You ok, Max?" said Carmen.

"Just give me a moment." Max tried to gain his composure. Then it happened again and this time Max didn't have the bag of barf open and ready. He bent over and out came the remainder of the pizza from the night's dinner, splattering the front of the black Escalade, his jeans, and his new Nikes.

"Oh, that's terrible," said Kevin, covering his mouth and looking away.

Max stood there retching, smelling like puke and rotten body fluids from the corpse. He knew the girls watched and while he didn't want to appear weak, he couldn't help but feel like the saddest kid ever.

Maxine yelled back at him from out in the street. "There's nothing we can do about it now, let's get going! Things will be better at the house!"

Riley put her arm around Max and helped him move. The teens stumbled out into the fog-cloaked road and shuffled up the uneven sidewalk toward Carmen's house several blocks away.

The sounds from the police scrambling around the station drifted off into obscurity as the distance between them grew. They heard no police sirens.

"Thank God," said Max out loud. The police wouldn't know what they were looking for. If Max knew his father, the possibility of the slightest miscalculation could direct the Sheriff's gaze in the direction of the trespassing teens.

Regardless, Max intended to conduct his own, small scale investigation. He also knew he'd need the team who helped him break into the morgue. It was now a grave business. Investigating the murder would be his first attempt at a future career. His mother would be so proud.

"Thanks, Riley. I couldn't have done it without you and these guys." Max paused. They had managed to limp to the steps of Carmen's house. He sat down at the top, cradling his arm and smelling worse than the rotten barn. He whispered to his sister. "I think I broke it more. It feels like it might be swelling."

The vile fluids from the black bag had also saturated his cast.

"You're supposed to get a new one Saturday afternoon, dad's taking you, remember?" said Riley.

"I remember, but I don't know if I can wait —"

"Mom gave me your pills. You can take two blues. Isn't more better?"

"I don't know," said Max, "but it's throbbing. My fingers are numb. I don't care."

Carmen found the keys in her pocket and opened the large door to the Victorian.

"Hey, Max. Get your butt inside, we need to get you out of those clothes. I'll show you where the laundry room is...."

Maxine noticed Riley rubbing her leg.

"What's going on with your leg. Are you all right?" said Maxine.

"It'll be fine. I scratched it last week on a rusty nail from that barn. It's a little infected. My mom gave me some medicine to take for it, it's in my pocket."

"You look a little pale, too," said Maxine.

Kevin couldn't keep his mouth shut. "Who wouldn't feel like hurling after what we just did? I'm sick to my stomach, too."

Carmen stood inside the doorway watching the wary teens. The excitement of the night had turned like warm milk, replaced by exhaustion and fear.

"Everybody run inside before the police, or God forbid my mother, show up."

She barked at Max. "You! Inside! Washing machine, now!"

Carmen tapped her foot and snapped her fingers like an impatient parent. Riley stumbled but aided Max to his feet. They followed Maxine and Kevin into the house as Carmen leaned against the door frame. She backed away, wrinkling her nose when Max's jacket came close to touching her.

Carmen slammed the door shut and latched the deadbolt with a CLICK, trapping them all and the smell of the rotting corpse inside.

ⴹ ⴹ ⴹ

The entire trip to the morgue and back had taken less than two hours, landing the teens back in the Esteban house by ten o'clock. Within minutes the first tap-tap-tap from the monkey-shaped brass door knocker rang through the house.

"Who's that?" said Maxine. She yelled to Carmen who had attended to Max in the laundry room. "Carmen, someone's at the door!"

Kevin continued to munch some leftover pizza in the kitchen. He didn't want to know who knocked and kept looking down into the greasy pizza box. He shot a glance to Maxine who had braced herself against the open refrigerator door with one of Dr. Esteban's Vitamin Waters in her hands. She continued to take sips, trying to settle her stomach. They didn't budge. Carmen could deal with whoever waited outside.

The voice of a man thundered from outside. "This is Officer Reese. Are you kids home?" He tapped the knocker a few more times. Kevin heard the door handle rattle as the man checked the soundness of the lock.

Carmen dashed into the adjacent dining room and peered into the kitchen. She fiddled with a yellow number two pencil in one hand and motioned to Kevin and Maxine to smile. She fluffed her hair and crossed the living room to the door.

"I'm coming, I'm coming, hold on," she said laying on an exasperated, out-of-breath tone.

Maxine watched the affair play out from the safety of the open fridge. Carmen acted dramatic, flailing her arms and sighing.

Carmen approached the door and peeked through the peephole.

"Who is this again?" she said, chewing on the fresh yellow pencil.

"Officer Reese, miss. Are you kids ok? Can I come in?"

"Oh, sure, just a sec—" said Carmen in a loud tone. She raised her voice for the others to hear. "Let me unlock the door Officer. I don't know about this old lock, it's kinda tight."

The clicking of the deadbolt echoed through the house. Carmen unlocked the three locks on the door, methodically taking her time until the sound of footsteps racing up the stairs informed her the other kids were clear.

She unlocked the last bolt. The door opened. Officer Reese, along with a new officer fresh from the academy, stood just beyond the first step well back from the door.

"Good evening miss, I'm sorry for the intrusion," said Officer Reese. "We've had some issues down the road. It seems we had a break-in at the station and we're making sure kids are adhering to the curfew."

"Everything's fine," said Carmen. She stood frozen in her fluffy white terrycloth robe and fuzzy bunny slippers, chewing on the pencil.

"Are Sheriff Hunter's kids here, somewhere? Or your mom, Dr. Esteban?"

"Oh, sure, but Max bonked his arm again, so Riley's with him. She gave him a pain pill. Mom's out with some friends, you know. We're studying —"

"Is Max ok? I can take them home. Perhaps I should check on him for his dad."

Officer Reese and his partner took their covers off preparing to enter the house. Carmen guarded the door and placed herself across the opening like a sentry dog guarding a bone. She continued to nibble on the now severely dented pencil.

"I don't think my mom would want anyone coming in, sir."

"I really should talk to Max and Riley. Can you get them for me?"

"I suppose, just a moment. Maxine!" Carmen yelled, startling Maxine and causing her to drop the bottle of Vitamin Water.

"Hold on," said Maxine from the kitchen. She shut the refrigerator door which had been blocking her view of the front room and strutted toward the entrance.

"And who is this?" said Officer Reese. "I've never seen you before."

Maxine extended her hand, approaching the officers. "I'm new to Pine Plains, sir ... Dallas Finn, the new biology teacher, is my parent —
"

Officer Reese continued surveying the house, looking past Maxine, but he still didn't enter. The two girls barricaded the door with their bodies. Carmen nudged Maxine in the side.

"I'm going to get Max and his sister, I think they're upstairs," said Carmen. "The officer wants to see them." She clamped down and split the pencil in half in her mouth, startling the officers. She spat out some shards of wood and placed the two pencil pieces on the table next to the door before turning to get the boys.

"Max and Maxine, cute." Officer Reese's partner homed in on the names. "I like your hair. Isn't it Goth? You kids are into that these days —"

"I don't know, sir," said Maxine. "I like what I like. Dallas lets me do what I want. We're from the city, you know." She stood her ground in the doorway, as defiant as Carmen. She wouldn't let in any strangers.

The two police officers braced themselves in place with their legs spread. The newbie (his badge read Officer Tom Green) had placed one hand on his weapon and the other on his microphone. His thumb twitched against the mic's leaver. Static erupted from the radio and Sheriff Hunter requested the status of his son and daughter. Officer Green pushed the mic's leaver and spoke in a deep-voiced, official tone,

"We're getting them now sir. There are several kids at the Esteban house, a couple of girls, and —"

"And me," said Kevin who, having heard the conversation, left the kitchen to back up Maxine. Kevin's flaming red hair and large intrusive red freckles matched a ring of pizza sauce around his mouth. A piece of mozzarella cheese dangled from his chin.

"Better clean that up, kid," said Officer Reese, pointing to the mess and frowning. "You're Roy's kid, aren't you? Roy Baxter, and Hellen?"

"Yup, that's me, one of the six," said Kevin, who grabbed a tissue from beside the door and wiped the mess from his face.

"Amazing," said Officer Green to Officer Reese. "You told me, but I never believed you…"

Kevin was one of six kids born to the Baxter family. They lived close to Max's house on a smaller farm with a monumentally big farmhouse. Both of his parents, Roy and Hellen, were tall and blond with flawless tan skin. Three of Kevin's siblings had the same features as his parents (Roy called it the "good genes"), while Kevin and two other siblings were short and plump, with the red hair and freckles that drew gasps from anyone witnessing the whole family in public. Roy often referred to Kevin and the other two as his "recessive kids" jokingly. He often cited the biology behind the extreme difference in his children's appearances to anyone willing to listen to the wonders of genetics.

Kevin and Maxine stood in the doorway while Officer Reese gave Officer Green a science lesson. Riley ran down the stairs with Max in tow. Carmen followed them, gliding into the living room now in her mother's pink feather laced bathrobe, looking like a seductress.

"Here they are," said Carmen, her arms outstretched as though she were presenting an award.

"Your father is on the other end," said Officer Green, holding the mic out for Max and Riley to see.

"Hey, Bernard, what are you doing here?" said Riley.

"We're just checking up on you, you know. Your dad is very concerned about the curfew. We had some trouble at the station."

"What kind of trouble?" said Max. He stepped into the doorway pushing Kevin out of the way. "Anything we should be concerned about?"

Max looked pale and felt awful. He did his hardest to put on a cheery face as though nothing had happened, not wanting Bernard leaking any ideas to his dad. Max hoped the stench from the body had dissipated enough for the officers not to notice. He let out a sigh of relief seeing they were still on the front porch and not in the house poking around.

"Everything is fine, we've been here the whole time," said Riley, speaking over Max.

"Yeah, just eating pizza —" said Kevin.

"And working on our new school project," said Carmen. "No funny business, Officer ... what's your name again?"

"Officer Bernard Reese, ma'am," said Bernard.

Carmen blushed. "You're welcome to check up on us whenever you need to, Bernard."

Officer Green chuckled, watching the teenager flirt with his partner. Bernard had in turn grown red in the face and stumbled for what to say next, clearing his throat.

"You guys need to watch out. Keep the door locked as you did. Don't let anyone in. We have a not-so-nice person on the loose. They may have broken into the morgue tonight too, so be on your guard."

"How?" said Max. "Was it serious?"

"We don't know yet, but we're hoping to lift some fingerprints. There's some stuff on the floor too, so maybe we'll get lucky. You kids stay put, ok?" said Bernard. He looked at Max, scanning his body and pointed. "That girl said you bumped your arm. Is it ok? Can I have a look at it? What's with the clothes?"

Max faltered. He shot Carmen a nasty look and returned his gaze to Bernard. He had put on a large fleece shirt and some shorts from Carmen's father's closet (the man had left most his clothes after the divorce). His own clothes were going through a cycle in the Esteban's washing machine.

"Oh, I'm fine, hurts like it always does. Besides, I have the doctor's appointment tomorrow afternoon for a new cast. It's nothing," said Max.

Riley backed him up as a good older sister should. "He spilled juice all over himself, Bernard. And pizza sauce. That darn arm of his! But we're washing his clothes now."

Officer Green had turned toward the steps and whispered into the microphone. Max couldn't hear him but knew his father had been on the other end.

"Can you tell our dad we're fine?" said Max, yelling loud enough to wake the entire neighborhood. "Really, Bernard, we gotta get this assignment done. We're just now getting into it…"

Bernard looked past the group again, his eyeballs rolling inside their sockets and scanning the inside of the house. Satisfied, he grunted, backed up, and tipped his hat toward Carmen with a smile.

"Ok, well, remember what I said. Lock this door when we leave. Call if you hear or see anything, we'll be out all night because of this darn break-in. Got it?"

The kids were quick to agree, mumbling "Yes" and "Thank you" to the officers who turned and made their way down the steps. They disappeared into the fog. The red and blue lights from the parked police cruiser stopped spinning as the duo drove back toward the police station and the morgue.

Maxine shoved the door behind them into its frame, locking it tight. Max thought about the incriminating pictures on his camera and what Bernard had said about fingerprints and things left at the scene. Had they left anything behind?

His cast reeked. They had been unable to get the stench out, it had soaked up cups of body fluids. He'd have to carry it with him until his doctor's appointment and mask it with cologne and bleach. The poem inscribed on the cast by Bethany had turned into a blurry black mess with the only words remaining, "...my heart."

"I don't know about you guys, but can we call it a night?" said Riley, yawning.

Nods and tired grumbles came from all their lips.

"I feel like I've been run over," said Kevin.

"But we need to DO some work on the project —" Carmen moaned, still energized from the recent encounters. "My mom will suspect if we don't have something to show her ... we can't very well —"

"How about a nap. Just a couple of hours," said Maxine. "Your mom's not coming home now. We have all night."

"I'm in," said Max.

"Me too, where's my room?" said Riley, looking toward the stairs.

Carmen pointed at the sofa in the living room. "Unless you want to share a bed with Max," she said, pinching her nose and grimacing.

Riley got the point. She'd sooner sleep outside or on a couch than cozy up to her stinky brother. She patted Max on the back and lumbered away.

"The sofa, yes. Perfect. Gotcha."

Each member of the "morgue break-in team" retired to their respective areas of Carmen's house, exhausted from the night's excitement.

KILLER THE TREE

Sheriff Hunter collected Max late Saturday morning, the day after the break-in at the morgue. They still had no suspects and no clue why anyone would enter the morgue and leave with nothing. His mind reeled while driving the black and white patrol car with the murder and morgue on his mind. And the smell coming off Max in his nose.

"What could you have possibly gotten into while at that girl's house? Huh? You smell worse than roadkill, my god." Ace looked behind him. Riley sat hiding in the shadow of the driver's seat.

"Do you have any ideas?"

Riley didn't budge.

The car sped down the one-lane road toward Sharon Hospital.

Sheriff Hunter grilled his son and daughter on the matter. The only thing that smelled remotely like Max's arm was the old barn. The place still festered from the remains stewing in the last days of the summer sun.

Max also smelled like the morgue. A strange pool of stinky fluid had somehow leaked from the body in the fridge. Sheriff Hunter, no matter where he went, couldn't get the smell out of his head. He pushed all four buttons on his door, opening each window to vent the foul air and wrinkled his nose in disgust.

"Well, we were fishing around in the fridge," said Riley out loud. "They had some spoiled meat, right, Max?"

"Paris had spoiled meat? Are you serious? I don't believe that," said Ace.

"It's true," said Riley, formulating an alibi. "We had to throw it in the trash out back by their shed. Max took it out."

"Ah, ha!" said Ace. "I knew it! I told you both to stay inside. For you all to stay inside. Being my kids doesn't exempt you from the curfew."

"But their backyard is fenced, it seemed safe —" said Max, defending himself.

Sheriff Hunter slammed on the breaks, sending the patrol car veering into the dirt on the side of the road. He turned to scold the two.

"Nothings safe right now, got it? There's a murderer somewhere out there." He stared Max in the face. "If someone can get a giant pig into a barn with a rusty, frozen lock on it, that no one opened for years, don't you think they can get over a residential fence?"

"Sorry, dad —"

"Sorry isn't good enough. This goes way beyond grounding. You're going to help Coach Charlie for a while and do some one-handed work after school. I'll be picking you up before the curfew."

The police radio sputtered. A voice interrupted Ace's quality time with his kids.

"Ace here, Gertie. What's going on?"

Gertie Mae, the very grandmotherly emergency services dispatcher for Pine Plains, operated the radios for both the police and fire departments during the days.

"Ye' sir, we have another missing person's report, the daughter of Mrs. Waters, Melinda Waters. Her parents reported her missing. She didn't come home last night after her shift at Tower Pizza."

"No way," groaned Riley. She smacked Max on the shoulder to get his attention. "We just saw her. I knew something would happen."

Sheriff Hunter heard the comment. "She was at the house last night?"

Max jumped in. "Yeah, she delivered all the pizzas. Acted kind of sad."

"Yeah, Dad," said Riley. "She said we were her last stop and said she'd be heading home."

"Come to think of it, we saw —" Max stopped himself. He almost gave away their late evening trek across town. He turned and whispered to Riley, "Her Mitsubishi is the car I ran into, sis."

The radio crackled some more.

"We're also looking for her red Mitsubishi Mirage with the pizza shop sign on top," said Gertie. "Maybe it will turn up when these last pockets of fog lift."

"Put Bernard or one of the other guys on it. I'm taking Max to the hospital. It'll be a couple of hours."

"He's down at that barn with forensics," said Gertie.

"Get Officer Green on it then. I'll be back shortly. Out."

"Ten-four, Ace."

The radio cut out. Sheriff hunter opened the two rear windows wider, making motions like he'd puke any moment.

"If we were close, I'd make you walk," said Ace, pondering the recent news. "But your mother would kill me. So, tell me Max, when did your pizza show up? Was she out after curfew?"

"She brought the pizzas about half an hour before curfew, Dad. She knew she had to get back in time."

"This is just what we don't need now," muttered Ace.

"It'll be fine, Dad," said Riley. "I'm sure she'll be ok, she has to be."

"For all our sakes, I hope you're right. Things are getting kind of weird with the break-in and all. It's like a ghost did it. There aren't any clues."

"You have nothing, Dad?" said Max.

"Nothing. Some small smudgy fingerprints," —Sheriff Hunter put the car in gear and sped out onto the smooth pavement— "no DNA, no witnesses. We'll need to call in those Feds."

"You mean the FBI?" Max's eyebrows grew sharp upon his forehead. He imagined the town overrun with big burly federal agents. Maybe even the CIA or Special Ops would come.

"Cool!" said Max

"Not cool. They'll get into everything. No one will rest." Sheriff Hunter applied the car's accelerator and whizzed around the curves in the road, narrowly missing a deer and a couple of squirrels. Max and Riley grabbed the handholds above them. "You can expect the curfew to last a LONG time."

An extended curfew is what Max and Riley didn't want.

Max sat in this seat, holding onto the leather hand grip. His other hand rested in the sling strapped to his chest. His dad took his anger and frustration out on the police cruiser's acceleration peddle. Max noticed him grumbling under his breath. His father's face had turned a new shade of red, including his veiny hands now clenched to the steering wheel.

The radio sprang to life. Gertie's raspy voice came over the airwaves once again.

"Ace?" she called. "Your wife is on the line. The backhoe is ready to load them pumpkins. Should Earl and Steve —"

"Don't let them touch anything till I get home!" yelled Max. He looked at his father.

"Gertie, you heard Max. Can you tell them to wait?"

After a brief pause, Gertie replied, "They need to do it now... Say they only have it for a few hours, boss."

The radio clicked as Gertie waited for a reply. Max sat in his seat more fearful the Smith Brothers would damage his prize pumpkins than the police car's current speed of seventy on the winding backcountry road.

Sheriff Hunter rounded another bend, microphone in hand, waiting for Max to respond.

Riley thrust her forefinger between the two front seats. The dreaded, monstrous tree named "Killer" came upon them on the right side of the car.

"There she is, look," said Riley in awe. "How many over the past few years, Dad?"

"Nine... Five more a few weeks ago." He didn't slow down. "That tree takes more lives than anything else around here."

Max saw everything, including Killer, in slow motion while considering his options.

During all his planning to find out the dead person's identity, Max had neglected his garden, his pugs, and the Harvest Fair just a couple weeks away. Now his prized pumpkins were at the mercy of two of the dumbest, most irresponsible people in the entire town. Why his mother would insist on using the Smith brothers, he had no idea. He had thought they were coming the following weekend to haul the grotesquely shaped pumpkins to the school outbuildings for the upcoming weigh-in. Now they were at his home. Defenseless.

Max felt captive in his father's police car, which rounded curves at a high rate of speed. They were about to pass the most dangerous location in the entire town.

"Decision time, Max. What will it be?" said Sheriff Hunter.

"Uh…."

"Watch out, dad!" Riley shrieked. She clenched Ace's seat with both hands.

The car rounded the corner. As they passed the enormous oak tree, Killer, they all got a glimpse of the notches and chunks carved out of it from many bumpers, broken glass shards, engines, and in most cases, body parts, that had slammed into it, most late at night. Above the lower mangled flesh of the tree, about eight feet off the ground, the name "KILLER" had been carved by an angry Manny Hernandez who had lost his sister Penny on a snowy night the previous winter. An empty bottle of vodka and flowers remained scattered at the base of the tree, a testament to Penny's love of intoxicating screwdrivers.

A fresh mound of upturned dirt marked the spot the last of the Weatherby family met their end just weeks before.

The passenger side of the police car left the pavement. Sheriff Hunter grimaced. His fingers, Max realized, had turned purple from a lack of circulation. Ace cranked the steering wheel far to the left to keep the car on the road and, by mere feet, avoiding the tree.

Max recognized what looked like teeth still lodged in its bark. He screamed.

Riley fell back into her seat and turned into a ball. It all played out in seconds as Gertie yelled, "What's wrong?" over the speaker. Sheriff Hunter applied the brakes again. The car skidded to a smoky stop in the middle of the road.

"Gertie," said Max, grabbing the radio's microphone, "how about the Smith brothers go ahead and take them, you hear? Tell mom."

"Are you kids all right? What happened?"

"A close call with Killer, ma'am," said Max, now out of breath.

"Oh … I see," said Gertie in a low tone. She knew all too well Killer's reputation. She had lost her son years back to the same fate.

"I told you to take it slow. That turn's no joke, Ace," warned Gertie.

Ace drew in a big breath. "Everything's fine, Gertie. I'd never put my kids in danger."

"It's one of those things that sneaks up on you. Just be careful," Gertie warned him again.

"Are you sure?" said Max, looking at his dad.

"Hold your tongue, boy," said Ace. Max's father didn't like being challenged by anyone, be it an older woman, or one of his children. Even his wife. No one told him what to think or do. The last person to do it, Officer Green's brother, left the station with a bright red shiner and a bag of ice.

Riley said nothing, she knew better.

Max rarely guarded what came out of his mouth. He had become accustomed to chewing on bar soap and downing castor oil as punishment for his foul words and argumentative responses.

"Do you want your arm fixed or not?" said Ace.

Riley broke her silence. "That cast reeks, bro."

Max couldn't hold back.

"What good is trying to fix a broken arm, Dad, if the rest of you ends up wrapped around a tree?"

Sheriff Hunter responded, "Sorry," and left it at that. He felt edgy, as did Max and Riley.

The entire community of Pine Plains had been thrust into controversy. Local speculation over the recent murder had reached the newspapers. From the Register-Herald to the Poughkeepsie Journal, Ace knew, in a matter of days, the story would hit a major newspaper like the New York Times. With the now-missing Melanie Waters, he figured he should bump up the timeline. For the time being, staying calm and focusing on the road ahead remained his sole concern.

"Sorry. I freaked out," said Max.

Sheriff Hunter patted Max on the shoulder and looked past him at Killer. The tree still stood triumphant.

"You think we should cut that thing down?" he said to his kids.

Riley nodded "yes" and let out a sigh while rubbing the bandage on her leg. Max smiled, but shook his head "no."

"It's history Dad," said Max. "I think it's a burial ground of sorts, don't you think?"

Ace put the cruiser in drive and headed forward down Silver Mountain Road to the hospital. He opened all the windows in the car. He kept the speedometer below forty.

Library Whispers

Max had awoken Monday morning to find his arm no longer throbbing since Dr. Devlish applied the new cast. But not before the doctor questioned Max on how the current cast smelled and looked so rotten. Max lied. He received the same color—blue—with a new sling. The flesh of his arm healed well where the bone had protruded despite his recent clash with Melinda's car Friday night (he told no one, and Riley agreed to keep quiet). The appointment earned him extra points and a hand full of Tootsie Rolls at the front desk from the dizzying secretary.

Max decided he liked the secretary, though. He even received a hug out of it before she rushed away. She now worked on an upper floor on the other side of the hospital, far from the discharge desk.

What shocked Max more were the two new nurses staffing the desk at Sharon Hospital: an older man, with rotten Indian-corn teeth and a deeply wrinkled face, and a very plump lady with thick magnifying glasses and a mole on her nose. His father didn't stick around long enough to learn their names.

Max knew his mother had something to do with it.

N N N

Max had fed the chickens. He had collected dozens of eggs. The pumpkin patch was officially devoid of Max's prize heavyweights—they had been hauled to the school successfully for the Fair, undamaged. A first for the Smith brothers.

Max arrived at school without a headache from overexposure to bus fumes (though the rotting broccoli accomplished its job). He looked forward to researching his science project with Maxine, despite his revulsion for the librarian, Ms. Fox.

Max entered the school and turned the corner at the front office. Maxine leaned against his locker, waiting. She wore a different outfit, but the same black boots. She held a stack of books in her arms, looking gaunt.

"Hey, stranger," said Maxine. "Guess who's sick?"

Max shrugged.

"Carmen."

"From Friday night?" said Max, surprised.

"Don't know … might be the flu, or so I'm told. Carmen won't be going to the library with us." Maxine seemed happy about Carmen's condition, but Max didn't mind.

Girls can be kind of vicious, he thought and flashed her a smile.

"You know, my dad's picking me up after school. We're going out to the horse farm. You can come along if you want," said Max.

"What farm is that?" said Maxine.

"I forgot. You're new here. It's right next to the barn. I worked there on weekends and holidays until this happened." Max pointed to the cast.

"Oh, with the racehorses."

"Yup. I need to make some money, though. I'm going to check-in and see if there's something I can do."

Max nudged Maxine aside and unlocked his locker. He opened it and traded his coat for the books he would need first.

"Need any help?" said Maxine, acting eager.

"I've got it. I need to get used to it for a couple of months."

Maxine studied Max, who stood shorter than her. He noticed right away and fidgeted inside, taking his time to sort through a tin of pens and pencils. His hand jerked. The tin spilled, sending writing supplies cascading across the hallway floor. As Max leaned over to pick them up, the small digital camera used to photograph the body in the morgue fell out of his open jacket pocket. It slid beyond the mess and in front of the door to the central office.

Max followed the camera as it came to rest against the door. Standing next to it was Maxine, already squatting down to retrieve it.

The door to the office opened at the same time. Ms. Stout emerged as Maxine stood up.

"Excuse me, young lady, is that yours?" said the aid.

"Oh no, ma'am, it's his." Maxine pointed to Max, who, kneeling, had stopped picking up pencils and, instead, sat stunned at how fast Maxine had made it.

Ms. Stout eyed Max and put her hand out.

"I will need that. No cameras are allowed in school, you know the rules," said Ms. Stout.

"Oh," said Maxine, "but this is authorized, it's for our science project. See…" She opened the side of the case to reveal a vacant space where a battery should have been. "It doesn't even work. We're using it for a camera project in Dallas's class, so we'll need it when we do out research in the library."

Ms. Stout stood with her usual hands-on-the-hips look of disapproval. She wrinkled her fuzzy top lip.

"Very well. I'll check it out with, uh, Dallas, during, I think, the fourth period?"

"Yes, we'll be there," said Max, interrupting the exchange. "Then, the library with Ms. Fox."

Ms. Stout backed up and slowly closed the door behind her, never taking her eyes off Maxine, who stood defiant just feet away. Maxine turned and brought the camera back to Max.

"You better take care of this —" she said, handing it to Max.

"Where's the battery?"

Maxine fished the triple-A out of her pocket and put it back in the camera before handing it over. "Maybe we can look at this together? Between the bookshelves?"

"I haven't looked yet," said Max, who got to his feet with the remainder of the pencils. He cracked his neck. "I need to print them tomorrow with my mother's printer."

"We better get to homeroom," said Maxine with an exaggerated yell. She motioned to the office door. The shadow of Ms. Stout still haunted the door's frosted window.

Max wrinkled his nose. "What's up with her anyway? She smells like bacon all the time."

"Bad hygiene?" Maxine snickered.

Max grimaced and stuck his tongue out in disgust. The bleached halls of the high school were no match for a teacher with questionable personal habits and kids who refused to shower, like Tony Collins, the bully.

Max whispered. "She even rivals that body."

Maxine let out a single high-pitched squeak, which should have been a laugh.

As Max closed his locker, Maxine placed her hand on his upper back. While it was a friendly gesture, Max was unnerved by it. It seemed like a power move. He didn't know what to think. She seemed much more mature than him. She smelled better than the hallway, too. A million times better than the teacher's aide, like lavender and mint mixed together.

N N N

The morning passed uneventfully. Max found himself in line with Maxine, Kevin, and André. They stood single file for their trip to the library, quietly waiting for Dallas to lead the way.

Other students had become more vocal with their comments about the new teacher:

"What do you think, John? Man, or woman?"

"My mother said men have Adam's apples, they stick out. But I don't see one..."

"Dallas is flawless, that says something..."

"I brought Dallas an Apple, and some chocolates, and..."

The discussions were endless as students in the school jockeyed for the new teacher's favor. They worked hard to figure out the story behind the name and the lack of a pronoun.

Max turned to Maxine while André listened in.

"Do these idiots bother you?" said Max. He felt concerned. He knew she had to be somewhat annoyed or even bothered by the lack of respect from his classmates.

"It doesn't bother me. I think it's kind of funny, actually," said Maxine. She looked at Dallas, who winked and smiled.

Maxine smiled back. She turned to Max and said, "Dallas is used to it."

André shared his opinion. "The world is changing fast. If you want diversity you should come to France. We're always ahead of the Americans."

Dallas put a hand up, motioning to the students to quiet down.

"Ok, class. Follow me. You all know where the library is. Ms. Fox will take care of you once I've dropped you off. You have one hour today and another hour on Friday."

Kevin stood at the front of the line sniffing the air.

"Does Dallas shower a lot?" said Kevin, twitching his nose as though trying to figure out the scent. "Smells like … Dove."

Dallas looked down at Kevin. Kevin's head barely reached the teacher's waist. "Everyday young man," said Dallas. "Natural botanicals, always. No Dove. Commercial soap will kill you. It's," —Dallas grinned and pronounced each letter— "P O I S O N."

Kevin choked. He loved Dove and Irish Spring. Now he would have to calculate how long he'd have to live. He couldn't get it off his mind, and fell silent.

The line of seventh-graders snaked down the stairs and through the main corridor to the library where Ms. Fox waited. She tapped her foot and looked irritated. She crossed her arms, glanced at her watch, and rolled her eyes.

"About time, hurry up. You only have fifty minutes left. I imagine you'll waste most of that too," said Camilla in an accusing tone.

Dallas exchanged a tense look with the librarian and instructed the class to enter the library.

"Ok, everyone, make the best use of your time," said Dallas. "I want to know tomorrow what you discovered. You should have a good grasp of the library since doing your research earlier for Ms. Ballinger." Dallas gave Camilla another sharp look and finished addressing the students. "Ms. Fox here will be available to help you … good luck with that."

Max knew it was a jab at the librarian. A chill ran down his neck. He shuddered at the cold exchange between the two teachers.

The line passed quietly in front of Ms. Fox. Each student made sure not to brush up against her bony frame or create a noise that would draw her unnecessary attention.

Max snagged the table farthest away, where the line of windows met the stacks.

"What's the project?" said André looking over Max's shoulder.

"Soil analysis. Alkalinity and acidity. Plant health."

Kevin drew the back of one hand across his forehead, being dramatic. André followed suit. Both boys pretended to be relieved. Everyone in Max's group knew about the enormous pumpkins he had grown, having seen them in the barns behind the school. Max had to know everything about soil and ph. They'd get A's for sure.

"So, this means you have it all under control, right?" said André.

Kevin poked him. "Max here is the king of growing things. You can't grow five-hundred-pound pumpkins, and hundred-pound Hubbard squashes without knowing your soil, right, Max?

"I know a thing or two. I like horse poop the best —"

Maxine interrupted. "Because you know so much, how about these guys go get the books on the list? We can get that other book we talked about." She winked. Max knew she wanted to see the photos on the camera more than anything.

André and Kevin took their index cards and ran off to look up books in the card catalog. Maxine grabbed Max by the hand and led him down the row of bookshelves behind the table. When they reached the end, she pointed at his pocket.

"Let's have a look."

Max withdrew the camera, flipped open its view screen, and turned it on. It sprang to life. The last photo taken flashed on the screen.

"Gross," whispered Maxine staring at the screen.

"Must have snapped a shot when it fell Friday night."

The photo showed the SUV Max had barfed all over. It was a black and white blur of Max spewing pizza with the fuzzy, fog-shrouded street light glaring from overhead.

Maxine laughed again, muffling the sound with a sleeve.

"You laugh a lot, don't you?" said Max.

"Only recently," said Maxine. "I'm not the happiest person."

Max remembered the look on her face when she climbed into Carmen's car that Friday afternoon. Ms. Fox had detained Maxine in school. Max feared her story was more than she revealed. He left it alone. She was new to the school.

Max flipped the screen to the next picture.

"Those feet are nasty!" said Maxine.

Max remembered the anklet he had slipped off the dead person's blackened foot. It sat coiled in a ball at the bottom of his jacket pocket where it had remained. He fished the anklet out and showed it to Maxine.

"Maybe these … what do you call them … charms? Maybe we can find out where she bought them. Trace the body that way," said Max.

"I think those tattoos on that leg tell a story," said Maxine, pointing to the series of shapes and bluish outlines stretching from the rotten foot up the ankle and around the back of the leg's knee. "If we can find the tattoo shop that drew these —"

Ms. Fox dashed around the bookcase hiding Max and Maxine. Maxine gasped. Max twitched his shoulders and clamped down on the camera, burying it in the fold of his coat.

"Care to tell me what you two are up to?" said Camilla, who had an eagle's view of any student not adhering to the project guidelines. Those hiding in the stacks, talking, or not searching for books to use in reports.

Camilla craned her long neck to catch the two kids scheming. With a huff, she directed them to follow her.

"I'd like to see you two in my office right now. Come along."

Max whispered to Maxine as the three walked between two shelves of books. "She's your aunt, can't you do something?"

Maxine shook her head "No" and merely followed Camilla out into the main room with Max trailing. Camilla led them across the entrance steps to the library.

André and Kevin, along with most the library, looked on in horror: André pretended to play the violin. Kevin made a cutting motion across his neck with a finger as Max passed through the door to the librarian's dimly-lit office.

Camilla slammed the door closed behind them.

CAMILLA'S NOSE KNOWS

Camilla Fox sat on the edge of her desk with her arms folded. Her glossy long red fingernails contrasted against the steel gray of her blouse. Her eyes pierced Max. She disregarded Maxine.

"We did nothing wrong. We need to get our research done —" said Maxine. Camilla raised her hand in a rude gesture to shut the girl up.

"Little boys are only good for one thing," said Camilla to Max, "but I won't go into that now." Her pursed lips stretched into a devious smile.

On two sets of folding tables, Max noticed craft supplies: various sets of scissors, bottles of glue, needles, thread, and a massive spool of burlap. The figure in the center of the table frightened him the most, a familiar outline he'd seen before. It had two sets of legs, two sets of arms, a head, and was about a foot in length. The librarian had constructed one of the things from the barn—the same dolls Max planned for the Fair.

Max felt his chest tighten. He couldn't breathe.

Invisible insects seemed to scurry up and down his back.

He felt like he could faint.

"Are you ok?" said Maxine watching Max's face turn a grayish-white. Camilla also noticed.

"No, no," said Max, hesitating. "My arm hurts. I feel nauseous." He lied.

Camilla cleared her throat and grilled Max.

"What exactly were you doing with my niece behind those books?"

Max's eyes darted between the librarian and her art table.

The librarian has nothing to do with the incident, she can't, thought Max. It had to be a coincidence.

He remembered she owned the barn. Maybe she saw the dolls and had the same idea? Camilla didn't seem like the kind to slip up. Max had the distinct impression she was profoundly cunning. Someone who didn't make mistakes. She certainly didn't like children.

He also believed he needed to beat her to the doll-making finish line—make his before she ruined everything.

His eyes returned to Camilla. "We weren't doing anything, ma'am," he said. "We were talking about the project. We couldn't decide what books to get."

Maxine backed him up. "Yeah, we're working on soil and manure pH… It's a little involved."

"You seem a bit secretive, the two of you," said Camilla.

Maxine laughed. "We sent the other boys in the group to go dig up books. Max and I are the leaders, so we were talking things over."

"Don't you think you can do that at the table?" said Camilla.

Max wrinkled his nose. He smelled something familiar, a kind of wood from the forest. He couldn't wrap his mind around it.

Maybe a white birch tree, or silver birch? He thought. Silver birches in New York smelled a lot like root beer when their bark was removed. Many of them grew around the old red barn.

"I wonder what that —" Max hesitated. He knew not to open a door, but he couldn't help himself. "What's that smell? Is that some kinda perfume?"

"I'm not wearing anything," said Maxine. She looked at Camilla.

Camilla shifted her position. She uncrossed her arms and propped herself up with both hands on the edge of her desk.

Max stood up and, against his better judgment, walked toward the librarian sniffing the air.

"Yeah, I smell birch ... and moss." Max stopped just short of Camilla's black shoes.

"Definitely birch ... like root beer. Do you like root beer, Ms. Fox?"

"No, I do not," said the librarian, shocked at Max's audacity. He continued standing there.

"I'd prefer if you took a seat, young man," said Camilla. She pointed at the seat Max had left and wagged her finger. "Come on now, you need to —" She stopped.

Like Max, Camilla's nose twitched. She closed her eyes and tipped her head back, sniffing the air. Her nostrils flared. She opened her eyes and gave Max the craziest look he had ever seen from an adult, let alone a teacher.

Camilla reached forward before Max had the chance to return to his seat. She yanked him toward her by his shoulders.

"Watch his sling!" Maxine almost leaped from her chair, surprised Camilla handled Max so roughly. She stopped. Camilla sniffed Max's jacket.

"What are you doing?" said Maxine, horrified by her aunt's actions.

Camilla paid her no attention. The librarian was preoccupied with running her nose back and forth across Max's jacket. She sucked a torrent of air in when she reached Max's right pocket.

"What's this," said Camilla in an accusing tone.

Max shuddered and lost all feeling in his limbs.

Her freakishly strong hands cut off his circulation.

"I didn't do, uh, uh, anything," said Max stuttering.

"Oh, but you did do something," said Camilla. "I might smell like root beer to you, but you smell like…" She lowered her voice and whispered so only Max could hear, "…death to me."

She released Max from her grip.

Max stumbled backward. He had been leaning and lost his balance. His chest heaved as though he were out of breath.

The stench of fear consumed his mind.

Maxine spoke up. "We really should be getting back to work, Max. Your dad, the Sheriff, is expecting to look over your work tonight, right?"

"Yeah," said Max, acting sheepish. He continued to stare at the librarian. "I'm grounded. I have to show him all of my work." He spoke in a monotone.

Camilla looked emboldened. She had homed in on something, possibly Max's secret.

The more Max stood there crumbling, the more Camilla grew excited.

Anyone who looked at Camilla could see her mind working as her eyes shifted. Her lips spoke inaudible words. She quickly pieced the puzzle together on recent events.

"I think you're right. It is time to go and get back to work. I'm finished with you two," said Camilla.

Maxine nudged Max toward the door.

"And Max," said Camilla, gaining his attention one more time, "some things just don't come out in the wash, young man. You should wash that again, though I doubt it will help." She turned to Maxine. "Please stop at my office after school is out. Let Dallas know, will you?"

"Yes, Auntie," said Maxine. She opened the door. The two of them crept out. She closed it behind them quietly.

N N N

"She knows," said Max, "she has to. I'm so obvious."

"My aunt can be creepy, sure. And sometimes she's mean. But she doesn't know anything."

Max wasn't convinced. The creepy, witch-like woman had sniffed his jacket—the entire coat. She smelled the fluids from the dead body, right where Max landed.

She must know what it is, he thought.

He wanted to believe Maxine, but he didn't know her that well yet. She was related to Camilla, too. Max decided that meant he'd need to be guarded. He concluded, there in the library, to tell her only what she needed to know until he knew more.

He never told Maxine about the dolls. Riley and Joe were the only ones who saw them, besides the police and paramedics.

Max had gained the librarian's attention yet again. This time she might do something more than force him to clean chalkboards and put books away. He thought about the body parts and the big dead pig and thought, that could be me next! His mind drifted to Bethany's sister, who had disappeared, though her car appeared near the police station once the fog lifted.

Kevin stumbled to the table carrying several books and index cards with information on them. He noticed right away the tension between Max and Maxine.

"What happened?" said Kevin, slamming the books about poop and compost on the table.

"It's nothing," said Maxine. "Looks like you got some good books, though."

"Yeah, it looks like we need to get some manure samples," said Kevin.

"I'm going with Max after school to the horse farm after I meet with Ms. Fox," said Maxine. "We can get horse poop, cow poop, chicken poop...."

"This is going to be so stinking awesome," said Kevin.

"Like my jacket," said Max, mumbling and looking down.

Kevin had no clue what Max meant. Maxine nudged Max in the side.

Max spent the remainder of his library time fretting over the recent encounter with Camilla. He never thought the connection would be this close to home.

Clamoring in the Barn

Sheriff Hunter collected Max and Maxine with his police cruiser. He wore a pair of black aviator glasses, which hid his eyes. He remained silent during the quiet drive to Rojan with his lips pursed in a perpetual frown.

At the horse farm, Max had time to catch up with Cindy. Max found her in the dirty, cob-web infested front office oiling leather shanks. Sheriff Hunter left them, giving Max half an hour to show Maxine around.

Cindy gave Max a tight hug.

"Look at you, Mister Max, all fancy in your blue cast and blue jeans!" Cindy flinched upon seeing Maxine, who, being in the same frame of mind as Max's father, merely extended her hand without a word.

"Tough day?" said Cindy, noticing the girl's sad disposition.

"Family stuff," said Maxine. "You know."

Max shook his head in agreement. "It's been a crazy couple of weeks, Cindy. I'm so sorry I broke my arm."

"Oh, we have things under control around here." The sweat and dirt on Cindy's face told another story.

"You still have Alex helping out?" said Max.

"No, he quit right after the incident at that barn, you know ... his mother didn't like the idea of him working near a murder scene."

"Sounds like you need help."

"Not much we can do. With your arm broken, weekends are rough. Moreover, we've had reporters coming over and getting in the way." Cindy sighed and gave Maxine a once over, noting her decidedly non-country way of dressing. She raised an eyebrow, addressing the teenage girl directly.

"Did Max bring you here to apply for a job, miss?"

"Oh no, ma'am," said Maxine, surprised. "He's just —"

"Because if he did, we could sure use some more help. Mucking mostly."

Max interrupted. "Oh, no, she doesn't want a job. I am here to see if there's anything I can still do considering my arm and all."

Cindy's mind went to work on Max's suggestion.

"Maybe feeding?" said Max. "Watering? Odd things —"

"There's not much you can do without both arms, honey," said Cindy.

Max rolled his eyes and growled. Being told he was useless while his arm healed wasn't what he wanted to hear. Max needed money. He'd need to run with his plan-B of making the dolls to get him through December.

"Can I at least show Maxine around?"

"I've never been on a horse farm before, ma'am," said Maxine. She sniffed the air and gazed around at the antique tac equipment hanging on the walls, together with old photos of horses long gone.

"Show her around all you want, Max," said Cindy. "Watch out—we have a few feisty foals. They like to kick. Oh, and watch out for

Clamoring down in the lower barn. She's a real you-know-what. Mean as can be. She just arrived from the Henning farm up in Saratoga."

"We won't be long," said Max.

"And if you ever want a job, miss…"

"My name's Maxine."

"Strange," said Cindy, pulling on her stained leather work gloves. "Get to it!" She escaped through the door leading to the stalls, leaving the two kids to their wanderings.

𝘕 𝘕 𝘕

"She's very nice," said Maxine. "Aside from looking so boyish and a bit rough, she has good energy."

"Cindy's a fixture here. She runs the show," said Max, who laughed while leading Maxine out of the office and alongside the outside stalls. "I can't imagine YOU shoveling horse poop."

"I don't need a job, but it's tempting." She sighed. "Anything to get out of that house."

Max toured Maxine around the two massive barns on the hill. He showed her the outside paddocks where horses spent their days.

"I paint these with tar," said Max, pointing to one of the fence posts. "Kind of smells like road tar, you know, when they seal the roads on hot summer days."

"Why?"

"It seals the wood so it won't rot … and look here, at these bite marks…" Max pointed to several fence boards where a horse had chewed the wood, exposing the blond interior. "They chew these things up. I have to seal them up good."

Max picked up his pace. Maxine stayed close. They made their way from the upper barn, down the steep gravel driveway to the lower barn just as Big Don and a new man named Russ led the first horses to the stalls behind them. Max smiled but kept going.

"And you should never wrap the shank around your hand while it's clipped to a horse's halter." Max watched a new worker he had never seen before stop with one of the older mares while Cindy checked its foot. The mare grew agitated and threw its head up into the air, causing the worker to work hard to keep her stationary.

"If you wrap the lead around your hand, and the horse lunges," said Max—he motioned to Maxine what the worker did wrong— "you can dislocate or break your arm. They're powerful."

"What's in the lower barn?" said Maxine, who shuffled her feet in the dusty gravel lining the driveway.

"About thirty horses, and a stud in the back. It looks like they're already in, I'll show you some."

Across from the lower barn, Maxine spied a red tractor.

"What's that attached to it?" she said to Max.

"That's the spreader. We load it with horse poop. One of the staff drives it out to a field and spreads the poop everywhere."

"Where does it come out?" Maxine walked to the back of the long, stinky spreader and noticed a series of metal pieces dangling.

"Those things spin around," said Max. "Real fast. They grab the poop and shoot it out."

"Cool. It looks like it could do some damage."

"If you get caught in it, I suppose," said Max, cringing, "but I don't know how you'd accomplish that."

"Hmm." Maxine turned her attention to the open barn and walked inside ahead of Max.

The cement floors had been swept. All horses had been returned to their stalls and were busy eating fresh hay and pellets with their tails turned toward their stall doors. From square holes in the ceiling lining the backside of the stalls, Maxine noticed new slabs of hay falling through.

"Who's up there?" said Maxine.

"Probably John, or Luke, because it's feeding time," said Max.

"Can we go up there too?"

"Sure, but it's dangerous ... there's a lot of hay and straw stacked up. I mean a lot. We unload it from tractor-trailers every summer."

"These horses are gorgeous." Maxine stood transfixed by a golden brown thoroughbred

"They're all mares for breeding."

"This one too?"

The stall with the golden-brown horse in it had a name tag: CLAMORING.

"Some of them are mean, like her," said Max. "She likes to kick. Don't open her door if you value your life."

"Will she have a baby too?"

"Yes," said Max, "even though she doesn't look it, she's pregnant right now."

"Well, if she's mean, won't she hurt a baby?"

"They're called foals," said Max. Max turned his head to see farther down the aisle. "If she tries to hurt her foal, a nurse mare will take care of it—an Appaloosa—like the two down there."

Maxine made cooing sounds and clasped her hands in excitement. "Can I see one?"

"Follow me."

Max led her down the aisle to two stalls near the end. Two mares stood, appearing board.

"They're so strange looking," said Maxine. "All patchy; kinda dumpy."

"But they do a great job taking care of babies. One of the gentlest creatures around."

One of the Appaloosas turned around and stuck its snout through the metal bars blocking the window to the stall. All the stalls, made of pale brown wood, had their doors and walls secured with metal bars instead of windows. Maxine grabbed and tugged on one.

Max warned her. "You still need to watch out. They bite, too. It's excruciating." He pointed to his shoulder. "Last summer one bit me on the shoulder, clamped right down. I had a bruise for months."

Maxine pet the nose of the horse, looking at her through the bars. She loved the feeling.

"Feels like velvet."

More thumping and stomping thundered from above them. The regular workers were still in the loft.

"Can we go up there now?" said Maxine.

"Let's go," said Max. He guided her through a door in the middle of the barn, leading out to a sloping back lawn surrounded by muddy paddocks. She suddenly took his hand in hers. He didn't know what to do. He didn't expect it.

Max acted flustered. Pretending to be distracted, he rushed away, avoiding holding hands with the new girl. He wasn't ready.

Maxine sprinted after him. She let out a slight laugh. She knew how he felt, and it delighted her more.

Max climbed the steep, grassy hill. Maxine caught up quickly. When they crested the top, the large doors to the loft were wide open. The one man inside rearranged hay and straw bales that had fallen.

"Whoa!" said Maxine

"Yeah," said Max, "that's a lot of straw… The whole pile is about thirty feet high."

"What's that there?" Maxine pointed to a metal contraption running the length of the ceiling.

"That's a conveyor belt. When we load hay and straw, it comes up another conveyor from the tractor-trailer out front. It drops right here," —Max pointed to the spot where the bales would fall— "We pick it up real fast and stack it."

"Seems like a lot of work."

"It is. Dad thinks it's good for me."

"What do you think?" said Maxine

"Me? I make my own money, that's all I want."

Maxine eyed Max's arm. She knew he'd have little chance of finding any work with an injury that severe.

"I'm sorry you hurt your arm, I know it sucks."

The farmhand, Luke, spotted the pair. He dropped his work gloves, stuck his pitchfork in a straw bale, and headed over to see what the kids were doing.

"Hey, Buster," he said to Max.

Luke gasped with surprise when he saw the blue cast. "Well, man, that's quite the set up you got there."

Max smiled.

Maxine blushed.

Though covered in hay and dirt, Luke was in excellent shape. He was in his twenties.

Maxine didn't mind. The farmhand didn't have a shirt on.

"So, what are you two up to?" said Luke.

"Hoping there is something I can do," said Max.

"Not much you can do around here with an arm like that," said Luke. Then, like Cindy, he looked at Maxine and asked the same question: "Do you need a job, little lady?"

Maxine blushed a little harder. Her cheeks were bright red; she couldn't hide it.

"No, sir, as much as it appeals to me."

"Too bad, you look strong."

Maxine giggled. This time, Max flushed, and not for the same reason—Maxine's response to Luke bothered him. He didn't quite know why.

"We need to get a bag of horse poop, Luke ... and some straw, if possible."

"Why?"

"A science project in school... We're doing pH, soil acidity, you know...."

"Well, we got a butt load of poop right behind you," said Luke. "Pardon the pun, son!"

Outside the barn, in an alcove cut into the hillside, a high mound of fresh steaming horse poop waited for Max.

"Need a baggie?" Luke laughed. He pulled a Ziploc bag out of his back pocket, turned it upside down, and emptied crumbs from his previous meal.

"Here you go. You'll need something else for the straw. We have all those used burlap bags in the tac room. I imagine you can take what you want."

Maxine reached out and grabbed the small, plastic lunch bag. Luke held it for a moment, making her work for it. She giggled again.

Max put a finger in his mouth and pretended to puke.

"We should probably get some of the poop and straw. We need to go. Dad's coming back here in a bit," said Max. He ambled over to the pile and picked up chunks of horse dung with his useful hand.

Maxine skipped over to help. Luke closed the massive sliding barn doors behind her.

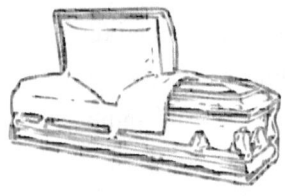

SUDDEN TRAGEDY

"Did you leave room for the two of you?" said Sheriff Hunter. "My God, Max, how much hay do you need? What is that darn smell?"

Max stuffed a large bag of straw in his father's trunk, and two large bags in the back seat. He left a little room for Maxine, who had to sit in the back. Max, of course, called shotgun on the front seat.

"Supplies, Dad. Got to get it while I can."

"What are you making?"

"It's for our science project, Mr. Hunter," said Maxine. She snickered. "That smell's fresh horse poop!"

"Wonderful," said Sheriff Hunter, his voice annoyed and reeling with sarcasm. He opened the windows. The two kids buckled their belts.

"What's this for?" said Maxine, pointing at the steel cage and Plexiglas separating the front seat from the rear.

"That, my dear, protects me from the criminals I chain up, right where you're sitting. The glass keeps them from spitting on me."

"Gross," said Maxine.

"A lot of crazy things happen in that seat, young lady," said Sheriff Hunter winking in the rearview mirror.

Maxine said nothing. Max, on the other hand, laughed with delight.

The police cruiser rolled down the dusty, gravel driveway, away from the barns. Cindy waved from the office and made a hand gesture for Max to call her.

She might have something for me after all, thought Max.

He decided not to make an issue of it by telling his father, who focused on making the right turn onto Silvernails Road.

"We're going to stop at Peck's Market on the way into town," said Sheriff Hunter. "Your parents won't mind, will they, Maxine?"

"I'm fine, sir, as long as you're fine with us being out after curfew."

"If you're with me, you're covered."

The police car crossed the Rojan Creek bridge and passed the barn on the left where the murder took place.

Sheriff Hunter didn't look. He took a deep breath and sighed.

Bright yellow crime scene tape wrapped the barn like a birthday present.

New chains and locks secured the front doors.

Additional cement barriers surrounded the building.

All exposed holes had been boarded over.

"Wow ... looks different now," said Max, peering over the steering wheel to get a better look.

"We've wrapped up things in the barn. It's cleaned out and locked down... You're never going in there again, got it?" Max's father sounded very stern. He smacked Max on the shoulder with the back of his hand.

Maxine scribbled something down on a pad of paper, ripped a piece out, folded it, and handed it to Max. Max unfolded it, making sure it faced away from his father. The words read: "I know of another cool place near here you can use for a hangout."

Impressive, thought Max. Maxine was as crafty as him.

He gave a thumbs-up but said nothing.

Silvernails Road continued to wind past the farm, past another dairy farm, and through the woods where it met up with Patchin's Mill. Upon making the right-hand turn onto Main Street, several miles from the center of town, the sheriff's radio sprang to life. It crackled and hissed as the operator tested the mic.

"Sheriff—Sheriff Hunter?" A man's voice cut in and out. He tapped it with his finger, but it made the problem worse.

"We—f—found her —" The radio went dead. Ace turned it off, rebooted the system, and turned it back on. He pulled the car over on the shoulder of the road and whispered for his two passengers to remain silent. He pressed the microphone button.

"Come in, base, Sheriff Hunter here." Ace gulped. "What's the news?"

Some more crackling came across the speaker. Bernard's voice, shaken, announced terrible news.

"We found the Waters girl. What's left, anyway. She's deceased."

Maxine gasped in the rear seat.

Max felt his face and hands go numb.

A coven of crows perched on a large branch jutting out over the car screeched over the announcement. The still air moved. Leaves were swept up from the ground and circled the vehicle in a torrent of wind.

Blood drained from Ace's face. Max put his hand on his father's arm to get his attention, but the man didn't move.

"Do you copy?" said Bernard. "Are you there?"

"Yeah, I copy," said Sheriff Hunter.

"Are you on your way back to the station?"

"Give me an hour, Bernard. I should go to the store first. The wife wants some steaks." His tone fell flat.

"Are you ok, Dad," whispered Max. He felt like he could start crying but held back.

Sheriff Hunter paused. He drew in another deep breath and let it out slowly. He put the cruiser in drive and slowly eased back out onto the road.

Maxine held on in the back seat, clutching the handhold overhead. She remained silent for the entire ride into town, as did Max.

Max took notice as they passed Evergreen Cemetery.

Several new headstones stood close to the road's edge. A green tent with chairs under it, and a large, green, carpeted box, waited for a funeral procession and casket.

Max thought of Carmen's mom. She preserved the same bodies now buried along the road's edge. He imagined her with a palate of paints, drawing eyes, lips, and noses on corpses in an underground room with no windows. Alone in the dark.

"I wonder what masterpiece Father Franks is burying today," Max mumbled, but loud enough for Ace to hear.

"What did you say?" said Ace.

"Behind us," said Max. "I wonder who's being buried today under that tent."

Ace craned his head, looking over his shoulder toward the section of the cemetery where the tent stood. One large, weathered headstone stood out among a family of shiny, yet substantially smaller new ones. A wrought iron fence surrounded them, designating it as a family plot.

"The Weatherbys...." Ace's voice trailed off.

The Weatherby family had been a force in the community since its founding many decades before. While wealthy, they were also the object of wild speculation among the townspeople, who spoke regularly of the family in hushed tones at parties and events. Each member died under unusual circumstances. Only recently had the last members of the doomed family dropped one by one.

Several weeks before, the remainder of the family—matriarch Mrs. Weatherby, and her daughter Janice and her three young—had died in a car crash. Mrs. Weatherby, ninety-five years old and legally blind, had plowed her car into Killer, the giant tree Sheriff Hunter narrowly missed the week before with his kids.

Past the Weatherbys' final resting place (haunted according to those who visited at night), Ace regarded the tent, and the occupant due to rest below it later that day.

"Old Mrs. Tweed," said Ace grumbling, not watching his words. "She passed last week ... the old hag."

"What was wrong with her?" said Maxine, who noted the sheriff's judgment of the deceased.

"Mean. Downright ornery. That woman always complained of home break-ins that never happened, and faulty carbon monoxide detectors that always worked." He growled. "She has used more resources from the police and fire department than the rest of the town combined."

"I forgot about her," said Max. He looked back as the silhouette of the tent disappearing behind the Weatherby monument. "She's being buried right next to—them."

Maxine knew the news distressed the sheriff.

"I'm sorry, sir. Now—Melinda Water's."

Sheriff Hunter stared straight ahead, taking his eyes off the cemetery.

Max knew his father had a right to be angry. The stakes in the murder investigation just grew now that Bethany Waters' sister had been found dead.

Max's mind flashed pictures of Melinda, buried next to the Weatherbys and the angry old lady whom his father seemed fine with meeting her end. He imagined her—having died too soon—floating around the graveyard at night, haunting the graves together with the Weatherbys. Melinda and her ghostly pizzas.

"Do you believe in ghosts?" Max blurted out.

Sheriff Hunter remained silent, guiding the car into the center of town where he'd make a left and pull into Pecks Grocery Store.

Maxine spoke up. She had settled back in her seat, happy the ride wound soon end.

"I believe in ghosts," said Maxine. "I've even seen a couple."

Sheriff Hunter chuckled under his breath but said nothing.

"How did you see them?" said Max.

"Our house is haunted. You know Dallas bought that Victorian down near Clinton Corners, right?"

Her pronouncement drew the attention of Sheriff Hunter.

"You mean the old Atkinson place?"

"That's the one, sir, yes. It looks incredible now, doesn't it?"

"The renovation is amazing. The house sure has some history, though." Sheriff Hunter shook his head in disbelief that the old Atkinson house had a family living in it. It sat vacant for many years due to not one, but two tragedies that took place within its walls. "Someone finally had some balls...."

"Yeah," said Maxine, "Dallas doesn't mind that someone died there. They're still there."

"Who's still there?" said Max.

"Their ghosts. They never left."

"No way."

"Yup. We can see them. I've even contacted one with my Ouija board."

Sheriff Hunter shifted around in his seat.

He puckered his face in disbelief.

"Maybe we should choose another topic, guys," said the sheriff. He waited for a response.

Max rolled his eyes. Maxine agreed with a simple "ok."

Max found that he liked her even more. She seemed more interesting than even Riley!

The police cruiser made its left-hand turn in the center of town. One block down, Pecks Market stood on the left. Cars choked the parking lot.

Sheriff Hunter pulled the cruiser into a handicapped spot in front of the store.

"Hey, Maxine," said Max, "isn't that Ms. Fox's Jeep?"

In front of the store, the red Jeep had been parked in front of the ice cooler. No one sat in it.

"They must be inside," said Maxine. Something stole her attention. "What's that?"

At the entrance, the sliding doors stood ajar. Several people outside peered in, pointing. One of them turned around and saw the police cruiser and waved for help.

"I better get in there and see what's going on," said Sheriff hunter. He adjusted his hat and stepped out of the car.

Max and Maxine jumped out and followed the sheriff into the store.

ANGRY WOMEN

Any commotion inside Peck's Market, or anywhere, was rare for Pine Plains. Rational people, such as the store clerks, Mrs. Mabel Smith from the bank next door, and PTA parents, had lost it before the sheriff's arrival. They yelled and screamed, snapping at one another like wild animals. Some stood and watched. Others had stormed to the back of the store, near the meat department, where the problem itself resided.

As the sheriff entered the store, two red-faced clerks, engaged in a debate about liberal politics at their stations, noticed him and turned to get his attention with exaggerated hand waves.

"Mind telling me what's going on, ladies?" said the sheriff.

Mindy Green blushed even harder at the sight of Ace. Her pink face turning deep red like it had been slapped. A short, paunchy girl, Tiffany Bowman, leaned over the counter's conveyor belt, staring out the door.

"Is Officer Bernard with you, Ace?" said Tiffany.

Another woman yelled from the back of the store, "Who do you think you're talking to…."

Several other angry, accusing voices chimed in.

"What's under there, anyway? We deserve to know!"

"You have something to do with this, don't you? It all started when you moved here."

Sheriff Hunter put his hand up, shutting up the overly-enthusiastic cashiers.

Max plodded forward, following his father down the cereal aisle. When they reached the end, access to the meat department proved difficult. Several women with their backs turned, and their arms crossed, observed something in the far corner near the entrance to the butcher's office.

"Ok, ok, let me through. What's all the commotion about," said Ace.

In the corner, Dallas had been backed against the wall clutching a large roast, looking very startled and a bit angry. Two women, within several feet of Dallas, had been badgering and berating the poor teacher when the sheriff arrived. He pushed his way through the women blocking the aisle, taking his hat off.

"Step back, ladies. Move aside," said Sheriff Hunter. He used his arms to sandwich his way through the two women.

"Are you ok, ma'am?" He addressed Dallas, not understanding the situation.

One of the women shouted, red in the face. Mrs. Dinsmore, the store manager, pointed a boney finger at Dallas.

"That's no woman. We don't know what it is," she said.

"Yeah," said dumpy Mrs. Smith, the local gossip. She had oily, flat brown hair, and always smelled like an ashtray. She stood out everywhere she went, with her SpongeBob printed pajamas bunched around her waist, house shoes, and soiled sweatshirt.

Dallas looked confused and noticeably upset by the encounter and stood in the corner. No gaps remained to run from the swarm of irrational and hate-filled women. They blocked the exits. They buzzed around, ready to strike like angry hornets.

"I did nothing wrong. Who do you people think you are?" said Dallas.

"It's all over town. You poor excuse for a —"

From the rear of the store, near Dallas, Maxine sprang. She placed herself in front of Dallas like a wall and held her arms wide.

Sheriff Hunter's face turned deep red. Max's chest heaved with anger while glaring at the unruly adults with disgust.

"That's my teacher, Dad. Dallas is the best." Max screamed at the ranting women towering over him.

One of the women growled. "My son tells me he doesn't know if it's a man or a woman. That's unacceptable in our school."

"Who can I blame? This is a public place of business," said the sheriff. Max's dad looked straight at Dallas.

Maxine stood in front, blocking Dallas, no one could get past her. She held a martial artist's stance. The look in her eye ensured anyone who looked upon her knew how serious she was.

"You kids shouldn't be here," said another woman. "This is between us adults."

Max never believed the parents of his classmates and the townspeople could be this cruel. Witnessing Maxine step in and defend Dallas impressed him. His father seemed the weakest person in the fray, though Max understood he was probably in a state of shock over the news about Bethany's sister. No one in the store knew the girl had been found dead.

"You should all be ashamed of yourselves," said Max, unable to keep his voice down and his feelings to himself. "Ganging up on Dallas, who's the newest member of our community and an amazing teacher. All my friends love Dallas."

"Quite a coincidence this one shows up the same time that body turned up," groaned Mrs. Smith.

The women tripped over their words, cutting one another off. They competed by raising their voices and creating dramatic gestures with their arms and hands.

Sheriff Hunter stood in front of them, blocking their view from Dallas and Maxine.

"Now, ladies," he said, "you all need to calm down. What you're doing is wrong. It benefits no one."

"It's mob mentality, Dad. We learned that in class." Max was pissed. He didn't care what came out of his mouth. "So much for looking up to the adults in my community —"

"Calm down, Max," said his father.

Max peered around Ace at Maxine. Tears had welled up in her eyes.

Dallas looked flat and unamused. Dallas clutched the large chunk of meat as though it were the most valuable possession in the store.

"As far as I'm concerned," said the sheriff, "everyone in this store is a suspect. Why? We have no suspects. Someone in this town did it. We're going to find out, it doesn't matter how pretty you are or how much you think those around you would never finger you. Watch what you say and those you blame. Things are going to get nasty."

Sheriff Hunter eyed each woman in turn. Some stood their ground. Others shrank away, diverting their eyes to boxes of pasta or specks of dust on the floor.

"Another thing," said the sheriff. "What you're doing here constitutes a hate crime. Bullying. Shaming. None of this, I mean none, will happen in my town. I'm warning you all now."

"Yeah," said Max. "What kind of precedent are you setting? I'm going to tell my friends and classmates what happened here today...."

"No, you're not," said Max's father. He returned his gaze to Dallas. "What's your name again?"

"Dallas Finn, sir."

"Dallas, I am so sorry for what happened here today. Would you like to press charges against any of these women?"

Dallas's throat cleared. Dallas's eyes moved around the back of the store, surveying those who brought the accusations. Many faces wore the masks of fear, mistrust, and ignorance.

"I don't wish to charge anyone right now, but I will think about it some more. I know you all can't help yourselves. What has happened in this community is horrific. However," Dallas paused, going inward and thinking of some witty response to make the situation a teaching moment. "You'll need to open your minds and work together. Otherwise, I fear you will tear one another apart."

"I think they should apologize to Dallas, Dad," said Max, butting in.

Maxine echoed his words. "Max is right. Who are you to attack anyone? You should be ashamed of yourselves."

Silence overtook the back of Peck's Market. Registers and conveyor belts at checkout stations ceased to move. The faint chirping of birds far out in the trees lining the street cut through the tension as those in the store held their breaths.

Mrs. Dinsmore spoke first.

"So, what is it? We still don't know what —" Max cut her off.

"This is Dallas Finn, Mrs. Dinsmore, our Biology teacher," said Max. "Dallas Finn, this is the store manager, Dirty Dinsmore. Oh, I mean, Mrs., that is…." Max's cheeks turned pink. He had spoken the unthinkable.

Mrs. Dinsmore had a reputation, though unsubstantiated. The people of the town knew her propensity to drink with her friends, among them Dr. Esteban, Carmen's mother. She also had a personal following with many of the local farmers. She'd personally deliver bagged groceries to several farm homes. On many occasions, when customers saw her return, her clothes had been soiled, and her hair out of place.

Mrs. Dinsmore's face grew redder than Max's. She scowled at him. Her face became a canvas painted with the dark colors of flaming shock and dark dismay.

"What did you just call me?" She looked up from Max and shook her head at Sheriff Hunter.

"Your son needs his mouth washed out with soap. Maybe a couple of weeks in his room, or scrubbing toilets again for the school."

Max blinked. Even Mrs. Dinsmore knew about his grounding the previous spring.

Dallas cracked a slight grin, trying not to laugh.

"It's ok," said Dallas, signaling out Mrs. Dinsmore. "I've dealt with people like you from the city. Nothing changes, be it a small town like Pine Plans, or the crush of Manhattan. Only, you can't hide your nature for long in a town like this. You all wear your true feelings like that thick, over-applied makeup you spread with a spatula across your simple, dull faces."

Mrs. Dinsmore covered her mouth with her hand. Her expression said it all.

"And," said Dallas, "I'll be taking my business over to Stanfordville Grocery, or across the border. We won't bother you any longer."

Dallas heaved the large, expensive chunk of meat back on the deli counter. The glass rattled as it slammed down on the surface with a THUD.

"There are too many negative adjectives to describe the people around here," said Maxine under her breath.

Max smirked. He liked it when horrible people got what they deserved.

Mrs. Dinsmore said nothing else and walked away. Behind her followed several other women, all with their noses in the air and huff's emanating from their throats. Mrs. Dinsmore's voice echoed through the front of the store: "Ok, enough tiptoeing around, back to work girls." The checkout conveyors sprang to life. Pecks' Market hummed once again, but not one person—customer or employee—spoke a word while the sheriff and the kids remained within earshot.

Sheriff Hunter stared at the meat display. Cold steaks—the reason he even came to the store—were piled along with plump chicken breasts and bright pink pork chops. Max had skirted around him to check on Maxine, who aided Dallas in picking up the contents from a satchel that had opened and spilled out on the floor.

Among the items were lip gloss, a mirror and comb, a ring of old skeleton keys, the automatic clicker for the Jeep, and other items. A giant wad of hundred dollar bills bound with a single, thick rubber band stood out next to an orange bottle of pills from the Pine Plains Pharmacy. The pill bottle had popped open, spraying red tablets from wall to wall.

"So, Dallas," said Sheriff Hunter, who watched the three kneeling on the floor, scooping items up as fast as possible. "Do you have any ideas about what's happening in this town?"

Dallas looked up from the floor.

"Sheriff?"

"Dad's name is Ace, Dallas, you can call him Ace," said Max.

Dallas continued. "A pretty sick person is among you. It could also be a transient. Or someone just passing through and saw an opportunity, and dumped the body."

"I suppose…" said Ace. "But that barn your librarian owns had been locked good and tight for quite some time. How they got the body and that pig in there is a major magic trick. Nothing had been disturbed."

"We better get home," said Max, seeing the clock on the wall. They had twenty minutes until the curfew.

"We better get going too," said Dallas. "But, Ace, let me think. Maybe I can come up with some theories."

"Any insight you can give is greatly appreciated," said Ace, hesitating, not knowing how to address Dallas. He understood, somewhat, what sparked the crazed women shopping in the store.

"I don't know what's gotten into people, I thought the people in this community were better than this," said Dallas, scooping up the last of the medication on the floor.

Once they got to their feet, Dallas shared a limp handshake with Ace and thanked him for interceding. The four of them left the store, single file. They headed their separate ways, but not before Ace secured seven steaks from the butcher.

Riley and Joe get Sick

That evening in the Hunter household, Ace sat quietly.

Max knew his father thought about how he would break the news about the death of Melinda Waters to the public. Ace had not returned to the station yet.

Bernard sat across from him at the table (he invited himself over as usual), picking at his steak and waiting for the verdict.

Max related the drama in Pecks Market while waving his mashed potato covered fork around. He explained the assault on Dallas and how Maxine stepped in and put herself in harm's way. Beth and Joe took measured bites of their food, careful to reduce munching or the clanking of silverware.

Riley, on the other hand, sank low in her chair with her head down. Beth kept an uneasy eye on her as Max forced most of his presentation Riley's way, trying to get a reaction.

Bernard reached over and felt Riley's wrist.

"She's freezing and pale Beth.

"Look up, Riley," said Ace. "Are you ok?"

Max ceased chattering. He noticed Riley's face looked almost blue. She didn't respond.

Bernard proceeded to check Riley's pulse by pinching her wrist.

"Her pulse is racing," said Bernard. "Has she had a cold or an infection?"

"Her leg," yelled Max, remembering the incident, "check her leg. She had that cut from the barn."

Ace threw his napkin on his plate and lunged over to Riley's chair, yanking it out from the table. He rolled Riley's pants leg up. Underneath, the gauze taped to Riley's leg, covering the gash from the rusty nail, glistened wet from fresh blood and green puss. It oozed fluid. Max also noticed he could smell its rancid aroma.

"Beth, her leg's infected. It smells —" Ace tore the gauze off, exposing the wound.

"I know what that is, we learned it in Dallas's biology class... Sepsis, it's mega bad," said Max.

"We need to get her to the hospital right away," said Bernard.

Beth flew around the table to look. Ace had removed the remainder of the gauze, revealing Riley's flaming red skin, yellow and green puss, and the wound itself, which had not healed.

"That's disgusting," said Max.

"You didn't see this before?" said Ace.

Beth looked dumbfounded. "It was nothing like this yesterday, I swear... Oh, my —"

"We need to go now," said Bernard. "If she has an infection, she's in big trouble."

While her parents lifted her out of the chair, Riley's body went limp. She barely moved. Her brow beaded with sweat.

Beth and Ace hauled Riley to the front door. Bernard ran out the door to his police cruiser. He hopped in, turned it on, and backed up to the entrance of the farmhouse.

"Come on, man, let's go with them," said Max, urging his oldest brother Joe to help.

Max worried for both Riley and Joe. Joe looked frozen in place at the dinner table with a nervous twitch in his chin, mumbling under his breath.

"Are you ok, Joe?" said Max. Max jostled his brother's shoulder, but Joe didn't respond.

"Mom!"

Beth and Ace were loading Riley into the police cruiser when Beth heard Max call her name. She ran inside, leaving Ace and Bernard.

"What's wrong now?"

"Joe is acting weird too, Mom."

Beth rushed over to Joe, grabbing him by the shoulders and turning him toward her with a jerk.

"What's wrong, honey?"

"I'm feeling queasy mom," said Joe, his voice quivering.

Joe had turned as pale as Riley.

"My God," said Beth, noticing his lips, "your lips are turning blue…"

"It's from the pie mom, that's all."

In the center of the table, amidst the other dishes, a blueberry pie beckoned to be eaten. Joe had stolen a slice before dinner. His mother had scolded him, telling him to wait, but he didn't.

"Well, honey, your librarian at school—Ms. Fox—wanted everyone to have a slice after dinner. Not before. She was very specific," said Beth.

Max's eyes grew wide. "What do you mean? The librarian?"

Beth eased Joe out of his chair.

"She stopped over earlier today and brought us that amazing pie…." Beth grunted. She gave Max a sideways glance while fumbling with Joe. "Nice lady… Says she's concerned about you and your grades."

Max didn't know what to say. He felt both scared and nauseous.

Camilla had been in the house. In HIS house.

"I don't think you should eat the pie, who knows what her kitchen is like," screeched Max. "And look… Joe's sick."

Beth rolled her eyes.

"Help me with your brother. You're both coming to the hospital."

Max looked at his mother and the pie. He knew, if he left it, anyone could get into it. He did what he had to do, regardless of the punishment that might come.

Before his mother could stop him, Max yanked the pie off the table and ran into the kitchen. He threw it into the hot soapy water filling one side of the sink. He put his good hand in and stirred it until the water turned a purplish-blue.

"What do you think you're doing?" barked his mother.

"The pie is no good mom. We need to kill off whatever's inside of it."

"That pie was perfect —"

"But she's evil mom… She did it on purpose."

Before Max could say another word, his mother grabbed him by the ear and dragged him out of the kitchen.

"Honestly, I don't know what's gotten into you. You better stop it this instant!"

Max squealed under the pressure of her fingers. He didn't dare pull away.

His mother could be quite the brute if she had the incentive.

Struggling would get him nowhere.

She released him at Joe's chair. Joe stood up, propping himself against the table and leaning on one hand.

"You, poor baby," said Beth. She put her arm around Joe's shoulders and led him toward the front door. Max kept his mouth shut and stayed on the other side of her.

The ride to Sharon Hospital zipped by. Max did not even know how he got there. The entire trip passed in a blur, except the moment they passed Killer, where things seemed to slow down. The gnarled tree passed by in slow motion, teasing Max. Its damp limbs brushed the top of the cruiser as if to snatch him up and claim him as its next victim.

Thankfully, his father had remembered, slowing down before the curve and avoiding inevitable catastrophe. The man looked exhausted and worried. The events of the day, and his job, played on his face.

N N N

Max spent two hours at the hospital in the waiting room. While he played "I spy" with Bernard, his parents sat looking stunned. They huddled together next to the water cooler and a pile of decades-old magazines.

Both Riley and Joe were admitted ahead of other patients, not because Ace was the sheriff, but because, this time, they looked on the verge of death.

When the emergency room doctor returned with the verdict, he confirmed Max's fears: Joe suffered from what looked like food poisoning. He had to have his stomach pumped and would be kept overnight for observation.

Riley, on the other hand, baffled the doctors. They suspected sepsis, but blood tests hadn't determined the extent of the infection on her leg.

"I'm sorry to say folks, but Riley is in grave condition. She's showing all the classic signs of a massive infection," said the doctor. The doctor looked much older than Max's previous physician. With deep wrinkles that showed his age, his eyes indicated the distress he felt for Max's sister. He looked over the family and spoke before having Max's parents follow him to another room: "I would suggest some prayers as well, as many as you can."

Beth and Ace stood up and followed the doctor into a nearby office.

Max sat with Bernard, who had also fallen silent with the terrible news.

"I know this all has something to do with her," said Max under his breath. He didn't speak directly to Bernard but voiced his thoughts out loud, engaged in an internal conversation.

"What are you talking about?" said Bernard. He hunched in his seat, leafing through an old copy of Time magazine.

"Camilla, the school librarian."

"What do you mean?"

"Well, she made the pie for one thing … Joe's the only one who had a slice."

"Seriously? What kind of pie was it?"

"Blueberry…"

"Well, that explains it, who likes blueberry?"

"Dude," said Max, irritated. "that's not the point. Camilla made the blueberry pie. Now Joe is sick. Fill in the blanks."

Bernard shook his head in disbelief.

"Now, what would make you think your librarian would try to poison someone with a pie?"

"Think about it," said Max, in full investigative mode, "she owns the barn. You and my dad are investigating this crime. She brings over a blueberry pie on the same day we're all eating together…."

"No. There needs to be more of a motive. That was a murder, including the slaughtering of that poor pig."

"Yeah, she's a freak man," said Max, becoming more convinced he was right. "The other day when Maxine and I were in her office —"

He almost gave away too much. Max shut his mouth before incriminating himself and his friends. Bernard wouldn't understand. Max knew Bernard felt disturbed over recent events, and the current state of Joe and Riley.

Max himself didn't understand yet. He had his suspicions. Plus, unbeknownst to anyone else, even with Maxine in the room, he hadn't made public his concerns with the art supplies in the librarian's office— the same supplies needed to make the creepy burlap dolls.

"Maybe we should pray. Can't hurt, can it?" said Bernard.

Max's parents remained in the doctor's office longer than Max expected.

They're probably discussing a treatment plan, or something worse, thought Max. He didn't like the silence. The waiting room had grown vacant, with he and Bernard being the last people to sit, waiting.

"I'm glad you're here, Bernard. I'm not sure what Mom and Dad would do without you."

"It's a small community, champ," said Bernard, tearing up. "We take care of our own, no matter what."

"Yeah, you're right," said Max. He let out a big sigh.

Max's lungs felt heavy. His breathing was labored as though he had run a great distance. His arm had ceased hurting but itched under the oppressive cast's thick, dry casing. The plaster cast was the least of his concerns. People around him were hurting bad, and he needed to do something about it.

"I'll pray, Bernard," said Max. "How about we pray for Joe and Riley, for the person from the barn we don't even know. For Bethany's sister?"

"Sounds perfect," said Bernard.

"I never did an official one before. Maybe you can start?"

"Sure. Here's how it goes...."

Bernard instructed Max on how to lower his head and close his eyes as a sign of respect and silent reflection. Max cupped his hands, mimicking Bernard so he could get it right. He didn't want to screw it up, too much depended on what happened from that time onward, he knew that.

Bernard gave thanks and prayed for those around them who suffered. He followed it by a long stretch of silence, which Max was happy to go along with—Max needed some silence and time to reflect on the next plan brewing in his early teenage head.

Maybe the illnesses Riley and Joe suffered were from some curse.

Max needed to find out—lure Camilla into a sneaky trap, or, if not her, whoever or whatever worked at destroying Pine Plains from the inside out. If his entire family stood in the crosshairs, maybe his plan to make the dolls to sell would draw the attention of the perpetrator at the fair, where he'd be—an easy target.

Max continued to follow Officer Bernard's instructions on praying, but sat silently, scared at what might happen next.

CARMEN AIDES MAX

With news of the Water's death and the spread of Sheriff Hunter's family crisis throughout the gossiping world of Pine Plains, Max chose to lay low for the remainder of the week. The school canceled classes until the following Monday. Many protested, citing the Harvest Fair should continue that Saturday as planned—the town's citizens needed something fun and entertaining to do.

With a vote of eight to zero, the City Council allowed the fair to proceed if it wrapped up before sundown.

Max decided on a plan. He would borrow his mother's sewing machine and, with the supplies, set up shop in the shed outside. Max would pump out as many creepy dolls as possible. He wanted money.

"These things will make me a butt load!" Max growled, grappling bags of burlap and stuffing. He dragged them with one arm from the back porch, through the torn screen door, and out to the shed.

Max reasoned that the people of Pine Plains would want a piece of history when they found out his creations were exact replicas of the dolls found in the rotten barn and linked to the crime scene. He also knew his crafts could draw the attention of the killer. He'd be that much closer to helping his dad and Bernard solve the case.

He wondered if—in the case of what seemed like Voodoo dolls—magic was involved. Events didn't add up. Impossible events.

"Maybe things will clear up for Riley and Joe if dad catches this murderer," he reasoned.

Thoughts raced through his head while hauling each item to the shed. The last thing—and a heavy one—was the sewing machine. Everything on the farm seemed to be industrial strength. His parents never bought anything without ensuring it included a lifetime guarantee. That meant everything, from furniture to farm tools, to the clothes they wore. Even the dinner plates. Everything had to last. Little changed on the Hunter farm. Hand-me-downs were typical. Max had his fill of wearing his brother's (what his mother called "gently used") clothes.

Max plodded along, pulling the sewing machine on his red wagon. He thought about the red and black plaid shirt he wore and inherited from Joe, the ripped Levis, and the mud-covered work boots of Joe's that got sucked into the mud whenever he miss-stepped.

"Max," he said to himself, approaching the shed, making sure not to veer off the path into the mud (it had been raining for days), "you need your job." He groaned as the wagon got stuck on a flagstone. "You need to make these dolls. People buy anything, and you like things your way, don't you, Max? Nice new shirt. Pants. Spend your own money. Everyone's happy."

He reached the half-open door to the shed, backed into it, stepped up, and pulled the wagon over the threshold with a jolt. The sewing machine wavered and nearly fell to the side. Max jerked the cart. It teetered back into place. Looking up, to his astonishment, Carmen Esteban trudged from the back door of the house down the path toward him.

"What are you doing here?" said Max, yelling across the yard. He couldn't hide the smirk that spread across his face and felt oddly conspicuous. He turned and laughed his way into the shadows of the shed.

"What are you laughing about?" said Carmen, stepping into the doorway. "I thought you'd be upset."

"I'm not laughing … I stubbed my toe!"

Max looked away from Carmen. A series of giggles crept from his throat. He pushed them back with a gulp—the last thing he needed was the girl thinking he was a loon, or happy to see her.

"You came just in time, I'm setting this thing up. I have a project to get done. Can you help me with this?"

Max jostled the sewing machine and attempted to pick it up with one arm and set it on a dusty workbench. Carmen hurried across the creaky floorboards and wrangled it away from him, lifting it and slamming it down.

"What are you doing with a sewing machine—out here?" She looked around the dim, dusty shed. A cord hanging from an antique, multi-light chandelier hit her in the face. She yanked it out of her way. The lights erupted. A million small crystals shot tiny rainbows all over the walls. "This is so cool!"

"Yeah, I saved it from the dump. I know it doesn't fit in, but this is my space, so…."

"I think it's super cool." Carmen had a better view of the room. "I assume this is an art studio, or —"

"It's my space, like I said," said Max, acting a bit defensive. He never had a girl in his boy-cave before. Now he feared being judged. "Right next to the garden where I grow the pumpkins, and out of the way." He paused and let her in on his plans. "I have a project I need to get done before the fair."

Carmen's hands explored the dark recesses of the shed.

"So, the sewing machine —"

"…is for the project, which I need to get done, so…."

"I won't get in your way," said Carmen. "My mom brought me over to check up on you, just for a bit. I'm so sorry about your sister and brother…."

"I know, it's a horrible thing," said Max.

Carmen stirred up some dust with her finger, inspecting it like a maid reviewing her handiwork.

"Does my cleaning pass inspection?" said Max, noticing her prying.

"It's a shed. It's supposed to be dirty," said Carmen. She snickered. A small laugh came out. "I'm sorry, I know I shouldn't be laughing." She stopped and stood next to Max, looking over his doll-making supplies, and spied the doll he had snatched from the old barn.

"Is that what you're making?" Carmen reached for the doll, but Max blocked her with his elbow.

"Yes. For the fair," groaned Max.

"Why?"

Max beamed. Someone he knew had come to visit. Carmen did let him stage his morgue break-in from her home, so he knew he could trust her.

She arrived at Max's shed wearing a thick, yellow slicker over her faded blue jeans and a hooded, pink sweatshirt.

"I like your ensemble," said Max, using a funny French accent.

Carmen laughed a little harder at his shaky attempt to be silly.

"But seriously, why are you making dolls?"

"Can you keep another secret?" said Max.

"I didn't break the last one, did I?"

"No."

"Well then...."

Max turned and unfolded a black metal chair for Carmen. He lumbered over to the door, peered outside—he didn't want anyone to see—and pulled it shut, latching it from the inside. Sitting in his chair, he told Carmen everything he believed; everything he suspected.

✄ ✄ ✄

"You seriously think Ms. Fox has something to do with this?" said Carmen, shocked at his story.

"She owns the barn," said Max. "And I've seen her red Jeep following us. Also, the way she sniffed the jacket you washed when she held me and Maxine captive...."

Carmen rolled her eyes in disbelief. "I don't know about this, Max. You might be losing it."

"Yeah, I have a good reason, it's called Riley and Joe. Something's seriously wrong around here." Max's voice cracked. He didn't want to have to explain himself to anyone.

"Ok, say you're right. What can you do? I mean, your dad won't believe you. Ms. Fox is smart. I mean, intelligent. So is whoever's doing the murders, considering they left no clues —"

"Except for the dolls!"

"So, there were more of them?"

"Yes," said Max, "four in all, hanging over the dead things like some magical, voodoo-like spell or something."

"That's one of them?" said Carmen, pointing to the doll propped up on the window sill. Bits of newspaper and what looked like hair poked out of its mangled body.

"Yup. I'm copying it. I made a template from it last night." Max puffed out his chest and let out a deep breath. "People will buy them up when they know what they are. I might even be able to lure the killer in."

"And then?" Carmen probed for answers.

"Well, if we can get a read on people—you know, see how they respond to the dolls—we can narrow the field of suspects."

"Not a totally bad idea." Carmen warmed to his strategy.

"Then, I can present my evidence to dad, but not until then."

"Do you need some help?" Carmen's eyes played over the supplies stacked next to the sewing machine.

Max looked at the supplies. His templates were ready to cut the shapes out of the burlap. Before his grandmother passed (*God save her soul in Evergreen Cemetery, where the Weatherbys haunt the graves,* thought Max), she had taught him a little about sewing—anything she could show knowing her mind quickly faded and she had eager, young grandkids with too much free time.

"How much time do you have?" said Max. "Aren't you only here for a short while?"

"Mom's having tea with yours. I can go check —"

"Make it fast," said Max, interrupting. "I have to get this done. Maybe you can cut the shapes out for me."

Carmen giggled and ran out the door. "I'll be right back!"

Max sorted supplies. He planned on making a ton of dolls, to maximize his profits at the Harvest Fair.

He knew he'd be mocked by older boys when they saw his creations, but he didn't care. Max had the law on his side. He was also very muscular for his age and the newest member of the football team after all. He liked stirring things up, causing the kind of trouble that wouldn't lead him spending a week in his room.

"These'll raise some eyebrows," he muttered, plugging the old, yellowed Spiegel sewing machine into the electric outlet above the supplies.

He tinkered around with thread cones and had everything ready when Carmen came dashing back through the door.

"Mom said I can stay … if you want, of course," said Carmen, panting.

"I have all day, do you?"

"Yup, mom's going into town. She had some epiphany about the body parts. Something about tattoos. She'll be up to her elbows in that body's juice in no time."

"Yeah, that juice Camilla smelled on my jacket," said Max, "you remember. There were tattoos all over that leg."

"Did you see the pictures yet?"

"I looked them over—lots of clues, like the swirly bird tattoo on its ankle." Max talked while continuing to thread the machine.

Carmen tapped her foot and groaned like she had something on her mind.

"You know, Max … your mom has, I think, the same tattoo on her ankle."

"What?"

"Yeah, the same bird, with the black swirls all around it. I saw it bright as day while she sat there —"

"I've never seen it," said Max, turning to meet Carmen with an accusative gaze. Carmen just shrugged her shoulders.

"Go look for yourself. Your mom is sitting at the table right now, whispering."

"I'll just do that," said Max in a huff. Like Carmen, he ran out the door, intent on proving her wrong, but he wasn't gone for long. The blood had drained from his face.

"I was right, wasn't I?" said Carmen, noting Max's creeped-out expression.

"I can't believe it," said Max, "it's been under my nose all this time. What do I do?"

Carmen pulled up her chair next to his and put her hand on Max's knee.

"It just means there's a popular tattoo parlor somewhere around here, that's all," said Carmen. "But it's a good clue, right? I mean, you can ask your mom where she got it."

A devious look crossed Max's face as the blood returned. The revelation his mother was a link to the dead body, while disturbing, was a positive sign. He thought hard about what to do. Pieces to the puzzle were coming together.

"We need to find out where it's at—get over there and snoop around."

"That's easy," said Carmen.

"What do you mean?"

"I overheard your mother suggesting the Metamorphosis Tattoo parlor across the Hudson River in Kingston to my mom. Mom's going over there to get one tomorrow —"

"That's perfect!" said Max.

Carmen ran out of the door again.

"Where are you going?" said Max. "We need to get this done...."

"To see if we can go with her tomorrow," said Carmen, her voice trailing off.

Max shook his head and finished threading the sewing machine. He had the dolls figured out: tan burlap, black thread, odd buttons for eyes, straw stuffing, and the precious little red hearts the murderer had affixed to each in the barn.

"Yup," he said under his breath, smiling at the tattered doll on the window sill. "These should freak them out nice and good."

METAMORPHOSIS

Max, with Carmen's help, completed one-hundred dolls the day before accompanying Doctor Esteban, and his mother, to the tattoo parlor in Kingston, New York. Beth sat in the front passenger seat of the Volvo rattling on about her motherly duties and her concerns over Riley, while Max and Carmen sat in the back, whispering.

The plan was simple: get to the tattoo place, hit up the owner about the tattoo on his mother's leg while his mom was distracted, and beg for a list of clients who got the same one.

"This shouldn't be too hard, right?" said Max. Carmen wasn't too sure about his plan.

"Don't businesses have rules about handing over personal, client information?"

Max shook his head. "Don't be so literal," he whispered. "There are ways…"

Max produced a large, reusable hemp grocery bag he obtained from the previous year's Pine Plains Farmer's Market behind the Stissing House. It had large handles and felt sturdy enough to hold anything from vegetables to books.

"We can use this. You distract while I steal," said Max.

"You can't just take stuff, that's illegal." Carmen rolled her eyes at the idea. "It's all probably on a computer, anyway."

"These places always have journals. Artists don't like technology, like computers."

"Let's hope so. Leave me out of it if you get caught," said Carmen.

Max chuckled, "I have the law on my side."

"Stealing is stealing."

И И И

Beth turned around in her seat to check on the two kids in the back. They were just about to cross the Kingston-Rhinecliff Bridge spanning the dirty Hudson River.

"There's a ton of history here," said Beth. "I challenge you to recite one piece of historical fact about this bridge … either one of you."

"It's a continuous under-deck truss," said Carmen, matter-of-factly. "It was supposed to be a suspension bridge, but the bedrock wasn't stable."

Beth raised her eyebrows in surprise. Max did the same.

"I don't recall ever learning that in class," said Max.

Carmen smiled. "I'm sure you were flying paper airplanes that day … you, Kevin and André."

"Airplanes?" said Beth. "You're a straight-A student, Max."

"He's still a boy," said Carmen.

"And you're still a prissy —" Max stopped himself. Being trapped in a car with three women, he knew he would have no case. So, he shut his mouth and looked out the window. "Anyway, the toll is for eastbound traffic only—a dollar fifty." Max shot a look at Carmen. "See, I can fly planes in class if I want."

Beth smiled. "That's my, Max!" She laughed.

Carmen giggled and put her hand up to her glistening "Dior Addict Ultra-Gloss" covered lips. "You almost said it! I'm a prissy—what?"

"Almost," said Max. "But I know my limitations."

Beth drew in a dramatic breath, acting surprised. "Limitations? You? My son? When pigs fly."

Doctor Esteban, who preferred to be called by her name, Paris, barely listened. She laughed when necessary, but kept her eyes on the road. She turned the car toward the off-ramp once they reached the other side of the river, aiming it south where she'd take the 9W toward the tattoo parlor a short distance from the Hudson Valley Mall.

"We're almost there," said Paris. "I'm a little nervous."

Beth consoled her while Max and Carmen listened in from the back seat. "This is easy and fun, you'll see. Getting a tattoo is like kittens licking your skin."

"Hey, mom," said Max. "I have a question."

"What, honey?"

"Well … what is that tattoo you have on your ankle? You know, the bird…."

"Oh, that." Beth turned to Paris and whispered something. Carmen's mom gasped, surprised at the secret Beth divulged.

"Seven?" she whispered back.

Beth turned toward Max. "That tattoo was one of the first I ever got. I was very young, your father and I had just gotten married."

"But what does it mean, mom?"

"I don't know, honey. I think it is supposed to have some mystical meaning, like living forever or something."

"Forever?"

"Yes." Beth sighed, acting dramatic. "Your poor, aging mother might live forever ... imagine that!"

"Maybe I should get the same one," said Paris. She hummed under her breath. "I know I've seen it somewhere else, though...."

Max gave Carmen a meaningful glance, forming his lips into an "O." They had seen it before, at the morgue, including several of their friends. Max figured the symbol hid more meaning than he had realized. He leaned over to Carmen and whispered, "Maybe it's a conspiracy."

И И И

The Volvo did a U-turn and parked along the street at the Metamorphosis tattoo parlor. The four got out.

"Can we come in too," said Max. "I want to look around."

"Me too," said Carmen.

"Well, for a moment," said Beth. "But I want you to go hang out at the pizzeria next door, as we discussed. I don't want you watching."

"How long will it take, Mom?" said Carmen.

Paris looked at Beth for help. Bath counted with her eyes and recollected her own experience in her head and replied, "Really, no more than two or three hours."

"That's not bad," said Carmen, "at least I brought a book —"

"Oh, you two won't need to read, they have games in there and the pizza buffet." Beth motioned to the store next-door with the pizza name on it. The pizza shop and the tattoo parlor looked the same. Both were built from local stone, almost like barns, and were very old.

"The same gentleman owns the pizza shop as the tattoo parlor," said Beth. "We might get a good deal." Max's mom rummaged around in her purse and produced a wad of money. "Here's some money for the pizza. There's plenty for the games."

"Cool!"

"This better not hurt," said Paris, looking at the front door to the Metamorphosis tattoo shop. She looked a little nervous. The rickety old buildings did not inspire much confidence, they had been around a very long time.

"Ian and Jasmine are wonderful. They know what they're doing," said Beth.

"Well, let's get this over with." Max watched as Carmen's mother, a doctor no less, nibble on a fingernail. Her eyes darted around. She took deep breaths, trying to calm herself.

Max felt electrified. The trip promised to be the most fun he had in a while. He could tell Carmen felt the same. She beamed from the plans they had hatched.

Inside the shop, the rough plaster walls were cluttered with jagged cutouts from magazines and books on the art of tattooing. Framed photos of previous clients hung precariously from nails in sporadic spots between windows, posters, and small trinkets for sale.

Beth and Paris engaged in a conversation with Ian. He hovered over Carmen's mom reclined in the duct-taped, green doctor's chair.

Max noticed Dr. Esteban perspiring. She dabbed her forehead while being shown sketches of tattoos with skulls, thorns, and swords.

Max's mother stood over Paris, pointing at things she liked, making suggestions. She kept turning back to one page and looking toward the tattoo on her leg.

"It's awesome seeing newbies come in," said the other tattoo artist, Jasmine, "especially older women reclaiming their youth."

"My mom's not old. She's in better shape than most people half her age," said Carmen, annoyed at the insinuation her mother was a washed-up old dowager.

"I've seen it all, it's ok. We know Beth, she's been a regular," said Jasmine. She thumbed through a large black binder on the makeshift counter used to separate the office from the rest of the store.

Max noticed page dividers with letters of the alphabet on them. The letters divided what he believed were client records by the last name.

"I bet you've had loads of people in here," said Max, digging for information.

"Over the past couple of decades? They're all in here, little bud," said Jasmine.

Carmen leaned on the counter, peering into the book. "Do you remember all the tattoos people have gotten?"

"Every single one, it's all right here."

Jasmine leaned on one arm while turning pages, looking bored. She smelled like stale cigarettes and patchouli oil. It's creamy, dirty scent blocked out all other odors, aside from what Carmen guessed was the damp rot from black mold.

Jasmine's arms were covered in mismatched tattoos, all shoved together. They ran up her hands, over her bare shoulders, and up her neck. She wore several pieces of jewelry in her face, but her lips—thick with black lipstick—stood out the most.

"Our friend Maxine would love this place," said Carmen to Jasmine, "don't you think Max?"

"Thought you didn't like her," said Max, calling what he thought was a bluff.

"She's all right—a bit creepy, though."

Jasmine smirked. "You think we're creepy?"

"I didn't say that, but you know … the goth thing is a bit abnormal." Carmen stared back at Jasmine while gnawing nervously on a green pencil she found in a rusty can on the desk.

"That's abnormal, young lady," said Jasmine, puckering her lips in disgust.

"She does that in our class all the time," said Max.

"Do you have any idea how many dirty hands have picked that up?" said Jasmin. "They don't all wash up after using the bathroom…."

Carmen stopped whittling like a woodchuck. She had been unaware of what she did and spat pieces on the floor in front of the counter.

"Do you have a bathroom?"

Jasmine chewed a little harder on her piece of gum, smiling. She pointed to a narrow door in the back of the store. Over the door, a sign hung with the figures of a man, a woman, and a question mark.

"Is that the girl's room," said Carmen.

"That's the only bathroom we have, sweetheart. You might want to keep anything in there out of your mouth too. And you thought that pencil was dirty!"

Carmen huffed and skipped over to the bathroom. While she closed the door behind her, Max couldn't help hearing her exclaim, "Gross." He turned to Jasmine, who continued to flip through her binder.

∦ ∦ ∦

"So, Jasmine, I have a question. Maybe you can help me."

Behind them, Dr. Esteban had chosen the same tattoo as Beth and sat back with a hospital gown draped over her silk pants suit. Beth sat in a wooden chair next to her as Ian prepared his needles and inks for the procedure. They were fully involved in the coming horror soon to befall Carmen's mother. It was the perfect time for Max to obtain the information.

"Yes, babe?" said Jasmine. She blew a strawberry bubble while looking down at Max. She popped it, making a sharp smacking sound and laughing as Max jumped back.

"So, you see that tattoo on mom's ankle?"

Max pointed behind himself. Jasmine's eyes followed. Beth had worn aqua blue Capris and white shoes. About six inches of her ankles were exposed, including the tattoo.

"Yup, I see it, bud. What's your question?"

Max turned away from Jasmine to avoid her breath. Patchouli or not, the rancid smell of tobacco made his stomach turn.

"I heard that some other people have the same tattoo. I wondered —"

"Oh, that one is popular, yup—has some mystical significance. I do one of those at least once a month. Use special ink too."

"Really?"

"Sure. People believe things. It's one of the reasons they choose certain tattoos." Jasmine looked Max in the face, studying him. "Someday, you too will probably be covered in them. Once you get one, you get another and another... You should see your mom!"

"She has more?"

"Honey, people are freaks under their clothes."

Max cringed at the idea. He looked over his shoulder at the gun Ian held in his hand and the needle sticking out the end of it.

"Mom told Paris—over there—that it's like kittens licking —"

Jasmine broke out in hysterical laughter, almost screaming. Her face turned red. Ian and the ladies looked over at her, and Max, who was caught off guard by Jasmine's thundering voice.

"What?" said Ian.

"Kittens ... licking!" Jasmine could hardly get the words out of her mouth. Ian got the point and chuckled, loading fresh ink into the apparatus. Paris looked confused while Beth pretended to know nothing. She gave Max a disapproving look.

"So..." said Max.

Jasmine calmed down. She took a drag on her vapor pipe.

"You're a hoot, kid."

"I'm glad I made you laugh," said Max. "I assume that the needle doesn't exactly feel like a tongue."

"No, it doesn't."

"But back to my question."

"What is it, Hun?

"I know this sounds weird," said Max in a whisper. He leaned as far into the counter as possible. "Do you have a list of the people who have gotten that tattoo? The one on mom's leg."

"Why would you need to know that?" said Jasmine. A crease formed above her eyebrows.

"It's a numbers thing ... something we're learning in school. Hard to explain." Max lied.

"Well, they're all in here." Jasmin pointed to the binder. "But, it's kinda private."

Then it hit Max. He remembered the leg with the tattoo on it. It also had the anklet on it, the same anklet he took before running from the morgue. It lingered in his jacket pocket. He had worn the same jacket from the morgue. The same coat Camilla had sniffed.

Max fished the anklet out of his pocket and plopped it on the counter under Jasmine's nose.

"What's that?" said Jasmin.

Max made sure no one watched. Carmen was still in the bathroom. He was glad she had not returned yet—her remarks about goths rubbed Jasmine the wrong way. Carmen's presence right now might ruin his chances.

"The person wearing this anklet also had one of those tattoos, and a lot more. Maybe you remember who it was —"

"Anklet honey, that's what it is." Jasmine picked up the jewelry and studied it. "Looks familiar..." She opened the binder. "We have pictures. We catalog each piece we make, you know, for testimonials."

She proceeded to look through each page, flipping them quickly. "I know it's here somewhere...."

Jasmine flipped one more page and slapped her palms down on the open pages. "That's it!"

"What? You found it?"

Max heard someone clear their throat behind him.

"Max," said Beth, "aren't you and Carmen going to get some pizza? Better hurry, mister. Time's ticking."

Carmen exited the bathroom at the same time. She meandered between two chairs, looking at photos on the wall while walking by her mother. The buzzing from Ian's needle signaled he worked quickly, injecting toxins into Paris who grimaced, turning her head away from the shoulder the man mutilated. Carmen stopped, looking at the image of the drawing next to Ian and the image appearing on her mother's shoulder. She mouthed the words to Max, "OMG."

Max waved to Carmen to come to the counter.

"So?" said Max, turning his attention to the binder. "What did you find?"

"This is the one, but I can't show you the page, it's private."

"Well, can you describe the person?"

"No."

"Oh, come on!"

"Sorry, kid." Jasmine swished around behind the counter. She took another drag on her vape pipe and coughed up some phlegm. She took a sip of some Mountain Dew soda. "I have to pee."

"I can watch the counter," said Carmen, who stood beside Max. "I won't let anyone see your book, least of all, Max."

"Ian!" Jasmine yelled across the room. "I'm going to pee!"

Ian nodded and kept on drilling into Doctor Esteban's arm. Jasmine handed the anklet back to Max and rushed around the counter, out of sight.

"Quick," said Max, "that page, the one right there, is the person…"

"No way," said Carmen.

"Yup, she recognized the anklet, which was on the leg."

"Good thing you took it."

"No joke," said Max. He knew Carmen had a cell phone, something her mother demanded so she could keep in touch at school. He needed it. "I need you to take a picture of the open page, quick."

"But mom might —"

"Just do it. It's our only opportunity." Max urged Carmen with is eyes. "I'll buy the pizza, come on...."

Carmen grumbled and pulled her phone out.

Ian eyed the kids. Beth looked at them and pointed to the door.

"Pizza. Now."

"Ok, mom," said Max. "Carmen's just getting a picture of that cool tattoo on the back wall behind the register. Hold on."

Max lied, but he didn't care. He needed to know who owned the leg. No one else, after all this time, had a clue—not the police, not Carmen's mother, the mortician—no one.

Carmen took her opportunity. She held the camera over the binder and clicked a series of pictures. She moved the camera around because she couldn't see the screen. Max blocked the activity as best he could.

"Done," said Carmen. "I think I got each part of the binder." She stuffed the camera back in her pocket and turned around as though nothing happened. "Awesome pics you have on your walls, mister!" She yelled at Ian. He just shrugged and kept carving her mother's arm. Beth shrugged, too.

"Ok, Mom, we're going," said Max.

Paris had one last request. "Honey, I don't want you to lose that phone. Put it in my purse, over here." Carmen's mother pointed to the brown Coach leather bag below her chair. Carmen obeyed.

"But we need to see those photos," whispered Max.

"We'll look them over later ... it'll be ok, I'm hungry," said Carmen.

Max agreed. Lying, deceiving, and manipulating to get what he wanted was an exhausting chore. It always left him hungry.

The Harvest Fair

The Pine Plains Harvest Fair commenced Saturday, early in the morning, before the sun turned the day's bright, crisp skies a brilliant blue. Not a drop of rain, or snow, had been predicted by the weatherman, Mr. Storms. The people of Pine Plains couldn't have asked for a better start to the day. The weatherman assured everyone a warm fifty degrees would settle in at noon, at the height of the day's activities. A brisk thirty degrees would descend on them once the sun disappeared through the trees and vendors packed up their booths.

Max's mind reeled.

"I need to see that camera when Carmen gets here," he puffed.

Max dragged straw bales around the tent with his right hand to the side of the most massive barn, which contained his prized, colossal, award-winning pumpkins. No awards had been given out yet, but he knew he was the winner. His pumpkins were the largest of any lining the entrance to the barn, entirely orange with no splits or scars and unaffected by previous frosty nights.

Sheriff Hunter overheard Max. He had been skirting around the tent, helping drive stakes into the ground, and tying weights to the tent's legs. The wind might blow later in the day.

"What about Carmen?" yelled Ace.

"Oh … I'm expecting her to help today, Dad," said Max. "And André is coming. Maybe Kevin —"

"You never told me what's in those big boxes. What are you putting out today?" Ace pointed at four boxes that, unbeknownst to him, contained the dolls Max and Carmen made days before.

"It's a surprise, Dad. Something I made to sell because I can't work at the farm."

"That's news to me," said Ace. He kneeled next to one of the boxes and coaxed the top panels open.

"It's a surprise. Don't look, dad!"

Ace put his hands up like a criminal caught in the act. He continued kneeling and looked around, ensuring everything was in place. Max's arm was still in a delicate condition. His son couldn't do everything on his own. Ace had to be at the police station early Saturday morning. Doctor Esteban had some new information. She had things to show him downstairs in the morgue that could help him solve the case of the dismembered body and the abused pig.

"It's all yours," said Ace. "You sure you don't need help changing anything? Lifting those bales?"

Max had to muscle the straw bales into place with one hand. They were ninety-pound, wire-bound blocks of compressed straw. Max decided to surround three sides of his tent with the bales and stack several as places people could sit and relax. He had them perfectly angled, so those who used them had a perfect, unobstructed view of what he had to sell in his booth. He knew marketing was vital.

"You taught me to be self-sufficient, Dad." Max continued pulling another bale into place. "If I need more help, I'll ask André when he gets here. You've done enough. I know you have a lot on your mind. Besides, look at my arm." Max flexed his bicep. It stood out round and full. Much bigger than other kids in high school. "I feel pretty strong."

Ace looked surprised and shook his head in disbelief.

"Not bad. I see why Coach was so upset losing you for the season." He checked his watch. "What's the schedule for today?"

"It opens at nine. Animal judging at eleven. Pumpkin weigh-ins at noon. We're packing up at six," said Max.

Ace rose to his feet, feeling his waist to ensure his weapon and other items were in place. He cinched his belt and twisted around to view the different vendors. Several farmers had started arriving.

An enormous pink tent had gone up at the entrance to the fair. Buzzing around the tent, pulling supplies off a large Dodge Ram pickup truck, were Mrs. Waters, her daughter Bethany, her two sons, and a slew of middle and high school girls—friends of Melinda. The group hung balloons from the tent. They placed piles of free logoed water bottles on the table, each one emblazoned with the face of Melinda. The posters and banners all shouted the same phrase: JUSTICE FOR MELINDA.

"Isn't this going to be fun." Ace groaned in an irritated, sarcastic voice. Max heard him and trotted over to his father's side.

"What are they doing?" said Max.

"I think it's a protest, or fundraiser, for the Waters girl." Ace straightened his hat. "I'll go check it out. You ask for some help if you need it, don't ruin that arm again."

Max flashed a thumbs-up and a big, silly, toothy grin.

Ace swaggered away through the early light of the morning.

The sun graced the horizon with an orange glow. Yellow and red-leafed maple trees stirred as a slow breeze wafted up tent panels and table cloths around the fairgrounds. A warm air current circulated through the coolness of the lingering nighttime air like a snake.

Max watched his father approach the Waters' tent. Mrs. Waters broke into a crying fit. The sheriff held her hand. Kids surrounded them and watched with stunned looks on their faces (some sad, a couple angry with arms folded, most with no emotion at all). Sheriff Hunter's lips moved.

Dad's probably reporting on the status of the investigation or saying how sorry he is, thought Max.

Max stopped hauling straw long enough to notice Bethany crying too—not her usual annoying self. Max felt sorry for her. He felt the same way now that Riley was in critical condition. Max believed the evil librarian Camilla had also poisoned Joe. He still didn't have proof, but he planned on getting it.

✂ ✂ ✂

From across the parking lot, past the Waters' tent, Max spied the Volvo Doctor Esteban drove. It pulled up along the curb. Carmen jumped out, slamming the door behind her and waving at her mother, who pulled away. Carmen raced toward Max, waving her cell phone over her head.

"You won't believe this!"

Carmen wore a pair of pre-ripped jeans, a checkered red, black, and gray button-up shirt tied at the waist. Her blond hair had been parted with pigtails jutting over and behind her ears.

"What's up, Ms. Daisy?" said Max, chuckling at Carmen's outfit.

"I thought it was appropriate for today. I wanted to have some fun," said Carmen. She plucked a sprig of wheat out of the dried floral arrangement on Max's table and chewed on it while pushing buttons on her phone.

"You thank you's in the South?" Max drew out a southern accent, but his voice cracked in the middle of it. Puberty had hit, and with it so went the old Max.

"Funny," said Carmen, still trying to catch her breath, "but you're going to freak when you see this."

Carmen opened the file on her phone with her picture archives. She scrolled, scanning a list of photos until she found what she wanted. "Here it is. Oh—this one's blurred. Oh, look at this!" She handed the phone to Max and screamed loud enough to draw the attention of everyone within a hundred feet. "Twins!"

Max looked down at the bright screen on the phone. His eyes lit up as an "Oh, my God," escaped his lips. On the screen, a woman—very tall, with thin limbs, a sharp nose, and very well dressed—sat in the same tattoo chair Carmen's mother had. She had hiked up her long, gray dress to reveal the same tattoo Max's mother had. Like the leg in the morgue— and now the one on Paris's shoulder. Below the symbol, the anklet circled the top of her shoes. She smiled and stared directly at the camera.

"It's the librarian…" Max lost his breath and stood with his mouth hanging open.

"It's not Camilla, Max. That's her sister—her identical sister."

Max couldn't hide the stunned look on his face. He looked out past Carmen, who had her back turned toward the parking lot. Sheriff Hunter had left the Waters family and lumbered to his car. Bethany, still soaked with tears, looked over at Max with the saddest expression he had ever seen.

Max's eyes moved from Bethany to Carmen. "I meant the librarian. She's the murd—" Max couldn't finish his sentence. Carmen knew what he wanted to say and covered her mouth with her hands in shock.

"Do you think so?"

"It all makes sense … somewhat," said Max, his eyes piercing the air as though he were trying to catch thoughts fleeing from his head like bats in the sky. He looked back to Carmen. Bethany continued to stare in his direction. Max moved his head so Bethany couldn't see.

"Something's very wrong, Camilla owns the barn. She smelled my jacket. Now her twin sister's laying in the morgue, and…."

Another thought occurred to Max. Dallas and Maxine are also related to her.

He couldn't tell Carmen, not yet. They needed more answers.

"I don't know if you should hang those dolls up, Max," said Carmen motioning to the boxes. "If Ms. Fox comes to the fair and sees them — "

"We'll have our proof."

"We might be in for some major trouble," said Carmen.

"Who cares. I still need money. We still have more questions than answers." He was determined to make a kid's fortune from all the work he and Carmen did in his shed. They had finished one hundred dolls and would offer them for ten dollars apiece.

"If you think so, I'm game." Carmen rolled up her sleeves, cracked her knuckles, and put her hands on her hips. "So, what can I do?"

"And I thought you were the shy one in class," said Max. "What's your game, girl?"

"People change."

"I guess so," said Max. He thought about the many new and disturbing things he had been learning about the people in Pine Plains.

The more he learned, the more it became apparent the people he knew from his youth had a lot more going on in their lives—their secret lives—than he ever knew.

"Maybe," said Max, "you were just pretending to be shy when all along you were just playing everyone … putting on an act."

Carmen didn't protest. Max might be right. She pretended to brush it off and continued to wait for him to give her directions.

Max looked around at his booth. He needed to hang the dolls from hooks surrounding the tent's edge. They had decorated poster boards with advertising created from felt letters and photos pasted on with glue. He had Christmas lights that he needed to string. Max even brought a large, orange cooler with lemonade, and a thousand cups.

"Let's finish setting all this up. We should be good to go," said Max.

Carmen made a salute and dug into the boxes of dolls.

N N N

When the first light from the sun poured through the trees, illuminating the hundreds of tents and games at the Pine Plains Harvest Fair, Max's tent already had a small crowd around it. Max had not yet put out the signs advertising the dolls, but there they were. Figures hung from strings affixed to the metal poles running the length of the white pop-up tent. Dolls had been piled up in two artistic heaps on the table.

"Crazy bunch of dolls you have," said one man, staring from a distance with his young daughter. "Kinda disturbing, kid."

"You'll see what they are in a moment, mister," said Max, shuffling around the booth, preparing for the onslaught. "I need to get the signs out."

In the center of the table, facing the entrance to the fair, Max had also placed the original doll. It rested in a small fish tank, with a board on top and rock holding it down. The thing leaned against a chunk of quartz, making it look like it stood at attention. Its mismatched button eyes seemed to stare out into the yard, one eye bulging as though it expressed real excitement at the people arriving.

"They're perfect," said Carmen. She stood in front. While the tent illuminated in the orange sunrise, she took a series of pictures.

The fair was about to open. The public filled the parking lot.

Carmen joined Max behind the table. She plopped herself down in a blue, fold-out camping chair, stuffed her open can of Pepsi in the holder, and looked out at the crowd.

"Here they come, boy. I already see Dallas. Looks like Maxine, too. Out there in that red Jeep. See?"

Max saw the red Jeep pull into one of the teachers' reserved parking spots. Maxine exited the rear, while Dallas rounded the front.

The passenger side front door flew open.

"Oh no, it's her," gasped Max.

"Here we go," said Carmen.

"My heart's racing."

"So is mine."

CAMILLA GOES BERSERK

Camilla took no guff from anyone: not her naughty, disrespectful students, the gossipy, whiney teachers, or the clueless, out of touch parents. Even the school's superintendent and principal shrank away in her presence. She always got her way.

As the librarian descended from the red Jeep, she planted her well-manicured feet in sparkling new Prada shoes on the pavement. She emerged from the vehicle, looking like a runway model with a "don't-mess-with-me" attitude.

"Would you get a load of that!"

Carmen noted the difference from far away. Others, much closer to the parking lot, caught themselves stopping to gaze upon the celebrities before them.

Both Camilla and Dallas were stately, very tall, towering over anyone in Pine Plains. They were well poised and seemed to glide more than walk. Each was always adorned in the highest fashion—many times in couture, a sure sign of their city origins.

Camilla wore a classic sleek, beige, Armani dress with shoes and a purse to match. She had worn her hair down.

"Is that her?" said Max. "I thought she was ancient."

"Looks like she dropped twenty years," said Carmen.

"A little less intimidating, too." Max wasn't fooled.

Indeed, any wrinkles on Camilla's face had been smoothed away. Her skin glowed, chasing away her natural milky, pale complexion.

"Dallas still looks like Dallas, I love the suit," said Carmen.

Dallas arrived looking like a very tall woman, but in a stylish, fitted men's suit. Dallas continued to mystify those in the community with a combination of qualities unusual for a small, farming community. Most people had, by this time, stopped questioning so ferociously. Pine Plains was also a booming retreat for the city's wealthy (they owned all the large homes), and a second home to many in New York City's performing arts community.

The social climate of Pine Plains continued to change. Most of the residents didn't like it.

Maxine wasn't alone in her style, either. While she wasn't sleek like Dallas and Camilla, Max noticed she wore an equally upscale version of goth. She was much more on point than those students in the school who acted out or tried to find themselves through lousy fashion and the application of clashing accessories.

While Dallas and Camilla stopped at the hood of the Jeep engaged in some discussion, Maxine made her way, at a brisk pace, toward Max's tent. Her eyes were wide. She was aghast at what dangled from its metal supports.

"What are those? Oh, how creepy—how awesome!" said Maxine. She stopped short of the table's edge and regarded Max's creations with a mix of amazement and envy. "Wish I had thought of something… Too cool, man."

"I helped him out." Carmen swished around behind the table. Her pigtails twirled around on the sides of her head.

Max smiled and shrugged. "I sewed, she stuffed."

"Awesome, guys. I'm so jealous," said Maxine.

"You should hang with us… That's if you want to," said Max. "Plus, you're not going to believe what we found out —"

"Max!" said Carmen. "We can't tell everyone."

"But she helped us with the morgue. We're all friends here, we're kind of in this together." Max argued in favor of divulging the tattoo information.

Carmen had something else on her mind, something Max had neglected to consider.

"Can you stand here behind the booth for a moment, Maxine?" said Carmen. "I have to help Max finish something in the barn, with the pumpkins."

"Sure," said Maxine. "I do need to walk around with Dallas, though. Don't take too long."

"We won't."

Carmen took Max's hand. She pulled him over some stacked straw bales, but Max stumbled, trying to keep up. He didn't have another hand with which to protect himself.

"Would you slow down? What's gotten into you?" said Max.

Carmen stopped him when they reached the shadowed interior of the barn.

"Man, you're dense sometimes," said Carmen.

"What do you mean?"

"The photos, dipstick. It's Camilla's twin," said Carmen. "Are we ready to let THAT cat out of the bag?"

Max thought about Carmen's concerns. She had a point. It dawned on him Camilla was Maxine's aunt. Dallas and Camilla were cousins. Maxine, in Max's estimation, didn't have a clue. He didn't know how much she knew. She was new to Pine Plains. Max still didn't know many things about her.

It happened again. The hairs on the back of Max's neck stood up as fear spread through him. He didn't just put a simple puzzle together. Rather, Max had erected a jail, and he now lived inside it.

He chose to play it safe.

"Yeah, you're right," said Max, his heart thumping. "Let's wait."

Carmen beamed. She felt vindicated. She had successfully persuaded someone she was right, and it empowered her.

N N N

Max and Carmen shuffled their way through dirt, animal droppings, and straw on the way back to Max's booth. When they arrived, Maxine had taken the original doll out of the fish tank and examined it, comparing it to what hung overhead.

"Not bad, mister," she said, "you created perfect replicas." She paused, squeezing the original doll, and one of the newly stitched versions. "They feel different. This one feels crinkly inside and smells funny. The new one, I see, has straw in it."

"I had to take the stitches out of that thing to make the template," said Max, pointing to the new thread he used to sew it back up. He had poked all the loose stuffing back in. He didn't want anyone to see what was hidden inside. Max knew the doll was part of the crime scene.

"That works," said Maxine. She placed the old doll back in the tank and covered it with the board and rock.

"Time to put the advertising out," said Max. He grabbed the two sandwich boards, each indicating the price for each doll, how he made them, and what they represented.

Carmen voiced her concerns out loud, again, while watching Max arrange the boards. "I hope this works, Max. You know that no-one knows about these things, right? Or, what that thing in the fish tank is?"

"They're just dolls," said Maxine, unfazed.

"Uh, no-duh," said Carmen. "And made from the same doll Max stole from the murder scene!" Carmen yelled. She got her point across to Max and Maxine. She also managed to turn heads as far away as the Waters' tent, the parking lot, and everyone around Max's booth.

Eyes shot toward the booth. Bethany, who had been organizing shirts with Melinda's face on them, turned upon hearing Carmen inform the entire populace at the fair. A look of curiosity, mixed with shock, poured from them all as they gazed upon not just cute, burlap dolls, but exact replicas of an item found in the barn where the murder took place.

People were more curious now that they knew MAX was the boy who discovered it all.

"HALLOWEEN'S COMING FOLKS!"

Max had pulled out a megaphone and yelled like a circus announcer. He intended to get as many people to buy his dolls as possible. The potential profit was a thousand dollars, more than enough to make up for the temporary loss of his job on the horse farm.

"GET A CREEPY, EXACT REPLICA OF THE VOODOO DOLLS FOUND AT THE MURDER SCENE OVER IN SILVERNAILS...."

The megaphone did its job. Just as André showed up under the tent, parking himself next to Carmen and Maxine, people approached Max's booth. They read the brief history of the dolls on the sandwich boards.

Hands plucked dolls from the tent's metal beams. André whipped out his iPad, swiping cards and collecting cash.

N N N

A scream, louder than the megaphone, pierced the roaring crowd. From the parking lot's edge, Camilla—towering over even the tallest men—rushed toward Max's booth. It was still early morning. The crowd could have been bigger. She managed to shove many people out of her way with her long, sinewy arms.

"You little brat! What have you done?"

Camilla charged like a rabid bull.

Max put the megaphone down. Maxine crept back into the recesses of the tent to escape her aunt's gaze. Carmen and André stood their ground—they were merely helpers. People threw money at them, demanding a piece of history. Someone had to collect it all.

"Calm down, Cam," shouted Dallas, who paced Camilla about twenty feet behind.

Camilla raged, out of her mind. Having reached the front of the line of eager buyers, she stopped dead in front of the fish tank. Her lips stopped moving. She clamped her mouth shut and stared at the mangled doll sitting inside. On her perfectly polished forehead, a protruding vein pulsated. Her face turned pink. Her eyes grew red. Her shoulders rose and fell as she hyperventilated.

Camilla craned her head toward Max.

My God, she's going to kill me, thought Max.

Max had dropped the bright red megaphone on the lawn but hadn't moved an inch from his original position. While many people skirted around Camilla, oblivious to her rage and just wanting to get their hands on a piece of history, some stepped back. They had never seen the school's librarian act in such an unprofessional manner. Several took out cell phones and recorded the scene with their cameras. Others held their babies close as the tykes cried.

Camilla scared a good number of people. She looked ready to pounce and rip Max's head off.

"It was you," Camilla whispered, creeping toward the boy. "The one who broke into my barn…"

"I didn't mean to, ma'am," said Max. He stuttered. He felt he could pee his pants at any moment.

Dallas appeared and stepped between Max and the librarian. Camilla straightened to meet Dallas's gaze. The librarian's face had lost its elegant look from earlier. The confused expression of a woman frightened for some unknown reason replaced it.

Camilla looked at Max, and back at the many dolls for sale on the table.

"But he … the barn …the —" Camilla stopped short of voicing something more telling.

She took one more look at the kids selling dolls. She saw Carmen Esteban, the mortician's daughter, looking back at her with no expression. André, the French foreign exchange student, rang up sales like an excellent merchant. Behind them were straw bales and the barn with Max's enormous pumpkins ready for the weigh-in, but nothing else.

"Where's Maxine," said Camilla. She held her head. "I think I need to go home."

"Are you going to be all right, Cam?" said Dallas.

"I'll be fine. These kids just shouldn't be doing what they're doing."

"Are you safe to drive?"

"I can take care of myself, you know that," said Camilla. "So, you're not coming?"

"We're here. I want to enjoy the fair."

"Suit yourself."

"So, you're ok, right?"

Camilla placed her cheek close to Dallas's, gave Dallas a light hug, and whispered something Max couldn't make out. He guessed it wasn't in his favor.

Before heading back to the red Jeep, Camilla, towering over Max, gave him a predatory grin. She pointed at the megaphone still laying where it had fallen.

"I'm guessing that thing won't work now. Oh, I hope your father doesn't ground you for all of this. I'm guessing he doesn't know what you've been up to." She flashed a sly, toothless smile, issuing a stern warning before walking back to the Jeep. "Watch what you get yourself into, Maximilian. Some things should be left to us adults. We're stronger than you. Good luck with those pumpkins you worked so hard to grow.

Camilla looked past Max at the barn, at all the pumpkins and giant squashes lining the entrance. She drew a sign in front of her in the air with her index finger.

"Don't taunt the boy, sis," said Dallas, who's eyes rolled in disbelief.

"I'll be back to pick you two up in a few hours," said Camilla.

The librarian charged away and departed in the Jeep.

Max picked up his megaphone and flicked the switch to ON, but it was dead.

A Pumpkin Deflates

Police Officer Bernard Reese pulled up next to the Waters' tent two hours after Camilla left.

The Pine Plains Harvest Fair vibrated from the swell of people as Barnard made his way toward Max's booth. The time for the pumpkin weigh-in had come. Ernest Hollow stationed the crane next to the barn with chains hanging from it. Each pumpkin sat on a wooden platform, ready to be hoisted to the scale.

Max had sold ninety of his dolls. What remained hung from the tent, ready to be claimed.

"Bernard!" Max yelled, seeing the officer heading his way.

"What is this all this about?" said Bernard, seeing the last ten dolls. "What are those things?" Bernard stopped. He had seen them before. His eyes rested on the fish tank, and the tattered thing sitting inside it. "What did you do?" He let out a long wisp of air.

André laughed behind the table, excited at what they had accomplished.

"Max made nine-hundred dollars so far," said André. "Can you believe it?"

"How did you get that?" said Bernard, pointing to the doll.

"From the barn," said Max. "Before the ambulance hauled me away."

Bernard scratched his chin, deep in thought. He regarded the doll and Max. What had possessed the boy to take evidence, he had no clue. How the sheriff's son managed to make and sell them was another matter. He looked at the sandwich boards with Max's advertising and the explanation.

"You told everyone where these came from?"

"I thought they'd find out sooner or later," said Max, backing up his plan. "People think they're cool. Crazy and scary, considering the story behind them."

"Do you know what they were stuffed with, Max?" said Bernard. He took his hat off, placed it on the table, uncovered the fish tank, and pulled the doll out. "Hair, Max. Human hair..."

"Well, I found some in there, I know, but it's just hair —"

"From potential victims, Max!" Bernard glared at Max. "Some crazy person did this. It's witchcraft. Evil, Max."

"Well, the ones I made are stuffed with straw... Harmless."

"Doesn't matter. Your father is going to freak out when he finds out what you did."

"But I needed money. I can't work with this arm —"

Bernard put his hand to Max's face. The officer fumed at what the kid had done. To make things worse, Max had involved several other kids in his plan: the mortician's daughter Carmen; the French exchange student; the new teacher's daughter Maxine who stood behind Max, trying to be obscure in the shadows of the tent.

"Carmen! Oh, my God...."

Bernard's face went pale. The blood drained from his skin as an idea flashed through his mind. Carmen was Doctor Esteban's daughter.

Had the kids standing before him been the ones who broke into the morgue? It made sense. Carmen could get the key. Her mother had been away that night, the night Bernard checked on the kids with Officer Green. It would also explain why the fingerprints they found had no records, there would be no reason for the prints from these middle-schoolers to be in the system.

Carmen looked at Max and André. She pointed at herself when Bernard called out her name in surprise.

"What?" said Carmen. She felt singled out. "Are you ok, Officer?"

Max jumped in with news. "Uh, the weigh-in is happening in a few minutes. We should go back to the barn."

Bernard was shocked. He felt sure his face showed it, but he debated, in his mind, whether to address his theory at the fair. The kids all looked utterly innocent. Max had made money. No one was in harm's way.

After a moment, Bernard got his head straight and put his hat on. Dallas gracefully pranced across the open lawn between the booths and stopped by his side.

"Hello, Officer. I hope you are having a splendid day," said Dallas.

Bernard was unnerved by the teacher's appearance. He didn't know what words to use. He kept his response short.

"Yup, uh … nice day for sure. It looks like the pumpkins are about to be weighed." He looked at Max, his eyes telling the kid he had every reason to feel guilty.

"Splendid," said Dallas, who peered into the tent. "Maxine, what are you doing back there? Come out where it's sunny."

Maxine shuffled between two tables and eased up to Dallas, looking sheepish.

"Are you ok?" said Max. He was concerned with Maxine's change in mood since Camilla had raged in front of his tent. Maxine has been in trouble before with the librarian and had gone into a similar spirit on other occasions. Max had seen it firsthand.

"I'm fine. I'm used to Camilla," said Maxine. "It was supposed to be such a fun day too."

"It still is," said Max.

The loudspeaker on the barn sprang to life. Ernest Hollow's high-pitched girly voice shouted over the roar of the fair. The time came for the Largest Pumpkin weigh-in. He directed anyone involved to gather at the barn, watch the show, and get their pictures taken riding a pumpkin.

Max felt elated. While he had been overly nervous after Camilla's scene, he felt much better. They grossed nine-hundred bucks at the booth and his pumpkins were the largest of any at the fair.

"Let's go," said Max.

Max left the tent. Carmen followed, continuing to look at Bernard with suspicion. Max took Maxine's hand and headed to the barn. Carmen took his other hand, jerking them faster forward.

"Cute," said Bernard, seeing the girls swoon over Max. He looked at the tent. André still operated the booth. "You stayin' there?" said Bernard.

"Yeah, I can see the contest from here... I have ten more dolls," — two more people, having seen the dolls, ran up and took them, throwing twenty dollars on the table—, "I mean, eight dolls to sell." He smiled, stuffing the cash into the blue money bag. The boy beamed and hummed some obscure French song under his breath.

Bernard walked to the barn.

N N N

The tall, white barn housed all the agriculture exhibits. Chickens, goats, cows, sheep, and all manner of farm animal mulled around in the stalls and cages. Judging had finished. Most enclosures had been adorned with white, red, or blue ribbons.

Pumpkins flanked the barn's entrance. The smallest of them was lifted manually, with men placing them on the large, industrial scale. When their sizes rendered them too big, the crane was needed; it lifted each pumpkin, the weight was recorded, and it was returned. Max had the last three—and the most giant—pumpkins in the show, so he had already won. He was particularly excited over his largest specimen.

"I used a new manure mixture this time... It's larger than any of my previous pumpkins," said Max. Pride beamed from his face. "It has to be more than eight-hundred pounds."

"I think you're right," said Carmen, "it's huge. I can't wait to ride it!"

"Me too," said Maxine. "This is my first fair."

"Ever?" said Max.

"Yup. I'm from the city. All we have there is cement."

The crane settled in to weigh the last pumpkin. Max watched and held his breath while Carmen chewed on a fingernail.

Maxine stood with Dallas, both staring with their eyes wide open. Bernard stood like a statue, he tucked his thumbs into his belt.

The chains were attached to the platform. The crane lifted the behemoth pumpkin, swung around, and lowered it onto the scale.

Max cheered. "Nine-hundred, and thirty pounds!"

A cheer quickly took over the crowd as people did high-fives, exchanged money from bets made earlier in the day, and stared at the new record.

The digital display on the scale changed.

"What's that?" said Carmen, noticing the numbers on the scale begin to go down. "Why is it doing that?"

Max stared too. Nine-hundred and thirty—twenty, ten, eight-hundred and eighty, sixty —

"What's going on?" said Max, shocked at the display.

Charlie Wise, Max's coach, operated the crane. He hopped off the machine and ran over to the sale.

"Why I'll be," he exclaimed, dumbfounded. "I've never seen that before... Must be broken."

"Look!" A woman standing a little farther off pointed to the pumpkin. "Is that thing deflating?"

"What?" Max whipped around in time to see the pumpkin begin to pucker and fall in on itself.

"That's impossible," said another man. "They don't just do that."

Another person yelled, "Cheater." Several more followed.

"No, I didn't," said Max. "You can't cheat on something like this ... look at it."

He was right.

Max backed away.

A horrible stench wafted off the pumpkin.

More people backed up from the scale. Others near the barn shuffled away from the other pumpkins that had also begun to shrink.

With the space around the barn cleared, the people of Pine Plains had a perfect view of evil at work. Each pumpkin fell in on itself, shriveled, and turned into a pile of mush. Max's nine-hundred and thirty-pounder split into several gooey pieces and appeared to melt like a candle off the side of the scale.

Max looked at Maxine, pointing to the parking lot where Camilla had returned to the Jeep.

"She did it."

"What?" said Maxine. "Who?"

If Max was pale before, now his face glowed red hot with both anger and fear. Camilla had pointed to the barn before leaving. She had made a sign in the air after mentioning the weigh-in.

Max mumbled under his breath, practically hyperventilating. Bernard heard him.

"It's my fault," said Max. "I shouldn't have made the dolls. She knows. It's her."

Bernard kneeled next to Max, seeing his distress. The boy held his arm, which was still mending.

"What are you talking about?" said Bernard. "Who is 'she'?"

Max looked at Bernard with tears welling up in his eyes. People were looking at him. The entire crowd had gone quiet, but as with all people, they stirred and mumbled among themselves, backing away from the barn and returning to other areas of the fairgrounds. Some left for their cars, but most shook off the tragedy in front of them.

Max also witnessed Dallas, Maxine, and Carmen—each of them overcome with what they had seen. Max leaned in to whisper in Bernard's ear, "The librarian, Camilla. She's the one."

"Maybe we should wrap things up early. You can come with me," said Bernard.

Charlie Wise stood next to the scale scratching his head in disbelief.

"If I didn't know any better," said Charlie, "I'd say it's some kind 'a blight ... or the recent frost maybe softened them up?" He looked closer at what remained of Max's prize beauty. "I'll be, it's already starting to mold...."

Carmen silently returned to the booth and counted the cash sales with André.

Dallas whispered something in Maxine's ear and left for the parking lot. Maxine turned to Max and patted him on the shoulder.

"Excuse me," said Maxine. "I'm sorry. I don't know what to say."

Max looked at her, upset. "If you knew something, you'd tell me, right?"

Maxine paused and said, "Of course." She looked over her shoulder at the mess and turned her gaze to Bernard. "Can I speak to Max for a moment? It's somewhat personal. Girl stuff."

"Are you ok?" said Bernard. Max nodded. Bernard left the two kids to talk.

Maxine waited for the officer to leave and addressed Max. "I need to talk to you." She looked around, making sure no one heard. "How about we go for a walk around the track. I have some ideas."

Max, visibly upset, left with Maxine as a group of men cleaned up what remained of the dissolved pumpkins.

GIRLY FEELINGS

Max shuffled across the dewy grass to the school's outer field with Maxine. They didn't make it far before Carmen caught up.

"Hey, Max," said Carmen, "wait up!"

Maxine craned her head and shot Carmen an annoyed look. She had been clutching Max's hand, but let it go when Carmen burst between the two of them. Max noticed and stumbled to the side from the force of the impact.

"Sorry to interrupt. I wanted to let you know you sold all the dolls. Way cool," said Carmen.

"That's awesome," said Maxine. She cocked her head at Max. "Isn't it, Max?"

"Yeah, I suppose so." Max wasn't in the mood. He knew he should be excited to have made his money, but the betrayal he felt from the librarian seemed much worse.

"What if…" Max couldn't bring himself to say what was on his mind in front of Maxine. Camilla was Maxine's family, and he didn't want to hurt the new girl.

Carmen did it for him.

"Maxine," said Carmen, thinking of just the right words to say, "I know your family consists of Dallas—who's way cool by the way—and Camilla, but, girl, your aunt's a freekin' witch, or something."

Maxine practically choked. "I know she can be rough, but she's not all that bad —"

"No," said Carmen, readdressing her point. "I mean, she's an actual, spell-casting, mean-spirited, murdering witch."

Max groaned. He wanted to tell Maxine what they had found at the tattoo parlor, but he was too shy, or too much of a coward, to hurt her feelings. He let Carmen do the talking as they neared the fence separating the lawn from the track enclosure.

"Now come on, don't be calling my aunt bad names," said Maxine. She stopped in place with her arms folded in front of her, blocking Carmen's path. "I think you should say you're sorry for that."

"But we have proof! We have pictures. We know about her sister. Your other aunt."

"She doesn't have a sister," said Maxine, looking quite confused and on the verge of slugging Carmen.

"It's true," said Max. He still looked down sheepishly. "We tracked down the tattoos on the body's leg. You need to see what we found."

Carmen shrugged and nodded her head, yes.

"You mean to tell me you both think Camilla's a witch?" Maxine's jaw dropped in utter shock. "My aunt? A witch?"

"Or something else…"

"Prove it," said Maxine. She crossed her arms higher, standing in defiance of the information the pig-tailed farm girl presented.

"I have the camera right here." Carmen opened her phone, scrolling to her pictures. She selected the snippets captured from the tattoo parlor.

"See. It's the same tattoo. Oddly, adults seem to be getting the same one. Look at her face. She looks just like the librarian."

Maxine looked over the photos, sliding them across the screen. Her eyes widened the more she studied the evidence in front of her.

Max grumbled, reluctant to offer up more information, but finally got up the nerve.

"Do you remember the day we were in her office? How she smelled my coat?" said Max.

"I do," said Maxine. "It was pretty weird."

"That was the same coat I got the body-fluid stuff on," said Max. "And remember the art supplies on her desk? She had the same doll sitting there, and the supplies…"

Maxine's face grew pale. Typically, very white, she still managed to drain away what little blood flowed under her skin. She dropped Carmen's cell phone on the ground. Carmen dropped to her knees to retrieve it from the wet lawn.

"Watch it!"

"What is it?" said Max, seeing the look of fear on Maxine's face.

"Maybe you're right," said Maxine.

"You mean you believe us now?" said Max.

"Maybe. It's a lot to take in." She paused and grew strangely still. "My aunt has many gifts. Education. Skills you don't know about." Maxine sighed. "But witches are evil."

"Maxine?" Max had another, more critical concern on his mind. "We need your help. I think —" Max stopped himself. He almost said some things that could hurt his friend Maxine. After all, Maxine was Camilla's niece, and Camilla was Dallas's cousin, from what Max understood. He could lose Maxine. She could run back to tell what she had learned from him and Carmen. She could also help them, but he knew that the phrase "blood is thicker than water" meant she could put her own family first.

Max laid it all on the line.

"Maxine, they found Bethany's sister. She's dead. Camilla brought my family a pie the other day, blueberry. Joe was the only one to have a piece, and now he's extremely sick. And Riley..." —Max teared up at the thought his sister, critical in the hospital with both a feeding tube jammed into her and a respirator breathing for her— "might not make it. They can't figure out what's wrong. It was just a scratch."

Carmen whispered. "I can't figure out why someone would want to do this. What's in it for them? Why hurt people? Especially kids."

A moment of silence ensued as Max stood there, upset. He waited for Maxine to respond.

Maxine looked stunned. Blindsided.

"Oh, God." She began walking through the gap in the fence and out onto the track.

"What is it? Do you know something?" said Max. He followed her with Carmen close behind.

"More like remember," said Maxine.

"Remember what?"

Maxine, followed by Max, looked back toward where the fair continued to swell with more people. While the recent unexplained deflation of the pumpkins had become the stuff of long-term gossip, the town's people seemed to have already forgotten. They mulled around laughing, smiling, and eating their cotton candy and funnel cakes as though nothing had happened.

"Your small towns are so strange," said Maxine, looking at everything around her. "People are so quick to get on with things, covering up what they still know and hide inside." She paused, and said,

"I suppose we do it in the city too, but the noise and jarring movement all around make it so much easier. It's not so obvious."

Carmen tapped her foot and fidgeted. "So, what do you remember?"

"Well, I don't like keeping secrets." Maxine took in a deep breath, followed by a knowing sigh. "I do have another aunt. She doesn't live here, she still lives in Europe."

Max stood as still as possible, listening.

Maxine continued. "Her name is Alana. She's stunning. People always gasp when they see her, she could be a model." Maxine paused, deep in thought. "She was supposed to come out for a visit last month."

"So, she never came?" said Carmen.

"No. My aunt never showed up. Even though Dallas and Camilla told me to stop, I've tried calling her many times since. She never picks up."

Max didn't know how to respond to the revelation. He and Carmen might have caught onto something quite sinister. If they had found Maxine's sister, it only meant one thing: she was probably dead, in pieces in the morgue.

Maxine was also at the morgue that night, thought Max. She was a force during their break-in. She had fearlessly led them to the location through the dark, creepy streets, past the unsuspecting police. She had even helped with the body.

Now she'd be stuck with the knowledge one of her aunts may be the murder victim. To make things worse, both Max and Carmen believed her other aunt, Camilla, was at fault.

"Dallas told me something bad was about to happen," said Maxine in a shaky voice. "Maybe this is it."

"I think we need your help again, Maxine," said Max.

"She has yelled at me so many times, telling me how bad it would be if I hung out with you... That you were all bad people."

Maxine threw Carmen and Max for a loop when she told them her next revelation.

"I'm not even Dallas's daughter. I'm adopted."

"You're kidding me!" said Carmen.

Both Carmen and Max looked shocked.

"Wow, that's crazy, man," said Max.

"Well, you don't exactly look like them. You're a lot shorter, and a little dumpy," said Carmen.

Maxine's mouth dropped open. Max noticed she held back what she truly wanted to say. Max would have been less forgiving.

"Thanks for the vote of confidence. I thought us girls were supposed to stick together," said Maxine.

"Listen," said Max, "We can't start fighting against each other. People's lives are at stake."

Carmen huffed and looked at Maxine. "Max is right. I'm sorry, it's just that —"

"You like him, I get it," said Maxine.

"I do not!"

"It's written all over you, Carmen, don't kid yourself. When you like something, you protect it. You're protecting Max."

Carmen gulped. Maxine caught her.

Despite Max's propensity to always find trouble, his mother had also taught him to be sensitive to others. He didn't want to upset Maxine. Or Carmen.

This could get all over school, thought Max. He could be plunged into more drama than he was currently embroiled in. The doctor had also made it painfully clear the need for less drama if Max wanted his arm to heal faster.

Max deflected from Maxine's pronouncement. He gave Carmen a quick smile and changed the subject back to Camilla.

"You know," said Max. "It doesn't seem that even you like Camilla. I mean, she looks younger every time I see her, and today—Wow!"

Carmen bit the carrot Max dangled. "Yeah, Max is right. For someone so vile, how is it that she looks better and better?"

"Well," said Maxine, "she makes a lot of this soap. She uses fat in it. She claims it's like the fountain of youth or something. Dallas likes it —"

"You mean Dallas uses it too?" said Max.

"Well, sure."

"How does she make it?" said Carmen. "I mean, Max has a shed for his crafts. Does Camilla have a special place she makes her soaps? Could we see?"

Max looked particularly interested in Carmen's leading question. They might have found a motive, though Max still couldn't figure out how the pieces fit. He did believe Camilla was the murderer.

Strange, unexplained events were going on in Pine Plains—things that needed explaining.

"I'd seriously need to check it out," said Max. His voice cracked. After Camilla had seen Max's dolls for sale, and how she had freaked out, Max believed she was deeply involved. She probably knew too much.

"You know, Maxine," said Max, "your aunt Camilla made this strange motion in front of my tent while she looked at my pumpkins—some kinda symbol. Really weird."

"She believes all kinds of crazy stuff. That's my crazy aunt."

"Well, after she did it, don't you think it's strange what happened to all the pumpkins and gourds in the barn?"

Carmen had another idea. "Maybe a curse?"

"So, you really do think my aunt's a witch?" said Maxine.

Max and Carmen both shrugged.

"Maybe just a little?" said Max.

Maxine fumed. If smoke could come from her ears, it surely would. The fact her friends would suggest her aunt could do such unspeakable things—such horrible things to the people she knew—was unfathomable.

"It really hurts me that you would believe something like that," said Maxine. "I thought you guys were better than that."

Max stuttered. He had no intention of hurting Maxine, but he knew Camilla was involved. Being the librarian's niece meant Maxine might also be in danger. Max thought of all the times they were due to meet, and how she had shown up crying after meeting with Camilla.

"Well, we're just worried about you," said Max. "I don't know if you live together. Plus, you've been upset after meeting with her."

"Fine..." Maxine cut Max off. "How about you two come over? I can prove to you that Camilla is harmless."

Maxine's response was exactly what Max wanted. The look on Carmen's face indicated she was on board. She would want to come along, though it was always a fifty-fifty chance she could.

"I sincerely hope you're right," said Max.

Max did wish, deep down, Camilla wasn't at fault. The jitters he got deep inside when his heart fluttered were a warning he couldn't ignore. His father often told him to trust his intuition. Max's told him he was right. They were about to enter the beast's lair.

The Old Atkinson Place

Dallas Finn had purchased the three-story, dilapidated Atkinson Victorian a year before moving to Pine Plains. During that year, her cousin Camilla directed the reconstruction efforts on the old house while taking up residence as the school's head librarian. Camilla also claimed the basement of the house for herself. It had a private exterior entrance and was perfect for a small business she had launched in New York City.

Several days after the fair ended, with his sister still fighting for her life in the hospital, Max accepted the opportunity Maxine had handed him. Sheriff Hunter allowed him to go home with her on the bus, making sure Max would be ready at five o'clock sharp when his father came to pick him up.

"How are we supposed to get in there?" said Max. He stood with Maxine outside her home as the school bus departed.

The cracked and faded double wood doors leading to the basement we're chained and double locked.

"I kinda figured she'd do that," said Maxine, scratching her brow. "She'll be in the library until six. She has two kids in detention. She's making them clean blackboards."

"Can we get in from inside the house?" said Max.

"It's locked inside too. The only other way I can think of is an old Dumbwaiter, with a tray and a pulley. It was made for trash and clothes, and taking boxes to the basement."

"You sure that's safe?"

"Do you know any other way?"

Maxine tried offering him options.

Max thought she should have told him the difficulty of getting in before he took another bus driver's route. The bus was dingy. It never got cleaned. Crumbs and candy wrappers were strewn all over the floor. The kids on that bus were out of control and didn't remain in their seats.

"I'll take you inside."

"My dad said this house has a lot of history," said Max. "Remember? We talked about it in the car the other day, after you went to the farm with me."

"I remember. I didn't lie," said Maxine. She smiled. "There is a ghost here. Maybe you'll get lucky and see her."

Maxine led Max around the side of the house.

The lawn remained thick with crunchy brown leaves.

Large thorny rose bushes lined the outside walls. English Ivy, ordinarily green, had begun to rust and hung greedily to the brick foundation. A thigh-high white, picket fence with spiked crowns jutting skyward surrounded the central lawn and the driveway on both sides.

Maxine climbed a steep set of old, red brick stairs onto the palatial wrap-around porch. It had a gray, glossy wood floor and ornate wood carvings—like vines—swirling around large, gaping openings between the railings and the roof. Dried up, potted plants swayed in the breeze as they dangled from hooks.

"This place is crazy-cool, and creepy at the same time," said Max. He took in all the fine details. He remembered when the house resembled a burnt-out shell, all blackened and falling apart. "You did an amazing job."

"Dallas did an amazing job… Even more so, Camilla. She's the handy one around here," said Maxine, "she can fix anything."

"Including her face?" Max grumbled under his breath.

"I know I wasn't supposed to hear that, but I did," said Maxine.

"Sorry."

"Don't be. You're just not informed yet. You'll see."

Maxine produced a large skeleton key, the kind Max only saw at the museum in Hudson. It had a clover-shaped end and consisted of three fat, flat pieces of differing size along its length. She placed it in the door's lock, turned it, and the door clicked.

"Come on."

Maxine opened the door, pushing it open hard. The door was solid oak and creaked as it moved.

Max couldn't believe what he saw. "It's so modern inside. I expected old wingback chairs, oriental rugs, and crazy candle holders, but not this. Cool."

"Yeah," said Maxine, leading Max to the kitchen, "bet you didn't think Camilla had this kind of taste. She does love new things…."

Everything looked fresh and new. Geometrical red sofas were paired with white and black accents. Crisp white and gray walls proudly displayed paintings from modern New York artists. Paper, Asian lanterns, instead of old brass lights or crystal chandeliers, were perfectly placed and created a warm glow. The massive, spiraling staircase had been resurfaced. A red-carpet cascaded down its center. It wound its way down from the upper floor, fanning out into the living room like a monstrous tongue.

Max walked along in awe.

"This is nothing like my house. We live in a dump."

Maxine laughed. "I hardly think so. This is just Camilla and Dallas, exposed. They are true city people."

Maxine opened the kitchen doors.

"I know we don't have much time. Here's the chute." She pointed to a large, brushed copper door and frame. The door hung about four feet off the floor and was about three feet tall and two feet wide.

Maxing opened it up. Inside, a similar copper platform (like a mini elevator) had been meticulously restored.

"So, people used to lower things down with this pulley." Maxine pointed to a rope inset in the wall.

"And it still works?"

"We never use it, but the rope is good," said Maxine, who proceeded to lower the platform, "see…"

Max looked inside the dark hole in the wall.

"Who should go first?" said Max.

Maxine smiled a devious smile that Max feared, meaning he'd be making the first run.

"I'll lower myself down right behind you. Look, it's big enough for each of us…"

"Oh, I don't know," said Max, a bit worried. His mind conjured up images of the rope snapping, sending him crashing down into the dark basement, and breaking more than his right arm. He also formed a picture in his head of a ghost waiting for him in the dark, ready to snatch him up and devour him for dinner.

Maxine never hesitated. She proved herself a fast worker when they traveled between Carmen's house and the morgue. She was intent on getting this job done as fast as possible. Entering the basement before Camilla came home was no exception.

"Make a decision," said Maxine. "And, don't worry about the ghost, it stays upstairs."

"You just had to say it, didn't you?" Max shook his head in despair, but proceeded to work himself up into the mini-elevator. "Do you have a step stool?" He couldn't get in with his broken arm. The cast was too heavy and awkward.

Maxine reached behind the oversized stainless steel fridge, grabbed a step stool, and unfolded it, allowing Max easier access. He almost wished she hadn't found one, but, it was his idea. He had to know if Camilla had any secrets.

Once Max had curled up inside in a fetal pose, Maxine smiled and lowered the platform down into the dank, musty recesses of the basement. It only took a few seconds. In no time, Max stopped moving. He pushed hard where the basement door would be, and it sprung open, slamming against the basement's wall.

"OK!" shouted Max. "I'm out. Get your butt down here."

The platform disappeared, clanking as it ascended back up into the kitchen. In no time, Maxine lowered herself down to join Max.

"I have a flashlight," said Maxine, standing up next to Max outside the elevator, but in total darkness.

N N N

"Have you ever been down here," said Max, his voice quivering. "Man, it's so dark."

Maxine launched herself from the elevator's small door and grunted, sliding up next to Max. He felt her because of the heat coming off her body. The ruffles in her pleated skirt brushed against his leg.

"What am I smelling?" said Max. He made a sniffing noise. "I smell mothballs. Rotting meat. And something else. Cologne."

Maxine agreed. "It smells bad down here. I am wearing my La Vie Est Belle perfume though."

Max felt scared. He smelled something similar before, in the morgue. This time the hair on his neck pointed out like little spikes. A chill ran up the back of his head, setting his scalp on fire.

"I guess you better turn that flashlight on."

Max heard a fumbling sound. A thump issued as Maxine dropped the flashlight on the floor. Her movement indicated she picked it up.

The flashlight clicked and sprang to life. It flickered a faint dull yellow.

"Darn," said Maxine, pissed at herself. "I just put new batteries in, I must've damaged it."

"It's enough," said Max. He pointed toward the far corner, close to the steps leading to the outside door. "Look."

A set of four light switches hung on the wall. Overhead, a series of bare lightbulbs graced the ceiling.

Max practically moaned: "It's like being back in the morgue...."

As the two looked around, they noticed similar equipment like a long industrial sink, a large silver table in the middle of the room, and a large storage freezer had all been built into the basement. What startled Max the most were two other items: a large, thick, butcher block table littered with knives, meat cleavers, and a circular saw, two buckets, and a fresh pile of shop rags. A large, round metallic vat stood four feet high from the floor and had a thick industrial lid clamped down on top.

"Oh my," said Maxine, dismayed by all of Camilla's equipment.

"So," said Max, "what small business does your aunt have?"

"She makes decorative candles, like soy. They melt very slowly. Also, soap."

"So, where are all the candles?"

The basement had little storage. Nothing indicated anyone made candles, no waxy smells or supplies.

Max freaked out by what he saw next, almost screaming when he saw it.

"What the — is that?" He pointed to the ceiling.

Obscured by one of the giant lightbulbs, hanging directly over the large stainless steel vat, was one of the dolls. It had small doll hair on its head and what looked like a tiny red uniform shirt.

"Well, that's new," said Max. "All the other dolls had—l—l, little red hearts on them."

Maxine stuttered just like Max. He looked at her. In many ways, she acted and sounded like him.

"It's probably just one of your dolls. Cam was totally pissed."

"But she never bought one. I have the money to prove it."

"Then what's it doing up there?" said Maxine. She shrugged her shoulders. She didn't know.

Max knew. He was in the worst place he could possibly be.

In front of them, the vat, cool to the touch, waited for inspection. A small red trickle down its side indicated it held a secret.

"I want to open it —"

Maxine pushed Max aside and barged past him. "It's probably just red wax," said Maxine. She climbed up on a two-tiered wooden footstool, lifted the lid from its edge, and pried it upward and off the vat. Maxine shined the dim flashlight into the container.

"Do you want me to turn the lights on?" said Max.

He didn't get an immediate reply from Maxine. She stared into the container, motionless.

"What do you see, Maxine?"

Still no response.

Max grew more scared but muscled up some courage and joined her.

"What's in the —"

Max looked inside. He stood on the vat's edge and stared down into its depths.

Maxine whispered: "You're right ... she's not making candles...."

Maxine couldn't speak. She backed off the shaky footstool, ran to the wall, and leaned against it.

"I think I'm going to be sick."

Max continued to stare. Maybe he was used to it now. It didn't bother him. Perhaps he was in shock. His rigid body wouldn't let him react.

Remains littered the bottom of the vat. Floating in a pool of jelly-like red goop were the missing body parts from Camilla's sister in the morgue. They had also found the final resting place of part of Bethany's sister, and the remainder of the pig.

Maxine cried and threw up.

"What could she possibly be doing down here? How could this happen?"

"You really knew nothing about this?" said Max.

"Nothing. Absolutely nothing."

"It's a good thing we didn't have Carmen with us," said Max.

Maxine turned around. She looked deeply wounded. She wiped her face on the back of her arm, disgusted at the carnage before them.

Max slowly approached her and put his arm around her, giving her a firm hug.

"What do we do now?" said Maxine.

Max had only one answer. He had seen things like this in horror movies on television. In cases like these, they always had to vanquish the evil-doer.

"I think we need to meet up with the others, we're going to need help," said Max. "Something has to be done."

"I know," said Maxine. She paused a moment and asked, "Can you not mention this to your dad or any other adults? For now?"

Max had no problem keeping his discovery to himself. Involving anyone currently on the case could implicate them all. He preferred to take matters into his own hands. With the help of those who helped him break into the morgue, he knew they could hatch a plan, though he had no clue what that would be. But acting too quickly would merely prove his parents right—he couldn't stay out of mischief.

"You bet," said Max. "You can count on me."

Maxine looked around at Camilla's private room. Tears streamed down her pale, almost ghoulish face. Her overly applied mascara and black eyeliner ran in two streaks.

Her crying was replaced quickly by a look of deep anger that Max found hard to ignore.

"I wonder what else she's hiding," said Maxine.

Maxine prepared to rummage through items strewn about the room when Max heard a noise.

"What's that?" said Max. "Is someone outside?"

"Oh, my God, we have to get out of here," said Maxine. "She's not supposed to be home yet."

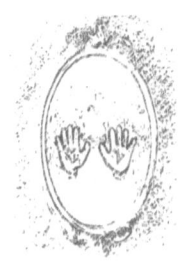

CAMILLA IS EARLY

The Jeep, either driven by Dallas or Camilla, roared to a stop outside the basement's exterior doors. Max couldn't know who had arrived, he had seen both teachers driving the Jeep on other occasions.

The vehicle's engine cut off. The distinct opening and closing of its massive steel door echoed through the basement.

Maxine ushered Max toward the wall and the chute. Max protested.

"My pants are caught on something —"

Maxine yanked Max hard. His pants tore above his Nike's.

"These are my favorite jeans!"

"Sorry," said Maxine, "I think getting out of here is a little more important, don't you think?"

Max grumbled, trying to see the extent of the damage in the dark.

"Hurry up, idiot," said Maxine.

She didn't wait for him to check his pants. She pushed him toward the opening in the wall and helped stuff him in. Within seconds, she had hoisted him to the kitchen, where he quickly got out. A moment later, she did the same.

"Ok," said Maxine, a bit winded. "We better sneak up to my room— pretend we know nothing."

Max watched her peer around the kitchen. Maxine opened the doors to the dining room and peered out. No one had entered the house yet.

"I think I hear the doors to your basement opening," said Max.

He was right. They heard banging outside the window as the locks were unclasped. Chains were removed from the doors.

"Camilla," said Maxine. "Dallas never opens those doors... Doesn't even have a key."

"We better get going now," said Max.

Maxine nodded her head in agreement. She and Max tiptoed across the dining room floor. Several of the old wood floorboards creaked while they approached the stairs, and they quickly scurried up.

As they reached the landing, Max had a horrible thought.

"Oh, we're in big trouble."

"Shush," said Maxine. Max's voice rang out in the hallway, almost a shriek. "What is it?"

"We never put the lid back on the container!"

Max held his cast close to him, protecting it with his other arm. Maxine's eyes bugged out. Her face grew a soft shade of pink.

"Maybe she won't notice," said Maxine. "After all, both the doors are locked. Maybe she'll think she just left it open."

While Maxine stared down the steps, Max's eyes focused on the hallway spanning the second floor of the house.

Though the house had been renovated, Dallas had left old, antique items in place. A muted yellow wallpaper with a brown paisley print clung to the walls. The original frosted glass sconces remained glued eerily near the doors, creating a tunneling effect. A silky, floral carpet runner spanned the hallway from end to end. A French bureau with an ornate gold framed mirror graced the wall.

The prickly hairs on Max's neck stood on end, sharper than they had ever been.

"What is that?"

He pointed to the mirror. He expected to see himself and Maxine, but instead, a woman, dressed in an off-white, late 1800s dress, with her hair pulled back in a ponytail, stared back.

Maxine whispered. "That's her. That's the ghost."

"You gotta be joking me."

"No joke, kiddo. That ghost owned this place…."

"I don't like this, one bit."

A shriek and a yell sounded from the basement. It reverberated through the metal ducts, which acted like horns, amplifying the horrible noise. The space around Max and Maxine was filled with the librarians cursing—the kind no child should hear. As Max stared at the mirror, even the ghost disappeared.

"She sounds pissed," said Max. He ducked into the shadow of the hallway, out of view from the stairwell. "What do we do?"

Maxine was deep in thought, listening to the crashing and banging from the basement.

The noise stopped. A deafening silence filled the house once again, but not for long. The exterior doors of the basement slammed shut.

The front door to the house flew open with a bang. It slammed into a side table, toppling and shattering a large, purple glass vase filled with sunflowers.

Camilla's voice, raspy and profoundly irritated, pierced the interior of the house.

"I know you're here, you little brat," said Camilla, hissing. She screamed, "Maxine!"

Maxine made little noise, hoping Camilla would turn around and cease her tirade. However, the school's librarian was the keen, suspecting sort, and didn't give up so easily. She stood in the doorway to the house, her head jerking left and right.

"I can smell that coat of yours, Max," said Camilla, who sniffed the air like a dog on the scent of some counter-top treat. She chuckled and cleared her throat. "You left a little something downstairs —"

"It was me, Aunt Cam," said Maxine, who made her presence at the top of the stairs known by gliding out onto the first step.

"You get your butt down here, now."

Camilla didn't play when she demanded compliance with her wishes. The severity of Maxine's—and Max' s—situation oozed from every part of the woman. Her eyes glared like a cat's in the headlights of a car. She held a fighting stance, hardly the elegant woman from the fair with the perfect couture outfit and flawless face. She spread her legs and hunkered down like she'd throw anyone who crossed her to the floor. Her face, while still pale, had taken on an aged, weathered degree of severity. She bared her teeth.

Maxine didn't budge. She stood defiant.

"We didn't do anything wrong," said Maxine.

"Liar!" said Camilla. She held out a small, square piece of Max's jeans with blood on them. "What's this?"

Maxine stumbled while trying to speak. Max saw how frightened she was.

She shouldn't be punished because of me, thought Max.

Max did a great job of getting away with his antics in the past. He'd generally let the blame fall on his brother and sister if he could get away with it. He even had his tears under control, making them pour from his eyes at will. This tactic always garnered him sympathy, specifically from his mother and others, though Ace began to catch on and was less sympathetic.

Maxine was about to get herself in even hotter water.

"I did it," said Max. He walked out next to Maxine and stood his ground. "But it's not what it looks like…"

Camilla pursed her lips and put her hand on her hip. "You didn't DO it? Is that what you want to be saying to me, boy?"

"Uh … yes," said Max, formulating his lie and buying time. "Exactly. Uh, Maxine showed me the kitchen. I opened that door in the wall, you know, the one with the pulley? I tried to hide from her, like hide-and-seek, but it fell. She had to come down and help me out."

Fake tears came to Max's eyes.

Max noticed Camilla's shadow, cast by the setting sun, stretched out across the living room floor. Unlike Camilla, who stood still, trying to collect herself—*and undoubtedly planning something horrible for me,* thought Max—the shadow seemed to move, stretching itself closer and closer toward him. The shadow was boney and angular, resembling a dead tree branch.

"I don't believe you, you've been prying," said Camilla.

"I really didn't mean it."

Camilla inched inside the house, a few feet closer to the stairs. She boxed in the two kids. If they came down, she'd have them for sure. Max didn't know of a back way out.

"What else did you see?"

"It was too dark, Auntie," said Maxine. "Not even I could see… I know it's your private space."

"But that lid was lifted!"

"Max fell on it, banged it," said Maxine, "and I guess it fell off."

"Hogwash!" said Camilla. "Prying eyes … prying eyes. Naughty little intruders. Bad children, always getting in the way."

The librarian took a few more steps, landing her on the first step of the staircase. Max couldn't help but see the likeness between her and the ghost in the mirror. The differences were small but significant. Aside from what the spirit wore—a dress from the late eighteen-hundreds—they shared the same long brown hair. Both were tall and had the same beak-like nose, like that of a vulture or a hawk. Sharp and cutting.

"Please, Auntie," said Maxine, "it was an accident. It will never happen again."

"Oh, you're right about that, sweetie," said Camilla, taking another step. "It won't happen again. You're grounded." She stopped mid-step and pointed at Max. "And you Mister sneaky pants... I'm taking you home. We're going to chat along the way."

"Oh!" Max let out a frightened breath. He didn't like the idea of being captive and alone in the Jeep with Camilla. "I can get home —"

"I insist," said Camilla. Her eyes returned to Maxine. "And you, young lady… When you're back at that horse farm on Saturday, you're going to quit. You're no longer allowed to work."

Maxine working for the Rojan Horse Farm, was news to Max. He looked at Maxine, momentarily irritated she never told him she had accepted the part-time position Max himself lost due to his bum arm. Maxine noticed his look and shrugged.

Camilla took a deeper breath.

"This has gone on too long," she said, coming to some dark conclusion that was all too noticeable to Max. "I think the three of us need to go to the basement —"

This is it, thought Max. *I'm going to end up like her sister, or poor Melanie Waters. In that pot!*

"But Dallas deserves to be in on this," said Maxine.

"Dallas is weak. I have to make all the decisions around here," said Camilla. She stared Maxine in the eye. "Do you know what it takes to maintain this body? This face? My standing in the community? Moreover, to have the energy to deal with you and all those little imbeciles in the school. And all those brainless teachers, and the ignorant parents?"

As Camilla advanced on the two kids, taking measured steps toward them, her face seemed to melt. The skin on her forehead began to sink over her eyes. Her cheeks lost their plump, round perfection, adding to the jowls that hung from the line of her jaw. Her eyes lost their brightness as her deep, black irises opened.

"What's going on with you, Auntie?" said Maxine, a look of shock forming on her face.

N N N

Unbeknownst to Camilla and her captives, Sheriff Hunter had driven up the driveway and parked next to the Jeep. He had gotten out to look around the Anderson home, amazed at what Dallas had accomplished since he last saw it. He had made his way to the front porch and saw the front door open.

"Is anyone in there?" said Ace, trudging up the broad steps toward the porch.

Upon hearing his father's voice, Max felt an overwhelming sense of relief. He wanted to call out to his father but stopped when Camilla noticed they were no longer alone. What happened next frightened Max even more. Camilla, hearing Ace approach, transformed back into her well-groomed, professional self, within seconds.

She turned and descended the steps.

"We're in here, Sheriff," said Camilla, calling for Ace to come in.

Ace's hard-soled boots clanked. He walked through the front door to the house. Max saw him look toward the stairs, but his attention was stolen by the shattered vase and flowers sprayed across the living room's floor.

"Is everything ok here?" he said, looking back toward the stairs.

"Wonderful," said Camilla. She became a different person. Not only had her body been restored, but she also sounded like a flirtatious school girl when she spoke.

Ace smiled back, totally unaware of what had transpired minutes before.

"You're looking beautiful today, Ms. Camilla," said Ace.

"Why, thank you, Sheriff." Camilla tossed her hair, as all women did in the presence of the town's sheriff. "We had a little accident. Max didn't mean it." She looked over her shoulder at Max who looked back speechless. "And he's sorry, aren't you, Max?"

"Uh ... huh," was all Max could muster. He stood there in disbelief.

"Was it expensive?" said Ace.

Camilla lied. "It's an antique, costly, but boys will be boys, right Sheriff?"

Max watched as Maxine almost spoke up, but stopped.

We're in the beast's lair, thought Max. *Everyone's in danger.*

Ace was furious. He wasted no time showing it.

"I'll make sure he gets the proper punishment, Ma'am," said Ace. He shook his head in disbelief at Max, who sank where he stood.

"Max," said Ace, "you're going to pay for that vase, starting with that money you made from those things you sold at the fair."

"But Dad, I didn't —"

"Not another word," said Ace. Camilla looked delighted. "You caused a lot of trouble by alerting the town to something they had no business knowing. You stole evidence —"

"But people have a right to know, Dad. And those dolls are harmless."

"And now I want to know if it was you that sabotaged the pumpkins. Did you do something to spoil them?"

"Dad, I won… Why would I do something like that?"

"Why do you ever do anything you do?" said Ace.

Silence overfell the living room. Ace fumed with anger. Camilla almost clapped her hands, excited by the punishment the boy would suffer. Maxine stood on her step—Max knew—trying to figure out what she could do since she had to live with the evil librarian.

"And I have another idea," said Ace, adding to the librarian's delight. "Next Saturday, instead of coming to the picnic and prayer-in for Riley— with all that cake and ice cream—you'll help Cindy on the farm all day, tarring fences. Without pay."

Max tried to speak but was cut off.

"All you need is your good arm," said Ace, knowing what Max was about to use as a way out.

"When will he be there?" said Camilla.

"Cindy and the other workers are going to be away. They're driving a horse to the Henning farm. Max will be on his own all day.

"What about the barn? The murder scene?" said Maxine. "I thought it wasn't safe."

"Officer Bernard is working with a forensics team from the FBI at the old barn. Someone will be close enough to deter anyone from coming around," said Ace.

"I like it," said Camilla. "Maybe send him out to the back forty, so he can't get into any mischief."

"Perfect," said Ace.

Max knew he was in trouble. He couldn't tell his father about Camilla now, not with his reputation in the toilet. After so many mistakes, his father would never believe him. He also knew Maxine would be working that Saturday, though Camilla demanded she quit.

"We need to settle this," said Max under his breath, but loud enough for Maxine to hear. Maxine reached behind her and grabbed Max's hand, signaling she agreed.

"It's also my last day working there, Sheriff," said Maxine, yelling down the stairs. "I'll be in the barns. We won't see each other."

"I'll be out of town," said Camilla. "Dallas can pick them up if you want." A slight smirk spread across her devilish face.

Ace tipped his hat. "Are you ready to go, Max?"

"Like I have a choice?" Max descended the stairs and yelled, "Dad?"

"What?"

"How's Riley?"

"She's in bad shape… Let's not talk about it right now. Get down here."

Camilla paralleled Max after he reached the bottom, leading him out the door. She held tight to his shoulder with a cold hand. She glanced back at Maxine, and said, "Go to your room, young lady, you have homework for tomorrow, I believe. Make sure to lock the door from the outside before you close it."

THE MORGUE BREAK-IN TEAM RECONVENES

Max officially decided the librarian was out to get him. She was something other than human. Just what, though, he couldn't figure

Maxine had also disappeared. She had called in sick for the rest of the week but managed to get a note off to Max. She would still be mucking stalls on Saturday by herself, in the lower barn, and suggested Max try tarring fences along the creek near the barns. She insisted.

Carmen wasn't pleased either. During third-period Biology class, while Dallas droned on about brain synapsis and the wonders of the spinal cord, Carmen pouted in the far corner. She sat in her old seat next to the window, whittling down a new number two pencil with her beaver-like teeth. All the while, she kept tabs on Max, who sat in the front row, his eyes fixed on the teacher's lesson.

He didn't seem to care.

Max was taken by surprise when Dallas called him by name. "Max Hunter. Can you please recite, based on what I just taught you, the regions of the human brain?"

Max had been watching the teacher speak, but never heard a thing Dallas said. His mind wandered between their basement, the apparition in the mirror, and Camilla's transformation while cornering him in their creepy old Victorian trap.

"Uh," said Max, at a loss for words. "Uh, I think—the occipital lobe?"

"Yes," said Dallas. "And?"

"Uh, and, the temporal lobe. The frontal lobe. The cerebral cortex…"

"Go on, you're doing fine," said Dallas, surprised by Max's ability to recite the parts of the brain not yet taught in the day's lesson.

Several students laughed closer to the back of the room. André, sounding bratty in his native French, barked out, "Cerveau antérieur, et—," but stopped.

"We just need the three regions of the brain, Max," said Dallas, who also responded to André, "Tu veux rentrer tôt à la Maison? En France?"

André grunted like he had been slapped. Never had Max heard Dallas speak in another language like a native. André was even more surprised, responding to the teacher, "No, ma'am, I don't want to go home early… Sorry."

Dallas winked at Max.

"Uh, yes. Well, the frontal, mid, and hindbrain?" said Max.

"Perfect. Smart kid," said Dallas. The teacher seemed to squint at Max. "That's quite the arm you have there. Show me your bicep."

Max flinched at the request. He had worn a short sleeve shirt for the day. His unbroken arm was clearly visible. Despite his injury, he hadn't lost any of his strength, or the work he had accomplished in the school's gym in preparation for football season.

Max drew his arm into a flexed pose. His bicep popped. Several veins bulged out.

"I see why Coach Charlie was so eager to have you on the team," said Dallas. "I think you'll heal just fine."

Dallas addressed the rest of the class. "The brain controls all functions in the body, class. Feed your brains by eating your veggies! And someday you can have an arm like Max's!"

A few groans emanated from the students. Some rolled their eyes.

Max put his arm down and shrank lower in his chair, embarrassed.

Dallas looked at the clock on the wall and turned back to the class.

"Ok, my eager little students. Time for you to break into your groups again, same as before. You'll be discussing the regions of the brain and their functions."

Max headed back to the large, round table near the window. André, Kevin, and Carmen each shuffled from their stations and plopped themselves down at the chairs circling the table. Dallas turned some classical violin music on, something Dallas had learned from a specialized school abroad where students learned better in the presence of music.

Max noted the tension at the table. He had been the talk of the school since the deflating pumpkin incident, and the creepy dolls he had sold.

The kids were frightened of the deaths. Everyone was annoyed by the tightened restrictions from Sheriff Hunter.

"Man, how could your dad do that to us?" said Kevin, whispering. "My mom drives me everywhere. I don't get a break."

"Me, either," said André. "At least Kevin is hideous, no one would kidnap and kill him, but me —"

"Take that back," said Kevin, reaching over the table to slap the exchange student.

"I only meant that we French are more desirable," said André.

"You mean snobby, stuck up, and —"

"Stop it," said Carmen, who wasn't in the mood for pubescent male bickering. She shot Max a nasty look. "I think YOU should explain what happened yesterday—why you went to Maxine's without me."

"Well," said Max, "do you want the long or short version?"

"Don't be a jerk," said Carmen. "Just explain yourself."

Max felt a little hurt by Carmen's angry mood and her attack on him.

"Your mom kept you home, didn't she?"

"That's not the point...."

"Sure, it is. Life does go on with or without you, Carmen."

"But we're a team."

"And that's why we need to talk shop, now, instead of this stupid project." Max pointed at each of his friends. "I need your help."

"When do I get my cut of the profits from the fair?" said André. Carmen shrugged, backing up André since she, herself, had also helped.

"Dad confiscated the money."

"What? How?" said André. "It's not his."

"I know," said Max. "Our horrible librarian lied and blamed me for breaking an expensive vase in Maxine's house, right in front of my dad. He believed her. He's making me pay for it." Max gritted his teeth. "She broke it herself while beating the door down yesterday before she cornered Maxine and me... Before Dad came. After I saw the ghost."

Confusion spilled from the faces of Carmen, André, and Kevin.

"What are you talking about? Ghosts? The librarian's not that mean," said André.

Max looked Carmen in the eye. "It's her," said Max. "Camilla. She's the one. She's not what she looks like."

"What do you mean?" said Carmen.

"That body? It's her sister, right? Don't you get it?"

"What?" said Kevin, shocked at Max's statement. "How do you know."

Max gulped, shocked at even what he said. He whispered under his breath, so none of the other students could hear.

"Maxine and I broke into Camilla's secret room in their house… Body parts were in a big container, or cauldron, or whatever it was. She makes something with them."

"That's nuts," said Kevin.

"Yeah," said Max, "but she caught us. Luckily my dad came at just the right time, but he's clueless. She knows I'd never tell him because he would never believe me after all of the trouble I've been in."

"I don't get it," said André. "Why would the librarian kill people? It doesn't make any sense."

"Because she's not a real librarian," said Max. "She's something different. Something evil, I can't explain."

Carmen cleared her throat. She listened to Max's explanation. Knowing more than the other boys, she voiced her theory.

"Max is right, you know," said Carmen. "She may not be human, or at least not completely. Somehow, she stays young from something she gets from those she kills, including that poor pig."

"You mean, like a vampire?" said Kevin.

"No, nothing stupid like that, silly," said Carmen. "Certain parts, like heads, organs… Didn't you notice only certain parts of the dead were missing? She uses them, but I don't know how."

"And what about those badly made dolls?" said André.

"They were perfect replicas, thank you," said Max.

"That's not what I meant," said André. "I mean, the one in the fish tank. The one you took. It was all raggedy. Even you said the police found others. Some with hair."

"That's right," said Carmen. "It's one of the reasons you got in trouble. Officer Bernard said they're stuffed with things like human hair —"

"Which made them evidence," said Max, coming to some dark realization the dolls themselves had special significance to the killer. "But..." Max paused, unsure. "There were four more dolls strung up in the barn after I hid the first one... The day I found it all. Two had hair on top of them, like girls."

"Oh, do you think they represent people who haven't been killed yet?" said Carmen. "Mom's going to be pissed."

"Pissed?" said Kevin.

"Yup. Mom hates working on murder victims."

Max cupped his chin in his free hand and leaned into the table, balancing on his cast. He was glad to have the collective help of his friends to sort out the pieces. He had been so busy reacting to what was around him. He had little time to formulate a proper, teenage-boy-style theory on what was going on in their town.

"So," said Max, creating his list, "the first victim was a woman. Carmen and I believe it was Camilla's sister. If the four dolls hanging overhead represent people on her list, it means the one I took was for the body in the morgue, the sister."

"Sounds good to me," said André, nodding his agreement.

"Go on," said Kevin. "Brainstorming like Ms. Ballinger taught us in English class is useful after all."

Max continued.

"If Carmen is right, they're killed because she needs them for something," said Max. He reached the moment where what he found in the basement made more sense, including Camilla's changing appearance. His face went pale.

"What?" said Carmen, noticing the blood drain from his face.

"Woah, dude. You need some water?" said André.

"No ... no, I'm fine," said Max. "It makes sense now."

The three looking at him sat on the edge of their seats, waiting for Max to come up with some crazy revelation.

"This is what I think," said Max. "Camilla's been getting younger. She suddenly got very old in front of Maxine and me, like some creature. When Dad came in, she returned to her younger self in seconds."

"You serious?" said Carmen. "Wish I had been there to see it."

Max continued. "She was making something with the body parts in that big container. Maybe Carmen is on to something. What if she needs them to stay young?"

Max got blank, anxious stares in return.

"Plus, she owns that old barn and several acres by the farm. It was the perfect place to store what she had just killed."

"And?"

Max continued. "She's something. Maybe a witch. Maybe even an alien."

Kevin chuckled. "That's funny, man. Now you're going over the edge."

"Can you explain it?" said Max irritated. "Maybe you'd like to take my place, Kevin. I found it all, and she's coming after me. Also, Riley's body isn't responding to the doctor's treatments. I need to do something before more people die, including Riley."

"How does this affect Riley?" said Carmen, concerned for Max.

"She got scraped by one of the nails in the barn. The infection's not that bad, but the doctors can't figure it out."

"Maybe," said Carmen, "if it's magic, it can be undone, if we," —she gulped at what she suggested— "if we kill the one who did it."

"You're suggesting we kill the librarian?" said André, growing excited. "I never knew a trip to America would be this cool. I know it's all made up…."

"You're stupid," said Kevin, shaking his head at André's suggestion.

"Well, you have that mess on your face, so what's the problem?" said André, pointing at the patches of red freckles scattered across Kevin's cheeks.

"Cut it out," said Carmen, acting as the mediator between the much less mature boys.

"I have a feeling she's going to come after me on Saturday," said Max. "When I'm working on the farm, out in the paddocks, painting fences."

"Why are you doing that," said Carmen.

"Dad's making me help pay back that vase. Cindy and the guys aren't going to be there, but Maxine got a job and will be in the barns mucking stalls."

"She shovels horse poop?" said Carmen.

"They offered her a job. I guess she jumped on it."

"That's gross."

"Well, I do it all the time. I mean, I did. Besides, who can blame Maxine, we all need money."

"Who cares," said Kevin. "Don't we have bigger fish to fry? Like, isn't there like a monster in the school or something?"

Max looked up sheepishly at his friends. Any of them could be next, three dolls were left. Bethany's sister was the fourth doll.

Max didn't bother to mention the ghost in the mirror and its striking resemblance to Camilla.

Max glanced at Carmen, who had joined him on the trip to the tattoo parlor. It was where they saw the same tattoo drilled into her mother's shoulder. The same one on the leg in the morgue. He didn't know what to think, he'd have to wait to figure it out.

"What do you think, Carmen?" said Max. "Is that all we need to talk about today?"

"Well, I don't know…"

"Well, there's nothing else we need to discuss. Right?" Max winked at her.

"I suppose."

"Then, we need a plan."

André's excitement flared up again. The prospect of another adventure, while an exchange student in America, pleased him. Nothing like this ever happened in his hometown on the Sein River.

"I'm game," said André. He looked at Kevin. "That's the right expression to use, right?"

"Yeah, you got it right, buddy."

N N N

Dallas, checking the clock overhead and comparing it to a wristwatch, called time for the students to stop. The teacher proceeded to rifle through a stack of papers on the desk.

The kids bustled about the classroom, shoving each other as they trudged toward their work desks.

Kevin pointed at the teacher and whispered, "So, what do you think? Isn't Dallas related to the librarian?"

Max shrugged. "I don't know what to think. Dallas is too cool. I don't get an evil vibe."

"Neither do I," said Carmen.

"But," said Kevin, "how do you know?"

"Hey!" André yelled and quickly covered his mouth with his hands.

"What is it?" said Carmen, more irritated than before.

"Well… Doesn't that mean Maxine could be part of it, too?" said André.

Max had never thought Maxine could be on Camilla's side. Maxine seemed more like an innocent victim. She had acted just as dumbfounded as Max.

Camilla had even told Maxine to lock herself in her room when the librarian escorted Max down the stairs. Now Maxine wasn't in school, which worried him.

"I suppose we need to consider all possibilities," said Max. "I think she's a victim in all this, but we need to focus on the librarian. We have to stop her."

"When?" said Carmen. "How?"

"I think she'll strike this Saturday when I'm alone tarring fences. When Maxine is alone in the barn."

"It seems you won't be alone after all," said Carmen, eyeing up André and Kevin. "What do you two say?"

"I'm here for the complete American experience," said André, cinching his tie and acting official.

Kevin was less enthused but agreed. "If it means saving a life, I suppose I'm in."

"What exactly are we going to do?" said André. He still acted confused.

It was a good question. The kids still didn't know what they were dealing with.

Max watched as each of their faces contorted while thinking their private thoughts about witches, ghosts, and fighting villains. Suddenly, someone tapped him on the shoulder. Carmen looked past him, shocked to see Bethany had approached their table.

Without hesitation, Bethany, with a deep sadness in her eyes, yet angry, spoke up.

"I know you don't like me, Max, none of you do, but … I want in too. I know what you're up against."

No one at the table spoke. The kids were shocked Bethany had returned to school at all since her sister's death, let alone made a gesture to help them.

Max felt unusually happy to see Bethany. She had not yet been a part of their group, so how she knew anything was something he wanted to know right away.

"You're welcome to join our table tomorrow. Right, guys?" He had to get approval from the others. Their blank stares indicated they didn't know how to respond. Even Carmen's face didn't change from the possessive expression she wore when Max was near, so he took her response to be a "yes."

"Ok," said Max. "Sit at our table tomorrow. We'll fill you in."

Dallas watched from the front desk as Max shook hands with his classmates. They silently agreed to discuss a plan the following day, at the same table.

Max also noticed Emily Puckett, the poor farm girl from the outskirts of town whom Dallas had taken a liking too. She helped Dallas sort papers.

Emily filled a file box full. After Dallas whispered in her ear, Emily put her tattered yellow, button-up sweater on, grabbed the box, and headed to the door. She stopped, but only for a moment. Dallas thrust some car keys at her, which Emily snatched with a free pinky.

Max guessed she'd take the box out to the car for the teacher.

In the back of Max's mind, he wondered how long poor little Emily had left before she ended up in Camilla's big pot.

Was Dallas involved?

A Beast in the Shed

Max didn't eat much at dinner. Everything tasted bland. The four-cheese macaroni and cheese his mom made loaded with bacon and breadcrumbs, had none of its usual pizazz. The large pizza, covered in fresh goat cheese, garden tomatoes, and homemade red sauce, all from his garden, was barely touched.

Just the three of them ate. Riley was in an induced coma. The doctors offered no good news, just the grim reality things could take a turn for the worst in the coming weeks. Joe felt better but continued to recover at home in his bedroom, where he remained for the night's dinner.

Max's mom and dad sat at the table, both in silent reflection. Max could only wonder how major their worries were.

Needing a breather from the depressed mood, Max excused himself halfway through the meal. He decided to go to the shed to tinker with art supplies and gourds that were drying.

He shuffled to the front door. His father stopped him. "Make sure you turn the floodlights on in the backyard and the one outside the barn. I don't trust anyone, even on our property."

"Yes, Dad," said Max, turning to open the door.

"Wait," said his father. Trailing behind Max where the four pugs: Rufus, Jack, Trapper, and Buddy. "Take them out with you. They need to go piddles."

Max knew he had neglected his pack. So much had happened over the previous month, he barely saw the four pugs, now three years old and energetic as ever. They sniffed around his feet, waiting eagerly to do their business. Their tails twirled and curled. They panted like it was one-hundred degrees outside, but it was only forty.

"You guys ready?" said Max, stirring them up.

The pugs buzzed around like bees and bobbed their heads left and right.

Max opened the door saying, "Ready," and the grumble shot through the door, out into the darkness. Max quickly turned the floodlights on to ensure he could see the directions they went in.

The first large barn and the shed loomed a few hundred yards ahead. At night, they looked like tall red skyscrapers with white window frames, monumental against the pitch black.

Max flicked the second switch. The floodlights on the barn, combined with those from the house, lit up the yard like it was mid-day. A winding path of flagstones connected the rear door of the house to the barns. Near-naked white birch trees guided the way, their sharp fingers jutting into the sky. Dozens of small metal and stained glass wind chimes hung from their branches, clanking, tittering, and whistling in the light breeze.

Max ambled down the path. He noticed little Trapper stood by himself at the corner of the shed, staring into the dark behind it where the garden spread out. His tail was stiff. His scruff stood up. The pug held one paw up while staring at something with intense interest.

"Come in, boy," said Max, calling out to Trapper. He watched the other three attempt to pee on a dead, thorn-covered rose bush.

"Don't make me come and get you."

Max, being cautious, left the path and jogged over to where Trapper peeked behind the shed.

Something dull flashed by farther out in the field, possibly a deer. The ground remained littered with the scraps of unformed squash, tomatoes, and other vegetables the deer regularly grazed on before the first snow liquefied them. For a moment, the shadow seemed tall, not long. More like a person than an animal.

Trapper growled.

A raccoon suddenly scurried out from the shed's edge, almost bumping noses with Trapper, who turned tail and ran back toward the house.

"Jeez!" Max screeched, startled from the equally freaked out raccoon that hissed at him before plunging back out into the darkness.

"Thank God there's no other way for you to get into the shed, buddy," said Max, "except the front door. And that's locked up good and tight."

The striped bandit scurried off. It glared back at Max with glowing eyes.

"You're lucky you can see in the dark, buddy."

The raccoon was not the only one watching. If questioned, Max would undoubtedly say the shadow, crossing the yard farther out, looked at him as well with a set of golden-yellow eyes that outshined the raccoon. The shadow fled, in any case. It disappeared as quickly as it appeared.

"Those darn hairs again," said Max, rubbing the back of his neck as a shiver ran through him, causing him to shake. He suddenly felt less safe. Trapper was no fool. He had joined his three brothers. They already scratched feverishly at the door, eager to return to safety.

Something overtook Max. He yelled out into the shadows, "If you ever touch any of my pugs…" His moment of bravery didn't last long. He turned and ran to the shed door, unlocked it, quickly slamming the door behind himself.

Once securely locked inside, Max decided to put away his doll making supplies. He had one specimen left, a new burlap doll he had made for himself. His father had confiscated the original from the fish tank after the debacle at the fair. It sat with the others in the police office, secured as criminal evidence. Whose hair was inside it, Max didn't know. No one had told him.

"This place is too quiet," said Max, mumbling a nursery rhyme under his breath.

He heard a slight shuffling sound in the corner and whipped around to spy whatever moved. There were no mice or rats. The raccoon had not made it inside.

"Burlap rolls go in the burlap bags…"

While deciding what items went where his gaze fixed on the workbench. His back faced the door.

Max crumpled the paper templates into balls, throwing them over his shoulder. They bounced off the wooden wall behind him. He hummed the same rhyme under his breath, all the while shuffling knives and scissors across the shelf surface. The breeze outside amplified. Bare tree branches scraped the side of the shed

For what seemed like no reason at all, his scalp felt energized. The hair on his head and the back of his neck stood on end. A chill ran through him. He quivered momentarily.

"Like the devil just walked by me," whispered Max under his breath. His parents taught him that a certain cold shiver, like the one racing through him, meant something evil passed nearby.

For the first time in his life, he felt his parents were right. Max froze in place, sensing something wasn't right. He wished the pugs had come in with him, instead of running to the house.

Maybe it wasn't such a good thing he was there alone.

His hands went numb while he clasped a long set of shiny silver shears.

Behind him, a thunderous knocking shook the door.

Max didn't turn around.

A few seconds later, knocking shook the shed again, this time louder and more erratic.

"...Who, who's there?" said Max. He tried to yell, but the words came out of him in a gurgling sound.

About 30 seconds later—bang, bang, bang—what sounded like multiple fists hitting the door sent shockwaves through his body.

Max held the shears up. The blade's surfaces shined with the brilliance of mirrors. As he twisted them to see what was behind him, he spied one of the dolls hanging from a noose about eight feet up. What separated this one from others was that it had not been there before. One of its arms had a miniature cast fashioned to it.

The door's locked! Max screamed in his head. His eyes quivered. His lungs clenched as the air rushed out of them.

Knock, knock, knock.

Whoever was at the door tapped lighter until it faded out, leaving Max in total silence aside from the wind.

Max lowered the shears and slowly turned around. His eyes fixed on the doll.

"How did you get up there?" Max grabbed hold of a ladder leaning against the wall, unfolded it, and dragged it under the doll to retrieve it.

When he climbed to the top, something moved behind him. A shuffling sound was followed by a thud and the metallic clatter from tools that spilled onto the floor.

Max wasn't alone. He had put himself in a vulnerable position, perched atop the ladder, with a broken arm. The shed door was locked from the inside.

"Well, well, well… I finally have you all to myself."

Camilla stood behind him. Her breathing was labored from some exertion Max could only guess at.

How did she get in here, Max asked himself? Who was at the door?

He didn't want to turn around. He closed his eyes, pursed his lips, and held his breath, as if doing so would make it all go away, like in his youth. Max would have nightmares where he woke up with his sheets soaking wet wondering if there, indeed, were monsters under his bed. He didn't want to see Camilla. He had a sense that she would look horrible.

"You've caused a lot of trouble, young man," said Camilla, in a forceful yet private tone. "So much so, I fear, I may need to take you next instead of that sweet, little Emily…"

Max felt her presence. The air in front of him seemed fresh and light. Behind him, her presence was heavy and suffocating. He thought he could be dragged down, deep into the earth below the shed where he'd remain, hidden. Alone in the dark. If she were a demon from hell or some loathsome ground dweller, it surely meant his end.

"W … why are you doing this?" said Max, unable to keep from stuttering his words.

"Doing what?" said Camilla. "What is it, exactly, you think I am doing?" She hissed, drawing out her words.

"Killing people."

"Is that what I am doing—killing people? Your parents do a good job of keeping their secrets, don't they? As do all the people in this tiny little town…"

"It was quiet until all this happened —"

Max heard a metallic sound, like knives being sharpened. Camilla fiddled with something behind him, but he still couldn't open his eyes. He had become part of the ladder, unable to move, fixed in place.

"What are you going to do to me?" said Max. He felt one eye well up. Don't cry, you, idiot.

"You're young and full of life," said Camilla. "Your youth is my youth. I take what I need and discard the rest. In fact," —she continued, always the teacher, always a professional— "those I take, through me, live forever, when you think about it."

Max forced his eyes closed even harder while grasping what the evil librarian said.

"You'll be found out. You can't keep doing this forever. I'm not the only one that knows —"

"And that's a shame, really," said Camilla. "Every one of you brats is on the list. Every adult—your parents, your teachers, your friends—will suffer the same fate. Trust me, it's for the best. Your quiet little town is perfect for us. Close to the city, but far enough out in the woods to be almost unnoticeable. You're going to have many new teachers in your school next year, not that you'll be meeting any of them."

Max felt Camilla step on the first rung of the ladder.

"What about your sister? Dallas, and Maxine?" Max hoped to keep Camilla talking. If she were talking, she wasn't killing him.

"My sister? Hah! She was of no use, but, it seems, she was good for something. She had to go." Camilla's breathing increased in volume. She stood within inches of Max. He felt her. "And Dallas has no clue. Has the money and the connections, but that's it."

"Is Dallas like you?" said Max.

"Oh, yes, though, I have to admit, it is hard to tell, isn't it?" Camilla sighed. "As a shifter, Dallas is currently trapped somewhere in between. I know people have been wondering. You kids have been poking your noses around."

"And Maxine, ma'am? Is she normal —"

"As normal as a person can be after they've crossed over, unfortunately," said Camilla, clanking the metal instruments in her hands together.

Max was glad Maxine wasn't a monster. He still didn't know what Camilla meant by "crossed over." Max assumed Camilla was a monster, and the more she talked, the more reality set in that he was in significant trouble.

"Let's get this over with," said Camilla, "I don't have all night, though, I don't sleep, so it doesn't matter. I imagine your parents will come looking soon —"

Max leaned on his cast, sandwiching it between a rung of the ladder and his body. He held himself in place. With a slow movement, he put his unbroken hand on the shears in his pocket.

"What are you going to do to me?"

"Oh, slice you, cut you up fast and tidy, you know how it is," said Camilla. She was all too happy to freak the kid out even more before ending him. "Then, I make my special creams."

Max held tight to the shears, ready to defend himself the best he could. Camilla was right on him, but she stopped just short of towering over him on the ladder.

"How about you turn around, my little one," said Camilla, "I want to see your eyes…"

The hairs, yet again, became stiff on Max's neck.

This is it, he thought, just do it, Max.

Max eased one foot around the other. With his eyes still shut he turned around. He felt Camilla's breath in his face, she was incredibly close. She smelled like the body in the morgue. Max curled his lip in disgust and parted his eyes enough to catch a glimpse of what grappled the ladder in front of him.

Camilla appeared even more hideous than he ever imagined.

Staring back at him, inches away, was something barely human. The creature looked nothing like the school's beauty-queen of a librarian.

Covered in fine blond hair—like the pugs, but nowhere near as cute—with a pig's snout, long, razor-sharp teeth and glaring red eyes, was a beast fit for the worst of nightmares. It held several sharp knives in its hand, all pointed directly at Max's chest.

The beast smelled. Not just its breath, but the entire creature reeked of old decay, something Max imagined people buried six feet under in Evergreen Cemetery smelled like as they laid there rotting.

Max almost let out a swear word that would land him in deep water with his parents and their church's pastor, Father Franks. He'd be a step closer to an eternity spent burning in the pit of the underworld.

"Scream!" said the creature with Camilla's voice. It hissed and spit as it prepared to strike Max.

Max screamed, just as commanded. He threw the arm with the cast on it backward, shaking the ladder. In one swift motion, shutting his eyes in fear, he drew his hand back and plunged the shears into the neck of the thing in front of him.

The ladder collapsed backward. It hit the shed door, slamming into it and forcing it open. The ladder, together with Max and the nasty version of Camilla, crashed to the ground outside.

The sound must have stirred anyone within a thousand hundred feet. A rush of barking emanated from the house. The back door flew open. Ace and Beth, along with the four pugs, ran out, down the flagstone path toward the shed.

"Oh, my God! Oh, dear," screamed Beth, outpaced by Ace, who reached Max within seconds.

"Get her off me!" Max screamed and flailed, rolling off the ladder and onto the grass.

"Are you ok, honey?"

Max thought Camilla was still on him. He continued fighting his father until he calmed down enough to open his eyes.

"It's ok, son. What hurts? What were you doing?" Ace checked Max's body for any more breaks or cuts, as did Beth, both fussing over him.

"She attacked me," said Max. "She —"

Camilla was too cunning. The beast librarian had disappeared before the ladder even hit the ground.

It dawned on Max that she outmatched him. If she could get into the shed—and into that locked barn a month earlier—without leaving a trace, she could probably do anything.

"Who is 'she?'" said Beth. "There's no one here, honey."

Ace looked up from Max, and scanned the yard, still lit up in all directions from the floodlights. Nothing moved except the four pugs who sniffed around Max's face, licking him and panting from the night's excitement.

"Are you sure nothing hurts?" said Beth.

"I'm fine, Mom… The arm seems ok. I'm sorry."

Ace looked a bit mad, though he kept his eyes on the yard, continuing to look in all directions while tending to Max. "You keep doing this, mister. You have to be careful," said Ace. "Let's get you inside."

"What were you thinking?" said Beth, noticeably trying to stay composed, dusting straw off Max's clothes.

"I dunno," said Max. His nose started to run. "I'm sorry…"

Max's parents helped him stand. Together they stumbled back into the house. Ace looked down at Max with a look of disapproval, and sympathy, and said, "You're still working Saturday. I suggest you rest up."

Once inside, Beth took Max upstairs.

Ace returned to the barn to put the ladder away and close the shed. He surveyed the damage to the door. He never looked up and saw the doll. He never saw the eyes peering at him through the dark, far out in the field of dried up corn stalks. He did, however, find a set of fabric shears. One blade was shiny as a mirror. The other blade was coated with fresh blood. He figured Max had cut himself someplace he had not seen and returned to the house to tend to the undiscovered wound.

A RETURN TO ROJAN

Max never got to make plans in Biology class with his friends the next day. The principal canceled classes so students could mourn the passing of Melinda Waters; her wake was that morning, and her funeral in the afternoon. Max found out she would also be buried close to the Weatherbys and grumpy, old Mrs. Tweed. That part of the cemetery was beginning to take on a new significance. Max wondered what it meant.

The murders in Pine Plains remained unsolved. A killer remained on the loose.

Max spent part of his day visiting Riley at the hospital with his mother, rather than attending the funeral. He spent the day quietly thinking, analyzing his encounter with Camilla. He had almost been her next victim.

Saturday arrived. Max sat in the police cruiser with Ace, heading toward Rojan Farms and his day out in the fields taring fences.

"Do I have to do this, Dad?" groaned Max. He held his cast and put on a sad face. Undoubtedly, his father should give up and take him home.

Ace wasn't deterred.

"That look only works on your mother, so give it up, buster," said Ace, wearing a scowl on his face and focusing on the road. "Besides," — he grabbed his coffee cup and guzzled— "we're almost there. As I said,

Bernard will be close by. It's such a perfect day to be outside. Look at that sun."

The morning couldn't have been any more beautiful, Max agreed. While a bit nippy, the frost would soon burn off. The weatherman did call for sun and mild temperatures ahead of a front and the first snowstorm forecast for later that night.

"When will you be back to get me?" said Max.

"Oh, around four, I think. Nine hours should be enough for you. You got your lunch pail, and thermos. They can go in the wagon with everything else. Couldn't be any easier." The wagon Max used to pull the two five-gallon buckets of tar were piled in the cruiser's back seat

Max grumbled at the idea of having to work on such a perfect day. Plus, he wouldn't be paid. Even worse, his father had confiscated his harvest-fair money, so he would have nothing with the holidays coming.

For a moment, Max's lack of personal income seemed to overshadow everything else. His mind returned to Camilla and the fact she wanted to kill him and his friends.

Max's decision to be an investigator had really backfired. He never realized the work and sacrifice that went into the profession. He never knew there could be such a downside.

Ace cleared his throat. "Did your mom tell you a couple of your friends called this morning, looking for you?"

"Nope, not a word," said Max. He was a bit miffed that he only now learned about the calls. He had no clue what might happen while he was alone out in the fields with no friends around, no plan, and the possibility Camilla might attack.

"Yeah," said Ace, "especially Doctor Esteban's girl, Carmen."

"What about her," said Max.

"She was all sweet and lovey-dovey when she called... Checking up on you. Making sure you're ok...." Ace kissed the air.

"Oh, I wouldn't say that," said Max, "she's just a friend —"

"Might do you some good," said Ace, glancing at Max from the corner of his eye. "Maybe a girlfriend is just what you need —"

"Dad!" Now Max's father went too far. The man even laughed lightly, obviously delighted he got a reaction from his son.

"I'm just saying, things are going to start changing for you. You're going to start going through some physical changes —"

"Ugh." Max sighed and shook his head. "We don't need to have 'the talk' do we? Not now..."

"I know you kids know a lot more at an earlier age than we did."

"Some things," said Max under his breath, "but I can wait a little longer on the rest, thanks."

Ace smiled. "That's nature for you. You can't get away from the inevitable, mister. Soon enough, you'll be a grown man, out of the house and on your own."

"And until that time..." said Max, stopping his father, "I'll be fine with football next year, cross country, working, concentrating on school. Normal things."

"And you need to stop getting into trouble," said Ace. "How are you supposed to get into a good college, or have anyone take you seriously if you don't shape up?" He pointed at Max's arm. "Broken legs and arms can really get in the way, Max."

"Point taken, Dad." Max sighed. "I'm a little young to be dating, too, so don't go there."

"Good. That's the correct response," said Ace. "You need to start thinking about a future career too ... like police work, or as an investigator, or forensics...." Ace had no clue Max had already begun his training investigating the murder in Pine Plains, dealing with the worst kind of criminal: a ferocious, narcissistic monster named Camilla Fox.

"I'm doing that," said Max. "Maybe I can take your job one day."

Ace smiled and tussled Max's hair with his big hand.

"Sooner, the better," said Ace.

N N N

The police cruiser rounded the bend past the Broadrick Farm. The first fields of the Rojan Horse Farm—dotted with horses—came into view. The large, steel training center passed them on the left as the car wound its way to the intersection where the creek ran under the bridge. Another police cruiser sat on the edge of the road in front of the old barn. The barn had even more yellow crime scene tape wrapped around it than Max remembered.

Max noticed the creek ran high over its banks. Despite the dry weather, a recent heavy rain farther away sent a torrent downstream. The water was high enough that Ace pulled his car next to Bernard's, parking closer to the road to let Max out. The creek had inundated the barn by about a foot and rushed close to the road's edge.

"You better be careful when you pass over that rickety bridge to get to the forty-acre," said Ace, looking down the creek to where Max would be heading with the wagon.

Max shot his dad a salute. "Yes, sir."

Max wondered if Maxine would still be working in the barns. He had not heard from her since descending the staircase in their Victorian. A lot had happened. Camilla, looking unhuman, had attacked him in his shed. She could have done anything to Maxine by this time, including Dallas.

I did stab her in the neck, thought Max, remembering the shears. What if she had already died because of him? His parents still knew nothing. Max wasn't going to tell, no matter how freaked out he had become.

He had so many unanswered questions. No one was around to help him figure it out, except his friends. They were just as naive has he was.

None of them had heard back from him.

Max's heart thumped harder while opening the car door. The reality of his situation became more apparent when his feet hit the hard dirt and pebbles on the road's edge. He looked out past the rushing water in the creek; past the old barn, now looking worse than ever, like it had aged another ten years; out into the pastures where the helpless horses stood, chewing hay, incapable of coming to his rescue if he found himself in trouble.

He glanced up just in time to see a familiar figure walking down the hill from the farm's driveway. Bernard slowly swaggered over the bridge. He vigorously brushed something off his blue uniform, his hands patting and swiping his shoulders and down the sleeves. As Bernard got closer, Max noticed a look of annoyance on his face. What looked like pieces of straw haphazardly dangled from his hat. His lips moved. He cursed under his breath, looking like a crazy person arguing with some internal demon.

Max laughed. "Hey, Bernard, what happened, man?"

"That darn horse—Clamoring, I think you call it—tried to kick me..." Bernard removed his hat and shook straw and chunks of manure off its brim. He wrinkled his nose in disgust.

"I hate dirt, but this ... this is disgusting."

"At least it's not cow poop," said Max. "Nothing is nastier than cow poop."

"Nothing?" said Bernard. "Are you sure?" He finished picking bits of poop from the hat and placed the cap back on his head.

The officer crossed his arms.

"Your little friend with all the black makeup sure talks a lot. She even confessed to helping you break into the morgue."

Max had been found out. Bernard figured it out at the fair, but only now confirmed that he knew. He hoped his father hadn't heard.

"When did she tell you that?" said Max, whispering.

"Just now ... in the barn."

"So, she is here," said Max under his breath. He was glad she was still alive.

"Yup ... down there, cleaning stalls. I'll tell you," said Bernard, "that girl has got some muscle on her, sure knows how to use a pitchfork." He looked Max in the eye. "She's honest, too."

Ace poked his head up from the trunk. He had been searching for the equipment Bernard needed and hadn't heard their conversation.

"Hey," said Ace, snapping his fingers and lowering the trunk to get Bernard's attention. "You need to help me with this thing." Ace grunted while trying to pull something from the trunk. "I didn't know these generators were this heavy. What do you need it for?"

"Uh, boss," said Bernard, not prepared for the question, "I'm meeting those two agents here in a little while. They requested a power source for some equipment they need to use."

Ace mumbled. "Don't know what that could be, but, ok..."

Bernard squeezed Max's shoulder, saying, "Hold on, our talk's not over with."

He ambled over to the back of the cruiser and helped Ace jostle the generator out of the trunk.

"How are you going to get this thing around here?" said Ace, looking around. Water was close to the road. "Do you have a wheelie or something you're using?"

"Darn," said Bernard, laying on some drama, "I forgot the dolly."

Max waved from the passenger side of the car. "I have an idea."

"And what's that? "said Ace. "You need to start getting that tar out of there —"

Max groaned. "I was going to suggest Bernard could use the wagon, Dad."

He shook his head. "What about the fence?"

"Oh, well, how about I paint the paddocks near the barns? They're close. It would be easier." Max threw his attention to Bernard, whom he figured would probably understand what he was getting at. "What do you think, Bernard?"

"It would make the day easier… What do you think, Ace?"

Ace looked the rushing water. It seemed higher than earlier, which meant more of the valley could be flooded. The rushing water was terrible, able to carry people away, never to be seen again. Max could easily fall in because the kid was prone to clumsiness and getting himself into trouble. It was the last thing Ace needed, and his guard was up.

"While the work needs to be performed out there," —Ace pointed across the creek, out into the depths of the largest field on the farm— "I am inclined to agree with you."

"You really should spend time with Riley," said Bernard. "She needs her father."

"Yeah, it's pretty bad…" Ace Sighed. "We have some decisions to make today."

"Like what? "said Bernard.

"She's not getting any better. We might have to consider making arrangements."

"What do you mean arrangements, Dad?" said Max, alarmed.

Ace clammed up and looked away from Max, involving himself in hefting the generator. It was clear he did not want to talk about Riley. Bernard saw the tension and closed his mouth as well.

Max opened the rear door to the police cruiser and grabbed hold of the red wagon, pulling it out onto the side of the road. He placed the two five-gallon buckets of tar on it, supplies, and trudged towards the bridge, pulling it with his unbroken arm.

"Hold on, buddy, where are you goin' there?" said Ace.

"Thought we decided we'd paint up there?" said Max, pointing to the many paddocks lining the bloated creek.

"Well?"

Ace looked like he was thinking, but no words came out of his mouth.

"Dad, the sooner I get the stuff up there, the sooner I have the wagon back to you."

"Ok. Ok," said Ace. "Just make it fast."

"Yes!" Max was happy. He got his way. Thanks to Bernard, Max would have access to the farm's bathroom. He would be closer to Bernard and, just what he wanted, he'd be closer to Maxine.

As Max made his way up the hill on Silvernails Road, he noticed the perfect weather predicted seemed less than ideal. Clouds thickened ahead of schedule. The temperature seemed to drop several degrees since they arrived. Was it possible the cold front came earlier than predicted?

Even the trees crackled as the wind whipped up the dead leaves of fall. Max looked over his shoulder while he crossed the bridge and saw Bernard running down the street after his hat.

Man, he's fast, thought Max.

Bernard sprinted about five-hundred feet. Max was surprised and thought, maybe, he'd ask the officer to go running with him, cross country, once his arm healed.

Max turned back toward the hill and continued pulling the wagon.

A Parade of Cars

Max returned with the red wagon, a bit winded. He hustled down the hill as fast as possible. He never realized the time off with a broken arm had made him so weak.

Ace had already left.

Bernard waited on the side of the road, leaning against the police cruiser, picking his teeth with a twig.

"Took you long enough," said Bernard.

Max rolled the wagon in front of him and asked the vital question: "I see Dad's gone. How are you supposed to get that thing in the wagon?" Max pointed at the generator.

Bernard looked down and almost blurted out the wrong words. He gave Max an "I 'm-so-stupid" look. He had the police car's radio microphone in his hand, clicked the button, and called Ace's name.

The radio crackled with static. Not even Girty Mae picked up.

"That's strange, never happened before," said Bernard, noticeably agitated. He tried several more times with the same result. The radio merely buzzed.

"I'll have to take this car and go get your father."

Max was surprised that Bernard seemed unprepared.

"So… Do you want me to stand here on the side of the road with this thing?" said Max.

"Ace can't be far…"

Bernard looked Max in the eye and diverted his attention to the generator, the taped barn with the rushing water around it, then up into the sky. Clouds began to lower. The air grew colder by the minute. "If you can just watch it for a few minutes, he can't be far."

"Yeah, I suppose, but —"

"I have no choice, Max." He tapped Max on the shoulder, opened the door to the cruiser, and hopped inside.

Leaving Max was probably the worst thing he could've done. Max didn't like it. Bernard made a U-turn and quickly sped down the road, back toward Pine Plains.

Max was left standing with the large generator and the red wagon. He had left all his supplies in one of the paddocks near the lower barn. He had no water, no food, and no clue when Bernard would return.

A series of cars passed Max.

Father Jim Franks, in his beat-up old Ford hatchback, flew up the road and slammed on his brakes in front of Max. The man opened his passenger side window.

"Everything ok, young man?"

Father Franks looked a lot different than he usually did in church. Max regularly saw the man in typical priest's clothing: a black suit, white shirt, slicked-back black hair, and a fresh look on his face on Sundays. Today was another matter. As Max peered through the open window, he noticed the man had a half-buttoned shirt that was untucked—very untidy. His hair was a mess. He kept sniffing like he had allergies.

Max leaned in the window to let Father Franks know he was ok. The overwhelming scent of hard liquor, mixed with beer and cigarettes, overtook him. He quickly backed away.

"I'm fine, sir. It looks like you should probably get home," said Max. He wrinkled his nose in disgust. He couldn't get the smell out of his head.

"You sure?" said the pastor. "I can take ye' home." The man let out a baritone-like belch and began to hiccup uncontrollably.

Max flinched and stepped back farther.

"Just waiting for dad, but thanks."

Father Franks gave a feeble salute and put his car in gear. He sped away, kicking up gravel and dirt, sounding like a drag racer while speeding up the hill.

Good thing he's not heading toward Killer, thought Max. He didn't know if he would ever get the new images of the town's pastor out of his head. It would surely spoil church. Had his father seen the man, Max knew a DUI would've been handed out.

The air grew cold. Max swore he felt small raindrops from the oddly growing, single cloud overhead. He had planned for a warm, sunny day. As he shuffled around in the dirt, snapping dry weeds with his shoes and looking down, he wondered if his day tarring fences was doomed to end early.

A new yellow Camaro rounded the corner and eased up next to Max, as quiet as a black cat sneaking by. Another passenger door window opened. Inside, Mrs. Waters and Bethany sat with McD's Cafes in their hands.

"Of all the things to find on the side of the road!" Bethany yelled out the window.

Max jumped. He tripped and stubbed his toe on the generator.

"Darn, why'd you do that?" said Max, grabbing for his foot. "I didn't even see you. You were so fast."

"More like super quiet ... loser," said Bethany. She chuckled. "Looser" was her favorite name for Max. Why she chose to use it, Max never knew, but he became accustomed to it. She was two grades ahead of him, so he let it go.

"This car's super quiet, unless mom's gunning for Killer or taking the corners so stinkin' fast," said Bethany, who leaned out the window.

Max looked up sheepishly, still rubbing his shin. "How are you doing, anyway?"

Mrs. Waters held tight to the wheel and barked at Max. "As best as can be expected, considering the delays at the Sheriff's office. They work slower than sap in winter, I swear —"

"They're doing their best, ma'am," said Max. "It's all Dad does, but I have a feeling things are about to change. We'll get 'em."

Bethany's mom blew air out of her nose, sounding like a cow clearing its sinuses. She looked at the barn, now more submerged by the creek. She tilted her head to look at the growing clouds overhead. The spiky limbs of a willow seemed to reach for the car, bowing low as if to snatch it and drag it into the rushing water.

"You shouldn't be out here alone." Mrs. Waters seemed uneasy. "Who left you here?"

"Bernard. He'll be right back."

However, Bernard wasn't back. Neither was Ace.

Bethany confirmed Max's fears.

"A large tree, you know, that enormous one leaning at the intersection at Patchin's Mill? It fell across the road after we passed—blocked the whole thing. It's a good thing those other cars made it through. That red Jeep sure cut it close, right Mom? But I swear that darn tree seemed to wait for it."

"We'll have to take a long way around to get back to town," said Mrs. Waters. "Don't expect anyone any time soon, Max. Do you want a lift?"

"I can't. I've got this generator to protect and a ton of fence to paint up by the barns." Max pointed across the road toward the muddy paddocks lining the hillside along the creek.

"Doesn't look fun," said Bethany.

Max didn't hear her. He no longer felt the pain in his shin and forgot the cast hanging in its sling. The sky itself seemed to lower and close in on him. He looked down the road toward town, frightened by the red Jeep hurtling his way.

He thought he should get rid of Bethany, and seek the safety of the barns as fast as his tired legs could carry him. The generator was too heavy for anyone to move, so he'd leave it where it was.

"I think I'll get to work," said Max. "What are you doing today, Bethany?"

Mrs. Waters cut Bethany off, pulling her out of the window's opening.

"Miss here is going to help me clean a house today ... just a bit up the road ... Judge Coffee's place."

"The whole time?" said Bethany, annoyed she'd have to work. "Can I ride his bike too? Maybe at lunch?"

"What bike?" said Max.

Bethany perked up. "So, the judge has this Cannondale mountain bike he never rides, you know ... and sometimes I like to take it out when I go with Mom to his house, out there on the lake ... it's a sweet ride."

"IF you get your rooms cleaned," said Mrs. Waters, interrupting.

Bethany beamed. Her eyes sparkled. She gushed at Max. "I can zip down here for a few minutes to see what you're up too; make sure you tarred enough fence; make sure you're ok."

This time Max didn't protest. With danger looming so near, the more people that showed up, the better off he'd be. He knew Camilla liked doing her evil work in private, away from prying eyes. She'd want him alone when she attacked.

Mrs. Waters put the Camaro in first gear and revved the engine. Bethany sat back like she was about to blast off, clutching the center console and the window frame. The car sped forward up the steep Silvernails hill, but not before Max caught Bethany's last words.

"See' a loser!"

Max shook his head and let out a pathetic sigh.

The last car to cross his path was a new Range Rover, black and perfectly waxed. Coach Charlie sat in the front, staring straight ahead like he was in a trance. Max just watched. Unlike the pastor and Mrs. Waters, Charlie didn't slow down. He didn't even seem to see Max while speeding by. As the pastor, Charlie's face was red and quite bloated like he was about to pop.

Like that dead pig, and those darn woodchucks on a hot day, thought Max, watching the Range Rover scream up the hill.

Charlie was another piece of unfinished business. Max never made it to detention with the school's coach. He decided, if he managed to survive Camilla, he'd be more than happy to do "the time." He'd be back on the football team for the next season. In the meantime, he'd see Charlie, and most likely that jerk Tony, in the school's gym, lifting weights and laughing at each other's bad form.

MAXINE SAVES MAX

Max stared toward the top of Silvernails hill for several minutes after Coach Charlie sped away. His eyes deceived him. Though he had no reason to cry, his eyes teared up, feeling red and inflamed, as though he caught a severe allergy or something more horrific like pinkeye. The burning felt intense.

A wave of crippling fear traveled from his feet up through his head. His heart pounded in his chest. His breathing became short and labored. Max felt as though he could scream, though no words came out.

Max thought he saw something that could not possibly be there, both at the crest of the hill and in the heavily treed forest on both sides. Like an old crackly black-and-white film played from an old projector, with all its distortions and choppiness (he had watched several movies like this before, on an old projector, in a musty old museum in Hudson), the view before Max twisted and contorted. His vision became colorless, merely black-and-white—an old picture from a hundred years before. He rubbed both eyes, trying to stamp out the image and come back to reality, but nothing changed.

The road running up the hill no longer looked paved, but rather, was only dirt and gravel. The large trees on either side no longer looked majestic. Their hungry, thin limbs reached and stretched out over the road seeking to pluck someone up. They even moved. The end of the branches resembled hands that flexed and pinched.

Max blinked, but the change in his vision remained the same.

Just over the bridge, an old cemetery with gravestones that time and weather had flattened, looked reborn. All the stones were now erect as though they had just been planted there. Their polished surfaces showcased the names and dates carved into them.

Max's feet froze to the spot. He felt nothing, not even his wretchedly broken arm. His eyes traveled back up the road where, at the top, an old buggy pulled by a single black horse raced down the hill. A woman perched on the firm wooden seat at its front.

If he didn't know any better—he blinked several times again in succession—it was the very ghost he saw in the mirror at Maxine's house. A replica of the librarian, Camilla, with an unusually broad smile.

The clouds overhead churned and rumbled. A flash of lightning streaked from overhead and crashed behind him. Max shut his eyes tight, bearing down on what he saw, trying to push it out of his mind.

"You don't see this… It's not there…" said Max, garbling his words under his labored breath.

"Water!"

Max's eyes flew open. He caught himself looking down.

The water from the creek had risen halfway to his knees. It flowed behind Max as well, cutting off the road to Pine Plains.

A clap of thunder shook the ground. A light brighter than the sun flashed overhead.

Max twisted to see the old barn.

A lightning bolt had drilled a smoking hole in its roof. Flames shot out. The old barn had begun to collapse, undercut by the rising water.

Max found it strange that the water had risen so quickly. No reason existed for any of it, not even some recent rain.

The long line of yellow crime scene tape had also detached from the barn and wrapped itself around Max's ankle, connecting him to the structure as it collapsed farther into the water. He didn't think anything of it. His attention had fixed on the mess unfolding around him.

Max looked back up toward the hill. The water would cut off the bridge at any moment. It was his only escape route.

He was in deep trouble.

Max needed to get his butt to the safety of the barns quickly.

ℳ ℳ ℳ

The generator was a loss, completely submerged by the creek.

Not a single car approached the Silvernails intersection—none from Pine Plains, none from the top of the hill. Total silence, aside from rushing water, enveloped the valley.

Max couldn't wait any longer. Bernard and his father were probably tied up in Pine Plains, unable to get through due to the downed tree, or any other number of factors. Max could only guess. What he did know was he had been left there and had to count on himself. No one could save him if he were swept away by the stream. Worse yet, what he had seen when his vision turned from color to black-and-white meant his fears about the librarian were well-founded. He could be the next on her list.

"Get yourself together, Max." Max slapped himself in the face. He had seen people in the movies do it to wake themselves up. He gathered his strength and rushed forward through the rising water toward the bridge.

The current ran strong. The water churned like thin, muddy pudding. Debris and branches, and bits of trash floated by.

The water had reached Max's knees. Something below the current tightened around his ankle. He couldn't move his leg.

Max raised his leg and found the yellow crime scene tape had knotted itself, squeezing his ankle tight. As he yanked his leg, the tape only tightened more. Max had an even harder time balancing on the other leg, all while trying to keep his balance. He didn't want his cast to get wet should he fall.

However, things got much worse.

The other end of the tape remained connected to the collapsing barn, which by this time, moved off its foundation, carried by the water's strong current.

Max tried again, but the tape only tightened. He felt it cutting off his circulation.

"Oh, man, I'm screwed," said Max. His heart sped up to what felt like ten times its average speed. He felt his lungs clench.

His leg buckled from the pull of the tape. The old barn cracked and splintered. Finally, after standing for decades, it pancaked into the rushing water.

Max, unfortunately, went where the barn went. All its boards separated into a heap. The broken barn drifted toward the bridge, pulling Max with it.

"My arm!"

Max screamed before falling and being pulled under the water, dragged by his leg. He flailed and reached with his arms, but felt no scraggly trees or brush to clutch with his hand.

He imagined the barn's wood jamming, together with broken trees, against the bridge. If he became part of the jam, he was doomed to drown. The crush of water would pin him against the mess, like people he heard of dying in rafting accidents. Their bodies would be pressed against a rock underwater. No matter how hard they tried, it was never enough. Sometimes they'd break free. Other times, their bodies would only surface after bloating from decomposition, only to be found farther downstream weeks later by an unsuspecting hiker or a wayward dog.

Max wasn't ready to decompose. He was only thirteen. He just started puberty!

He pushed and forced his head above the dirty water. When he opened his eyes, above him, a hand reached down from the edge of the gray cement barrier lining the side of the bridge. The hand and arm were fuzzy. Max had a hard time focusing. Someone in a dark blue long sleeve shirt with a pair of tan gloves had leaned over the barrier. Max heard the muffled sound of a girl calling his name.

"Max!" He knew the voice, but the knotted tape pulling on his leg forced him back underwater.

Before submerging for the second time, Max—surprisingly—saw more movement to his right, beyond the bridge.

A woman! The same one he saw riding the old horse and buggy, with her long, dark hair streaming out behind her. Her pale arms were outstretched as though trying to reach Max. She rushed toward him and toward whoever appeared on the bridge.

"Help —" Max tried to scream, but water entered his mouth. He gurgled the last of his words before choking.

As he went under, he heard a struggle above him. Two female voices screamed.

"Away with you," demanded one voice.

"He's mine..." howled the other. High-pitched screaming, mixed with cackling and uncontrollable excitement, filled the air above the bridge.

Max went under as the tape pulled him down. Regardless of the muddy water, he instinctively opened his eyes upon reaching for the surface.

A brilliant flash of lightning and a loud clap of thunder shook water. Several more flames—reds, blues, and greens—seemed to come from over the bridge where the screaming continued.

Suddenly, it all stopped. Someone with vice-like hands clamped down on Max's wrist. In one fast motion, Max was yanked toward the surface.

The person who pulled him up was incredibly strong.

His cast came out of its sling, feeling like a massive weight determined to pull him back down to the depths of the swollen creek.

Max sprang from the water like a missile leaving the confines of a submarine far out in some deep ocean. The oddly strong crime scene tape was no match. It tore away. Max found himself flying over the edge of the bridge. His body slammed down on the concrete. The air he had been holding left his lungs in a quick, painful gasp.

When he opened his eyes, Maxine stood over him, her chest heaving. Dark streaks ran across her face in the shape of fingers.

Maxine breathed heavy. "She's gone, for now. We have to get going —"

Max squirmed. The back of his head hurt where it had bounced off the pavement. He had also swallowed some of the muddy water. His stomach churned. He thought he could puke.

But he was alive, and that's all that mattered.

"Come on, kiddo, we need to get you inside," said Maxine.

Max looked up and focused his eyes. Maxine didn't look like her usual, goth-like self. She loomed over him wearing dark brown work boots, brown Dickey's work pants, and a barn jacket covering a thick, red sweater. She still had the leather work gloves on, though they were drenched with water from pulling Max out.

He couldn't believe he looked at the same girl.

"You're freakin' strong," said Max, slowly sitting up from the pavement and dragging his broken arm to his lap. "No wonder Cindy hired you."

"Enough of that," said Maxine, "how's your arm?"

"Heavy ... soaked."

Maxine kneeled to help him with the water-swollen cast. She raised it, careful not to let any of the material chip off. Max tilted enough for her to slide it through the muddy sling. He held it open with his free hand.

"Thanks."

Maxine stood up, backed a couple of feet, and reached for Max to help him stand.

When Max reached for her hand—to his surprise—his eyes fluctuated yet again. Colored scenery disappeared and was replaced with the strange black-and-white, film-like quality. When he looked up at Maxine, he gasped.

"It's like you're not even there!"

Max's eyes shifted. Maxine no longer looked like herself. An outline of her shimmered, like crystal clear water with the sun beating off it. Stars of various sizes and intensities, with rainbow hues, sparkled within her. She seemed made of light, a stark contrast to the whites, blacks, and grays coloring the surrounding landscape.

She no longer reached for his hand. She took a glove off and spread her hand flat and slapped him on the cheek.

"Get a hold of yourself. We have no time for your fantasizing."

Max screeched, "Hey!" He rubbed his cheek and grimaced. With no help at all, he sprang to his feet.

"Come on," said Maxine in a gruff tone, ignoring Max's protests. She turned her back to him and, at a brisk pace, hurried back toward the barns.

Max blinked rapidly, striding forward. His eyes stung as though sand or pollen had gotten in them. The color of the fall leaves and the raging gray skies returned. Even Maxine looked normal.

Max glanced behind himself while following Maxine. The creek's water had risen another couple of feet, inundating most of the bridge. What remained of the barn, co-mingled with other debris, clogged the creek's flow under it. The jam caused a flood, the likes of which Max had never seen in the valley before.

Lightning flashed. Thunder rumbled through the billowing gray and green skies. Green clouds always meant the approach of a significant storm, and the possibility of tornados. Wayward clouds began fusing, blocking out what remained of the tranquil blues and yellows of the morning. The perfect fall day vanished hours ahead of schedule.

Max had not yet asked Maxine what happened on the bridge. What happened to her face? Who screamed and yelled at her while he nearly drowned in the toxic soup that was once the clean, sparkling creek? He quickened his pace to catch up. His body hurt more than ever. He felt like vomiting.

They were in terrible trouble.

RACE TO THE BARNS

It took Max and Maxine just five minutes to leave the bridge, jog up the long, rocky driveway under the canopy of maple tree skeletons, and arrive at the first barn. It had been cleared of horses for the morning's chores. The stalls were empty, ensuring Maxine would have no problems mucking.

Maxine rushed through the barn's front door into the office, narrowly missing Max while flinging the outer screen door open.

"We need to think fast," said Maxine.

She leaned against the office desk, slouching from the exhaustion also clearly written on her face. She had spent the morning cleaning stalls before hearing the commotion down at the bridge. Her clothes were soiled. She smelled of horse poop and the puddles of lime-infused horse urine hidden under the old straw. Max had grown used to it, the smell didn't bother him. In fact, he felt more at home.

Max regarded Maxine with new interest. The more he hung around her, the more mysterious she became.

He continued breathing heavily. "I don't know how you can be so strong," said Max. "I don't know anyone else who could have pulled me out … except maybe my dad."

Maxine snapped at him. "Well, your dad isn't here. Neither are any of your other friends." She rubbed her temple. Her eyeliner had smudged. It dripped down her damp face making her look like a ghoulish clown. "I was petting that horse Clamoring when I heard you down there. She's the only mare left in the barn. Grumpy old thing, too."

"She bites. You should keep away from her."

"I know. Cindy told me." Maxine looked away and turned her ear to the door as though listening for something. Max figured she was deep in thought. Possibly stalling.

The winds outside picked up in intensity. Small stones and twigs bounced off the sides of the barn, dancing off its thick wood shakes and frosty windows. The building shook, creaking with each blast. Max knew the barns well. They were built a hundred years earlier and lasted through many the assaults Mother Nature threw at them. Their foundations were thick cement. Their lower walls up to the base of the windows were constructed of large rock cemented together. Thick wooden walls and massive support beams framed the stalls, ceiling, and lofts.

Nothing can bring one of these barns down, thought Max.

He also knew the lower barn was more massive and had a fully stocked loft of golden straw, and hay. It had many more hiding places should they need them.

As the rumbling outside grew, he shivered from not knowing what happened to his father and Bernard. He wondered how Riley fared in the hospital—with all those tubes and wires keeping her from slipping away to someplace even more frightening.

Max couldn't imagine life without his sister in it. It scared him to death.

"Are you ok?" said Maxine, noticing Max on the verge of tears.

"No, I'm not —" Max's torment choked the office. He looked up, visibly overcome with grief, and stared Maxine in the eye.

"Who is she? What does she want?" Max's eyes welled up. Anger took over from where his tears stopped. "Why does she like to hurt people?"

Maxine opened her mouth, about to speak, when something louder than the wind knocked at the door. A THUD and a series of harried bangs rattled the screen hidden behind the solid wooden door locked from the inside. The rhythmic pattern of the banging suggested a person stood on the other side, desperately trying to get in, but no one screamed or cried. No one spoke a word from outside the barn's door.

"It's her, isn't it!" said Max, convinced Camilla had caught up to them.

"No, it's someone else," said Maxine. "Camilla doesn't need doors." She hesitated and added, "She's still flesh and blood. She can be stopped."

That admission by Maxine took Max's breath away. He gasped. His mind conjured up images of the sleek librarian passing through walls like a ghost or squeezing through thin openings like a deadly black widow spider or centipede. What Max experienced back in his shed, with Camilla looking like a beast from deep in a dark, unmoving forest, gave him an even more profound sense of dread. She could probably do anything she wanted; go anywhere; be anything or anyone. She could take him and everyone he loved out with a flick of some razor-sharp claws, or—like his poor prized pumpkins—work her will in some unspeakable, magical way. She could destroy whatever she touched.

Max had no clue who, or what, he dealt with when it came to Camilla. She was crafty and took great care not to alert any adults. He also realized he knew very little about Maxine.

Max froze. He felt encased by the office's walls. Maxine stared at the door from the middle of the room, unsure. Whoever stood outside—desperately, and without words—tried hard to get their attention.

"We need to open the door," said Max, "it could be anyone. Everyone knows I'm here today."

Maxine agreed. She inched closer and reached out with one hand toward the lock. Stronger gusts of wind replaced the banging on the door. It rattled the barn's windows and caused the door's hinges to flex and splinter the frame. She jumped back and took a breath before lunging at the door.

In one swift move, she pried it open, revealing the tattered screen on the outside.

"A tree fell!" said Max, pointing.

Indeed, one of the large trees lining the driveway had come crashing down from the force of the wind. Not only had it fallen, but the wind had picked it up and tossed it into the side of the barn, shattering the screen door. Its gnarled branches had been scraping at the door the entire time.

Maxine sighed in unison with Max.

"Would you look at that," said Max. He had looked beyond the remnants of the busted tree. The weather had not only become stormy, but the bright, sunny morning had mutated into something far worse.

The sky had become a low ceiling of dark, turbulent clouds. Light, misty rain began to fall, turning the top of the driveway into a muddy mess. Trees swayed and bent toward the driveway as though reaching for anything trying to pass by. Outside, down the hill from the barn, Max and Maxine heard the horses cry.

"Those horses need to come in," said Max. "Did Cindy teach you how to lead yet?"

Maxine, looking dazed, shook her head "no." Cindy gave her basic tasks first. Maxine spent most of her time cleaning.

"You mean, go out in THAT?" said Maxine. Max didn't buy her concern. After all, she had just saved him from certain death by drowning. She had been in a fight on the bridge.

As the two looked out the door, the rain intensified. The day became as black as night with a full moon.

Someone, out in the rain, ambled up the driveway.

"I see someone," said Max. "I think it's —"

Two figures rounded the hill. They ducked as tree branches thrashed the way, while pulling hoods over their heads, attempting to shield their faces from the driving rain.

"It's André … and Kevin."

"How'd they get past the flooded street?" said Maxine.

"More like, how'd they get here? I mean, they don't drive yet."

Indeed, the two boys were André and Kevin, peering out from under their hoods, surprised at the large tree lying in front of them.

André yelled when he saw Max in the light of the doorway.

"Are you two, ok?" They stood about twenty feet away, blocked by the tree's trunk, which had come out of the ground, dirtball and all. "I think you had a tornado, man."

"Who brought you?" said Max, yelling over Maxine.

Maxine continued to stand with her arms crossed. The look on her face and her lack of response made Max feel a bit uneasy, as though she suspected something he couldn't fathom.

"We were at your house, man," said Kevin. "Our mom brought us over. There's a problem at the hospital. Your mom took my mom with her, so we took her car to go find you."

The two boys had their backs to the driveway. They grabbed onto branches and climbed over the tree's corpse, dodging limbs that popped up, determined to swat them as they crossed. Both Max and Maxine's faces grew terrified as they looked past the boys, out into the rain, at a third figure coming up behind them at a brisk pace.

Maxine seemed puzzled. "Max … I thought Bethany's sister died?"

Max saw what Maxine saw: Melinda Waters, in the same pizza delivery driver outfit, raced toward them, speed walking. Her facial features came into view. The closer she got, the more frightening she became. Melinda's face contorted into a severe grimace. Her mouth spread into a deranged smile. Her eyes glistened against the rivulets of water cascading down her cheeks. What looked like blood poured from under her pizza ball cap. It trailed between her eyes and poured off the tip of her nose. She held a wet pizza box under one arm.

Melinda clenched her hands into fists and ran at them, screaming: "You little turds. I'll kill each one of you. It's all your fault…"

André turned first when he heard the voice. Kevin was bound up in some branches, one leg caught in a v-opening where a branch split. André screamed in French.

"Oh, mon, Dieu!"

"What?" said Kevin irritated. He was engrossed in his debacle. He worked to free his entangled foot, but his oversized sneaker wouldn't budge.

"It's that girl. She's demonic!" said André. "Look!"

"She's supposed to be dead!"

Max screamed and ran into Maxine while plunging forward into the door's opening. He shoved her aside and propelled himself out onto the trunk just as Melinda reached the roots of the tree.

She stopped abruptly and was met with four sets of wide teenage eyes. Max remained hunched over Kevin while attempting to reach for his friend's foot.

Melanie stood there. She didn't pant from the run. Her mouth had clamped shut, but her devilish smile remained stretched from ear to ear. More of her blood poured, endlessly spilling on the ground like a faucet had been turned on, emptying her skull. Only her eyes moved; they shot left, then right, in sharp, superhuman movements. She fixed her gaze on Max.

"You!" Melinda's eyes glared at Max. "You know where she is. Where is she?"

Max was, again, frozen from fear, but only momentarily. Maxine spoke up.

"Who are you looking for —"

"That pesky, prissy, overindulged blond girl, you rat," yelled Melinda, her eyes still darting feverishly around.

Max's mouth felt numb, but he had plenty to say in his head. Unlike what often came out of his mouth, his thoughts were a different matter. They were the one place he could keep his secrets to himself; have private arguments; talkback without his mother hearing; even curse from time to time.

The only blond girl I know is Carmen, thought Max. His mind trailed off. *She's pretty....*

Melinda stopped looking around and fixed her gaze on Max.

"Yes, that's the one... The one who stiffed me on my tip, that pizza-grubbing little thief!"

This time, Max spoke. "Uh, Melinda, you're supposed to be dead — "

"Dead? I'm not dead, you little creep! I'm working. I have pizzas to deliver. I never got paid for the last box. I checked as I sat in my car, counting the money that blond twerp gave me..."

Melinda choked on her words. Her throat gargled. She looked dizzy. Her skin, to Max's amazement, took on a pale, grayish hue, like the body that lay in the morgue. She looked confused.

"I have a horrible headache," said Melinda. "It feels like something hit me ... when my car window shattered, I can't remember..."

Maxine had inched her way into the barn's opened door. She remained inside where the rain couldn't have its way with what remained of her makeup-smeared face.

"Melinda," said Maxine in a soft tone, "we were there. You got paid. You left."

Melinda cried. "I want my money for that fifth pizza. I need to pay for this old clunker-of-a-car. I have track tomorrow..."

Melinda didn't stay for long. Not having seen the blond-haired girl, she began to wail in hysterics. "Oh, no. She's coming. She's almost here. I can't take any more. It burns..." Her eyes flashed left and right. Blood poured from under her pizza ball cap turning her entire face red. Max thought, *she couldn't possibly have that much blood in her body.*

André and Kevin had both turned as white as Melinda. Unlike Max and Maxine, they, however, continued to remain as still as possible considering the impossibility of the recently-buried Melinda Waters standing in front of them. Flashes of lightning and cracks of thunder made them shiver violently.

A bolt of lightning hit the peak of the barn's roof, showering Max and everyone below with sparks. The energetic remnants of its powerful current ran down wires into the ground.

The barn's roof had been lined with lightning rods from end to end, one every five feet. It was their savior.

Each of them screamed. At that moment, Max finished freeing Kevin's foot from the tree's grasp. When they all looked back at the base of the tree, Melinda Water's had vanished.

Farther down the driveway, another figure—tall, refined, and with a dress and long hair flowing as though unaffected by the rain—seemed to float slowly toward the barn.

"Camilla!" Max gasped.

The three boys quickly, yet clumsily, skittered along the tree and back into the barn's office. They barreled into Maxine, almost knocking her over.

Maxine took a moment to look out the door with an emotionless, deeply aggravated look in her eyes. She slammed the door shut and broke the key off in the lock.

THE STORM RAGES

"Man, we just saw a freekin' ghost!"

Kevin's chest heaved from the excitement on the tree. He witnessed something he only saw in movies. He didn't believe ghosts existed. Nothing so strange had ever happened in Pine Plains before—their dull little town. He just sat there panting, staring at the floor in disbelief.

André ran to the bathroom. Sounds of retching and coughing emanated through its walls and under the door for them all to hear. The French exchange student was a bit timid, even more than Kevin. André wasn't prepared for what Max had brought upon them all.

Between coughs, André yelled from the bathroom, "What the heck is all that about?" The sound of throw-up hitting the water in the toilet, splashing, forced him to gag more. "What's going on in this crazy American town…"

"I'm sorry, André," said Max, yelling back at the closed bathroom door.

Max was sorry he had pursued the elusive truth: who was murdered, who the killer was. In doing so, he brought danger to all his friends and his family. It was his idea to go to the barn the day Riley scratched her leg and was now on the edge of death in the hospital. His sister was a victim because of his own stupid, irresponsible decisions.

Max looked around the office and fixed his eyes on a giant spider web blocking a corner, covered in dust. The spider was long gone. He felt himself begin to cry.

"I'm so sorry... I should've left it alone."

Kevin looked up. "Man, no one would know anything if you hadn't gone into that barn."

"But I didn't even tell my dad. He's the sheriff. Not even Bernard, or my mother. I tried to handle it myself."

"But you didn't try to do it yourself," said Maxine. "You asked for help, Max. Help is what you got."

Max met Maxine's gaze. She hid so much from him.

"Tell me you don't have something to do with this," said Max. A shiver ran through him. His body quivered as a current of cold, electrified energy ran through his limbs. He felt his heart temporarily stop and start. His lungs grew cold. His skin felt as though it met arctic air—ninety to twenty in ten seconds.

It wasn't an illusion.

André stopped throwing up, and yelled, "Wow, did your winter just arrive?"

Kevin put his shaking hand to his mouth, exhaled, and watched his breath steam up in front of his face. Max's breath did the same as the room turned into a freezer. Both the boys looked at Maxine. She stared at the closed door as though she could see through it. Her breath didn't steam up like theirs. She didn't even look like she breathed.

"Are you ok?" said Max, concerned. Maxine only continued to stare.

Then a voice, with words drawn out in long, ghoulish—yet feminine—tones, spoke from outside the door. The wind continued to slam into the barn, trying its hardest to push the building over. Boards splintered. The sound of glass panes shattering along the barn's walls accented the dread in the office, and the devilish voice from outside.

"Maax … eeen…" said the voice. Max knew, without a doubt, the school's librarian, in all her secretive and mysterious glory, had found them.

She always knew we were here, thought Max. *She knows what's she's doing, her next victim, and she'll get it.*

André exited the bathroom and stood in the doorway. "Who was that?" His shirt was wet. Specks of undigested food glistened on his chin.

Maxine cleared her throat, took a deep breath, and seemed to moan rather than speak.

"It's Camilla."

"Who?" said André.

"The librarian," said Kevin, being careful to keep his voice down for fear she'd target him.

"The librarian? You mean the school's librarian, Ms. Fox?" said André, looking confused. "Why is she here? Shouldn't we let her in?"

"She's not here for —"

Maxine raised her voice, showing an emotional side the boys had not yet seen. She screamed at the door. Her voice was dreadful—tear-laden.

"You can't have them! I won't let you!"

Something crashed inside the barn, where the empty stalls lined the wide cement walkway. A metal pail, maybe? Perhaps a pitchfork falling off its mount? Max couldn't tell. More clanking followed the noise.

"She's inside," said Kevin. He mouthed the letters OMG, his breathing from fright.

"She's just a lady," said André.

André was severely uninformed. In Max's opinion, he was no more knowledgeable than the rest of them, except for Maxine, whom Max sensed was on the verge of giving up her owns secrets.

Maxine wasn't one to appear weak, despite her gothic fashion and shy way about her.

"We need to get to the lower barn," said Max, "I know some hiding places."

Maxine got a crazy look in her eyes while turning, twisting toward the commotion inside the barn.

"Oh, I left the tractor running too, in the lower barn, right in front of Clamoring."

André didn't understand. He looked from one frightened face to another, shaking his head, unaware of what was about to happen. He was ignorant, as Max and Maxine were, that the librarian was not only the Pine Plains murderer, but also something else—a beast that Max had already seen.

"What's going on, guys?" said André?

Max spoke first.

"Camilla's not just a librarian," said Max. "She's the owner of the barn where we found the bodies."

"We know that from the news," said André. "So, what?"

Max looked right at him. "She's responsible for the murders."

André jerked upright. He had been slouching, but in hearing Max's news, his face changed. He was now just as scared as the rest of them.

"You can't be serious?"

"I'm serious," said Max. "I've been, well, snooping around, Carmen too. We found evidence."

Maxine spoke up. "There's more too it … it's all my fault."

All eyes turned to Maxine. She told them a story.

"Camilla is Dallas's cousin. Their family comes from deep within East-Central Europe—countries like Romania, Hungary, and Russia."

Silence filled the room until another clanking sound shook the inside of the barn. The wind howled even louder, rattling the windows.

Maxine continued.

"Dallas adopted me when I was just five. My family had been killed—something about a riot and houses burning, stuff like that. I don't remember. Dallas found me alone in an empty room, down the hall from where Mom and Dad lay. I was poisoned, as were my siblings. I'm the only one who survived. Dallas took my hand that night and carried me out of the burning house; took me to a dacha outside of town where they lived; fed me; gave me a place to sleep; bound my broken ankle to a board..."

Max couldn't believe what she said. He had thought she was just an overindulged girl from New York City, going through middle school changes like the rest of them.

She was the first goth girl Max had known. He found it interesting that several other girls had adopted some of Maxine's ideas since she arrived weeks before.

Maxine continued to speak while slowly inching her way toward the door. Her ears twitched like a cat's.

She prepared to sprint through the barn, down the hill to the lower barn.

Max knew she was ready to take the lead.

Maxine wept. "We're not like the rest of you. Even immigrating to New York City years ago, after a couple of years in Paris, we still stood out. I mean, look at Dallas. I know everyone is talking. So, Dallas bought that house outside of town. Camilla came here first to set things up. It's supposed to be nice and quiet here, but she couldn't stop. She's so obsessed with herself…"

"You came here to get away from your past?" said Max.

Maxine looked over her shoulder but didn't make eye contact.

"A fresh start —" She paused. "For me, for Dallas and Camilla." She sighed and said something that shook not only Max, but Kevin and André. "Wherever we go, strange things always follow. Ghosts. Creatures not seen in millennia. Strange events. Death. People get hurt."

The storm felt unnatural. Max knew that for sure.

"Camilla is responsible for this weather," said Maxine, "and the creek running high, almost sweeping Max away."

"You got caught in that water?" said André, shocked. "It was over the bridge when we got here, blocking the driveway. We had to leave the car —"

"No one's coming," said Kevin, interrupting André, who, in his fear, destroyed the English language. "They might make it down Silvernails Hill, but no one will come directly from Pine Plains. There's no word from your dad, Max."

Max figured his father and Bernard, with the rest of the police, had been cut off, dealing with other matters as the storm raged.

They were on their own. Camilla had them right where she wanted them.

"As I said," said Maxine, "Camilla doesn't need doors … she's just playing with us."

Another clank from inside the barn broke the silence. Flashes of blue lightning, directly followed by roaring thunderclaps, indicated they were in the brunt of the storm.

Maxine turned toward the others, leaned her back against the door to the barn. Her hands fell to her sides. The look in her eyes indicated she was about to say something profound.

"I'm sure you've all heard of things like 'shapeshifters,' right?"

"Uh, duh," said Kevin. "There's enough stuff like that in the movies these days... What are you getting at?"

"Camilla and Dallas are both like that, only, Dallas decided to control it. Camilla doesn't care. Shifters are supernatural beings. You don't want to get on their bad side —"

"I don't think it matters, in Camilla's case," said Max. "Didn't she start this?"

Maxine stood frozen.

"She killed people," said Max, "and we're also on her list."

"What do you mean by 'we?'" said André. "What does she have planned?"

Max's mind returned to his recent plunge into the basement at Maxine's house, and the large metal container containing a stew of body parts. Camilla killed specific people, even the pig. All for some purpose. Max didn't understand, not until Maxine mentioned her obsession with staying young.

Max looked back at Maxine. "She uses parts of people to," —he gulped— "stay young. We're next."

"Camilla's been around a long time," said Maxine, muttering under her breath, not looking Max in the eye. "She sees things you can't see with your own eyes. She uses it to her advantage. She couldn't have lasted for so long without it." Maxine became increasingly excited. "You need to understand, I owe her, and Dallas, for saving me..."

In a whisper, Max reminded her, "But, she killed people Maxine. Somehow, Riley's illness is connected, and she's in the hospital, and could die." Max coughed and felt his stomach. It hurt, badly. Waves of nausea made him want to vomit.

Kevin and André sat stunned. Their mouths hung open in disbelief.

The front door to the barn's office began to splinter and bowed inward from some overwhelming force on the outside. Max thought he heard high-pitched laughing through the whistling of the wind as it poured through the crumbling door.

ESCAPE

"Run!" yelled Max.

Maxine quickly turned and threw open the door to the stables. All four kids took off down the aisle. They turned down the barn's length and out the opening where the tall, rolling doors stood open.

"Follow me," said Maxine, screaming over the wind and pouring rain.

Max kept pace with her despite the pain in his chest. Kevin and André tailed them, grunting and groaning with each step. They stomped through a torrent of water pouring down the driveway.

In the pastures, horses ran the length of the dark wood fences with wild looks in their eyes. As Max looked toward them, he noticed the creek consumed half the paddocks and most of the land leading to the training center. Much of the fence separating the fields from the stream was now missing or leaning against the current.

Max didn't have time to worry about horses. Horizontal rain stung his face like sharp pebbles. Somewhere behind them all—if Maxine's statement about Camilla not needing doors were correct—the librarian could be anywhere, ready to fall upon them. Who knew if she was alone.

They had just seen Melinda Waters. She was supposed to be kickin' it with the Weatherbys in the cemetery under all that freshly laid sod.

"Over here," said Max, shielding his eyes while running to the lower barn.

The enormous sliding doors were closed tight. The massive, steel latch had been dropped in place. An old, rusted lock with a large keyhole dangled and had been clamped shut. It still swung side to side as though someone had just taken their hands off it. The red tractor continued to rumble inside.

"This wasn't here before," said Maxine. "What the —"

Rain poured down. Horses bayed and cried in their paddocks. The big, industrial light hanging below the roof's overhang burst to life. It sensed the darkness closing in. As the muddy driveway illuminated, Max spied several shapes approach from different directions. He backed up against the doors, paralyzed.

André screamed and pointed to a towering, fuzzy, white creature lumbering down the driveway.

"Ce ne peut pas être réel!"

"Oh, it's real, all right," said Maxine.

"Look!" said Max.

By the paddocks, several figures—floating, not walking—shimmered and advanced on them, the wind at their backs. Leading the pack, the only two Max recognized were Melinda Waters (scowling beneath her Tower Pizza ball cap) and the ancient-looking ghost from the mirror. The others, while human in shape, fizzled, cutting in and out like an old black and white television with a broken antenna.

"Are you seeing this?" Kevin burst into tears and cowered behind Maxine.

"Screw this," said André using some American slang.

The hairy, white creature and the ghosts converged on them. André dropped his Mag light and barreled around the corner of the barn. Kevin screamed: "Wha—what are you doing?" He shoved Maxine and lunged around the corner after André.

"You freekin' gotta' be kidding me!" said Max. "Those jerks —"

Max lost his breath as Maxine spun him around and forced him toward the fleeing boys. He tripped, stubbing his toe on a loose piece of cement. A jagged splinter of wire ripped at his arm, tearing his windbreaker. Mud bubbling up around the barn's outer wall tripped them up, but they made it to the side door in time to see Kevin sliding through it.

The creature wailed. It shrieked, letting out a series of rolling grunts like a gorilla. Its heavy footsteps slapped the puddles and shook the ground, adding to the roar of the storm. What remained of Melinda Waters screamed, "Gimme what's mine!"

⚡ ⚡ ⚡

The dry warmth of the barn's interior had mixed with the tangy scent of urine and lime powder. The unmistakable fumes from the running tractor choked the air. Maxine had only cleaned a quarter of the stalls and the manure spreader was empty.

Clamoring was startled when the four kids arrived soaking wet and screaming.

The horse pranced around the interior of her stall, flaring her nostrils. The tractor sputtered while it sat there, turning the air rancid and toxic.

"Wha' do we do?" André sobbed behind the half-full manure spreader with Kevin huddled and crying at his side. Max heard them right away and ran their direction.

The side door slammed shut. A loud CLAP rang out behind Max when he reached André. When he turned around, Maxine was no longer behind him. Max joined them, squatting low to the ground behind a rear tire.

"This isn't real. This isn't real..." repeated André. He had shut his eyes.

Kevin craned his neck toward Max. "What was that thing? A y-yeti?"

Max remembered Camilla in his shed. She had been every bit the beast as the thing outside, but a lot smaller. Still, teacher sized. Not a grotesque giant, white-haired ape, or abominable snowman, or as Kevin suggested—a yeti. Whatever she had become, it had nothing to do with the beautiful woman she wanted the town to see.

She commanded pure fear.

He met Kevin's eyes. "It's Camilla —" He paused, choked by the revelation. "She has only one goal right now. To get rid of me and anyone else standing in her way."

Kevin whispered. "But I had nothing to do with it —"

"We're friends ... and now you know. That's all she sees."

Kevin gasped. His red freckles converged, making him look like old Frankie Potter after a long night at Bernie's Pub. The man's skin was so red and taught from booze, that whenever Max encountered him mopping floors at school, he'd shrink away, convinced the man would explode if Max startled him.

"Did you see her skin change at the Fair?" said Max.

"Yeah. And?"

"When things aren't going her way, the real Camilla comes out, not the perfect person she kills to look like. She can't help it. We're the only ones who know."

"You mean," said Kevin, "once we're gone, she can keep fooling everyone?"

"Yup. Dad and Bernard have no leads. They suspect nothing. With us out of the way, Camilla can do whatever she wants; be whomever she wants. She's been getting away with it so far, man."

"So, what do we do now?"

Max pondered their dilemma. No answers entered his mind.

Maxine had disappeared. She was the only one with any information that could help them.

Max's back throbbed. His stomach burned, as did his eyes. Oddly, he felt nothing from his arm. It was the one body part that didn't hurt.

He knew he'd have to fight when the time came.

N N N

CRASH!

Something slammed down on the loft's wooden floor, directly over Max.

WHAMP!

The side door slid back open. Raging wind rushed in, blasting a cloud of straw and dirt into the air. André screamed when Kevin reacted by jumping on him, forcing him head-first into the spreader's tire. The two boys crumbled into a heap on the floor, a ball of flailing arms and legs.

"Could you both shut up?" said Max.

The noise overhead and the roar from the open door were not what concerned Max. Behind him he heard heavy, labored breathing. He felt a hot breath on his neck. There were no entrances in the rear of the barn where it backed into the hillside. No windows. No doors. Just a stack of hay and straw against the cement wall.

The stud, Chichester, was not in his stall, which was also behind them.

Clamoring continued to prance along the wall to her stall at the front of the barn.

Max had a feeling he shouldn't turn around. His feet became one with the cement floor.

André and Kevin stopped moving altogether. Max saw them shivering. They stared at him, sensing the same presence behind them.

Whatever it was, it suddenly stopped making its horrible noise. The barn fell silent. Even the wind seemed to cease its never-ending tirade.

"Like I said…"

Max heard a familiar, terrible voice echo from behind. It was slick and sophisticated, and very sure of itself. "Little boys are only good for—one—thing—"

Max felt his skin and bones go numb. His feet became limp. He thought he could fall right over. He couldn't sense the floor.

"Oh, please don't hurt us —" he began to say, but what happened next happened fast.

Max felt an intensely cold rush of air against his backside. A scream from André followed it. As Max turned toward his friends, faster than his eyes could focus, André vanished, together with the thing behind them.

"Camilla!"

Max screamed at the same moment Kevin yelled, "The librarian —"

As if flooding into the barn from a large, metal drainage pipe, the voice of Camilla reverberated all around them. Max had climbed through such pipes in the past. They were always full of slime, stinking debris, and spiders. Max decided such a place was perfect for someone like Camilla, regardless of how Maxine defended her.

Camilla droned on. "One down, pass it around ... three, four, outside your door..."

Another torrent of wind broke the silence, rushing through the side door. This time, instead of straw and dirt blowing into the barn, Max and Kevin—both with enormous eyes—witnessed something dark enter the barn's light.

A massive, smoky shadow blocked the barn's wooden walls to the ceiling overhead. It morphed in and out of the distinct shapes of Melinda Waters, the ghost from the mirror, and a giant, dark orb that resembled the dead, mutilated pig.

Another pulsating mass of body parts joined the shadow. Max knew they had to be those from the dead body—Camilla's murdered sister.

Smaller globs of distorted light zigged and zagged between the ghosts. The whole spectacle remained stationary in front of the running tractor.

Kevin rubbed his eyes. "I am not seeing this, no way. It's not real, man."

"She's playing tricks on us," said Max. "Maxine said when she's around, strange things start to happen."

"Yeah?" said Kevin. "Where's Maxine? Where's André?" He choked when they both witnessed the next transformation from the things in from of them.

Maxine Waters looked like she melted into the body of the ghost from the mirror. They, in turn, joined with the pig, and the swirling, ghostly body parts. The entire mass before them grew into a monstrous, swirling black phantom with a single, quivering yellow eye. It hovered in the center of the barn, from floor to ceiling. It stared hungrily at the two boys.

Kevin tried to scream but only forced out a gurgle.

Max felt himself hyperventilate as his heart pounded in his chest. The hairs on his neck were too frightened to show themselves by standing up.

Camilla's amplified laugh shook the walls. She was in the loft. Max had no clue what happened to André. Camilla probably held him as bait.

The massive, pulsating phantom in front blocked the only way in or out of the barn.

Max felt sick too. Each minute he spent hiding from Camilla, he felt worse. His vision fluctuated. His abdomen felt like swelled, and it throbbed in pain. His arm was useless in its cast, making his ability to defend himself extremely difficult. At the very least, he had to protect Kevin, who was at the barn because of Max's stupid decision to uncover the truth.

Max decided he should never have gone into that old, red barn. He should never have tried to do the police's work for them.

DEFEAT

Death was certain for Max, that he knew.

As he stood there, trapped with Kevin by his side, Maxine returned. She didn't hesitate to show them what she could do.

"Maxine!" Max called her name.

Maxine stood at the front of the running tractor with the towering phantom before her.

"Oh, man," said Kevin. He gasped. "What is she doing?"

Max thought the same thing.

While Maxine still wore her work clothes, two things about her changed dramatically. Her pale white skin became almost translucent, so much so Max could see the different colored arteries and veins running beneath the flesh on her face and neck. Her eyes, no longer dark brown, glowed a bright blue, like little lightbulbs.

When she turned toward Max and slightly parted her lips, he swore he saw razor-sharp teeth. He couldn't be sure, his vision also deteriorated minute by minute.

Maxine looked like Max's vision on the bridge.

Maxine climbed to the driver seat atop the tractor. She balanced on her dark brown work boots, spreading her arms wide, facing the massively expanding phantom. Its shadowy mouth opened. Louder than the wind roaring outside, and the screaming of André overhead in the loft, Maxine let out a shrieking yell that forced Max to cringe.

Kevin covered his ears.

Maxine lunged at the phantom.

Max screamed, "No, Maxine, no!"

Kevin said nothing. All color had bled from his face.

Maxine waited for no one. She made that clear to Max when she paraded the "morgue break-in team" those many nights ago through the fog and chaotic yards of Pine Plains.

"I said you can't have them!" Maxine raged as Max had never seen. She leaped and hurled herself through the air.

While the phantom was ghostly, with no real physical body, Maxine managed to clamp onto it with her arms and legs spread, like a rock climber. She was eye to eye with the monster. Its body pulsated and bulged.

"Oh, my God!" said Kevin.

Max reached over the filthy edge of the manure spreader. Rather than wait, he snatched one of several sharp pitchforks. He handed one to Kevin and grabbed a second one for himself.

"She's not doing this alone." Max felt anger well up inside himself. "We're on our own, Kevin," said Max. "No one is coming to help us."

Kevin gave Max a wild look. "W-what are we supposed to do against THAT?" He looked in horror at the phantom, which had doubled in size.

Max also noticed a girl's shouting had joined the screaming from André upstairs. Then it too stopped.

"There's someone else in the barn ... upstairs!" said Max.

He didn't know what to do. André needed their help, but the thing in front of them blocked all the exits from the barn.

"That's not her," said Max, yelling to Maxine.

Max believed the thing in front of them was a decoy. While he and Kevin focused on the phantom, André was in danger.

Maxine ripped and tore at the monstrous phantom with her fingers and teeth. She had become a monster herself. Now Max knew what she had been hiding from him.

Maxine wouldn't hurt Max or Kevin. She fought to save them from the many ghosts that turned into the towering form in front of them.

Max yelled. With his free arm, he ran toward the monster. He threw his pitchfork like a spear as close to its eye as possible.

Kevin screamed from behind him and did the same.

The pitchforks flew through the phantom as if it were smoke. They crashed to the floor on the other side, in front of Clamoring. The horse to reared up, kicking the inside walls of her stall.

"I got this," said Maxine. She gave Max and Kevin a glance. "Get upstairs. Save André!" She turned her head back to the phantom and planted her teeth in it.

What happened next gave Max the room he needed to run by the monster. Maxine began to draw the phantom into herself. The apparition shrank before their eyes. Enough space opened by the tractor for the two boys to escape.

Max took another pitchfork. He grabbed Kevin hard by the hand and jerked him along the stalls and out the side door as the monster whaled and lurched.

"What about her?" said Kevin, out of breath. They ran from the barn, not looking back.

N N N

Max ran up the hill through the drenching rain and howling wind. He was freaked out but didn't look back.

Kevin stopped talking and followed Max up along the grassy hill to the side of the barn's loft. What they found at the entrance, hanging from the top of the slightly parted doors, sent a fresh wave of fear through them.

"Look!" said Kevin.

Above them, five new dolls hung from the sliding doors' track. Pieces of twine from hay bales had been tied together. Each doll hung just above their heads from their signature hangman's knots. One of them, with no hair, had blood leaking from its fabric heart and coursing down its leg.

A scream rang out.

Max forced the doors apart and lunged inside the loft. Kevin followed him in, narrowly missing the doors as they slammed shut behind him, guided by some invisible hand. He skidded on the loose straw covering the old, wooden floor.

Several dim lightbulbs shined from the high ceiling, revealing the length of the hay elevator. Colonies of spiders in ancient, dust-choked webs littered the rafters. Mounds of loose hay and straw had been gathered up in front of the towering wall of freshly placed bales from a recent delivery, perfectly stacked by Luke.

Luke was still in the barn.

"Oh, my god. Luke!" said Max.

Luke's hands had been skillfully bound with leather shanks. He hung from the metal elevator overhead, motionless. His head dangled in front of his overalls.

Max didn't notice any blood.

"What did you do to Luke?" Max yelled into the depths of the loft.

"Oh, man, this is terrible," said Kevin. He looked around the barn. "I don't see anyone else, maybe —"

Someone cried, hidden by the dim light along the loft's wall. Max had a hard time seeing, but three dark forms—one much taller than the others—stood close enough for him to make out a scent he had smelled before. It made his skin tingle, and his hands went numb.

"Who is it?" said Kevin, whispering.

"It's her. She has them."

"You mean, the librarian?"

"Yup. She has André, and someone else —"

Growling overwhelmed the crashing wind outside and the rain on the roof as the tallest figure moved. It held its oddly long arms out to its sides, grasping what Max guessed were the collars of André—and someone else. He still couldn't get a good look.

"As I said, little boys are only good for one thing..."

Camilla's voice echoed through the loft. The unmistakable scent of birch trees lingered on the air surrounding her, as though she had rubbed them all over herself. Max didn't know how. The overflowing creek had destroyed the red barn, and the trees were inaccessible. He didn't care. He held a pitchfork out in front of him while Kevin, too scared to act, stammered and quaked where he stood.

"I—I'm not afraid of you," said Max.

"You should be!" said Camilla. She snapped. "I can do what I want, to whomever I want. Neither you, not your father, or anyone in this town, can do a thing about it." She laughed. "You have no idea, you little brat. In Pine Plains, I'm the least of your worries. You just had to poke your sorry little nose where it didn't belong. So, now, I need to clean up your mess."

"I just want my friends —"

"Your friends?" said Camilla. "Your friends should have known better than to listen to you, dear, little Max." Her words ended with hissing. She chuckled. "Everyone has a use. Little boys for their mischief and their foolish curiosity. Little girls for their intelligence and beauty."

The dark figure of Camilla turned toward Luke. "And strappin' young men, like this beauty here, for their strength."

Kevin managed a pitiful whine through his running nose. "Wha— what you goin' da' d—do to us?"

Camilla immediately dropped the bodies of André and—to Max's horror, and disbelief—Bethany Waters, while entering the light. The kids hit the wooden floor. André groaned, his arms barely moving, but moving none the less, which Max was glad to see.

Bethany had no marks on her. She was covered in loose straw and dirt from the floor. Max noticed her chest rise and fall. Camilla had given her something to knock her out.

She's still alive, thought Max.

Camilla knew his thoughts. "Not for long," she said. She lumbered forward. The dim light hid nothing else. She was somewhere between the librarian they all knew, and the beast that had almost killed him that night in his shed.

Max couldn't believe it was Camilla. The thing in front of him clasped its hands in delight. It had them cornered. The doors were shut tight behind them. Luke, André, and Bethany had been disabled and were of no use.

Kevin bawled at the sight of her and fell to his knees.

Maxine fought for them down below.

Max remembered what Maxine had said: "Camilla is still flesh and bone." How Camilla managed to place the dead body, and pig, in the old red barn was still a mystery.

What lingered in his mind were Maxine's words: "She can be stopped."

Camilla loomed over Max, stalling. Her hairy, un-clothed body no longer resembled that of an educated, well-dressed woman from New York City. She seemed more like a demented, furry, white monster.

Maybe Big Foot? Thought Max. *Possibly some form of a werewolf from ancient Europe? Perhaps even a demon?*

Regardless, she was hideous. Two small tusks jutted up from her lower jaw. Her bright, yellow eyes shined in the darkness.

One thing Max was sure of: Camilla had miscalculated what she saw in Max.

Her entire plan seemed based on scaring them. After all, what kid wouldn't buckle when faced with a beast much more massive than themselves, with rows of razor-sharp teeth, growling and hissing, and baring claws that could rip them in half in seconds? Whatever ability she used to create the phantom was just another way to distract her pray while she moved in for the final kill.

Beyond Camilla, against the wall, light shined up from one of the holes used to drop hay to the horses below. It wasn't more than fifty feet away. Based on its location, it was directly over Clamoring.

Max whispered to Kevin. "I want you to run," —he pointed to the hole— "as fast as you can. Jump over the hole."

"What? Uh…"

"Just do it." Kevin shook his head, ok, and Max yelled, "Now!"

Kevin sprang forward toward the hole. As Max planned, Camilla did the same. Fortunately for Kevin, the beast, sure of herself, moved a bit slow.

Max sprinted forward behind her, holding the pitchfork with one hand. It was his opportunity to prove himself. Despite his broken arm, and despite missing out on football season, he used every drop of rage in him and directed it toward Camilla.

Max muscled forward and lunged on top of her. Kevin had jumped the square opening just in time, plastering himself between two beams, ducking down and covering his head. As Max landed on Camilla's back, she stumbled. The two of them fell through the opening in the floor and into the stall below.

Camilla shrieked, "You vile little...."

Kevin heard something that rivaled the clamor from the storm outside. André heard it too because he lifted his head off the floor and locked eyes with Kevin. Even Bethany began to twitch as the shuddering from the floor jostled her awake.

✁ ✁ ✁

Clamoring continued to kick everything in her stall, including the beast that fell through the hole.

Max had crumbled in a heap in the corner of the horse's stall and watched as Camilla and Clamoring battled. He held his stomach and his broken arm. The pain was intense.

As the beast circled one way—with the pitchfork lodged deep in her back—Clamoring countered and turned. The horse reared up and kicked her with both back legs. Camilla couldn't get away, not until the stall door slid open.

Still kicking, Clamoring ran from the stall and galloped toward the front door, which was locked. She stopped and panted from the excessive bout of kicking, snorting and circling as Camilla stumbled out into the aisle.

The beast didn't look back at Max. It would have had been the perfect opportunity for her to finish him off. Max knew he was in bad shape. He wouldn't have the strength to fight her off.

Max kept his mouth shut.

The beast hitched and jerked her way out in front of the tractor. She stumbled over the two pitchforks Max and Kevin had thrown earlier. Angry, she kicked them aside. She continued to follow the horse's movements.

Camilla drew another sign in front of her just as she did at the fair before Max's pumpkins deflated. Before she could complete it, Max watched as Maxine silently sprang from the tractor. Just as Max had, Maxine used her full force to attack the beast.

"I said," —Maxine screamed, while running by the door— "I won't … let you … have them…."

Max witnessed Camilla being thrown across the barn's concrete floor by Maxine. Next, he heard Clamoring neigh and grunt. With a high-pitched whinny, the horse kicked Camilla so hard the beast flew back toward the tractor. Her monstrous body flashed across the entrance to the stall with Maxine quickly following.

Max heard another loud thud—the sound of the tractor's manure spreader revving to life.

Camilla screamed an inhuman scream that Max would never get out of his head. He didn't have to guess what happened to her. He had used the spreader enough to picture Camilla being swept into its blades and shot out the back. The screaming stopped. A final rustling THUMP gave up her position in the bales of straw and hay stacked along the barn's rear wall.

Max managed to twist onto his knees and climb to his feet.

Maxine appeared in the doorway to the stall.

Max looked at her and said, "Thank you," while stumbling forward.

His eyes swam.

His gut was on fire.

His arm had been re-broken in its soggy cast.

"You did great," said Maxine, tenderly placing her arm around Max and helping him from the stall. "You saved several people today. I'm sorry she did this. I never realized —" Maxine broke down in tears.

Max saw that she looked like her old self again. He hesitated to bring up what he had seen her do, figuring it would be best to wait another day.

"It's ok," said Max. "We had no choice."

"I know." Maxine cried.

Maxine turned around, realizing the tractor was still running. She left Max standing there and walked to the tractor to turn it off. She splashed through a massive, oily-looking puddle on her way, not seeing the danger behind Max.

Before Max had time to react, Clamoring charged. The horse turned and kicked him. Both of her rear hooved feet contacted his chest and his head.

Max flew backward, landing on the solid cement floor. He saw the sun's rays pierce the door and windows. Maxine raced toward him with André, Kevin, and Bethany stumbling behind her.

The storm ended as fast as it had started.

Max's vision went blank.

A New Day

Morning arrived on another cold Sunday. The sun's rays bounced off the far wall of Max's hospital room. It illuminated several dozen colored vases stuffed with fragrant evergreens, red roses and holly, limp red and green balloons on strings, teddy bears (one dressed as Santa in a football jersey and sitting on an open card from Coach Charlie), and boxes of mostly-eaten dark chocolates. Machines beeped and chirped, feeding off Max from wires glued to his skin.

The smell of anesthetic and fresh plastic-filled his nose.

Max didn't see any of it right away. The room was dark when he woke up. Black as midnight during a new moon. He couldn't move his eyelids. Pressure from thick padding weighed down by adhesive tape sealed them shut. His eyes felt tired, dry as sand, and they stung.

He felt weak and could hardly move. A searing pain traced his abdomen from one side to the next. His broken arm had been placed in a suspended sling, hovering next to him, well off the bed. Two sounds signaled that he had awakened: Max smacking his dry, cracked lips, and a sudden low, pulsating alarm just annoying enough no one could ignore it.

Max heard a voice. "Mr. Max, are you awake, sweetie?" If he didn't know better, he awoke in the presence of Nurse Carver somewhere deep within Sharron Hospital.

Another voice, excited but groggy, rang out behind her.

"Oh, wow, is he awake?"

"Yes," said Nurse Carver, "he's coming out of it now, it's a miracle."

"Oh, I better call his parents ... and my mom!"

Max listened, regaining consciousness.

"It's been so sweet of you to be here all weekend, Carmen," said Nurse Carver on the other side of the room.

Max remembered Carmen. He had last seen her at the Harvest Fair. They had walked in the lawn together discussing —

Max's body bolted upright, tensing the wires connected to him. His chest heaved. His heart pounded. The machines chirped rapidly. Several buzzers blared. Something poked him in his abdomen. He noticed a tube ran down the side of the bed. A thick needle, piercing the vein in his hand, pinched when he flexed his fingers.

Something even stranger seemed to be attached to him, below his waist, where nothing should be.

"Doctor!" Nurse Carver's soft-soled shoes swept across the floor. She poked her head through the door, calling for help.

Carmen appeared at Max's side, he felt the heat of her hand on his arm. She pressed his hand between hers and squeezed.

"It's ok, Max. Shush, settle down, everything is going to be all right." Carmen tried to soothe him. She sounded tearfully happy.

Max fell back into the fluffy bed. He worked to gain control of his breathing but gasped when he spoke.

"Is she... Is she still here? Did she get away?"

Carmen knew what he meant. After another funeral (this one for the farmworker, Luke), a lengthy investigation with few answers, and some new changes in the town of Pine Plains, she didn't want to overwhelm him with too much information. Facts were the responsibility of his parents. They would tell him when the time was right. Carmen pressed his hand between hers and waited for the doctor to arrive.

Nurse Carver parted Max's gown and checked him over with her stethoscope.

"It's ok. It's over," said Carmen.

Nurse Carver whispered for Carmen to make her calls.

Carmen let go of Max's hand and took her phone out into the hallway. Max heard her high-pitched voice call his parents first. He heard her confirm with, "Twenty minutes? You're welcome, Mrs. Hunter." She hung up and called her mother.

Max settled down and let the nurse do her job.

Doctor Devlish arrived shortly after.

"How are you feeling, buddy?" said the doctor. His cold, gloved hands inspected under Max's gown, pressing on his abdomen. He peeled back something that felt like tape and gauze.

Max heard Carmen in the doorway.

"Can I observe, sir?" she said.

Doctor Devlish giggled, saying, "Not till you're a lot older, honey. But thank you."

"I'm twelve, sir. I'm not a kid anymore," said Carmen with a huff. "I'm planning on being a doctor someday, like my mom."

Max sighed, happy Carmen wasn't going to see under his gown. His spirits were higher knowing she was in his hospital room when he woke up. He didn't mind her holding his hand either.

"Sir," said Max. His throat was dry, and he had to work at talking. "I'm not sure how I feel. Something's up with my eyes, and my chest hurts." He paused and wiggled the fingers sticking out of his cast. "I'm guessing I broke my arm again."

The doctor grunted. The grunt sounded judgmental.

"Your arm was the easiest part of all this, young man, and ready to lose the cast," said Doctor Devlish. "Fixing your eyes, and with your liver failing ... well, it was what we call touch-and-go for a while."

"A miracle, if you ask me," said Nurse Carver. She fiddled with machines. It sounded like she scribbled on paper with a pencil. "Can't believe she ... of all people ... was the only match."

"What are you talking about?" said Max.

The room grew quiet. Doctor Devlish excused himself and walked to the doorway with the nurse.

"We need Doctor James in here, asap, to examine the new liver," said Devlish. "And, get his eye surgeon, Doctor Finn I think the name is, and that brain specialist. Blood. Urine. Catheter. Feeding tube, you know. I bet he's hungry."

"I'll assemble the whole team," said Nurse Carver.

Carmen said nothing until she arrived back at Max's bedside.

"See, it's all going to be just fine!" Her voice trembled, alerting Max. "They just need to examine you since you've been out of it for a while —"

"How long?" Max managed to speak before coughing.

"Man, you really are out of it," said Carmen. "You've been asleep since getting kicked by that horse..." Carmen held his hand again. "Christmas is in a week."

Max couldn't manage a "What!" or an "OMG!" though the words formed in his head. His throat was gummy. Only a few gurgles came out. He cleared his throat and swallowed.

"I think I need some Kool-Aid."

ᴎ ᴎ ᴎ

Before Max had a chance to count how many tubes were plugged into him—one where nothing should ever be; he felt that one with no effort at all—his parents arrived. Riley rushed through the door first. She hopped on the doctor's low, rolling chair, and sailed up to his bedside.

"Careful, sweetie," said Nurse Carver, snatching up a yellow fluid-filled tube in Riley's path.

Riley laughed regardless and planted her elbows on the armrest near Max's broken arm. She leaned over and kissed him on the face.

"I knew you'd be ok," she said. "My little brother is one bad as—"

"That's enough!"

Joe squeezed through the door, as eager as Riley to see his brother. Riley and Joe got as close as possible to Max without disturbing any of his equipment.

Beth emerged from the doorway with Ace on her heels. Max's parents briskly walked to his other bedside, both with tears in their eyes.

"You almost had us there, chump," said Ace. He jostled Max's leg.

"But you're back now," said Beth, wiping her cheeks with a tissue. "That's what matters."

Max didn't hold back either. He didn't need to act now that his family stood over him. He couldn't see them through his bandaged eyes but began crying. His face turned bright red, his nose gushed.

Unable to wipe his nose, Riley reached over with a tissue and blotted it for him. Max looked toward her and cried harder. Nurse Carver reached for his face, inspecting his bandages.

"Now, now, be careful, honey… Watch those eyes, don't make too much of a mess," said the nurse.

"I'm s—sorry." Max blundered through his words. "It's all my fault. I thought you were going to d—die, Riley."

Joe smiled.

"It was amazing, man. The same day it stormed we thought Riley was a goner, but she woke up. The doctors checked everything. It was like she never had sepsis at all."

"We still can't figure it out," said Max's mom. She looked at Riley with love in her teary eyes.

"Carmen, come over here," said Riley. Carmen had kept her distance while Max's family talked to him. She eased over to Max's bed and stood next to Riley.

"Carmen's been here a lot, looking out for you," said Riley. She winked at Carmen. A few giggles erupted from her mouth. Max didn't see it. Carmen jabbed her in the side with her elbow but smiled.

"And we have a surprise for you," said Beth.

Joe laughed. "It's a big one!"

"I suppose so," said Riley, grumbling.

Ace walked to the door, looked out into the hallway, and flicked his index finger. "Maxine? Come in here, please."

◢ ◢ ◢

Maxine poked her face into the ICU's doorway, sheepishly looking at Max, unsure how he would respond. His face remained covered in bandages.

Max held his breath, shocked she was allowed in the room. A flood of memories poured through him. He stopped crying while hearing her thick, hard-soled boots walk across the tiled floor. He had no way of knowing if anything about her had changed.

"Are you ... different?" said Max. He didn't know what else to say. Fear spilled over him, not knowing who knew what. He had no memory of events following that day in the barn.

"Same old Maxine we all know and love," said Joe

Love? Thought Max. It was strange for Joe to say such a thing.

"Yup," said Riley, "black, black, and blacker. You can't tell her from the cow when she's down there milking her."

"What?" said Max.

"Well," said Riley, "she pulls it off."

Why would Maxine be milking a cow?

Maxine arrived at Max's bedside. Like Carmen, she rubbed his arm to let him know. She felt warm. Max was glad. According to Joe and Riley, she still looked like a goth, nothing like the raging monster Max saw fighting her aunt.

"Oh, man," said Max. He gasped. "Those ghosts..." He took a deep breath and asked Maxine, "Why are you milking a cow?"

Joe and Riley both chuckled. Max heard his mother nibble on a fingernail, the sound was oddly deafening for something so small.

However, it was his dad who spoke up, and not in his usual police-business tone.

"She lives with us now," said Ace.

"What? How —"

"It seems after her aunt did all those terrible things, Dallas had a breakdown and had to take some time away. She's back in Europe for now. We're Maxine's legal guardians, kiddo."

Max's lungs clenched.

Maxine rubbed his arm vigorously. Max felt her anxiety.

"She's amazing around the farm," said Joe. "Got your eggs all under control. Her room's right next to yours."

Max didn't know what to say. He was happy that everyone seemed ok. His family had suddenly grown. He was excited to know that Carmen had spent so much time with him while he slept.

Riley being healed was, indeed, a miracle.

Max knew that Camilla was no longer a threat. The murders in Pine Plains were at an end.

But Max felt an uneasiness in the room. A communal thought remained unspoken. A moment of silence ensued until he broke it by coughing.

Max did better, more energetic, more awake. He needed to pee badly but wanted the thing down there removed so he could go on his own.

"Folks, we really need to see his parents now," said Nurse Carver. "We're going to begin disconnecting Max from these machines. Everyone needs to leave."

Max, unable to see, and immobile in the bed, had a question. The nurse had said something long before his family showed up that baffled him.

"Nurse," said Max. All eyes turned to him. His family ceased talking. "I'm confused."

"What is it, dear?" said Nurse Carver.

"I heard you say something to the doctor earlier... I think it was something like, 'I can't believe she was the exact match.'" No one spoke. Nurse Carver groaned a little. "What did you mean by that? Who was an exact match for what?"

Joe, like a good older brother, wanting so see Max's reaction, giggled, and began to talk.

"Man, you still don't know?" said Joe.

"Joe, let him rest," said Ace. "It's not the time for this —"

"But he deserves to know, Dad. It's why he's even alive. Man..."

"Know what?" said Max. His heart beat faster. "Seriously, I want to know. What's up with me? Is something wrong?"

Max heard muttering between the nurse and Max's parents as they stepped away toward the corner of the room. He heard words like, "I don't want to jar him," "...high blood pressure," and "not out of the woods..."

"Just tell me already," said Max, loud enough to get their attention. "I feel fine, really."

"I suppose he can know," said Ace. "He's a strong boy. He can handle it. Besides, he'll have to know sooner or later, might as well be now."

A devious look spread over Riley's face.

"I think Maxine should tell him."

For the first time, Max felt Maxine's hand (still cupped to his arm), sweat.

"Max," said Maxine. She gripped his arm a little tighter. "I'm so happy your parents took me in after the mess Camilla made. Your family's been so good to me. You're so blessed." She hesitated.

"Go ahead," said Beth. "It's ok."

Maxine released her grip, telling Max what happened.

"I don't blame you if you're mad at me, Max."

"I'm not mad at you. Why would I be mad? This happened to you, too," said Max. He wanted to reassure her, but the tension in the room told him he was about to learn something he'd hate. He was glad he couldn't see their faces.

Better off staring into nothingness while being handed lousy news, he thought.

"Well, Max, you were badly hurt when Clamoring kicked you. It seems you had also gotten an infection from the dirty water in the stream."

"Your liver gave out," said Beth, interrupting.

"That horse kicked you in the head too, man… Ruined your eyes," said Joe.

Maxine continued without looking at Max.

"Well, no one was a match for your blood type, but —"

Joe loved interrupting, and blurted out, "The librarian died. She was the only one with your exact blood type. How crazy is that! Luke died too, but he was too fit. Definitely not a match for you."

"Cut it out, Joe," said Ace. He looked at Max, who also turned his sightless eyes in his father's direction. "What they're trying to say is Maxine's aunt was an exact match for you. She happened to have an organ donor card."

"What do you mean?" said Max. His voice began to shake. "What did you do?"

Ace cleared his throat and spoke. "Your mom and I agreed to the transplants. It was the only thing to do. We had no time."

"You mean…"

"Yes, you received Camilla's liver and her eyes, and several blood transfusions," said Ace.

Max heard him tear up. Beth and Nurse Carver huffed, muffling their crying with their hands. It seemed Max didn't need his eyes at that moment. He heard everything. The sounds painted a bold, colorful picture of what had happened.

Ace muttered, unlike the self-assured sheriff he customarily portrayed.

"It seems, Ms. Fox's death also saved your life."

"A miracle, if you ask me," said nurse Carver under her breath. "Just amazing."

"Yes, it is a miracle," said Beth, echoing the nurse.

Max half-screamed, half-choked. "What?" He felt the air bleed from his lungs.

The machines beeped erratically. More buzzers sounded.

Carmen joined Maxine. Both held onto Max's arm for comfort.

N N N

Max Hunter spent the rest of his day probed by specialists.

The doctors tested his new liver and blood. They removed all manner of tubes, hoses and wires from his body.

He even got to pee on his own.

The doctors had not yet unwrapped Max's eyes. He waited in the dark for the eye specialist who continued to call in, late leaving his other practice in Yonkers.

The Hunter family had returned home after a couple of hours visiting, telling him some friends would be over to visit later in the afternoon.

Max received the news he would spend one more day in the ICU. He would spend several more days recovering in a private room while the doctors made sure he was strong enough to return home.

He might even return home before Christmas Eve, the one thing he focused on the most.

He also thought he might ask Carmen to go to a movie with him.

Close to evening, the eye specialist finally arrived. The man entered Max's room with a crowd of interns. Max heard them chatter to each other, excited to see a new set of transplanted eyes.

Behind them, Max's friends—André, Kevin, Bethany, and Carmen—poked their faces in. He had only seen Carmen since waking up and longed to find out how the others were doing. They waved at Max and protested as Nurse Carver forced them down the hallway to wait in the waiting room.

The doctor's stiff dress shoes clapped across the floor as the group entered his room. The man stopped at Max's bed.

"So, young man, let's see what we have here," said the doctor. He undressed Max's eyes, unwinding a spool of crusty gauze.

Max wanted to know more about the doctor. Talking calmed him down.

"So, what's your name, doc?" said Max.

The man chuckled. "Doctor Finn, young man. From Yonkers."

Max knew he heard that name before. He had to think hard. None of his friends had that last name. He didn't know anyone on the police force with it.

"Finn," he grumbled to himself, puzzled.

The doctor finished removing the gauze and began to toy with the thick pads covering Max's eyes. Days of moisture—from fluids that oozed from his eyes, and crying—made the pads stick to his face. The doctor instructed the students watching his procedure, reminding them to be "client-centered" and to "take their time."

"I know!" said Max, unable to contain himself.

Doctor Finn startled and stopped for a moment. "Know what?"

"Dallas had the same name, Finn—Dallas Finn. She was our Biology teacher."

"Fascinating," said the doctor. He dismissed Max and turned to his students. "Be extra careful when patients are this excited. Any wrong moves can lead to damage of the localized tissues, resulting in a longer recovery time."

"Didn't you hear me?" said Max.

"Just hold still, son, we're almost there…"

Doctor Finn carefully removed the two pads, revealing Max's messy, yet well-healed eyes. Max felt the light in the room hit him. A yellowish blaze overtook his vision. His eyelids were closed, forcing the doctor to unstick them. They were cakey and crusted with dried, smelly chunks.

The procedure took a few minutes. When Max was instructed to carefully, and very slowly, open his eyes, his reaction was quite different than that of the others in the room.

"Look at those beauties," said Doctor Finn, proud of his work. "Corneas to die for. He's a lucky boy."

The fresh, young interns gasped.

Doctor Finn patted Max on the shoulder and said, "Young boys like you, my friend, might normally be good for one thing, like sports, but," —he paused and smiled— "with those eyes, you'll be able to do anything you want. You're one lucky boy."

Max gasped. He'd heard that before.

A man with a round face and blond hair stood over him. Round, black-framed glasses rested on his nose. He wore a blue shirt cinched with a yellow silk tie and a crisp white lab coat with his name—Jules Finn, MD—sewn over the check pocket. He stared Max in the face, scanning his excellent work.

When Max blinked, as instructed by the doctor, he focused. Max lost his breath.

Dallas Finn seemed to loom over him in shades of black, gray, and white—smiling. Max blinked again, and the teacher vanished.

"Like I said," said the doctor, "anything." He winked at Max, and walked away with the interns, discussing preventative care for their young patient.

ᚾ ᚾ ᚾ

The room grew silent once again.

Carmen entered, followed by Bethany, Kevin, and André. They stomped and shoving each other in excitement. They almost crashed into his bed. Carmen pushed her way through and held his hand.

Max smiled and told them what he remembered.

Each one interrupted with their own experiences on that stormy day at the Rojan Horse Farm.

André had been next on Camilla's list of victims. Max had arrived with Kevin just in time to distract her.

Bethany said she had figured out the librarian had something to do with the murders and feared for Max's life. After seeing Camilla's red Jeep race past the falling tree on the day of the storm (by this time, everyone knew to whom the Jeep belonged), she knew Max might be in trouble. She made sure she had access to the judge's bike to check on him.

Unfortunately, Bethany was also no match for Camilla. The school's evil librarian had made another sign in the air with her finger, and Bethany had fainted.

Carmen had seen nothing. Her mother was away with some friends in Kingston, getting a fresh tattoo from some guy named Harvey Duke. She left Carmen at home to look after the house but had left Duke's business card in case Carmen had to call her.

None of the kids told the authorities what they had really witnessed at the barn that day. A simple explanation of how Camilla had attacked them in the barn, together with doll-making evidence in the librarian's office, ensured the librarian was blamed for the murders. Her dolls had hair from each of the victims stuffed inside them.

"When they searched Maxine's house, they found nothing," said Carmen. "They looked everywhere, even the basement. Dallas's schedule showed Dallas had nothing to do with the murders." She thought for a moment. "It seems Dallas was always with that tattoo artist, Harvey Duke, when something happened. Or in school."

"Don't you remember, Carmen?" said Max. "That Harvey Duke name was on the leg in the morgue."

"You're right," said Carmen, surprised she had forgotten. "Do you think there's a link?"

Bethany chimed in. "So, you were the ones who broke into the morgue? You should have brought me along. You better include me next time. You better!"

Max smiled and nodded his head, yes. Carmen smiled too. After Bethany showed how much she cared (biking to the farm in the violent storm), how could Max not like her?

"Let's talk more about this after Christmas, ok?" said Max.

"Yeah, man, you need to get better," said Kevin. "Coach Charlie, and even that jerk Tony, was talking about needing you on the football team next year. Tony's totally eager to break you in, bro. He's got it in for you. Oh, and," —Kevin pulled a seed packet out of his back pocket and handed it to Max— "this is for you." Max looked at the pack. It read: Wallace Whoppers Giant Pumpkin Seeds. Kevin pointed at the packet. "Maybe you can outdo yourself next year. These are supposed to be the best."

"And guess what," said André. "I'm staying longer. Through next summer, at least."

Max relaxed. His friends were alive and seemed just as determined as he was.

He looked forward to the holiday, hoping to be home in time for Christmas with his family and his fur-babies, the four pugs. Now that Maxine lived with them, life would never be the same—indeed, it would prove to be more interesting.

He knew he couldn't tell Riley or Joe his secret. Not yet.

Having Maxine around meant there'd be more of them to go sledding. Max would have more help on the farm. But he would need to keep an eye on Joe, who had ogled Maxine in school.

Another thought dawned on Max while he thought about his growing family. He gasped from a rush of disappointment, mumbling under his breath, "That means Maxine is like ... a sister now." He thought about Joe's interest in the girl, and his own. Max cringed, and groaned, "Gross..." talking to himself in the dimming light. "Maybe having another sister will make it easier."

"Did you say something, Max?" said Carmen.

Max looked up at Carmen and the others, not realizing he had drifted off into his private thoughts. He cracked a smile.

"I've got a lot to think about, is all," said Max.

Another thought flashed through his mind. Maxine had mentioned she knew of another building Max could use as a hangout. Max intended on hiking there over the holiday. He decided he'd use the time to get to know Maxine better. He would treat her as a sister. Only a sister.

Nurse Carver finally entered the room and asked the kids to leave. The time had come for Max to rest. The group waved as they meandered out of the hospital room. Before the door closed, Carmen ran back to Max's bedside and, without warning, planted a kiss on his cheek. She giggled and ran off, having accomplished one of her own goals.

Max Hunter closed his new eyes. His mind faded. He dreamed he stared from a mirror on a wall at the end of a long hallway. At the end of the hall his friends and his family looked back at him, smiling, but only for a moment. They too faded.

Tony, Max's nemesis, stared back at him. The boy grinned. His eyes sparkled. Tony punched one hand with a fist, inviting Max to fight. Coach Charlie Wise stood behind Tony, egging him on. Sheriff Ace Hunter stood off to the side with his arms crossed, waiting for Max to make his move.

Darkness overtook Max. He grumbled before falling into a deep sleep, "Bring it on."

The End

COMING Fall 2020

Mischievous Max – Book Two

Look for the next installment of **Mischievous Max,** due Fall 2020!

Maximillian (Max) Hunter has the eyes, the liver, and the blood of the evil beast Camilla running through his veins. Maxine, his second sister, has a lot of explaining to do now that his family life has changed. The town he thought he knew so well is leaking its secrets faster than the flood that almost took his life.

Are you interested in BETA READING? Contact us from our contact form on **www.BeauDurand.com** for a chance to win one of one-hundred beta reading opportunities and an advanced, free copy of the next Mischievous Max novel!

Visit our web site: www.BeauDurand.com for new novels, contests, and more. Twitter @realbeaudurand, Facebook @realbeaudurand

Follow developments with Max Hunter and the Mischievous Max series at www.MischievousMax.com!

Photo © Durand Publishing

Beau Durand

Beau is the author of the Mischievous Max series, the Nemesis trilogy, the VICTOR BLACK quadrilogy, and numerous individual novels coming for young adult and adult readers of modern horror, mystery, suspense, and science fiction.

Beau graduated from Hawaii Pacific University with a B.A. in International Studies and Russian Translation. He currently lives in Colorado Springs, CO, has four amazing pugs, drives a school bus for the city's largest school district, and owns a weight loss company.

Watch for Book Two of Mischievous Max, Fall 2020.

Visit www.BeauDurand.com for new novels, contests, and more. Twitter @realbeaudurand. Facebook @realbeaudurand.

www.ingramcontent.com/pod-product-compliance
Lightning Source LLC
Chambersburg PA
CBHW020242200626
46816CB00001BA/83